BROKEN DEVICES

Karen Myers

BROKEN DEVICES

The Chained Adept: 3

Karen Myers

PERKUNAS PRESS • Tyrone, Pennsylvania

Broken Devices

The Chained Adept: 3

Perkunas Press
2635 Baughman Cemetery Road
Tyrone, Pennsylvania 16686
USA

PerkunasPress.com

Author contact: KarenMyers@KarenMyersAuthor.com
KarenMyersAuthor.com

Cover and Illustrations: Jake Bullock, http://ohbullocks.com
The Kigali, Zannib, Rasesni, Ellech, and Ndant languages:
    Damátir Ando,
    http://damatir-ando.tripod.com/conlangs.html

Trade Paperback
ISBN-13: 978-1-62962-036-7
ISBN-10: 1-6296203-6-X

Library of Congress Control Number: 2016946818

ALSO BY KAREN MYERS

The Hounds of Annwn

To Carry the Horn
The Ways of Winter
King of the May
Bound into the Blood

Story Collections
Tales of Annwn

Short Stories
The Call
Under the Bough
Night Hunt
Cariad
The Empty Hills

The Chained Adept

The Chained Adept
Mistress of Animals
Broken Devices
On a Crooked Track

Science Fiction Short Stories

Second Sight
Monsters, And More
The Visitor, And More

See <u>KarenMyersAuthor.com</u> for the latest information.

CONTENTS

CHAPTER 1

The Grand Caravan arrived that afternoon in sunlight fresh enough with the spring season to ignore the dust of the travelers and settle on the bright colors of their exotic robes and turbans instead.

Outriders had preceded them into Tengwa Tep, and the merchants and citizens of that entrepôt that could spare the time gathered on the southwest outskirts of the city as soon as the news had spread that the Grand Caravan had come, as scheduled, and that the trading season with *sarq*-Zannib and upstream Kigali had begun for the year.

Penrys rode well back in the caravan, dressed in the riding-length robes that all the dark Zannib wore, men and women, on horseback. Najud, her husband, was near the front, but the rest of her companions, as new to the caravan as she was, chattered excitedly about their first look at a Kigali city, its yellow brick golden in the light from the west, varied by the colorful stucco of its many residential and manufacturing compounds. By comparison, the caravan's first stop, a few days ago, had just been a large market town.

She'd seen cities before, in Ellech, across the northern seas. Here it was the children that caught her eye—dozens and dozens of them, screaming with excitement. Some were with a parent, but mostly they ran free, the littlest ones trailed by irritated older sisters or brothers. Unlike their elders, with the long single braid that almost all Kigali not in the military used, the children wore their hair loose or, at the most, gathered into a tail.

"Did they come to see the riders?" Rubti asked.

Penrys smiled at her sister-in-law's eagerness, a ten-years-younger version of Najud. She was an apprentice herd-mistress, a *dirum-malb* in her own language, and she'd been fascinated by the rehearsal the night before of the entertainment the caravan would provide this first evening, to entice the crowds to trade for the five-day stop before it swung west, upstream, paralleling the Junkawa, for the longest leg of its great circular route—to Jonggep, the Meeting of Waters.

Ilzay leaned across his saddle to catch Penrys's attention. "There's our setup place." The young man pointed to the left, into the open pasture that was bare of animals and clearly set aside for the use of the caravan, divided from the outermost commercial buildings on the west side of Tengwa by a well-used broad dirt road.

The caravan broke into its smaller components and the travelers began to unpack and erect their dwellings in the unchanging sequence they would maintain for the entire route. Penrys recalled Najud's advice when the caravan started from Qawrash im-Dhal to pick their neighbors well, since they'd be living with them for four months. That wouldn't be true for Penrys and Najud who would be leaving the caravan here tomorrow with their apprentice Munraz, but the other four would be hauling their two *kazrab* and trade goods on all but the final leg, parting from the caravan only once it had returned to *sarq*-Zannib and reached the land of clan Zamjilah on its way back home.

The six of them led their pack-strings of horses, five each, to their designated spot and began unloading their goods from the pack frames. Before the first of the three round *kazrab* had been raised, Najud trotted in with his own pack-string.

"Sorry, Haraq—we've been summoned. Can you take charge of getting our *kazr* up? Munraz can tell you where everything goes. I need to grab Penrys for a while, by order of our imperial… hosts."

A grimace crossed his lively face. *Sorry, Pen-sha. They're waiting for us. I'll stall them until tomorrow—we don't want to cross the river in the dark, I assure you. But they want to make sure I brought you. As, um, requested.*

Penrys felt the mix of exasperation and tension in his mind-speech. "Shouldn't we change our clothes?" She beat her sleeve with the riding gloves clenched in her hand and let the eloquent dust rise to make her point.

"No time. They'll have to take us as we are, at least on this side of the river where we can always just leave again."

With a sigh, Penrys waved her hand at what was left of their unloading and smiled apologetically at Haraq. "Have fun watching the riding exhibition if we miss it," she told Rubti.

She brushed the trail dust off as best she could and remounted her horse. Najud led her at a trot to the head of the caravan, passing the large *kazr* of the *zarawinnaj*, the caravan leader, and then crossed the road to the Tengwa side and slowed to a walk. He searched through the crowd of Kigaliwen, adults and children, who were watching the camp going up in the field, until he spotted two men, dressed somberly, and turned his horse in their direction.

"That's the dark brown of Imperial Security," he told Penrys. "Apparently they've been on the lookout for us."

When they reached the two men, they dismounted. Najud bowed in the Kigali fashion and Penrys followed his lead. When she noticed the older one staring at her neck, she raised her hand and unwound the colorful scarf she'd wrapped around it, a gift from a kind tailor's wife in far western Neshilik. At the sight of the heavy, brassy chain, settled close around her throat, with no method of removal, the official nodded.

"You are wanted as soon as possible in Mentsek Tep," he said. "Gather your things and follow us."

Penrys raised her eyebrows, and Najud shook his head. "We'll cross to Yenit Ping in the morning, Nip-chi, not in the darkness of night. By the time we load goods and horses, the sun will have long set."

He turned to Penrys. "Penrys, this is Nip Jochat, and Zep Pangwit who will be our guide into Yenit Ping, to take us to Tun Jeju. *Binochiwen*, this is Penrys of Ellech, my wife."

"So they didn't expect you to be married to my *tigha*?" Rubti was amused at the surprise Najud had described to her when they returned to their camp.

"News doesn't travel all that quickly," Penrys said. The scene of chaos that she'd left had fallen into order before she got back. The horses and other animals were tethered or herded in flocks on the far side of the camp, in the pasture set aside for the thrice-yearly visit from the Grand Caravan. In the middle rank were the *kazrab* of the caravan leader, the guards, and the permanent staff of the *Biziz Rahr*, scattered along its length, and then interspersed were all the traders traveling together in the caravan, one group after another. Some were regulars who undertook the journey every year and greeted each other like family, while others, like their own party, were strangers.

The final rank, along the frontage of the road, were the trading booths, still going up in the setting sun, bare and undecorated until the next day's early morning would see them transformed into colorful and enticing stops for the citizens and merchants of Tengwa Tep, and for any other traders who would rendezvous here before the caravan proceeded further into Kigali. Some would be buying, for the local region, and others would consign their own items for sale. Goods that went by water traveled in Kigaliwen hands, but the overland trade, along the route of the *Biziz Rahr*, was handled by the nomadic Zannib, by long custom.

Penrys had seen the process a few days ago in their first village, where the kinks had been worked out for the new travelers. The caravan's customers and trading partners would wait until tomorrow for their official business, but already they were gathering in the open space left beyond the *zarawinnaj*'s dwelling, waiting for the entertainment to begin.

As she pushed through the crowd with Rubti, Penrys could feel the exercise of the traders' professional skills, as much a part of them as the skills of a carpenter or soldier would be to another. She reached out with her mind and scanned the people—hundreds of them, in addition to those with the caravan. Across the road were the thousands in Tengwa Tep, and this, she knew, was just a small city, anchored by the caravan trade. The scale was overwhelming, and she concentrated on just the activity in front of her.

Over here, Pen-sha.

Penrys zeroed in on Najud's location from his silent call and steered Rubti in that direction. Along the westward-facing edge of the talkative crowd, their little group stood quietly—tall Haraq made taller by his turban, and young Ilzay, his eyes never still as they drank in and filed the behaviors of the people as though they were an exotic species of animal. Najud was there, younger than Haraq, with his face that so resembled Rubti's, especially when a smile flashed across it as it did now upon seeing them both. Munraz, their apprentice, stood by his side and smiled shyly at Rubti.

All the men wore the turbans that marked the Zannib, and as Penrys cast her eye across the crowd, she could see the colorful headgear bobbing like the blooms of tall flowers in a field of grass.

The Kigali men, some of them, sported the small emblematic caps of their rank or profession, perched moth-like on their heads. The universal single braid down the back for the adults, men and women, was in stark contrast to the exuberant curls of the Zannib women who wore their hair only casually restrained by scarves or pins, like Rubti.

Rima, the oldest of their party, had threaded the brightest scarf she owned through her own dark curls, until she seemed as youthful and uninhibited as Rubti. Penrys felt out-of-place in this crowd, with her shoulder-length brown hair in the sea of black-headed people. She hadn't stood out so much in Ellech, with its variety of hair colors, but here in the southern continent, any variation from black was unusual, and her skin tones and rounder eyes were wrong, too.

All around them she overheard snippets of conversation. Promises of spices and rugs, jewels and wool, exotic fabrics and dyes. Pearls from the Wandat Sea. Bargains being struck for consignments further along the route.

Suddenly the noise quieted, and Penrys looked west, into the sunset. A single Zan on a white horse had appeared. He bowed, and his horse knelt, too, before rising up to carry him at a gallop along the front of the crowd. Hands reached out to grab children and pull them out of the way, but Penrys could both see and feel how much the rider was in control of his horse, and how often they had done this before.

She felt the arrival of more riders, coming out of the setting sun, before her eyes wanted to leave the first one. They split into two groups of three and rode with their arms crossed over their chests and no reins at all. For a few minutes they wove through each other in intricate crossings, their faces impassive, using only their legs to direct their horses. Penrys could feel their concentration as they performed, something between a dance and swordplay.

With a shout and a flourish, all six riders moved as one and drew their *khashab*, the curved swords of the Zannib, from the sheaths mounted to the saddles. What followed was a stylized sword dance on horseback, first one group of three slashing and their opponents ducking fluidly away, and then the other. After the synchronized exhibit, they broke off into three pairs and traded a flurry of blows that never connected. Finally, by what signal Penrys was unable to detect, they stopped and struck their swords against their partners' swords in a single ringing clang that died out in the silence of the fascinated crowd, until the first hand-clapping began, and the children shouted in delight.

All six riders lined up and bowed, and than circled at a gallop and vanished back behind the caravan leader's *kazr* on the left, just as the sun finished setting.

Penrys glanced down at Rubti whose eyes were shining. "Think you can learn how to do that, in three months?"

Waking up from her trance, the girl turned a serious face to her. "Do you think they'd teach me?"

"Why not? Seems to me like it would be a fine thing for a herd-mistress to know."

That evening all seven of the travelers made themselves comfortable after dinner in the *kazr* that belonged to Najud and Penrys.

"Last time," Najud said, as he poured the *bunnas* for Haraq and then settled the pot on the metal plate that supported the stove. "No more *kazr* for us, in Yenit Ping."

He'd miss the comfort of the warm felt walls surrounding the round lattice-work shell, and all the colorful painted woodwork and textiles. It would all collapse down tomorrow into loads for two of the horses in his string, while the other two *kazrab* remained standing, for the four who would go on with the *Biziz Rahr* for three quarters of its circular route.

Tun Jeju, the Kigali officer of Imperial Security, had requested his presence, and Penrys's, in Yenit Ping, and Najud knew it was more in the nature of an order, an obligation already paid for in the form of a permit for a new caravan in the west of *sarq*-Zannib. He'd brought his apprentice along, but the rest were there to learn how the grandfather of caravans operated, as a model for the new one Najud intended to found.

"It's not too late, Munraz," he said. "There are other *bikrajab* traveling with the caravan—I could probably arrange for you to study with one of them instead, if you wish it. They're all older than I am."

Penrys rolled her eyes, and he corrected himself. "Than we are."

He could see that Munraz actually considered the offer, before shaking his head. "I'd rather study with you two, *bikraj*, and see the great city."

"All right, then. You'll find it… interesting."

Proceeding in order of seniority, Najud turned to Rima. The widow of a trader from clan Umzabul, she'd wanted to experience the Grand Caravan, from its base in Qawrash im-Dhal to its trading cities in Kigali, the better to prepare the other traders in her clan once the western caravan became a reality.

Najud looked to her steadiness to counter-balance his volatile younger sister. "Is there anything else you need, Rima, before we part? You're comfortable with your trade goods? Your silver?"

"It's not my first *biziz*," she said, with a smile, "though there's nothing like the *Biziz Rahr*, it's true. Penrys can take her loads of *kassa* into Yenit Ping, but I'll seed the market along the way with mine, and see if we can't stir up a demand for it."

The herbal infusion was an alternative to the dark and popular *bunnas*, and not yet well known outside of the far west, around the Wandat Sea.

Haraq was still a puzzle to Najud, even after two months on horseback together. Neither he nor the much younger Ilzay spoke much, and they shared a certain sobriety of character.

Penrys had broken Haraq free from a *qahulajti*, a wizard-tyrant, a few months ago, when the Kurighdunaq clan had been so disastrously drawn into the grasp of a young girl with overwhelming powers. In the process, Haraq had stuck to them both, and declared his interest in helping to create the new caravan.

Privately, Najud thought Haraq felt he owed Penrys some sort of debt for his life. That was nonsense—others had been saved the same way, including Haraq's own sister—but Najud was no longer surprised, when he turned around to warn Penrys of something, to find Haraq there before him, tending to the danger.

Ilzay was different. The Kurighdunaq clan was now so reduced in size, that its *ujarqa*, Umzakhilin, the clan leader, was considering Najud's proposal to help build a caravan base on the clan territory, like a Qawrash im-Dhal in miniature, as a way of avoiding absorption into the other clans of his tribe. Ilzay wanted a place in that. He was here to learn how a mature *biziz* operated, to help plan the infancy of a new one.

"You have all the letters for Umzakhilin and the others?" Najud directed the question to both of the men.

"We have everything, *bikraj*," Ilzay responded. "If Umzakhilin says 'yes' before you return, we know what to do. The rest of the work goes forward either way—the breeding of the horses and mules, and the announcements for the merchants and traders in the west."

"Good," Najud said. "I'd rather start the trading base this year, for greater stability next year, but even without it I'm determined to try for a first, short caravan next spring as an experiment."

"And Rubti, that means I'm placing a great responsibility on you." His sister returned his look with unaccustomed seriousness. "Just getting our herds from Zamjilah to Kurighdunaq will be a trial, even if those we spoke with when we passed through still plan to come with you. It's no small thing to uproot so many animals and people, and bring them to a new clan for an… uncertain adventure."

"I can do it, *tigha*," she said. "I may only be a *dirum-malb* now, just an apprentice herd-mistress, but I'm sure I can do it."

Penrys laughed. "Don't you think you'll be a full *dirum* if… when you succeed? If that's not a masterwork, moving so many animals three hundred miles west, I don't know what would be. Talk to the *dirum* of this caravan and learn everything you can. Stick to her like a burr and make yourself useful."

Najud said to Rima, "Take care of her for me."

"Well, I will," the older woman said, "but I don't see the least need to worry about it. You go off and give that old Kigalino what he wants, and we'll see all three of you in a couple of months."

Najud and Penrys shared a look. *If only it proves to be that simple.*

CHAPTER 2

"Is it a river, or the world's longest lake?"

With a sense of wonder, Penrys studied the view before her. She sat her horse with her two companions, each of them holding the lead rope of a pack string of five animals.

Below the bluff, worn by the river below, the flooded Junkawa flowed east. The roiled waters of the Mother of Rivers dominated the landscape. On the far bank, to the north, an isolated ridge stretched away into the blue distance. Its near end point, cut through by the river and erased from the memory of the land after that, was covered by the works of man—Yenit Ping, the Endless City.

She knew there were ways to travel the crumbling ridge down to Mentsek Tep, the lower town at its foot, diked and embanked against high water, but at this distance she could make out only the faintest smudges of color and structure. The western garden district that Najud had described was completely invisible, but the eastern industrial area was identifiable by the smoke that drifted steadily upstream at this time of day.

"That's the last piece of unfloodable land before the outlet, Munraz, a hundred miles away. The river broke through that ridge some unthinkable number of years ago, just like the game 'water cuts stone.' Some day the river will have its way again and they'll have to move the city further back."

Najud kept up a running education for his *nal-jarghal*, his apprentice. He'd visited the city before a few times, and Penrys had at least read about it and was familiar with Tavnastok on its river in Ellech, even if fifty Tavnastoks could have easily fit inside Yenit Ping, but Munraz was only eighteen and had never seen a city of any kind, there being none in central *sarq*-Zannib, the home of the most traditional nomads in the nation. The permanent settlement of Qawrash im-Dhal, the base of the Grand Caravan in eastern *sarq*-Zannib, had been startling enough, and then Tengwa Tep of the yellow bricks and colorful stucco on the south bank behind them had opened his eyes wider.

But this… this was the largest city in the world, by repute. Penrys had seen many illustrations, back in the Collegium of Wizards in Ellech, north across the sea. And there, stretched out before her, was the world's largest river to serve it, with a valley to match, hundreds of miles wide for much of its length. There were no bridges over the Junkawa until Gonglik, at the head of the Steps, in Neshilik, fifteen hundred miles to the west, and then only over the southern of the two main branches.

She opened her mind. Even from this distance she could feel the press of all the people across the water, swamping the population of Tengwa at her back.

"I hope the others will see this," Penrys said. "They may never get another chance."

"Rubti told me they were going to come and look before the *Biziz Rahr* moves on. After they get tired of the sights of Tengwa Tep." Najud smiled at the thought of his young sister's reaction.

"I miss them already," Penrys said. "After two months on the road together."

The click of hooves reminded her they weren't alone. Zep Pangwit, their guide, in his long brown robes, reappeared from below and waved them on impatiently to follow him down the broad diagonal track, terraced into worn steps, that led to the stone docks at river level.

Penrys had never seen a river harbor like this. A bare stone embankment stretched out from the base of the cliff, well above the spring flood level. It was two hundred feet broad, and worn lines memorialized the streets that would appear after the snowmelt had passed. Regularly spaced holes indicated the anchor points for the wattle walls that would be carried down the stepped road to erect temporary structures once the danger of flooding was over.

A massive stone wall west of the stepped road's outlet, more than thirty feet thick and a dozen feet higher than the current river level, jutted out from the bluff at an angle to deflect the force of the river, and in the backwater formed by it were dozens of solid stone docks, each one the width of three wagons. Both the top of the barrier wall and the docks were worn smooth by water, attesting to unusually high floods. A cluster of stone-flagged roads fingered out to access the docks, but they seemed very widely placed.

"What's this like at mid-summer's low water?" she asked Najud.

"Look *under* the surface, to the right of a dock," he said.

It was as though there were another stone dock, like a long stairstep, fifteen feet down, and her mind drew for her a path to a paved road that led to it, now underwater, from the branching network.

"It's like a staircase… How many steps?"

Zep Pangwit was off arranging transportation with one of the larger of the docked ships, a deep-bellied horse transport, but Najud supplied the answer. "Three—low water, high water, and the rest of the year."

"That's quite an investment. How'd they ever build them?"

"It was hundreds of years ago," Najud said, "but I believe they sank barges loaded with stone in low water until they had the bottom layers anchored for the breakwater and the docks, and then, over several years and only during the lowest water, they built permanent walls around those foundations. After they got above the low water level, it went faster."

He glanced around the handful of ships at dockside and grinned at Penrys. "You should see this place in summer when it's full of people. Once the high water passes and the merchants can set up outposts on the lower docks, the dockyard is crowded with temporary buildings. I've never seen them doing it, but I hear they can set up this whole place in a week, to kick off the trading season—they'll do that just after the *Biziz Rahr* leaves. And then they've got to use the signal flags to let Yenit Ping know when there's a dock vacancy, before they let another ship come in for mooring." He pointed upward at the bare patches forty feet up on the cliff, with stairways and paths cut into and above them for access.

Penrys thought of the lenses they must use to read each other's messages across the river, Yenit Ping and its satellite on the southern shore. It wasn't the technology that impressed her—she could see how everything worked, and Ellech could have duplicated it all—but the mute testament of how much wealth and organization and manpower it took to tame this giant river well enough to create these harbors on both sides. That was the part that was so hard to duplicate in the rest of the world. And Yenit Ping was an endless showcase of marvels like this.

Penrys fingered the chain around her neck nervously and bespoke Najud so their apprentice couldn't overhear. *Once we cross, we can't get back without help. We don't really know what Tun Jeju intends—what if it's just to keep a third chained wizard under Kigali control?*

Not too late, Pen-sha, if you want to stop. We can turn around and rejoin the biziz, or just head on back to Zamjilah or Kurighdunaq.

She smiled at her husband, and shook her head. *What, and give up your hope of a caravan in the west? Can't use the permits if we don't come when they call.*

"And besides," she said aloud, "aren't you curious about what they want?"

It took an hour, all three of them, to lift the packs from their horses at the dock and lead the animals through the hull access amidships to their tight stalls below deck. Penrys did her best to sooth them into compliance but a couple revolted in the unusual situation and had to be wrestled into place with ropes. They stood in place afterward, trembling, dismayed by the feel of the ship moving under their feet.

While the sailors latched and sealed the mid-ship hull gap, the three travelers helped haul the horses' packs up the gangway, and the crew lowered them via rope and a suspended pulley into the hold. The destination was nearby, but they would have miles of stubborn sailing to get to it, fighting the current, and the load, light as it was compared to the horses, needed to be balanced correctly.

While she worked, Penrys kept an eye on their guide. His face showed little, but her mind-scan revealed more. He disliked foreigners, as he counted both the two Zannib men, and found her particularly distasteful, probably a mix of her unknown nation, her alien Zannib clothing, and her shoulder-length hair, neither long enough for a proper Kigali braid nor truly short, like the rare women in the military ranks.

He felt shamed, as well—perhaps this errand, to guide them to the Imperial Security offices in the Yenit Ping, was somehow beneath him.

She reached out to the captain and his crew. Nothing odd there, just routine employment—though the curious glances at the

Zannib clothing of the party betrayed some curiosity. Zannib were an unusual sight for them, either at riverside or north of the river, where they were going.

Munraz was watching the sailors, too, and seemed able to follow the conversations. The nightly lessons Najud had given him in learning Kigali *yat*, once they'd crossed the border and had native speakers within reach to draw from, seemed to have worked for him—a good thing, since it would be less unsettling for him to get those mind-sharing lessons from Najud than from Penrys. He had enough of a problem with hero-worship, Najud had told her, and besides, she was a married woman now, not to mention eight years older.

Finally, all was settled, and the mooring lines were cast off, with just a couple of light sails for steering hauled up to help turn the bow out into the river current, inescapable even in this backwater. Then the captain set his sails to take advantage of the easterly wind and headed into the main stream. Najud had explained that the prevailing winds this close to the ocean ran to the west in the morning, and the east in the evening, and the seabirds hanging suspended effortlessly in the air confirmed it. Even with that help, however, it would take the ship the rest of the morning to tack upstream against the current to cross the few miles to the other side and then ride the current into the crowded central harbor of Yenit Ping.

Najud observed Munraz, with his teeth clamped shut, clinging to the rail of the ship with a desperate grasp and staring at more water than he'd ever seen before—a wholly alien environment.

"So, *nal-jarghal*… I forgot to ask you. Did anyone ever teach you how to swim, or should we add that to the list?"

Of course I can't swim. Where would I have learned?

Munraz bit his tongue on the ungrateful thoughts. His *jarghal* meant nothing insulting by the jest, he knew. *It's not the water I fear.* The river was just one more barrier erected between his old life and his new.

He wouldn't have returned home if he could have, not to that perverted life of the wizards of his clan—the inbreeding, a future of a terrified wife or a drugged one. Or none at all.

His right hand gripped the rail of the ship harder, in momentary remembrance of the knife it had held, the firm grip needed to cut the *qahulajt*'s throat, above the chain, still loose on her neck—she had yet to finish growing into it, so young she was, like a little sister. So dangerous. And so doomed. What his uncle would have done to her—it didn't bear thinking of. Munraz had denied him the prize and helped her die cleanly.

The senior *bikraj*, Khizuwi, had thanked him for ending the *qahulajti*, the necessary action to restore order. But Munraz agreed with Penrys—he couldn't hold the young girl responsible for all the deaths she'd caused, more like a natural disaster than deliberate malice. He could never say so—he didn't think mercy killing would be as acceptable an explanation as traditional justice. He thought Penrys suspected the truth, and understood, but time and distance hadn't made his hands feel any cleaner.

No, there's no way to go back, Munraz-without-a-family. The clan adoption had been good of Najud, kind. To a man with a fond family—what was one more orphan? It was something else he shared with Penrys, the shared glance when the exuberance of Najud's siblings painted such a vivid and cozy picture, and they both felt like outsiders, through no fault of the others.

No point in thinking of Penrys. She was Najud's, and rightly. She treated Munraz like a younger brother. He flushed remembering the one time he'd confessed his admiration of her to Najud, and had been reminded of the impropriety of it.

Their journey across *sarq*-Zannib to Qawrash im-Dahl had been interesting, seeing more of the world, though every time they were introduced the strangeness of a young *jarghal* and an almost-as-old *nar-jarghal* seemed to strike people, whether they asked about it or not. Najud and Penrys discouraged the questions, and he was grateful, but he felt as if his history were written on his forehead for all to see.

And then, once they'd joined the Biziz Rahr, Najud's professional interest had pushed aside some of their studies together. Was the man a *jarghal*, or a trader? And Penrys was no better. Maybe this was why apprentices studied with older masters, men who'd settled into their life's work instead of flitting from flower to flower like some unsatisfied bee.

For a moment black and yellow stripes wrapped themselves around his vision of Najud chatting at the rail with Penrys, and he added diaphanous wings before blinking them away and concentrating on keeping his stomach settled as the ship dipped and rose in the current.

CHAPTER 3

Unlike the half-empty harbor on the southern shore, the central harbor of Yenit Ping was full of life. The river rarely froze in winter, and traffic up and down the northern shore was active year round, though this was far from its busiest season. Signal flags the height of a man flapped, five and six at a time, from three stout masts, visible from the harbor and bluff of Tengwa Tep, Penrys assumed.

Their ship sought its modest mooring well away from the grand plaza of temples and imperial buildings, set back from the edge of the embankment, that displayed the order and power of Kigali for all to see. The three travelers and their guide leaned on a rail out of the way of the sailors, and the foreigners gaped at the sight.

"Is that where the emperor lives?" Munraz asked, happier now that they were no longer in the grasp of the main river.

Najud chuckled. "Hardly. He's up there."

He pointed up to the ridge with its cliffs, almost a quarter of a mile back from the level embankment. "The court and its functionaries live up there in Juhim Tep. What you're seeing are the central offices of government—they have satellite locations in Juhim, and scattered in smaller districts throughout the city, and in the lesser cities of the empire, but this is their central place. The temples, too, though the best of those are up in Juhim Tep."

"What I want to know," Penrys said, "is how they built this huge flat place so high above the river, with the ridge set so conveniently back."

Zep Pangwit condescended to explain the glories of Yenit Ping to these outlanders. "Our ancestors found the rubble of Tegong Him here, where the river had brought it down. All that was necessary was to break it up and level it out, until they were satisfied with the height above the floods. Of course, they broke off more of it as needed to make the cliffs steeper, for the better defense of Juhim Tep."

Penrys blinked. Pride and satisfaction were strong in his voice, but when she'd digested his explanation, she thought them well-merited. The civic and religious buildings were faced in a smooth white stone, but the older buildings she could see were the same red-brown as the cliff in the distance. The central portion of the city and the foundations of the embankment were all made from the stone of the ridge. What the river had started, the Kigali had continued, improving on nature. She wondered what it had looked like, before the empire.

From her reading she knew that there were famous hoists that hauled people, horses, and goods from Mentsek Tep at the base to Juhim Tep, but she couldn't make out any of the details from here. *What an impregnable situation for a seat of empire, like a castle with a moat of air.*

She opened her mouth to ask how the upper town was defended from the back, and then thought better of it. It would be probably be interpreted as military spying rather than academic interest.

The sailors uncovered the hatch to the cargo hold, and Penrys postponed her inquiries to help unload their goods.

"Try to keep up." Zep Pangwit's testy complaint woke Penrys to the fact that she was staring like any countrywoman while the traffic passed her by in both directions.

There was just so much to look at. The Kigaliwen she'd met in a military context had been orderly and professional. But these city-folk, with their innumerable interests and their busy errands were endlessly distracting—as many women as men, all carrying something or hastening somewhere, children and dogs underfoot and dodging the delivery wagons, and a few people on horses, like themselves. Now and then a closed litter passed behind its guide, its four bearers chanting rhythmically to keep step together. It made the bustling Gonglik with which she was familiar seem like a rural village.

Some of the Kigaliwen stared back at them, surprised by the sight of nomadic Zannib in the heart of Yenit Ping.

Najud had taken charge of Munraz and kept up a quiet buzz of conversation to defuse the young man's panic at the size and closeness of the crowds. Penrys swallowed uneasily and almost wished he'd do the same for her. The smells were as alien as the people. Tavnastok was nothing like *this*.

They finally reached their goal just off the grand avenue—a bonded stable that occupied part of a compound associated with a hostel where they could leave their horses and goods temporarily and be confident of finding them again. Zep Pangwit had no knowledge of what would happen after he delivered them to his superiors at the office of Imperial Security, but he couldn't drag them there in their travel clothing with eighteen horses. "Zannib barbarians," he'd muttered when he'd first seen what they planned to bring into the city. This was his solution to the problem.

As the designated leader of their party, Najud was bombarded with questions by the clerk of the stable who recorded all the answers neatly on a piece of papyrus—the names, ages, and citizenship of the travelers, the list of horses and goods, and so forth. Zep Pangwit tried to hasten the process along, moaning about them being expected by now.

Penrys paid little attention until the clerk's words "and to whom should the goods be released if you die or are imprisoned" struck her ears, and she turned on her heel to stare at him. "Very civilized," she commented to Munraz in *wirqiqa*-Zannib, and he grinned in appreciation.

"Najud said they're responsible for the safety of all our goods," Munraz said. "The penalties for failure are… severe."

Maybe so, but I hate to leave my power-stones here. Penrys hoped the hefty sack of pea-sized dull stones would pass for something of little worth, if anyone should look. They were far more valuable, anywhere wizards used devices, than the two small pouches of gold that Tun Jeju had awarded them, on the emperor's behalf, after their success in Neshilik six months ago.

"We should change clothes." She nudged Munraz in the direction of their personal packs. She rooted through hers and removed the new trousers, shirt, and boots she'd bought in Qawrash im-Dhal, and the green *himmib* Zannib robe, with the woman's stiff and embroidered bodice, one of several sets of clothing for both work and formal occasions that she'd purchased on Najud's advice when she re-equipped herself there. The permanent base of the Grand Caravan had everything a traveler could want.

The goat's-wool of the robe was soft against her cheek. She looked around for any sort of water source and found nothing except a pump for the use of the horses. She borrowed a clean bucket, rinsed it out and partially refilled it, and ducked into the tack room, shooing the grooms out that she found there and latching the door. She used her discarded shirt to do a quick wash with the cold water and redressed in her new clothing. A run of her fingers through her hair, and that was about all she could do to make herself presentable, under the circumstances.

When she emerged with the bucket in one hand and the dirty clothes in the other, she caught sight of her husband's grin and a sneer on the face of Zep Pangwit. The interested attention of the stable staff put her on her mettle, and when their guide opened his mouth to rebuke her, she lowered the bucket to the stable floor with a clang of metal and interrupted him before he could properly begin.

"That will be quite enough of that, Zep-chi," she said, in her most upper-class Kigali *yat*. "Is it my fault that you can't convey the invited guests of Tun Jeju to someplace with bathing facilities so that we can show him the proper respect when we meet, or would you rather we arrive in all our dirt, after traveling for two months and then laboring like stevedores to get here?"

Their guide flushed and pressed his lips together, and Penrys let her irritation with him help her keep a stern expression on her face, despite the wide eyes of Munraz, standing out of his sight behind him. "Your turn," she told him, handing him the empty bucket. "The pump's over there."

After months of wearing her Ellech workroom clothing and its replacements, and then the shorter robes and comfortable bodice that the women of Zannib adopted from men's clothing when riding, it was a challenge for Penrys to modify her stride and posture to accommodate the longer formal woman's robe and the stiff bodice.

She was grateful for the light trousers and low boots that went with it, allowing the robe itself to be open down the front rather than confiningly closed. Her glimpse of some of the wealthier women, as the party returned on foot to the government district, made the drawbacks of the high-necked tight gowns they wore clear. They were lovely, elegant and somber, but with no thought of horses—not that they needed them, since they either walked or were conveyed by litter.

Najud and Munraz strolling at her side behind the guide had no cause for complaint. Their style of attire was unchanged, though the fabrics were new and vivid. The turbans were larger, too. *Is that an armed anah im-ghabr?*

Najud turned his head at her silent question and nodded. She'd told him about something she'd read in Ellech, where a fighting people who wore turbans had a practice of including a metal skull cap for protection within them, as well as small concealed weapons and tools. The idea was new to Najud, but he'd been fascinated by the possibilities, and one of his outfitting excursions in Qawrash im-Dhal had resulted in an array of interesting sharp and pointed objects strewn on his bed in the *kazr*.

She herself wore a thin belt under the bodice, to hold the fancy knife Najud had given her for occasions such as this, useless for serious defense. A much longer and more serious blade was fastened at an angle behind her back. If she was going to have a stiff back from the bodice, the posture was at least useful for a concealed weapon.

Najud and Munraz couldn't wear the *khash*, the curved Zannib sword, openly here in the city, but she knew her husband had both visible and hidden knives, and she suspected Munraz of the same.

The quality of their clothing earned them a bit more space on the busy streets, but its foreign nature drew stares, more curious than hostile. It was obvious that the city-folk recognized their nationality, even if Penrys didn't quite fit in, and Zannib was an ally and trading partner, not an enemy, but it was strange to stand out so obviously in such a crowded place, with nothing but Kigaliwen in all directions. It made her skin twitch.

Even in Ellech, where she'd been clearly a non-native, they were so used to visitors from many nations in the harbor at Nachempolek that one more, even at inland Tavnastok upriver, was much less a matter of interest. *I don't think they see many foreigners here, in the heart of Kigali.*

She had a sudden vision of the immensity of the world, stretching out from this one point. Ellech was more than two thousand miles away from a harbor itself almost a thousand miles distant, and as far as she knew they were the only Zannib north of the river that bisected the fifteen hundred miles to the west, barring any ambassadorial staff maintained in Yenit Ping. *Not a good place to try and hide in, not for us.*

Her hand reached up involuntarily to touch her chain. Her instinct had been to wrap it in a scarf, but Najud had pointed out that it had to be why they'd been summoned. Better to display it proudly, he'd said.

He's a clever man, my husband, and well-traveled, especially for a Zan, but I think he may have mis-estimated these people. The Tun Jeju she remembered was subtle and intelligent, and though he'd done them no real harm, she was wary of him. It hadn't escaped her attention that it was not only his name on the caravan permits Najud carried, but also that of Menchos, an even scarier man in what seemed to be an analogous position for Rasesdad. The two of them, working together, would be formidable opponents, even if such an alliance between traditional enemies was unprecedented. And yet, there were the joint caravan permits Najud had received to attest to the partnership.

She smiled to herself. The permits declared they could be copied anywhere in Kigali, and Najud had taken the precaution to get copies made while in Tengwa Tep and place them into the hands of their friends to carry back into *sarq*-Zannib, just in case the originals were taken away again. This, in addition to the second official version of the originals that had arrived in clan Zamjilah's winter camp from Ussha and would be put safely in charge of Rubti when she returned that way.

Despite Penrys's suspicion, she knew Tun Jeju and Menchos would also make powerful employers, if they were both involved in this summons, and the permits for a new western caravan were prepayment for an unknown task. *Better wait until you know what they want before panicking.*

CHAPTER 4

The largest avenue of the city ran directly through the center of the government district. To their right were the scroll-roofed temples and the temple schools occupying several blocks of buildings. Some fronted on the avenue, and some on the harbor side to their right, facing a long, green park looking out over the harbor itself.

Najud glimpsed the busy civilian traffic enjoying the pavilions and pleasure grounds, but it seemed to him that the open space was also well-sited as a parade ground for military or guard units. *When's the last time that happened?*

The civic buildings were grouped to the left, serious and chaste, in contrast to the exuberance of the temples with their scrolled corners. This was the first time Najud had ever had occasion to enter one of these buildings. The city-folk he'd met steered clear of them as much as possible—nothing good ever came of going through those doors, they said. The most official notice he'd ever attracted before had come from introducing himself to the Zannib ambassador once, out of respect.

The headquarters of Imperial Security was not on the avenue itself, but around the first corner and halfway down the side street, on the east side. He squared his shoulders and followed Zep Pangwit up the slightly too high steps to the overlarge doors that dwarfed all who entered. "Say as little as possible, *nal-jarghal*," he said, giving Munraz a firm look.

Penrys cast a worried glance at him and then wiped all expression off of her face and composed herself.

Najud translated the signs carved high above the entrance— Vigilance on behalf of the Emperor is Peace for the Nation—and grimaced. They were about to be tossed into the cesspool of Kigali politics with neither alliances nor knowledge to protect themselves. He fingered the *lud* he'd slipped into his pocket and touched the official documents that sent for him at his breast, and hoped for the best.

Once inside, he tried not to stare at the imposing two-story high atrium. Fully three-quarters of the open space was behind walls with barred windows, and when he looked more closely, the arrow slits in the upper walls were obvious. Access to the interior was well-guarded by half-armored men in dark brown, and the handful of people huddled on the benches in the section nearest the door, awaiting their turn, seemed appropriately cowed.

Zep Pangwit strode impatiently to a barred window near the interior entrance and spoke with whomever was there, out of Najud's sight. Behind him, Najud heard the steady footsteps of Penrys and Munraz keeping pace with him and he led them, without looking back, to a place just behind their guide. The guards, a few paces away, did their best to ignore the presence of foreigners.

When Zep Pangwit turned around, he nodded in brief approval to find his charges there, suitably respectful. "We're expected. A runner's been sent to let them know we're coming."

He clutched two pieces of papyrus in his hand. One of these he presented to the first of the guards. "Entry for these foreigners. You may check for weapons and report, but do not remove them."

That raised both the guard's eyebrows and Najud's, and the two of them eyed each other. Najud's mouth quirked and he bowed. He displayed his visible belt-knife, lifted a sleeve to show another strapped to his left forearm, and then slowly reached through his right breeches pocket to the knife strapped against his leg. He replaced all of these blades under the guard's impassive gaze, and then waved his hand negligently at his turban and pulled out a small pointed nail, implying there were perhaps other objects there.

The guard looked at the note again, and its signature chop. "Leave him his weapons? You're sure?"

Zep Pangwit nodded. "By order of the *notju*."

Najud stepped aside to watch how his companions fared. Penrys smiled at the guard and presented her small belt-knife, and then stood back and drew the blade under the back of her bodice with a flourish and offered it hilt-first to the guard's view. Finally she lifted her left trouser leg to display the small knife strapped to her calf. "That's it," she told the guard.

Munraz was nervous, but he managed a bow. His only weaponry was the belt-knife and a small hand-axe, plain and in sight. When the guard cocked an eyebrow at the young man's turban, Munraz just shook his head.

"They're in your charge, *binochi*, but I'll provide an escort for these armed foreigners," the guard informed Zep Pangwit, and he passed them through the entrance with a burly and well-armed guard in their wake.

Zep Pangwit led them through the building as if he'd spent years there. For all Penrys knew, perhaps he had. Internal guard posts blocked off some portions from casual access, but Zep avoided those areas and took them confidently to the third floor. The travelers followed silently behind, and the footsteps of their escort in the rear resonated off the stone hallways.

There was little Penrys could see behind closed doors, and when she casually glanced at the minds behind them, all she could detect was the usual miscellaneous mix of humans, all of whom were native Kigali *yat* speakers. Beyond them were the thousands of minds of the city, in all directions except the harbor—it was as good as a compass for helping her keep track of where she was.

As they approached the northwest corner of the building, Zep stopped at a checkpoint. He showed his credentials one more time to the three men posted there, and scraped off his escort who turned on his heel to return to the ground floor as they passed through.

Another short corridor, and Zep knocked twice, then twice again on the closed door at the end of it. It was opened from within and swung back to allow entry.

Penrys squared her shoulders and followed Najud in, keeping an eye on Munraz to make sure of his readiness.

It was a large room, with the first external windows she'd seen since entering the building. Several people stood in clumps, and Penrys was distracted from her survey of the space when she recognized one group of bearded men as Ellech, and gray-haired Vylkar among them—her patron, the man who'd found her when she appeared, naked and empty of memory on a snowy hillside in Asuthgrata.

Despite her anxiety about the summons, she could feel the broad smile on her face as he looked up at the opening of the door and spotted her. He broke off his conversation and walked over to her. "I got your letter from Neshilik and it caused quite a stir."

More quietly, he added, "And relieved my fear after you vanished so mysteriously that night." He put his hands on her shoulder and shook her, lightly. "Have I taught you nothing about the right way to conduct experiments?"

"Sorry about that, *bilappa*, but it worked out for the best." She turned to the impatient man beside her who was running a measuring eye over the older man. "This is my husband, Najud, of the Zamjilah clan. Najud, this is Vylkar—you've heard me speak of him."

Najud nodded, and Vylkar smiled in satisfaction. "I thought it might end that way, from some of the things you wrote. At least you're both wizards."

A general silence fell upon the room, and Tun Jeju strolled up with Zep Pangwit who'd gone to report while Penrys was occupied. The *notju*'s thin, intelligent face put her on her guard.

Najud bowed in Kigali fashion with Penrys, and Munraz managed a clumsy imitation. "We're here, *notju-chi*, as you requested," Najud said. "The soonest we could come."

"With additions, I see," Tun Jeju replied, glancing at Munraz and raising an eyebrow.

"This is Munraz, our *nal-jarghal*," Najud said. "Our apprentice. We couldn't leave him behind."

"Aren't you young to be taking an apprentice, as I understand the Zannib customs?"

"Yes, but that's a long story, *notju-chi*."

"And we will hear it in its proper place." Tun Jeju clapped his hands twice to draw the attention of all the people in the room.

"Our last participants have arrived. Some of you have traveled from long distances at the emperor's request and have had to wait weeks impatiently while everyone else completed their journeys. I want to thank you all, on the emperor's behalf, for coming to help address a crisis that affects not only Kigali, but several other nations as well."

He gestured to a group of small tables clustered in the center of the room, surrounded by comfortable chairs. "Please, be seated. My colleagues of Imperial Security have information to share with you."

The handful of men and women in dark brown robes moved immediately to their seats and Penrys could finally focus on some of the more exotic attendees who'd been blocked from her view.

There were no other Zannib there, but the party of three of the tall Ellech of which Vylkar was a member was matched by three of the short, dark Ndanum in their long, diagonally draped robes—an older woman and what seemed to be two attendants, a young woman and a middle-aged man. There were also two Rasesni, both unknown to Penrys. Munraz looked ill at ease among all the older foreigners, but Najud resolutely seated him at their table, to his left, with Penrys to his right.

Tun Jeju remained standing while servants circulated to provide water, wine, or *bunnas*, as requested. Once the servants had left and the door was closed, he began to speak.

"The Kigaliwen, as you know, are not a nation of wizards. Most of us would say that *lupjuwen* do not exist, and certainly no Kigalino could be one. All of you here who are foreigners must have been amused at our beliefs. The wizards of *sarq*-Zannib and Ellech are well known, and the mages of Rasesni. And who has not heard of the witches of Ndant?" He nodded to the Ndane woman as he spoke.

"While waiting for our last participants to arrive, I have shared with each of you the news of the recent events in Neshilik, where these two," he waved at Najud and Penrys, "with the help of some of our Rasesni neighbors, stopped an attack by a rogue wizard who had carved his way through Rasesni and entered Kigali."

Penrys appreciated the subtle sarcasm she heard in his voice as he referred to the Rasesni as "neighbors" when they were in the midst of an invasion at time. He'd been there—he knew what he was talking about.

"I understand that a similar wizard was recently encountered in western *sarq*- Zannib, though I don't yet know the details."

He turned his eyes to Najud and Penrys, but it was Munraz who stiffened under his gaze, and that clearly puzzled him. "I look forward to hearing the whole story. I was convinced by what I saw in Neshilik, and there have been changes in how Imperial Security handles this new information."

Penrys blinked. *Just how high up is he in this organization? The title notju, Intelligence Master, doesn't really convey any sense of rank.*

"We haven't yet taken any steps with the ordinary untrained wizards we now believe live among us, as they do with all our neighbor nations. We plan to do so, but we have a more urgent concern. The wizards with chains."

All eyes turned to Penrys's exposed throat with the gold-brassy metallic chain that circled it closely. She felt her furry ears move back along her scalp, hidden by her hair, and her skin prickled. The Ndane woman gave her a cold stare.

Tun Jeju cleared his throat. "You know what we Kigaliwen are—we are organized."

This drew a few chuckles which eased the tension.

"We sent out a call to our neighbors asking for reports of people bearing chains like hers." He nodded at Penrys. "We also asked about people who had gone missing and had never been found—I'll explain that soon. And, of course, we searched our own nation the same way."

"Most of you here conveyed reports from your countries. And also—which we didn't expect—some of you provided evidence."

That brought Penrys upright in her seat, all concern about her uniqueness in this group put aside. *They found more? Alive or not?*

She glanced at Vylkar, and he nodded. *He found others?*

"The purpose of the next few weeks is to discover everything we can about these chained wizards, to evaluate the threat, and to determine what can and should be done about it. In all of our nations."

Penrys swallowed. *And here am I, in the center of a trap if they don't decide the right way.*

Munraz had no difficulty following the Kigali *yat* in the city, much less in this smaller space where he could follow one conversation at a time. Penrys had been right—it got easier with practice once you'd figured out how to tap it at all. He was more worried about the writing—there weren't any useful documents to use. Maybe his *jarghal* would come up with some, once they settled somewhere.

He'd had a few days to get used to the exotic appearance of the Kigaliwen in Tengwa Tep and the smaller villages they'd passed through after they crossed the border. He thought he'd started to see local differences in the city folk—short, broad-faced people and thin, elegant ones, for starters. *I bet they're from different parts of Kigali, originally.*

There were more Kigaliwen behind this Tun Jeju, quiet and attentive, like people who wanted to see but not be seen, and he remembered just where he was, in the building that housed Imperial Security.

It made him want to wrap armor around himself, somehow.

When he glanced around the tables, he wondered if there were others who felt the same way. The dark Ndant leader looked like not much would intimidate her, small though she was, but her young female attendant didn't seem very happy to be there.

The two Rasesni seemed pleased with their company and stared curiously at everyone. The Ellech reminded him a little bit of Penrys with their "I'm just watching, it's not my business" air of amused detachment. Penrys would typically dive in later after that initial hesitation—he wondered if these were the same. He'd heard of Vylkar, the man who'd found her when she appeared as a chained wizard.

No one had found the *qahulajti* he'd killed, and that was probably why she went wrong. Under the table, his right hand clenched and he forced it open again.

Why had his two masters been summoned, and he with them like a spare pack of grain?

"She's one of us, I tell you."

The groom who'd ducked out of the stable and slipped away from the compound kept his voice low despite his insistence. "She didn't cover the chain at all—left it on display as if she were proud of it."

His fingers crept to the the high neck of his tunic, a style which had been revived in the last couple of years in the working-class neighborhoods, not least because of the influx of new migrants to the city who adopted it. The collar hid many things, in particular the chain that marked the young man as someone of interest to Imperial Security, anywhere in Kigali.

Rin Tsugo listened to the report of his agent in an alley around the corner from the compound's entrance and considered what it might mean. When Jing Tajip had alerted him by mind-speech, it had pulled him away from his work in Chankau Tep, the industrial district—he'd wanted to see Jing Tajip in person and evaluate the truth of the matter.

"A brown-robe runner brought her in?" he asked. He wanted to get closer to Jing Tajip to keep the conversation quieter, but the chains around their necks prevented them from getting within arm's reach without pain.

"With a Zannib husband and some younger Zannib man, and those pack-strings they use for their migrations. Eighteen horses!"

"But she's not a Zan?" Rin Tsugo wanted to be sure.

"No, *wo-chi*. Reminds me of Dar Datsu. Straight brown hair, round eyes, not very tall."

Rin Tsugo winced at the reminder of the latest member of his band, his *gewengep*, to have been captured by the City Guard. "And the runner took her to Imperial Security?"

Jing Tajip looked around nervously at the very mention of the name. "That's what they were talking about when they left. I think they came because they were sent for."

He looked uneasily at Rin Tsugo. "I couldn't just follow them—I'd have been noticed."

Rin Tsugo waved the concern away and thought. The woman hadn't been arrested, at least not yet—she'd gone willingly, with some of her family. What was that about? Was she working for them? Why would the Zannib bring her?

There were people in their *gewengep* who looked like the Zannib, though everything else about them was Kigali. They weren't *real* Zannib. More than half of the brotherhood had the features of other nations, but otherwise they were all the same—chained, out of place, shorn of memories more than three years old, and on the run from Imperial Security. Only the ones that looked like Kigaliwen could venture out for paid work—all the rest earned their keep behind the walls of the battered compound they'd taken for their own in Chankau Tep. Unless Rin Tsugo sent them out for special tasks under the cover of night.

New members had been arriving weekly from upriver, ever since the decrees that began six months ago, making the villagers and farmers suspicious of the rootless laborers in their midst, especially the ones that looked like foreign crossbreeds. As long as no village talked about it to another, they'd paid little attention to the oddness of the one person without family who kept himself in the background and took jobs of low status to earn a living.

But once a decree came down from Imperial Security, looking for news of missing people or strangers with neck chains, all hands had turned against them. Many were killed, and their bodies presented to the *yankat*, the headman of the village, to satisfy the Imperial Security request. The rest had slipped away, blurring the attention of the villagers if they could. Rin Tsugo didn't know how many had made it to Yenit Ping, drawn by obscure news of refuge here, and how many were simply lost, but they were still arriving, some on foot, and some by river, down the Junkawa.

And the *gewengep* was responsible for all its members, and he was elected to lead it.

Rin Tsugo looked piercingly at the younger Jing Tajip. "You didn't try to bespeak her?"

"Merciful heavens, no! She was clearly a foreigner, in her Zannib robes. She might have exposed me on the spot."

"I want to see what's in her packs."

Jing Tajip backed away. "Can't be done. They're under the bond, and sealed."

"Not even at night?"

"They're guarded, and no groom has any excuse to look in on them. The guards wouldn't let me past, and I'd certainly lose my position."

"I won't ask you to do it now," Rin Tsugo said, "but the time may come when the brotherhood requires it." He held Jing Tajip's eyes until the young man nodded reluctantly.

"Good. Meanwhile, I'll put a watch around the Imperial Security building. She'll have to come out sometime, and then we'll follow her."

"What about Dar Datsu?" Jing Tajip asked.

"We don't know if he's in their hands or if the City Guard still has him. We'll keep an eye out for him, too." *But we're not likely to see him alive again, and Jing Tajip should know that by now.*

CHAPTER 5

Vylkar of Ellech was the first to report to the groups around their tables. He glanced at Penrys in apology, and began to speak.

"I encountered my first chained wizard three and a half years ago." He gestured at Penrys, so that there would be no confusion.

"It was winter then, in the north, and I was at my hunting lodge with my family in the uplands of Asuthgrata, when I heard a loud noise, here." He tapped his forehead. "I reached for the source, and brought men with me to look for it. And we found her, naked except for her chain, and speechless."

Penrys clenched her teeth and looked down. This was her earliest memory, the cold, wet snow on her bare skin and the torches of the riders flickering in the trees.

"By the time we got her home and warmed up, she had our language. When I probed her to see where she might have come from, she raised a shield, and so I knew she was a wizard, as I am."

He pursed his lips, half-hidden in his gray-shot tidy scholar's beard, as if to consider how to abbreviate the remainder. "I took her with us back to the Collegium of Wizards in Tavnastok, and there she baffled us all. Old Aergon resurrected an antique title— Adept, *hakkengenni* in Ellechen *guma*—and she spent three years with us, mostly in the library and working on devices, *ruanarys*, there being little to teach her in *beolrys*, the mental magic.

"Six months ago she vanished, but Tun Jeju has told you something of what followed and I'll let others carry that story. I received Penrys's own report about it just days before I got the Kigali request for information about missing people and chained wizards."

Vylkar cleared his throat. "At the Collegium, we thought Penrys was a unique mystery, but when we looked, thus prompted, we found we were wrong."

He reached into a pack, pulled out a chain identical to Penrys's, and tossed it onto his table where it clattered. "This was discovered on the remains of an unclothed man found inside a crypt in a country town, when they opened it for a new internment. He was not one of the expected inhabitants of the tomb," he commented dryly.

"The surprised funeral party called for help from the local magistrate, and it's from him I got the chain and the story. The conclusion was that, however the man had entered the tomb, he'd been unable to leave and so he died there. There wasn't much left, but the hair was black and curly, rather like that of a Zan."

Penrys swallowed. There were worse things than materializing naked in the snow.

"We do have people missing, and some of them are wizards. I've provided Tun Jeju with a list, but whether some of them are now wandering around some other country with a chain and no memory—which is what is being clearly implied—I have no way of knowing."

He paused. "Perhaps they were simply murdered by unhappy spouses and cleverly disposed of."

A nervous titter traveled around the tables.

"And so, I and my companions, Bildaer and Innurrys, came to learn more."

Nodding to Tun Jeju, Vylkar leaned back in his seat, and Mpeowake of Ndant stood up. She smoothed the layers of blue and aqua silk that draped from her left shoulder down to the sash at her waist and thence to her ankles. A tight bodice and long narrow skirt enwrapped her body beneath the outer layer.

She was small and dark and delicately built, with long straight black hair just beginning to go gray. Her eyes pierced those of her audience as she looked around the tables.

"We wizards of Ndant are pledged to our goddess, Pume Chowe. It's in her name that we work for our people. One who is born a wizard but will not take the oath is an abomination, a witch to be hunted and destroyed, before he can harm any of the innocent. I am the *mbaewe*, the leader of those who hunt, and these are my assistants." She gestured at the man and woman on either side of her.

"We do have missing wizards—we are a populous nation—but we have discovered none of these chained wizards, living. However, in the sea cliffs to the north of Shokona Bay, we have a three-year-old mystery. A bird-nester, descending by rope from the top, followed a foul smell and found two dead bodies, a man and a woman. There was no clothing, and the boy believed that they'd fought, using rocks. The woman was dark-skinned like the Ndant, but her hair was short and curly. The man was pale, with hair like fire." She pointed to redhaired Bildaer in Vylkar's party.

"Both had chains. We buried them under rocks in the cave, and the cave was sealed. It's high on the cliff and not easy of access. The chains are there—we chose not to meddle with them."

She sat down gracefully and folded her hands.

Tun Jeju turned his head to the older of the two Rasesni, both of whom wore the robes of priests.

"I'm Chosmod, and this is Mrigasba. My superior Menchos, who had met with his counterpart in Neshilik"—he nodded at Tun Jeju—"thought it better to send mages rather than come himself. Most of us work in the temples and the schools, or out with the people, not in the security services, though some of us do both." He gestured casually to include his companion and himself among the latter. "If nothing else, we have an easier time with Kigali *yat*."

That drew appreciative smiles from all of Tun Jeju's foreign visitors, and Penrys mentally kicked herself for not realizing that they were all wizards, every one of them—all shielded and buttoned down. She'd been so busy shielding herself against the overwhelming quantity of people in the city that she hadn't looked for anything more intimate than surface emotions from the people here in the room. She glanced briefly at Munraz, glad that Najud and she had worked hard on improving his own shield. His eyes were wide in this company, even as his body shrank in on itself and tried to disappear.

Chosmod cocked his head in Penrys and Najud's direction. "Tun Jeju has told you of our recent chained wizard, the one that was stopped in Neshilik, with their help."

Penrys reluctantly turned to Najud and held out her hand. He pulled out the small suede pouch from the inner pocket of his tunic, the one she'd given him to hold, since there was no place for it with her formal Zannib robes, and handed it to her.

She placed it on the table in front of her where it drew all eyes, and Chosmod waited for her to untie it. Her hand reached in and settled on the small fragment of chain, just three links, and she pulled it out and laid it quietly on the table. "This is what is left of the Voice's chain."

She looked at Chosmod. "Were other pieces found, afterward? I never asked."

"The area was searched and we turned up four individual links, but no partial links, no broken ones. And not enough to account for them all, though we're not sure how many that should be."

"Mine has thirteen links," Penrys said in a controlled voice. "I've seen another, with fourteen. I never counted the Voice's. The links themselves—all the ones I've seen—appear to be the same size."

Unexpectedly, Vylkar spoke up, waving his hand at the loop of chain before him on the table. "This has fifteen. The man was large."

Chosmod resumed his story. "After the threat of the Voice was eliminated, Menchos formalized the frantic information-gathering that we had been doing in Dzongphan. We consolidated the archives in the capital and pulled fresh information from the satellite temples."

"And from the harbors," Mrigasba interjected. "We heard many interesting stories there."

Tun Jeju nodded. "As did we."

"In our ports, as well," Mpeowake contributed.

Chosmod picked up the thread again. "The sailors had tales to tell from other ports. Nothing very believable, nothing different from other tales of demons and monsters hiding as humans."

Penrys tried not to wince at that.

"But the country folk had much to tell their priests, now that we were casting a wider net," Chosmod said. "We tracked down every report, and several of them yielded results. We brought those with us."

He glanced at Tun Jeju who said, "We'll be looking at that shortly, all of us."

"Alive?" Penrys asked Chosmod.

"No. None of them. And all recent—in the last three years."

There was a pause, and Penrys intercepted a significant look from Tun Jeju. *Must be my turn.*

"You've heard the story of my being found in Ellech. A… miscalculation while working with devices brought me unexpectedly to western Kigali, where I met Najud, with everything that followed with the Voice." She kept her tone bland as she recalled whacking the malfunctioning device framework she was building with the back of her hand in frustration and ending up in a Kigali military tent while they were under attack from a Rasesni device. Power calling to power, she assumed, though that was no real explanation.

"What happened after that… Najud invited me to see his country, his home. We traveled to central *sarq*-Zannib by way of the High Pass. And that's when we crossed the track of another chained wizard."

She glanced at Najud to see if he'd rather tell the story himself, but he shook his head faintly.

"To keep it brief, this was a young girl, maybe thirteen, who we think found animals, and only animals, for her first years and bonded with them, and then when she finally met people, tried to bond them to her like another kind of beast. It was disastrous for the people—hundreds died, most of an entire clan—but it wasn't an intentional slaughter, in my opinion, just a case of not understanding what would result."

"What happened to her?" Vylkar asked.

"She was captured and killed." Penrys carefully avoided looking at the rigid Munraz. "The Zannib wizards have a tradition of banding together to overwhelm and defeat a rogue wizard, what they call a *qahulaj*."

Mpeowake gave a sharp nod of approval at that.

"This girl was more powerful than any ordinary Zannib *bikraj*, of course. Stronger than me in some ways. But in the end she died."

She reached into the pouch in front of her one more time, and laid the loop of chain before her, stretching it out into a smooth circle. "Fourteen links, as you see. She wasn't full-grown yet so it hung loose on her. But tight enough."

Vylkar asked, "Did you recognize her nation?"

"She might have been from Ellech. Light brown hair, freckles, pale eyes."

Tun Jeju waited to see if she was done, and then spoke. "Our latest guests came from a direction and over a distance that made coordination with the the capital of *sarq*-Zannib difficult, but Ussha has sent us a separate report directly, via the ambassador. They disclaim knowledge of any other chained wizards, other than Penrys and the one who wore that chain, but they're looking now. Perhaps there will be other news, soon."

Penrys heard Najud's suppressed snort. She herself had difficulty picturing how people of foreign appearance with unremovable chains could possibly go unremarked in *sarq*-Zannib, but the country was large and the cities were small and few, so perhaps the reports hadn't yet traveled to the capital.

But news about her would travel at the same time. The whole country would know what she was. It was all too easy to imagine the reaction the next time she met Najud's people.

Tun Jeju pushed away from his table and stood up, and the rest followed his lead. "This is all just a start, and you have yet to hear the Kigali side of the story. We have things to show you, and things to tell you, before we can truly examine the problem. We'll start with the showing, if you will please follow me."

One of Tun Jeju's staff hastened to open the door ahead of the *notju*, and two of them lingered behind to monitor the last of the guests as they followed their host through the door.

Munraz opened his mouth to say something, but Najud shook his head sharply to silence him. "Later," he murmured. "Not here. Save it."

The exotic procession returned to the ground floor of the building, but not to the guarded entrance. Instead, they turned down one of the back corridors. There was a brief delay at some sort of internal guard post with a locked and barred entry.

Penrys was too far back in the line, and too short, to see exactly what was going on, and her audible frustration turned Najud's head. "Don't be so eager to look," he said, without his character-istic grin. "Might not like what you find."

He pointed down, as if to indicate where they were going. *He must have some idea. What would be below this, in the Imperial Security headquarters, behind bars? Prisoners? Special prisoners?*

Penrys reined in her impatience. True to Najud's prediction, they encountered another stairway that began in front of them and went down. The texture of the steps was coarse, and the rough stone of the walls was in sharp contrast to the smooth and polished surfaces she'd seen so far in this heavily guarded building.

When she reached the lower landing, she glanced at the barred and guarded entrance into deeper recesses of the structure. Her sense of direction told her that they were not only below street level, into the embankment that was built from the stone of Tegong Him, but outside the above-ground walls of the building. *Does it extend outward in all directions, like an iceberg?*

They descended three levels altogether, and when they finally passed through the guards and another barred entrance, Penrys felt nothing but apprehension from all the members of their party, even Tun Jeju and his staff. The marks on the walls below the first level were mute but unmistakable witnesses to highwater that had reached up through the embankment at various times, and it painted a picture for her of stone underpinnings that were solid but not waterproof, not when the Mother of Rivers decided to stretch herself in a flood.

Nothing down here but prisoners? Something that can be easily moved, if necessary. Or, perhaps, not moved at all.

The dankness of the atmosphere added to the sense of being underwater, though she knew the surface of the river south of her was still further down—the embankment was taller than a mere three flights of stairs. Still, the stairway descended beyond them to lower levels yet, obscure in the gloom. *If you go down far enough, do the walls become river mud?*

The first rooms on this level that they passed through were given up to the guards and their needs. Tun Jeju held up his hand when they reached one more barred and guarded door, and his staff faded away to the back of the crowd. "We asked throughout Kigali for news of chained people, and we miscalculated the effect. When Imperial Security asks for something, everyone assumes the worst. And there were many more of them than we expected."

Penrys felt her blood chill. What would it have been like, if the whole town of Gonglik knew who she was, because of her chain, and suddenly the dreaded and feared attention of Imperial Security had fallen upon her?

"Local authorities were zealous in their efforts to please us. Disastrously so, as you'll see." He waved his hand at whatever lay behind the door. "This was not what we intended."

Penrys thought his eyes flicked in her direction briefly, but she might have been wrong.

"Worse," Tun Jeju said, "some unknown number of people fled in alarm as the news spread of the local reactions. Some of them have appeared here, in the city, and they have no reason to trust us."

"Are they a threat?" Penrys asked. *Am I?* She suspected her undertone carried the rest of her meaning.

"Not so far, not that we know."

Penrys felt the walls closing around her, and pictured the gates between here and the outside, all three of them. The wizards around her, of unknown strengths and alliance, watched silently. She didn't know how much of her concerns appeared on her face, but something must have, because Tun Jeju looked her in the eye and spoke, just to her. "I make you an oath before these witnesses, Penrys-chi, that you'll leave this building as freely as you entered."

"Or you will answer to *sarq*-Zannib," Najud said. Penrys pictured the ancient ally of Kigali, small and disorganized, throwing itself valiantly at an indifferent, massive Kigali army.

Tun Jeju nodded to Najud, as if his warning carried weight. "Just so. The Zannib ambassador will be expecting your visit this evening, after we're done here."

She felt nothing but truth in her superficial scan of the *notju*, and let her rigid posture relax.

"All right, then. Let's see your collection, Tun-chi."

CHAPTER 6

The guard who had accompanied Tun Jeju on this level unlocked the entry to the prison and stood back to let the foreigners and the *notju*'s staff enter. A narrow corridor ran to left and right along the walls and another stretched before them.

It was quiet and much drier than Penrys expected. She looked up and thought she spotted ventilation openings in the low ceilings. The light was provided by oil lanterns hung at regular intervals between each pair of iron-barred cells, and the rest of the space was dark. No light glimmered from the rows on either side, so perhaps this central row was the only one occupied.

There was an odd scent in the air—not the stench of human occupation she had anticipated, but something she couldn't place.

Tun Jeju paused in front of the first cell on the left and pulled open its unlocked door. Two of the guards pushed past the rest of them and raised their lanterns high to hook them from the ceiling on the inside, and then returned to the corridor to let the others into the small cell, two or three at a time.

The Ndanum were the first to look. Tun Jeju stood outside and spoke to them all. "Our colleagues from Rasesdad traveled from Dzongphan and came almost all the way by river. This let them bring with them the fruits of their investigations."

Penrys couldn't interpret the expression on Mpeowake's face when she stepped out of the cell. She steeled herself and walked in with Najud and Munraz.

She had expected bedframes inside, but instead two tables filled most of the space. On each was a body, embalmed and preserved—the source of the unidentified odor. One male, and one female, she noted. Nude and chained. She knew that embalming could change the appearance, but neither looked like a Rasesni. When she reached down to push the hair aside, she found small, pointed, animal ears in the same place hers were.

It wasn't clear to her how either one had died, and that was disturbing. There were neither scars nor wounds on the front of the bodies. She glanced over at Najud and found his face locked into an impassiveness that gave nothing away, and his mind was a mirror of his face. Munraz looked distraught, and she laid a hand on his shoulder and told him, "There's likely to be worse coming. Prepare yourself."

She ducked back out of the cell to make room for Vylkar and nodded at him as they passed.

Silently she walked along to the next cell as Mpeowake left it and stepped in. The tables held chains this time, small neck-sized loops. There were no fragments, only intact circles of anywhere from twelve to sixteen links. Like her own chain, there were no stains, no marks of wear, no corrosion—they looked fresh and new, in some yellow metal neither brass nor gold, as though they'd just been made.

She shuddered. There had been living people inside each of these chains, like her. These two little piles spread casually on the tables represented more than twenty people.

She backed out of the cell and waited for Najud and Munraz to join her before moving to the next cell. This time the wrinkled nose on Mpeowake's face prepared her for something worse. Two more bodies, both male, but these weren't peacefully laid out. One had been killed at a moment when most but not all of his body had been covered in a thick white fur. His limbs were fully human, and his face, and his belly was still bare, as though the change had been interrupted.

But it was the other body that made her ears move back on her scalp. A long tail, like that of a miniature whale, extruded from the base of his spine, above the legs, and the rest of his skin seemed thicker, somehow, though the embalming process made it hard to judge. There were two unhealed wounds on his back, as though he had been struck with… with what, she wondered—a harpoon? Both had the pointed ears she expected.

When she rejoined Tun Jeju in the corridor, she saw he wanted to hold them all there before proceeding. They waited in silence for the last of the foreign guests to exit the third cell.

The *notju* spoke somberly. "When the villages and even some of the smaller cities received our request for information about chained people, it raised a panic. They seized whoever they could find, in the belief that they were dangerous, and weren't overly careful about it. Many died.

"The problem was, they were mostly foreigners. A village would have welcomed someone who had wandered in a couple of years ago, of presumably mixed blood. They would labor in the fields, or help with the fishing, or work as a servant. They tended to live alone—no one would marry a foreigner. They spoke Kigali *yat* without an accent, which was reassuring, but they had no ties, no family.

"So when we asked about them, suddenly all their suspicions were aroused. Many were captured and delivered already dead. Many more fled, and the news traveled quickly. We don't know where they went, but some are here, in the city."

He paused for questions but no one spoke.

"These few cells are the exceptional specimens. There seemed little point showing you the rest." He gestured to either side of them, to the rows beyond this one. "We'll give you the counts when we go back upstairs."

He had started to turn to take them to the next cell, when Penrys stopped him.

"No. I want to see them all." She choked it out as her voice thickened. "Every last one of them, you hear me? They died out of *your* carelessness, your indifference, not because they'd harmed anyone."

She noted the looks of distaste on the faces of most of the others and spoke to them directly. "I don't care if you want to skip them—fine. It's an ugly business. But these are ordinary people— they didn't ask for this. I want to look at their faces, people like me. I want to store that up, for the day I find our… makers."

She took a breath and tried to keep her fury from distorting her speech. "They can't get justice any more—they're gone. But I'm still here. By all that you hold sacred, I'll present a reckoning and make them accountable. If I live, I'll do it."

Stepping aside from the rest of them into the middle of the corridor, she turned her back and worked on controlling her shaking hands that itched for a throat to throttle. She made herself turn and rejoin Najud, so that they could see what was in the next cell.

There were four more cells of "exceptional specimens" to examine. Penrys gritted her teeth and maintained a chilly silence. One had a pair of wings like a bat. The worst was the woman with tentacles like an octopus emerging from the base of the spine. All of them had the ears—Penrys checked each one.

Why did so many of them die in their hidden forms? If she were suddenly killed here, her wings would still be secret. *Ah, but not if I had warning and was trying to get away. Then I might try anything.*

"How were they killed?" she asked Tun Jeju, when they reached the end of the row.

"It varies," he said, expressionlessly. "Some were seized and, when they resisted, they were harmed in the capture, or hung by terrified villagers. Or burned. That's where the loose chains come from, when there was nothing left to preserve.

"Each has his own history which I'll share with you, upstairs."

"I want a copy of that," Penrys said. "For all of them." She glared at Tun Jeju, until he nodded.

Munraz asked her, quietly, "Weren't any of them taken alive?"

Tun Jeju overheard him. "Yes, some were captured alive. And some have been caught here, in the city."

"Where? Where are they?" Penrys demanded.

He glanced at Chosmod. "Our colleagues from Rasesdad have provided the expertise to keep them alive but harmless."

He gestured across the aisle to the cells they hadn't seen yet. "We tend them, and none have died."

"*Sedchabke.* You've drugged them." Her voice was flat.

"You know it?" Chosmod asked.

"Oh, yes. I know it. Vladzan and Veneshjug saw to that, in Gonglik."

Something in her tone caused all of them to look at her as if she were a sudden threat.

"Vladzan died, in the Temple Academy," Chosmod said.

"Actually, it was in a basement storage room, under the stable," she said, blandly, "while he was conducting an experiment. On me. Veneshjug didn't die until he tried to use the Voice's chain for himself."

Najud positioned himself next to her, as if anticipating a fight that had any hope of being won, here, sublevels below ground under the Imperial Security building, surrounded by other wizards.

Penrys walked over to one of the guards holding the extra lanterns, and took it out of his hand. He was wise enough not to resist. She stalked over to the last cell on the other side of the aisle and held it high. It was empty, and she continued down the row until she found one occupied.

There were two women there, lying supine, under blankets, with their eyes closed. Penrys could feel the pressure of their chains against hers from a few feet away, not fiery as it had been with the Voice, but still perceptible.

"Najud, look at their necks. Please." She'd known from his footsteps that he had followed her. The cell door was locked, and she turned to Tun Jeju and stared at him, without a word.

He nodded to a guard, and the man produced a key and unlocked the cell. Penrys backed up two steps, and Najud stepped inside.

When he bent over the woman on the left, she saw him lift the chain, and then the hair around the ears. He checked the other one the same way and rejoined her.

"There's some damage, but you have to look for it," he said.

Penrys closed her eyes for a moment, and then turned to face the rest of the wizards. "*Sedchabke* is a drug used in Rasesdad to punish wayward mages, or so I understand. It paralyzes the body and, for wizards, it suppresses all powers, leaving the victim vulnerable to whatever might be done to him in that helpless state."

She looked at Chosmod. "Did you know that a chained wizard can't get near another one? The chains heat up and burn the flesh.

"These women are too close to each other. Their necks are burning, and healing, and no one noticed, no one looked for it. How long have they been there?"

She directed the last question at Tun Jeju. She didn't quite catch him wincing, but there was some hidden reaction there.

"Some of them for three months," he said.

"And you don't consider this torture. Or didn't it matter, because you were planning to kill them anyway?"

She unclenched her fists and turned away from whatever response he planned to make. She didn't feel like informing him that they could hear everything around them, when they were awake. Let him make his own discoveries.

Chosmod walked into the cell to make his own inspection. "She's right," he called out to Tun Jeju. "We need to move them all further apart."

Turning to Penrys, he asked, *"Brudigna,* would one per cell with an empty cell on either side be sufficient space?"

"Yes." Though she wondered what the point was of removing the pain when the odds that any of them were sane after months of the drug were remote.

"How long do you usually keep a mage under *sedchabke?"*

"A day or two," Chosmod said.

"So, not a few months."

Tun Jeju spoke, "It was this or death. We had no other way to contain them."

"Because they had attacked you? Damaged you? Threatened you? What crime had they committed?"

She took a deep breath to try and rein in her rage. "Perhaps they might have come willingly to you, offered to help. Like I did."

"We had no way to train them. We have no trained wizards in Kigali."

"So you just imprison them and torture them until they go mad instead."

"Or until we could hold this council." Tun Jeju made no effort at apology.

She closed her eyes for a moment at this. For the two months that Najud and Munraz had traveled with her from western *sarq-Zannib,* these… specimens had been suffering in ways she understood all too well.

"Stop the drug. Leave them alone. Imprisoned if necessary for now, but awake. Let's find out what can be salvaged."

"And if they choose to attack us?"

"You mean now that you've given them a reason to hate you?" Najud hissed at her but she wouldn't stop. "That's a chance you'll have to take. The cells are secure enough."

"Will you make yourself responsible for them?" Tun Jeju's question acted like a bucket of cold water on her fury.

She spared a moment for the vision of complications this would make in her life, but what choice did she have?

"I will."

Penrys avoided Najud's eye, certain this was not a task he wanted to accept, and who could blame him. In the company of so many wizards, she thought it prudent to avoid mind-speech with him. At least, that was the excuse she gave herself.

While the living captives were relocated under Chosmod's direction to individual and separated cells, she took a lantern from a guard and toured the other rows, the less "exceptional" specimens. There were a double handful of bodies, but she was ashamed to admit that she lost count as she went along.

Eventually she stood alone in a pool of light looking at the last one, a man, who seemed to share her ethnicity—not tall, not thin, brown-haired, pale-skinned. It had been impossible to be sure without seeing his living face, but she'd marked his resemblance to one of the captive men, and of that one to herself. There'd been one dead woman, too, that she thought was such a candidate.

There had even been an older woman that looked similar in her coloring to the teenage *qahulajti* that had been killed in *sarq*-Zannib.

The light of two more lanterns approached, bobbing in the hands of the men who carried them—Vylkar and, at last, Najud, with Munraz.

"They're done," Vylkar told her. "Time for us to go back."

He made no comment on her overreach of responsibility with Tun Jeju.

Najud stood quietly and looked at her. He sighed, and then said one simple word, "How?"

Half the weight she was carrying seem to fall away. Not "why" but "how"—he understood the "why."

She flashed a relieved smile at him, then shrugged. "I don't know. Some sort of school, I guess. I hadn't worked it out yet."

"Down here. In the dark. In their cells."

"I suppose so—don't imagine Tun Jeju's going to turn them loose anytime soon."

"All by yourself?" Vylkar asked.

"If necessary."

Najud shook his head. "Each of them will likely be as strong as you are, and there are five of them."

"They don't know what to do, not yet. If they did, they wouldn't have been captured." *Or killed. Probably.*

Vylkar looked down at her from his extra foot of height. She always felt short in the company of Ellech men and women. "You were freshly arrived and willing to learn. I had some idea of how strong you were, but you never gave me reason to fear you, and the others… well, they didn't take it seriously."

"But these…" he waved negligently at the next row where they had entered. "They've been undiscovered for three or more years, doing who knows what, whatever it took to survive. The two you've already met, before—they're dead. You know exactly what can happen."

"The Voice was an active threat," she said, "with a small army and some sort of plan. He had to be stopped and it could only be done by other wizards. I killed him, at the end, you know."

"With an hand-axe. Aye, I've heard the tale."

"But the girl we found in *sarq*-Zannib… She was just unlucky, and damaged."

"And yet she killed hundreds," Vylkar said. "And you killed her, too."

The silent Munraz spoke up, from behind Najud. "It wasn't Penrys, it was me." His voice was thick.

Vylkar turned to stare, and Najud told him, "We had a *bikraj* on the hunt who wanted her, for… breeding. We will kill a *qahulajti* in *sarq*-Zannib and though there was debate about her full responsibility for the deaths that occurred, there was no doubt of the cause. Munraz did the right thing, hard as it was. It lost him his family and clan."

"We're making too much of this," Penrys said. "Look, if I were imprisoned here, right now, what could I do? I can't make the guards march in and release me. I can't hide from the people on the various levels so that I could escape the building. I might be able to shield myself from a search by wizards, using their methods, but I'm still vulnerable to mundane attacks. And so are they.

"What's the worst that can happen? They bind together and knock me down. How do they get out of their cells?"

She felt a twinge of conscience as she spoke. She remembered, all too well, killing Vladzan after he'd given her *sedchabke* and then tortured her for his own amusement for the hours it took for her to purge the drug from her system, drain all his power, and then stop his heart. If she could do that, so could they. But she could defend herself, and they didn't know their own strength. She hoped.

"Not alone." Najud's voice had a tone of finality that she recognized. "You will not teach them alone. Besides, they need to meet wizards that aren't chained, and the only ones around are Tun

Jeju's guests. I doubt the Ndanum will cooperate—I was watching them while you defied Tun Jeju. But I'm here."

"And I'm an apprentice, a *nal-jarghal* like they will be," Munraz volunteered. "I'll help."

She shook her head helplessly. It was one thing to take a risk herself, but something else entirely to involve them.

Vylkar spoke up. "I think the Rasesni might contribute, too. They have a long tradition of training mages in their temple system."

He smiled down at her. "You always wanted to teach, when you were in Ellech. Here's your first class."

Najud added, "Tun Jeju spoke of finding ordinary people in Kigali, untrained wizards. They need teaching, too."

Vylkar looked at him. "A school for wizards, in Yenit Ping?"

Najud shrugged. "Why not? They're going to need it, now that they've recognized they have wizards among their people, like other nations."

"How will they find them?" Penrys asked. "Can't see them sending out a message throughout the land that says 'If you hear voices in your head, we want you.' And how do we keep the locals from killing them out of fear? How many bodies are here? How many chains?"

She shook her head. "The whole culture has to change. That can't be done by one person."

Vylkar cocked an eyebrow at her. "Still impatient, I see. Tun Jeju has a plan. He must have, or he wouldn't have invited all these wizards. Let's go find out what it is."

CHAPTER 7

Najud studied the Ellech party at their table, while they waited for Tun Jeju to resume the meeting. He'd wondered what Penrys's sponsor was like, from her brief mentions of him.

The relationship struck him as mildly affectionate, more like a distant uncle than a father. Vylkar had found her, when she appeared more than three years ago, and steered her into a suitable occupation at the Collegium of Wizards at Tavnastok, but Najud didn't sense any particular partnership between them. All the work she'd done on devices and research was on her own. Must've been lonely, surrounded by wizards, and not quite part of them, obscure and little regarded, except for the respect accorded to her power that had earned her the ancient title of "adept" before they left her to conduct her own experiments alone.

Lonely, perhaps, but lucky. Very lucky, considering what might have happened to her. None of those chained wizards several levels beneath them had been as lucky.

He caught his wife's puzzled glance and patted her hand, below the level of the table. Time enough to tell her his thoughts later, in a safer, more private place.

Tun Jeju cleared his throat, and the small conversations around the tables subsided.

"It's taken us more than four months to assemble all of you together in this room, plus two months before that when we began trying to discover just what might be hiding in plain sight in our empire.

"We have a mandate from the emperor to pursue this, but I'll confess that we're not sure how to do it. We would value your suggestions."

"Stop killing them," Penrys said. "That would be a good start."

Najud winced.

Her hand went up before the *notju* could defend himself. "I say that seriously, not in anger. I understand how that… slaughter you showed us might have happened, but you're better off if they can be persuaded to come to you willingly.

She shifted forward in her seat. "You have ordinary wizards out there," she said, waving her hand vaguely to the west. "And these chained ones. Both should be an asset to your nation. The chained ones are new, probably unskilled—a wizard learns skills partly from others, which is why we're good with languages—but where are the wizards these chained ones could learn from? The Voice may have met Rasesni mages, but the girl we found in *sarq*-Zannib met no one, and was less skilled because of it."

She shook her head. "I'm more worried about the ordinary wizards that have probably been living within your people for generations. Have they gone all their lives never knowing? Never meeting each other and discovering they could mind-speak? I think that unlikely. Don't you?"

After pausing a moment to wait for a comment, she went on. "I would expect there to be communities of wizards, doing what they could to study and teach, hiding their work from official notice. After all, if you don't think wizards exist, why would you look for them?"

Najud watched Tun Jeju who listened to her without changing his polite attentive expression. The rest of his staff was less successful concealing their uneasiness.

"So," she said, "where can they hide? In the temples? As scholars? In particular professions, like healers? You know your people far better that I do, *notju-chi*—where would they be? They're not like these chained ones, scattered and lost and three years old. They'd have been able to move or congregate."

"Once you've found them, you have to persuade them to come out of hiding. If you want wizards now, after all this time, you have to make it safe for them. Recruit them. Have them find the others, and start educating them. Make them part of your nation, valuable people. You're going to need them, because these chained wizards are a different matter altogether."

Tun Jeju finally interposed some questions. "How many could there be?"

Penrys snorted. "Najud, how many Zannib are *bikrajab*?"

"Perhaps one in a hundred or two," he replied.

"Mpeowake, how many are wizards, sanctioned or otherwise, in Ndant?" Penrys asked.

"That sounds about right."

"Vylkar?"

He pursed his lips. "Not quite so many. If half of them come to the Collegium at some point in their lives… One in four hundred would be my first estimate."

Penrys had only to look at Chosmod. "One in two hundred in Dzongphan or on the plains, fewer in the high hills," he said.

"How many people are there in Kigali, *notju-chi*? Divide by two hundred for an approximation." Penrys clearly relished the startled realization on Tun Jeju's face.

"It's like saying, how many are musicians, or quick with numbers, or fast on their feet. It's a family trait, like any other."

Vylkar glowered briefly at Penrys before interceding. "It's not likely to be that bad, *notju-chi*. Not everyone who has a turn for drawing becomes an artist. Just because they have a skill doesn't mean they want to develop it. Only half the wizards in Ellech work in the profession, doing research or teaching others."

Penrys looked at Tun Jeju unrepentant. "So divide that first number you thought of by two or three. Or ten. Feel any better?"

Najud kicked her, under the table.

She took a breath. "Look, I'm sorry to be abrasive about this, but it's going to take big actions to change this situation, and years. Many years. You must have thousands of people out there who've been hiding what they are all their lives. You'll have to make them trust you, and you'll have to make it worthwhile for them to expose themselves. You'll have to make the rest of the people trust them, unless you want a disaster like the one below ground here."

"Imperial decree," Tun Jeju said. "We thought we could arrange an imperial decree of welcome to our wizards and a blanket pardon for any past… irregularities in their actions to preserve their own safety."

Penrys nodded. "That's a good start. You'll want to recruit some yourself, so you'll know what to expect." She paused for effect. "Think what good spies they'd make."

Najud admired her deadpan expression while struggling to suppress a snort. That's what the two of them had been suspected of, by Tun Jeju, just a few months ago.

Tun Jeju ignored the gibe and spoke to Vylkar. "Ndant and Zannib train wizards by apprenticeship. The Rasesni, by recruitment into the temple schools. How is it done in Ellech?"

"We have a diverse system, *notju-chi*. Apprenticeship for many, but also regional schools, and the national research academy, for students and permanent scholars. From what I know of Kigali, I think that might suit your needs as a structure."

"I'll speak more with you about this." Tun Jeju turned his attention back to Penrys. "And the chained wizards?"

"On the one hand, they're wizards like the others and need to be trained. That's fundamental. They're stronger, and some of them may be dangerous. But you've got to stop killing them just because they exist."

She took a breath and looked around the tables at the other foreign guests. "All of you have reported missing wizards, except us, for *sarq*-Zannib, and we just don't know. Have any of your missing wizards re-appeared in chains?"

Mpeowake shook her head. "We haven't checked yet. We need the lists and descriptions of… all of that." She waved her hand delicately to the levels below them.

In response to a gesture from Tun Jeju, one of his men laid a roll of papyrus sheets tied with a red ribbon in front of the leader of each party.

As he moved around the tables, Tun Jeju said, "This is all the information we have about each… person below. Can you read Kigali characters?"

At least one head nodded in each group.

"Where are they coming from? Who's making them?" Penrys's words grated out between her teeth. "Did it only happen once, more than three years ago, or have there been others, before or since? Do we know all the nations they belong to?

"And most importantly, why? What's the point? What were we… they before? Are some of them your missing wizards? Were all of them wizards before they were chained?"

Najud watched her face take on an analytical look that he recognized. "And why are they different from each other? What are all the possibilities? There were surprises down there for me."

Tun Jeju said, "You'll begin your investigations of that, and whatever training you deem appropriate, tomorrow morning. It will take that long for the drug to wear off, I'm told."

"They'll need food, clothing…"

"Tell Gen Jongto here what you need, and he'll provide it. You are not to move them from that level nor let them travel beyond the entrance—I hold you responsible for them, and the guards have their orders."

She nodded. "It's a start. Let's find out how many of them are still sane."

In the end, all the tasks were distributed. The Ndant delegation would focus on trying to identify their own among the chained wizards, especially the living one among the five.

The two Rasesni lingered with Tun Jeju's team and the three men from Ellech to consider organization and infrastructure for identifying and training the assumed crypto-wizards.

Penrys was put in charge of everything to do with the chained wizards, both the dead and the living, with the resources of Imperial Security to draw upon, and she was still shaking her head at the magnitude of the task when she left at the end of the day with her husband and their apprentice. Zep Pangwit was their guide out of the building, sour-faced with the prospect of more time spent with foreigners.

They stopped outside the building when they reached street level and debated their next steps. She'd asked Najud if he wanted to stay with the group organizing the education of the wizards, and he'd shaken his head. "Our methods are different, and suitable for the Zannib, if not Kigali. I'm interested in what they'll come up with, but I don't need to be there."

"But you liked organizing the Rasesni mages in Gonglik."

"They were already wizards—this was advanced work for them. What they're working on up there…" He cocked his head back at the building. "That's elementary school. The wizards they find might surprise them, of course—maybe they're not all that untrained. Maybe they've already got hidden schools. They won't know until they start making themselves known."

"So, how *will* you spend your time?" she asked him.

"Divided between you two, and the city, of course." He waved a hand at Munraz to include him in the conversation.

"You will be in school, *nal-jarghal*, and so will I, when Penrys is working with the chained wizards."

Very softly, now that they'd put some distance between themselves and the foreign wizards, he bespoke her. *Maybe it's the chained wizards who will need organizing this time.*

She slid her eyes to him, avoiding Zep Pangwit's attention, and nodded slightly.

"But you can't be in school all day," he said cheerily, "so we will spend time in the city. I have a caravan to plan."

He smacked his hands together and rubbed them. "Now, we must organize ourselves—we need a place to sleep, and we're expected at the ambassador's tonight for dinner."

Penrys lifted the roll of papyrus sheets. "And we have homework to do. Where do we stay while we're here?"

Zep Pangwit interrupted. "I was told to bring you to your ambassador for the evening. Housing you will be his responsibility. And if you don't get started, you'll never get there." He turned north on the street, toward Tegong Him, and the bulk of the cliff face was a shadowed presence that dominated the blocks of compounds at its feet as the sunlight faded into dusk.

"One more formal affair, *nal-jarghal*," Najud called over his shoulder to the wilting Munraz. "At least we're already dressed for it."

Penrys raised her own sigh and followed them both.

"What were they doing there, all day?" Rin Tsugo asked the runner.

The young woman who knelt before him was still breathing hard from her long run through the darkening streets all the way from the diplomatic section of Mentsek Tep to the *gewengep* in Chankau Tep.

She shook her head. "I don't know, but we only started watching the place when the woman arrived, the Zannib-who-is-not-a-Zannib. I left Am Limzu there to see if anyone else interesting came out later."

"These Zannib with their *shaibo* guide ended up at the Zannib ambassador's compound. The guide parted from them there and arranged to return in the morning—I heard him. I assigned Paik Kanau to watch, just in case, but I think they're there for the night. She'll stay as long as necessary to be sure."

Rin Tsugo evaluated the story. Kit Hachi was reliable—that's why he'd put her in charge.

"Well done," he said. "They didn't see you?"

She reared her head back indignantly. "I was well-shielded. It's not my first follow."

He smiled. "Nor your last. Now go get some dinner."

She stood up, bowed, and left.

The smell drifting through the dilapidated corridors made his stomach growl, but he preferred to wait until the end of the meal, when fewer were there. Even after months in the artificially close quarters of the compound with others chained like himself, he couldn't shake the discomfort of watching all the diners sitting at their tables carefully spaced beyond the proximity range of the chains. Close enough to talk, but without intimacy.

When he'd been the only one with a chain in the village that had given him shelter, just another wandering laborer who was hired to help in the blacksmith's workshed, the family and their servants all ate together, companionably, warmed at the same fire.

Here, no two of them could get close. He missed the human contact, the casual touches among friends. You had to learn to restrain your gestures and keep your distance.

And he wasn't the only one. He had to remind all the ones with Kigali features, those who were the brotherhood's face to the city, that they needed to remember to relax when they were outside the compound's walls, to lose their new stiffness lest they stand out and prompt a second look from the City Guard.

Am Limzu coming in to see you. Sek Seto's warning from the compound's gate gave him time to settle back down cross-legged on his raised platform and compose himself.

The sound of Am Limzu's footsteps preceded him, and the gleam in his eye alerted Rin Tsugo. "*Wo-chi*, big doings at the *shaibo* lair today. The brown-robes are up to something."

He bowed briefly and sank to his knees, then launched right into his report without much of a gesture to formality. "I don't know when they arrived, but well after Kit Hachi left with her Zannib folks, a group of three Ndanum left, one of those slithery women and her two attendants."

He drew in the air to make the shape of her vivid, and Rin Tsugo suppressed a smile.

"Had to decide whether I should follow them or wait for more. So I waited."

He smiled. "Glad I did, 'cause the next ones out were two men from Rasesdad. Here, in Yenit Ping! All dressed like priests they were."

He winked at Rin Tsugo. "Well, all good things come in threes, I thought, and sure enough right after them came three men— must have been from Ellech. Tall and pale with hair all over their faces like bears. They chatted with the Rasesni ones, and then each group went off in a different direction. Made noises like they'd be meeting up tomorrow."

He spread his hands. "I hung around to see if there'd be anyone else, but after a while I figured you'd rather hear all this even if something else came out that wasn't just another *shaibo* or *duimur*, a lousy civilian."

Well-pleased, Rin Tsugo told him, "And you were right. I'll be setting up a schedule of runners for tomorrow. I want to know when they come, where they go, and where they're staying. Speak to your *togebi*, your captain, in the morning."

Sek Seto popped to his feet and managed to make even his bow seem cocky, before he spun on his heel and left.

Rin Tsugo shook his head. *How did he ever manage to keep a low profile in whatever village housed him? What did they make of him?*

There was no point speculating. The *gewengep* left the privacy of its members largely undisturbed. They revealed only what they felt they must. Once they found their way here and took the oath, they found sanctuary.

Time to draw up a plan for runners for tomorrow—three each for four groups of foreigners. That was a lot to try and conceal in the ordinary traffic that passed the Imperial Security building, but there were ways.

CHAPTER 8

"What do you think of the city so far, Munraz?"

The noise of the merchants and traffic had lessened, partly with the close of the day, and partly because they had entered a more wealthy and private district. Many of the compounds they passed occupied an entire block, and their discrete stuccoed walls were well maintained.

"There are so many streets they have to name them," Munraz said, trying to keep his voice down and avoid a scornful look from Zep Pangwit.

He cocked his head at the characters on the walls of the compunds or individual buildings at the corners, sometime accompanied by an illustration. The gates of the compounds were marked by the family names or, less frequently as they penetrated further into this district, by business concerns.

Penrys pointed out the tops of trees, all you could see of the gardens which she assured him were probably inside. She'd seen compounds like this in Gonglik, but Najud had told her they were modest compared to Yenit Ping. Now she believed him.

The compound that occupied the next block on the left was distinguished by the presence of two Kigali guards bracketing the gates in the middle of the block. In addition to the characters chiseled and filled with color on the wall, a small horse had been painted, at chest height, complete with the colorful abbreviated saddle of the Zannib nomads.

She read the characters and snorted. "Can you make those out?" she asked Munraz.

"South, horse, no-house…" he said, puzzled. "Wait, is that how they signify *sarq*-Zannib?"

"I expect so," she said, grinning.

Najud looked back to see what they were laughing about and read the characters for himself. "Could be worse. I think the sign for 'monkey' figures somewhere in the Ndant name."

Penrys glanced across the street while Zep Pangwit spoke to the guards. A young woman in a high-necked robe standing there looked away impatiently, as if she were waiting for someone. Not many were out in the dusk, and those that were all walked as if they were eager to reach their destinations. *Odd place to just wait. Watching us?*

She'd just about decided to drop her shield to look at her more closely when Najud distracted her. "Planning to come in?"

The gates had swung inward, and Zep Pangwit hastened past her, back the way they'd come. When she looked again, the woman was gone.

"He'll meet us again in the morning to take us to our first day of school," Najud said. "I invited him to stay but…"

He waggled his hand.

"So, you say you've met this fellow before? The ambassador?" she said, stepping up to accompany him side by side.

"His name's Talqatin. Three years ago, the last time I was in the city. It's a courtesy to let him know one of his countrymen is here. I was never invited to dinner, though, so this'll be a first for me, too."

The gates closed behind them, and Penrys got her first good look at a fashionable dwelling.

The height of the walls, ten feet and more, blocked out most of what was left of the noise of the street. A small graveled courtyard, with a gatekeeper's shelter to her right, defined the area just inside the closed gates. A mature tree of a variety she didn't recognize filled the interior right hand corner and towered high above the outer walls. The lower internal wall behind the courtyard was closed off from the back half of the compound by a double gate.

The smell and sound of horses drew her eye to the outer edge of the stable block which made up most of the right side of the courtyard. The curious heads which popped out of the openings with tied-back shutters to investigate the new arrivals made her smile.

"Do all compounds have their horses right up front?" she asked.

Najud grinned. "Probably not. Only the Zannib think of horses as part of the family, after all."

To the left and up two steps was the grand entrance to the house. She envisioned the size of the city block and realized the house must occupy all or most of the left side of the compound. Beyond the wall in front of her there must be access to the stables, and by implication, all the work areas for the servants, and probably their dwellings, too. And another entrance, she suspected.

A dignified Kigali, his gray braid swaying along the back of his formal robes, walked down the steps and bowed to them. "Please be welcome to this bit of *sarq*-Zannib, *binochiwen*. I am Mir Tojit, the *katsom* for the *likatchok* Talqatin. He has asked me to show you to your rooms and then bring you to him after you've refreshed yourselves."

Penrys rotated her head on her neck until the bones cracked and then accompanied Najud up the steps behind. She was more than ready for the day to be over. Too many people, too much death. On impulse, she gripped Najud's forearm and gave it a squeeze. At his surprised look, she said, "Just grateful there's someone here who's *not* a stranger and doesn't expect the impossible."

She glanced back to include Munraz. "And glad to still be walking around above ground unlike those poor *drepfarar* we saw, those lost souls."

It was chilly indoors, with all the stone walls. Cooler in summer that way, she supposed. There were two stories to the building, near the wall, with a grand staircase and two entryways leading deeper into the building. Mir Tojit led them smoothly up the steps and then straight back to another staircase. Penrys realized there must be another story for the central portion.

The third floor left the world of polished stone flooring for smooth and worn wooden floors and walls. Not servants' quarters, these, but more like the rooms of old retainers or lesser family members. Everything was clean and in good repair but not quite suitable for formal display, for public entertaining.

The change in sound as their footsteps transitioned from stone to wood relieved some of the tension Penrys had been carrying. Her shoulders dropped and she almost smiled. Mir Tojit stopped to open one broad door on the left and gesture them in. The room was small and lightly furnished. He crossed over to an inner door and opened it to reveal another room.

"This is intended for the two of you," he said, bowing to Najud and Penrys. "The *likatchok* felt that you might also need a workplace…" he waved his hand at the open doorway beyond, "…or perhaps you wish for another bed or other arrangement."

Najud slipped an arm around Penrys's waist and shook his head. "Are we intended to stay here long, then, *katso-chi?*"

"Did the *notju* not inform you? The *likatchok* invites you to stay here while you are working on this Kigali project."

Penrys ducked out of Najud's grip and opened a wardrobe. "They brought our things," she told him. She spun to ask Mir Tojit, "All the horses and packs, too?"

"The riding horses are here, and the pack animals have been moved to the stables we use when we exceed our own capacity, a few blocks away, along with their tack. All the packs are in your second room. We will be happy to rearrange anything that doesn't meet with your approval."

This was looking better and better. "And our student?"

"Come and see."

Mir Tojit led them back out and walked them further down the corridor. The door he opened revealed a smaller room, in a line with theirs. Its inner door opened back into the room in the middle. "Is this suitable, *binochi?*" he asked Munraz.

"It's very fine, *katsom-chi,*" Munraz said. Penrys noticed he looked rather worn, too.

"One more thing, and then I'll leave you to yourselves for an hour." Mir Tojit took them across the corridor to a small room at the end. As Penrys had hoped, after what she'd seen during her day spent in the Imperial Security building, this led to indoor plumbing for sanitation. Civic water engineering was clearly a strength in Yenit Ping, and a good thing for the health of its people.

They followed him back out to the corridor, and he handed each of them a key. "These are for your rooms. The inner room's doors bolt on either side. There is always a guard at the two entrances who will admit you at any hour, and someone will always be on duty at the main entrance to the house—you have but to knock. The *likatchok* understands that you may have duties that might call you out at unusual hours and he wishes you to have the freedom to come and go as you need to."

Najud bowed to him. "That is very generous and understanding of the ambassador. We'll try not to trouble his household unnecessarily."

"Ring the bell in your room if you need anything, at any time. I will return for you in a while."

He walked off with a firm step and descended the stairs.

"Nap," Penrys said, looking at the others. "I need a nap before a diplomatic dinner, and I advise you to do the same Munraz. Nothing like sleep to give events a little distance."

She left both the men and reentered the room she shared with Najud. The view through the windows from the doorway ran south and the abrupt end of the buildings many blocks away betrayed the beginning of the river. When she walked over and looked down, she discovered there was a bit of a garden two stories below, bordered by the outer wall and surrounded by the house. On the left was a compact tree, rising up to her left past the window. And on the right, across a cultivated space from the tree, where plantings were flush with the bright green of spring, stood a good-sized *kazr*— hidden, colorful, and completely out of place in the center of Yenit Ping.

Her peal of laughter drew Najud to her side, where he grinned appreciatively. "Do you suppose that's to contradict the 'no-house' sign out there for *sarq*-Zannib?" he said.

Penrys hooked a thumb at their packs in the next room. "Think we should break ours out and pitch it next door?"

Penrys eyed the Zannib ambassador warily. She'd met the Zannib-*hubr*, the traditional nomads of the central steppe, a class to which Najud also belonged. And the merchants and various functionaries of the Biziz Rahr were like others she'd met, though merchants tended to stay put in Ellech rather than travel.

But this was the first of the Zannib-*taghr* she'd encountered, what the nomads called the "slow Zannib," the ones who were settled into farming and agricultural districts. These were the most cosmopolitan, especially those living in the capital city of Ussha.

She looked him over in the small but elegant reception room— a man in his fifties, his curly hair a mix of pepper and salt. He and his wife wore robes similar to hers and Najud's, so at least she didn't feel as if she were attired as a country bumpkin. Munraz as always tried to fade into the background, but it wasn't easy for him, since he was already taller than Najud and likely to keep growing a while.

"Talqatin, son of Shaldaj of clan Umlaqlud, of the Nazghib tribe." The ambassador nodded his head affably to them while she smiled and nodded back. "My wife, Qulsharma, and our daughter, Baijukti."

The wife had a polished expression. *She's hosted dozens of encounters like this. No challenge at all.* Penrys was careful to let nothing appear on her face.

You could tell the daughter was happy to see countrymen, Penrys thought. Her smile was spontaneous, especially when she looked up at the face of the young man closest to her in age. Munraz shuffled a step back as though she were dangerous, and then belatedly nodded.

"And of course you know our names, but let's do it right." Najud's tone of good humor cut through some of the formality. "I'm Najud, son of Ilsahr of clan Zamjilah, of the Shubzah tribe. This is my wife, Penrys, lately of Ellech, and our *nal-jarghal* Munraz, adopted into my clan."

He smiled at them all. "There—that's done. And, yes, we're all *bikrajab*." That last was addressed to Baijukti, with a grin, and he winked at her.

"Aren't you young to be taking an apprentice?" Qulsharma asked him.

"Well, yes, *lijti*, but circumstances…"

"Ah, circumstances." Talqatin nodded. "I often hear of 'circumstances' when I'm visited by my countrymen here. Whenever I hear the word, I think of something that will end up difficult to untangle."

"In this case, I believe you're safe, *lij*—we've been getting ourselves into and, so far, out of trouble for a while."

Talqatin raised an eyebrow and looked faintly skeptical. "It's certainly true that your life appears to be much more complicated than when we last met, just a few years ago. Though it seems to me I remember something about a wager and a broken shop window…

Perhaps Najud could use an interruption. "Please let us thank you for your generous invitation to stay with you for… however long it's going to be." Penrys included both Talqatin and his wife. "We'll try not to disturb you."

"And how long *will* it be, *bikrajti*?"

Penrys wondered how much Tun Jeju had told him. "You know the *notju* has assembled wizards from Ellech, Ndant, and Rasesdad. And us."

He nodded.

"Did he explain why?"

When Talqatin shook his head, Najud took over. "*Bikrajab.* The Kigali have finally discovered they have wizards after all. You've heard what we've been doing, in the west of *sarq*-Zannib?"

"Yes, I've had a long report. More than one." He looked at the exposed chain on Penrys's neck. "There's been quite a correspondence between Ussha and Yenit Ping on what the two of you have been up to for the last few months. We've even heard a bit about Munraz's family."

"Not my family any more, *lij.*" Munraz's voice was quiet but firm. "My *jarghal* is my family, now."

"So I had heard."

Talqatin stroked his chin. "And then there's this *biziz* you think to found in the west. Not busy enough, *bikraj*, with your other responsibilities?"

Najud grinned engagingly. "We had an opportunity to wheedle concessions out of both Kigali and Rasesdad, and I plan to keep them, if I can. Why not?"

"So why aren't you there, working on it now?"

"Because those chained wizards you heard about, and me— we're not the only ones." Penrys swept one hand through the air at chest height. "The wizards Tun Jeju summoned found several, all dead, and many more have been found in Kigali, some living, and more in hiding. I think the wizards he's assembled are going to recommend bringing them all out into the open and offering training."

"Not the Ndanum," Najud said.

Penrys shrugged. "Too soon to tell."

"Anyway," she continued, "I'm the only one they know that they, sort of, trust. He made it a condition of the caravan licenses that we come and help with this. Whatever that's going to mean, or however long it'll take."

Najud added, "I don't see how it can be very long. What are the chances that the Kigali will want foreigners officially involved in their own institutions, even brand new ones?"

The whole group of them shared a Zannib smile at that.

A servant appeared on the doorway and caught Qulsharma's eye. "Our dinner's ready," she said. "Let's postpone business and hear about some of the adventures of our guests for a while. I've never seen Neshilik and the Gates where the Seguchi passes through into the plains. What's that like?"

How do they keep a formal conversation going like this?

Munraz politely answered all the questions addressed to him, but couldn't find the knack of tossing a question back, the way everyone else seemed to. Conversations came to him to die, and it was mortifying.

There were only six of them at the table, a low one suited to the all-Zannib diners who sat crosslegged on the floor. The food presented was as close to Zannib expectations as possible, given the foreign Kigali markets.

The ambassador and his wife sat at each end. To Talqatin's left were Penrys and Munraz, and to his right Baijukti and Najud.

Talqatin focused on Penrys rather than his daughter, of course, and the two of them went deep into Ellech culture and comparative methods of education. Penrys's hands flew when she talked unselfconsciously like this, and it didn't seem to bother her that the ambassador was more restrained in his movements.

When Qulsharma wasn't being entertained by Najud with tales of his travels, she turned to Munraz and asked him about his first impressions of Yenit Ping.

On the one hand, he was full of things he wanted to talk to a friend about, but on the other he knew she was just making polite conversation in her charming and professional diplomatic way, and he blushed to present himself as an unsophisticated back-country Zan to such a polished woman. And to everyone else who could hear him.

It tied his tongue and he stammered commonplace replies that discouraged further enquiry. When he caught a sympathetic glance from Baijukti, it just embarrassed him more.

As he listened to the others, his thoughts turned to tomorrow's work. Five chained *bikrajab*, likely to wake up mad. How could they all talk so normally tonight, as if that didn't matter?

CHAPTER 9

"You have to admire a woman who will use her own daughter to get a guest talking."

Penrys was curled up in one of the broad cushioned chairs in their room, not quite ready for sleep, and Najud was slumped in its mate, his legs stretched out at full length.

"He was like a bird hypnotized by a snake," Najud chuckled. "A very nice, plump, friendly snake. He couldn't take his eyes off of her."

"Good for him to meet someone his own age, someone polished and experienced, an international traveler. Besides, she's probably bored for company, too."

"I imagine she's met every Zan passing through, but that wouldn't be very many. And how many of them would be suitable young men, with an air of mystery and reserve? It's an effective technique—I wonder if he knows that yet?"

Penrys snorted. "Overrated. I prefer a man who can make me laugh."

"That's fortunate for me, then. I'm not very mysterious."

The small square table between them was covered with pages from the untied papyrus packet, the discarded red ribbon caught in a curl on top like a trail of blood.

She waved her hand at the paper. "This makes for sad reading, once you read between the dry numbers. So much waste."

With a yawn that felt as if it might take her head off, she glanced at Najud to check that he was still awake.

"What are we doing here, Naj-sha? What am I supposed to do with five of them in the imperial… dungeon, not to mention all the rest of them that must be around? All by myself? The job's much too big for one person.

"I'm not saying that maybe Vylkar and Chosmod and the others can't work up a system of education and training, and no doubt Tun Jeju can issue all the decrees he wants, in the emperor's name, but we're talking years of labor, something you dedicate lives to. We don't want to spend years here doing this."

Najud was silent for a moment. "Can you walk away from what you saw today, leave them in ungentle Rasesni hands?"

She shook her head. "That's the problem. I can't. But I can't let myself get sucked down by it, either."

With a shove, she twisted to face Najud. "I want their maker, our maker—that's what I want. All the rest—training the chained ones as wizards, answering their questions with what little I know, trying to protect them from Kigali fear—I'll do what I can, but I'm not some tutelary deity they can shelter behind. I'm just another lost one myself, luckier, but little wiser."

"It'll sort itself out," Najud said. "Just give it a little time. I don't believe Tun Jeju expects us to stay indefinitely. If he wants to build Kigali institutions for his wizards, he'll need to make formal arrangements, staff them, and so forth. That might be mostly foreigners, which'll gall them, but what else can he do? But it won't be this group doing most of the work in the long run—they won't want to stay for that without warning any more than we do."

"The chained wizards are bad enough." Penrys yawned. "Think how many untrained regular wizards there must be in a nation this size. It's a wonder they've managed to keep hidden, assuming they're there."

"These foreigners could teach us something about shielding," Char Nojuk commented sourly.

The senior members of the Char family who were gathered in the secured inner sanctum of their compound's small temple knew better than to comment. When the *samkatju* was frustrated, anyone who came to his attention could expect to pay part of the price.

Char Nojuk's gray braid gleamed in the dim light of the lantern. He glanced at his second daughter, the only one of his own offspring to manifest the *lupchit*, the wizard blood. "What news from Shwa Uchi? Anything out of the Ndant envoys?"

Char Dami shook her head. "All these foreign wizards, and every one of them shielded, night and day. His compound's well-situated to reach both the Ndant and Rasesni ambassadors, but it's not doing them any good."

"We have to know what the *shaibowen* are planning. Look at the mess they made of the chained ones. Are we going to be next?"

He glowered at his relatives, by blood and by adoption. "I told the council that delaying action for the new chained ones would be a mistake."

His nephew had the temerity to contradict him. "*Samkatju-chi*, we could never have adopted the ones that look like foreigners without raising an interest we didn't want."

"That doesn't excuse the delay. Nothing changed in three years. Now look where we are—many of them dead, and the rest scattered all over the place or making their way here, where even the *shaibowen*, the brown-robes, are sure to stumble over them if we don't notice them first and steer them. They got the latest from the City Guard, I'm told."

He wrinkled his nose. "That *gewengep* in Chankau Tep has the right idea—hide the foreigners away from the public eye."

Char Dami said, "But they lose the new arrivals, so often."

"What do you expect from untrained beginners? I've told the council we need to suck them into the families so we can disperse and control them, not keep them at arm's length, but do they listen? No! They're afraid of the unknown, like a bunch of old women."

"You've heard the stories out of Neshilik, *samkatju-chi*," his nephew said. "Strange tales. That's the same chained woman they pulled in from the Zannib. We don't know what the chained ones can do once they're trained. The council's just being prudent. Can't un-tell the secret once it's been revealed. The new ones don't need to know about us, not yet."

Char Nojuk just growled. He couldn't set himself against the council with just his own family—he'd never survive. The council took a dim view of anyone who jeopardized their own secrets and power base.

"Keep an eye on that Zannib trio when they come back in reach of the shop tomorrow," he told his nephew. "I want to know everything that's going on with the *shaibowen*."

Penrys drowsed in Najud's arms, grateful for solid walls and lockable doors. Despite the activities of a few minutes ago that had sent Najud into a smiling sleep, she couldn't turn her mind off.

Would any of the five be sane? Could they make themselves work with their captors or would they be implacable enemies after their harsh treatment?

She herself hadn't forgiven the Rasesni who captured her, and they were dead now. Tomorrow she'd find herself on the other side of the same coin, and she didn't relish the position.

And what about the rest of them, chained and unchained?

She lay in the dark, and for the first time in Yenit Ping she let herself search the thousands of minds in her near vicinity, looking just for that special spark which said "wizard" to her.

Nothing in the Zannib compound except the sleeping Munraz and Najud. She expanded casually to the next few blocks and bolted upright in her bed while she looked again.

Najud stirred sleepily by her side. "Hmm?"

"Wizards," she told him.

"Where?"

"Everywhere. In clusters. Like so many mice in their nests. As far as I can reach."

His eyes popped open. "Really? Can you show me?"

She let him in to watch while she ran through it a third time.

What's that one? And this?

She tasted the flavor. *Chained, I think. One just outside, probably spying on the place.* She remembered the woman she'd seen waiting across the street, and wondered.

"They're not lost, secret wizards, are they?" Najud said. "They're *organized*, or they wouldn't be in clusters like that."

She nodded. "But the chained ones are solitary, or in pairs."

Najud's voice carried confidence. "And they're not in the nests with the rest of the mice."

"Or at least not in this part of town. It's a very big place, and I can't scan it all."

"Maybe you're going to need to learn how. Meanwhile, you need to get to sleep."

"But this is…"

"Not as important as getting some sleep for tomorrow. I can see I'll have to take your mind off your problems. Again."

"But…" Najud's busy hands compelled her attention elsewhere.

"Well, if you insist…"

CHAPTER 10

They were both up well before breakfast. Penrys followed Najud down the stairs, and stopped a servant to make sure Munraz was awakened in half an hour.

"Is Talqatin still in the garden?" Najud murmured to Penrys, after he'd waved away another servant, looking to offer them refreshment.

She scanned and nodded. "In the *kazr*, by himself."

They'd passed the corridor that led to the garden last night, and when they stood on the outer threshold of the building now, Najud paused. The *kazr* to their right just fit the space, its six-lattice framework covered with felts and canvas. The stove wasn't lit—no smoke exited the *zamjilah* opening at the top. The surrounding compound wall blocked most of the early morning sound in this district of the city, and the breeze off the not too distant river stirred the spring leaves in the tree to their left, covering much of the noise with a natural susurration.

"*Tawirqaj.*" Najud's call was soft, so as not to disturb the household. In *sarq*-Zannib itself, he would have just walked up and knocked on the door frame of the *kazr*, but here, in a household's inner garden, he was uncertain of the proper protocol.

The ambassador answered. "Come, *lij.*"

They walked quietly through the plantings that were beginning to color up, and ducked into the *kazr*.

Inside, they found Talqatin seated crosslegged in front of a common portable worktable, two piles of parchment sheets on his left, and several wax-filled tablets for taking notes scattered across the rest of the surface. A basket for Kigali *yat* papyrus rolls sat beside him.

"You've caught me," he said, with a smile. "My servants will cooperate when I ask for a low table for a Zannib supper, but they want to see me at my desk like a true Kigalino. So I come out here to be comfortable and to get through as much of my work as I can, and use my office for official functions."

"And who can blame you," Penrys said. "I've gotten used to one of these myself, though I still like a desk and chair, in the Ellech style. Can't carry them on a horse too conveniently, though, I'll admit."

"Something I can do for you?" He addressed Najud, who had paused to collect his thoughts.

"Here we are in Yenit Ping," he said, "the largest city in the world. Very civilized it is, too. So civilized, that I thought for once I'd go prepared into a dangerous venture."

He eyed Penrys. "I'd like us to make wills, for the ambassador to hold, just in case. Munraz is our responsibility, now, and other things."

She blinked, and then nodded, and a bit of tension unknotted in his chest. He hadn't been sure how she'd react.

"Instead of just jumping off a cliff, as usual?" Her voice was teasing, but they'd really done it, in Neshilik. No need to explain to Talqatin, though.

"Just so," he said, smiling.

The ambassador picked up one of the wax-filled tablets. "I'll be happy to oblige you, *lij, lijti*. What did you have in mind?"

"It's simple enough. First I'd like Munraz to get back safely. None of this is his business. Getting him to my clan would be enough—he's a member now. That's if both of us... you understand."

Talqatin nodded.

"And in that case, too, I'd leave everything, especially my *biziz* licenses to my sister Rubti."

He glanced at Penrys and she shrugged. "I haven't got anyone," she said matter-of-factly, and he winced inwardly. "That'll be fine for me, too. Except for one thing..."

She looked at Najud as she spoke to Talqatin. "In my packs here there's a sack of small, dull stones. Those should go to... Vylkar, I suppose. In the Ellech delegation."

I forgot about those. Power-stones shouldn't be left in Zannib hands, true enough.

"All right," Najud said. "And if it's just one of us, everything to the other, of course." It quenched his appetite, just thinking of it.

"That's it?" Talqatin asked, his voice business-like.

"That's all."

"Easy. I'll have it for you to look over this afternoon."

"Um…" Penrys said. "Do you suppose we might sign something this morning, before we leave?"

Talqatin covered it smoothly, but Najud could see his surprise.

"Could be a tough morning," Najud explained.

"And a lively week," Penrys added.

Once inside the Imperial Security building, Zep Pangwit escorted them to the entry at the third sublevel.

Penrys wanted to survey the people around her for hidden wizards, chained or otherwise, but had trouble getting her mind off the anticipated problems they would encounter this morning.

By common consent, everyone who planned to participate in this first session congregated together first. Both the Rasesni were there, of course, and Vylkar from the Ellech party. Ijumo, the middle-aged man from the Ndant party, joined them, to Penrys's surprise. Tun Jeju did not plan to go in himself, but sent Gen Jongto as his representative. The *notju* held the master keys that would lock them in together, in case complete disaster ensued, and he held those keys in a separate location.

Penrys wanted to tell them that if they were overwhelmed and these chained wizards were knowledgeable, they could probably force ordinary people at quite a distance to help them. But, if they believed that, this impasse would never be resolved. And she didn't really think they knew what to do or how to join together, so she took the risk on herself. She thought Najud might know better, but he kept his council.

She glanced at him and he gave her an encouraging nod. She scanned the cells ahead of her and felt the five minds, their bright cores, so much brighter than the ordinary wizards around her. They were no longer asleep.

"It's time," she said, looking at each of them. "You all under-stand—you will observe, and I will lead. If it goes well, it will be quite boring." Her smile flickered at them.

"If things go very wrong, then you know what to do." That last was directed to the captain of the guard. He had orders to release an aerosol version of *sedchabke* which Chosmod had prepared. It would be a crude defense, but it ought to put them all down.

A guard unlocked the gate into the cell area, and stood aside, ready to slam it shut and lock it as soon as the last one was inside.

Penrys was relieved to find chairs set up inside, in two rows in front of the five spaced cells. The sound of the gate opening and then slamming shut with a clang had brought the five of the prisoners to the front of their cells. They were all clothed from the garments left for them.

She focused her attention on the minds around her—the wizards of unknown potential behind her and the five in front of her, and tried to shut out all other concerns.

Those chairs needed to be shoved against the opposite cells, or their spread-out audience wouldn't be able to see them. With a wave of her hand, she pushed the observers to move them back. Najud led the activity.

Then she hauled the chair she'd reserved for herself and pulled it forward a few feet, making sure the prisoners could see her, and sat down.

"Well," she said to them. "This is a real mess, isn't it?"

Some of them blinked, Not what they had expected.

"You were given a drug called *sedchabke*. They use it in Rasesdad to suppress the mind and body of a wizard, as part of their training."

A flicker of surprise rose from two minds.

"Yes, you're all wizards. Didn't you know?"

She stood up and walked in front of them, with her chain on prominent display. "So am I. So are most of them." She waved a hand in the direction of the audience.

"My first question is—are you all right? That drug isn't supposed to be used that long. No visions of dragons? No one gibbering?"

An involuntary chuckle broke from one of them. The mind-glows seemed healthy enough. Anger and fear were both to be expected, and there was plenty of that. Fair enough.

"M'name's Penrys. I was found, a bit over three years ago, in Ellech, by that wizard." She pointed to Vylkar. "Unclothed, with no memory." She monitored their reactions and nodded in satisfaction. "Sounds familiar, eh?"

"We're not the only ones. You must have heard us, yesterday. Over there, in those cells, are what's left of a bunch of others. And, of course, there're more to be found."

She could feel defensive shields rising, from those that knew how.

"Before you start worrying, let me explain what's happening. While you were making a life for yourselves in Kigali, I blundered into a situation in the west…"

She told them the story of the Voice in Neshilik, and then the poor *qahulajti* in *sarq*-Zannib. "So, you can see that the only chained wizards who had made themselves known to the Kigali so far were those two, and me."

They were still listening. "Now, you know the Kigaliwen… No wizards here, eh?"

More chuckles. Good. "This made them reconsider that position. So they decided to do something about it. They summoned some of us foreigners to tell them if they had any wizards in chains—that was a smart move. And they alerted the villages to find out if there were any there. And that was bad judgment, in my opinion. They didn't understand how many of you would look like foreigners and didn't think about what might happen."

The mind glows were sad now, or outraged.

"Yes, I can tell you agree with me. They know it was ill done— it's not what they wanted. In a panic, they asked the Rasesni to help with this drug, and you've been here a while, some of you more than others. They've been feeding you liquids and trying to keep you alive."

She waved her hand above her head. "You're down in the depths of the Imperial Security building in Yenit Ping, by the way, in case you've never been here before."

A snort or two. "I've been tasked by Tun Jeju, a *notju* I met in Neshilik, to try and fix all this. I got here yesterday, and here we are."

She sat down and waited for a response. None of them had given her a name yet and she tagged them in private, left to right, as Kigali woman, Rasesni woman, a man of her own ethnicity, Kigali man, and Ndant man.

The Kigali man said, "Why should we tell you anything, or cooperate?"

She shrugged. "Well, I can't think of any good reason, except that you're on this side of the aisle instead of that side." She hooked a thumb behind her. "Lot of dead people over there, though as far as I know none of them were killed directly by Imperial Security."

They need more context and fewer things to hide. "Did you know that many of them could modify their form? I don't know if all of you can, but some of them died that way, and me, well…"

She stood up again and invoked her wings. No one there besides Najud and Munraz had seen that before. Even Tun Jeju had never known exactly how she and Najud had escaped the Voice in Neshilik. There was more noise behind her than in front, but she ignored it and walked the full length of the cells, keeping enough distance from the prisoners that their chains didn't cause pain.

"I was lucky—I was recognized for a wizard and trained as one, and I've been working as one ever since. Kigali wants to start doing the same with its own wizards, and with all of you. Part of what I'm here to do is get you started."

She released her wings and sat down, then leaned forward with her elbow on her knees. "But, you know, they're scared of you. Those other two I told you about, they killed hundreds of people, and Yenit Ping is a big place. Any wizard can do a lot of damage, and we chained ones, once we're trained, we're stronger. Now, we don't lock up a strong swordsman, just because he *can* kill people. We arrest him if he does it, but only afterward, not before, just in case. That's what a civilized nation does."

She glanced at them all significantly in their cells. "Not very civilized, is this?"

One more check of the mind-glows of the prisoners. Lots of anger, still, but tempered from the first meeting, and much less fear.

Strolling over the the entrance gate, she called, "I want the key to the cells. You can keep this gate locked."

The startled guard on the other side looked to Gen Jongto for confirmation, and the man nodded. The key landed at Penrys's feet with a clink.

"First step. Let's at least get you a modest change of scenery." She walked down the row. As she approached each cell door, the pressure of the chains on each other forced the prisoner back. There was a twinge when she got close enough to unlock the door, but nothing too bad. When the door swung open, she stepped back.

Only the Rasesni woman contested her approach. She was a bit older than Penrys, and stubborn. Penrys dangled the key from her hand and shrugged, and the woman retreated back to let her unlock the door.

She spared a moment to see how her other audience was reacting to this bit of theater. Ijumo was somewhat alarmed but hiding it. Chosmod and Mrigasba shared with Vylkar a professional interest. Najud and Munraz were wary, like Gen Jongto.

"Ugly stuff in those cells over there, but you have as much a right to see it as we did, yesterday. Go take a look, please. Then come on back."

She walked back to the entrance gate. "Any way we can get five more chairs in here?"

Again the guard checked with Gen Jongto and got a nod. Penrys took the precaution of making sure none of the prisoners were near the entrance when it was unlocked and the extra chairs shoved in. She waved Najud and Munraz over to help her, and between them they hauled the chairs over to face Penrys's, outside of the cells, and as closely spaced as she thought the chains would likely permit.

The prisoners slowly made their way back and took a seat. Their demeanor was sober, and Penrys scanned and saw they'd finally moved past anger, mostly, into dismay. *Very suitable. Now maybe we can get cooperation.*

"So. Imperial Security makes its apology on behalf of Kigali and now we have everyone's attention. Time for some names."

Penrys introduced each of the people with her, ending with her own. "And this is Najud, my husband. And our apprentice, Munraz. I'm going to be doing a quick introduction to wizardry, and we thought he could benefit, too." She could feel the dirty look he gave her, and thought she caught amusement on the face of the Kigali man.

The young man who looked like her ethnic cousin spoke first. "They call me Dar Datsu. Where are you from?"

"Wish I knew," she told him. "You and the other man, over there, and maybe that woman," she hooked her thumb behind her, to the other cells, "you're the only ones I've ever seen that seem like we belong together."

The Kigali woman called herself Goi Ofa. The Rasesni woman hesitated, then announced, "Lai Tsumai. I didn't pick it."

The Ndant man stared at Ijumo in fascination. "Lir Pako. They were right, I do look like a Ndano."

The Kigali man shrugged. "Tse Lorping. Hardly matters, I can always get another name. None of them are real."

"Penrys is surely not my original name, either," she said, "but my past is lost to me, as I assume yours is lost to you. I've found that my body remembers some things my mind has lost, however, so if you find that you have a hand for something—music, say, or a craft—it may be an echo of what's gone."

"Why does this *notju* want us to be stronger?" Lai Tsumai asked. "Wouldn't that just make us more of a threat?"

Penrys could feel both her sneer and and the underlying fear that drove it. She glanced back at Gen Jongto to make sure he was listening.

"Because you may be dangerous if you get some basic training, but you're even more dangerous if you don't. You see, Imperial Security decided to look for you first, assuming it could look for regular wizards afterward. It didn't realize—there are lots of wizards in Kigali, in hiding. And they must surely know about you. You haven't been here all that long, but the other wizards… generations?"

That created havoc among the wizards behind her.

"You have no defenses, and you're going to need them. *That's* why the sudden training."

Gen Jongto interrupted her. "How do you know this about the other wizards?"

Penrys turned her chair around and faced the six foreign wizards. "You're not a wizard, Gen-chi, but the rest of you are. Come with me."

She bespoke them all, even the prisoners. *If you can hear me, try to just follow.*

Pulling them behind her like so many fish on lines, she mind-scanned the building for the inner glow of wizards. *See the one on the ground level, and the other on the upper floor?*

Rather than getting sucked into the particulars, she continued out to the street and the surrounding blocks. There were several in the immediate area, and one group of four.

I think these are chained ones, at a glance. She zoomed in on two more standing together, with a stronger core.

Why? Because they look like the five of you. She swooped in to look at the prisoners.

Or me. She let them get a good look at the power and texture of her mind before she raised her shields again and isolated herself.

Vylkar shook his head and turned to Gen Jongto. "She's right. You've got wizards all over, and two like these, probably watching the building because of them." He pointed to the prisoners.

"But who's in charge of them?" Gen Jongto said.

"Who, indeed?" Penrys laughed. "Want to bet it's no one person, but a bunch of factions? Wizards have politics, too, just like everyone else."

Vylkar and Chosmod both nodded ruefully.

"And these," she turned to the seated prisoners. "Two of you were picked up here. I'm sure there's at least one refuge in Yenit Ping, and maybe more."

She raised her hand before Dar Datsu could sputter defiance. "I'm not asking you where it is. I can find it just by looking, once I start. And so can you and, more to the point, so can the other wizards. They've probably been watching you all for three years or more."

"It's not a matter for 'control' any more, Gen-chi. Imperial Security can't control this. They've got to co-opt it somehow. And to do that, they're going to need to meet the leaders, since leaders there must surely be."

"My mandate is only for these prisoners," Gen Jongto said.

"They're not your problem, or at least, not yet," Penrys said. "You've gotten a hold of a few young lions that you're worried about taming before they finish growing, but you're surrounded by packs of wolves that could overwhelm you now and are probably just realizing that they're no longer invisible, at least not to the foreign wizards you've brought in. What are they going to do?"

She waved a hand at the rest of the wizards. "All the rest of these emissaries are concerned about any chained wizards that may be hidden in their own countries, and the whole general mystery of where they… we come from. But their ordinary wizards are already integrated into their societies."

Chosmod said to Gen Jongto, "Tun Jeju may already understand this. Or not. But I agree with Penrys—that's more urgent than these five here."

Najud said, "And yet, these must be trained."

Penrys nodded. "The whole lot of them. What about the ones in the refuge?"

She saw from their unshielded reactions that two of them were alarmed at the mention.

"You need shields, so badly. You're an open book to another wizard right now, and that's a very bad thing."

She looked back at Gen Jongto. "Here's my suggestion. We do some basic education this morning, and then meet with Tun-chi. I want to get training started in their refuge, wherever it is, as soon as possible so they're no longer so vulnerable. And we need a way to identify and protect the new arrivals as they come in.

"For that to work, Tun Jeju will need to be comfortable with some sort of provisional freedom, a working arrangement, for all of them. I expect that will be this afternoon's discussion, if it can be arranged." She caught Gen Jongto's eye, and he nodded.

She glanced back at the prisoners who were following the conversation intently as their fate was discussed. "Don't expect a decision tonight," she said. "You'll be, um, guests here until this is settled. But I'll be pushing to get you out of here and the situation, um, normalized."

With a sigh, she turned to Najud. "This is going to require the basics. I know you're better at that than I am—would you do the honors of getting them started?"

CHAPTER 11

In the end, Chosmod, Vylkar, and Najud each took a hand in impromptu lessons focused on shielding, and Penrys concentrated on testing the students.

They divided for the afternoon—Gen Jongto was swapped out for one of his colleagues to keep an eye on the proceedings, and he brought Penrys to Tun Jeju, alone.

The news had traveled ahead, of course. Tun Jeju's only overt remark was, "Wings? And why are you only telling me now?"

"I thought I'd reached the limits of believability without that," Penrys replied. "You were already strip-searching us for evidence of treason at the time, as you may recall."

Tun Jeju made no reply.

At the end of the afternoon's heated discussion, Penrys had to be satisfied with provisional approval to move forward with her plan.

Gen Jongto had related his observations of the morning and seemed to have convinced Tun Jeju of the reality of the wizard population.

"You're way behind on this, *notju-chi*," she'd said. "By generations, I assume. However your wizards are organized, they're out there. In their hundreds or thousands. They've managed to hide from you for a very long time."

He'd listened in dismayed silence.

"They've infiltrated your organizations—they're probably everywhere. But do they mean you any harm? Or are they more afraid of being found? Are some of them criminals? Undoubtedly. All of them? Unlikely. They must be policing their own members, or they wouldn't have been able to stay hidden so long.

"How do they manage their affairs? What are their factions? Their goals? They must have planned for this day to happen eventually—what will they want? Your search for chained wizards would have been the trigger."

She spared a thought for the five unprepared prisoners. "And speaking of them… They're a potential threat, but I think they're more likely to be a prize, for the regular wizards. They've been watching, they're interested—what do they want with them? Do they all want the same thing?"

She took a deep breath. "You want to get communications going with all parties, as quickly as possible. Before things get completely out of hand."

Tun Jeju held up a hand. "How?"

"Any wizard can find them, any of the foreigners you summoned. All you have to do is have them look for leaders."

"You," he said. "I want you to arrange it."

Her stomach clenched. She'd expected this, had even sought it out.

"If I'm going to be stalking around the city with my chain out for everyone to see, stirring up this fire, I'm going to make myself bait for anyone who's not happy with change. I'll need a visible representative from you to make it clear it's an official task, with the sanction of your office."

Tun Jeju nodded. "And guards."

"No, I think that's a mistake. It's a declaration of weakness. It makes any internal enemy think you're afraid. Besides, they're more likely to attack as wizards, and what good will Kigali guards do then?"

"You plan to present yourself as a… what? A herald? An ambassador?"

"Why not?" She shrugged. "I'm clearly a foreigner, someone relatively neutral—if anything, sympathetic to the wizards."

"A knife in the dark isn't going to care about neutrality," Tun Jeju commented.

They hammered out a few more details, and agreed to meet early in the morning, to confirm what she had in mind.

She left the room first and picked up Zep Pangwit who'd been told off to wait in the corridor outside for hours and was predictably sour about it. "They're waiting for you downstairs," he told her. "Your man and that boy."

She mind-scanned the lower level to check, and found all five prisoners back in their cells, presumably locked in, and all the other wizards gone. School was done for the day, apparently.

When she caught up with Najud and Munraz on the steps of the building outside, her scan picked up the two chained wizards that she'd noticed in the morning. "Wait here a moment, everyone," she said, absently. "I want to try something."

Without looking behind her to see their reaction, she walked down the street directly to the two wizards, a young man and an older woman. They both wore the high-necked robes that were so useful at concealing the chains, and the mutual distance of several feet that the chains enforced made their attempts at casual observation awkward, since they were clearly together, but standing too far apart to seem normal.

As she'd hoped, they were so startled at this direct approach that they were at a loss for how to react. She was within speaking distance before they'd recovered.

"I'm Penrys. Thought you might want an update," Penrys said, in a conversational tone. "Dar Datsu and the others are probably going to be released tomorrow morning. I thought I'd come with them to your place." She pointed east toward the industrial Chankau Tep. "I'd like to talk to whoever's in charge."

The older woman recovered first. She gave Penrys a wary look. "Who have the *shaibowen* got?"

"Well, the rest of the names they gave me were Goi Ofa, Lai Tsumai, Lir Pako, and Tse Lorping." She watched the reaction. "I see—those aren't all familiar to you. Well, any that aren't yours already were probably on their way to find you, so I hope that's not a problem."

The young man finally found his voice. "How do you know where to go?"

"Oh, are you worried someone talked?" Penrys let an amused tone color her voice. "I'm afraid you stand out like a beacon to anyone with eyes to see."

At the appalled look on the older woman's face, Penrys said, "Tell your leader, if he doesn't know, that you're being watched by the local wizards. Lots of them. That's part of what I want to talk about."

"I'll be here in the morning," the woman said, coming to a decision. "I'll let you know what he says." The young man opened his mouth to object, and she shushed him. "Can't you see there's little point in hiding?"

"I'll be bringing one or two other people with me, just so you're not surprised," Penrys told her.

The woman nodded, and both of them watched as Penrys walked back to the steps of the Imperial Security building's entrance, where her husband shook his head at her.

"What were you thinking?" Najud said.

"We have a new job," she told him. "Or at least I do. You'll love it. Thought we'd call on the neighbors tonight, after dinner, and get that ball rolling, too."

"This is madness," Najud said.

He'd listened after dinner as she recounted her conversation with Tun Jeju, and then with the two chained wizards outside on the street.

They kept their voices low in their room in the ambassadorial quarters, but Penrys could hear the steel beginning to enter Najud's voice and wanted to forestall a quarrel.

"Look, Naj-sha, if Tun Jeju hadn't been so clumsy with the notice to locate chained wizards, then this could be done with more planning. But once that happened, he ran out of time."

She could see he didn't quite understand. "These wizards have been here for who knows how long, hiding from the rest of the population. What does that tell you?"

Najud visibly reined in his temper. "They're organized. They have a way of bringing in new members and keeping the news from getting out."

"Right. And no one has ever spilled the secret? In generations? How is that possible?"

"Enforcement." His head nodded slowly. "They must discourage exposure."

"Discourage? They probably kill to prevent it. It means everything to them. No matter what, the Kigaliwen mustn't know that wizards are among them."

Penrys shrugged. "I don't know if it's because they're afraid the Kigaliwen will kill them, or if it's because they like being hidden to exert more power, whatever it is they're doing. Whichever, it isn't important now."

She leaned forward. "Don't you see? Ever since that Imperial Security notice, it's been clear that the presence of the chained wizards is known, even if the 'chain' part is clearer than the 'wizard' part. So it's just a matter of time before the whole thing is out in the open and they'll be exposed. What do they do when threatened with exposure?"

"They'll try to kill you!"

"Not if it's pointless, not if it's too late anyway. That's why we have to move as quickly as possible to get past that, to make it impossible to stay hidden."

Najud gave her a hard look. "It's not clever to force their hand. What if you make them feel they have nothing to lose? They're not all going to be long-range planners—what about the hot-heads?"

"There's not a lot of choice. The trigger event was none of our doing—all we can do is try to normalize the situation as quickly as possible. Besides, who knows better what the various wizard factions are up to than the other factions. We have to start somewhere."

"Not Munraz." Najud said. "Tonight or tomorrow morning."

"No, not Munraz. It's one thing to risk my own neck, but not a student's."

"And I'm coming with you."

"I was hoping you'd say that," she said, and smiled at him.

Penrys and Najud stood before the closed gate of a compound two blocks west and one south of the Zannib ambassador's. The symbol engraved and painted next to the gate declared it to be the Char family, famous providers of the purest and finest pharmaceutical products to the emperor.

Nervously patting her throat to make sure her chain was visible, Penrys struck the *wanbum*, the small gong suspended next to the gate with a knuckle. Before the reverberations had died away, a small hinged panel at head height pulled back and they were examined by someone on the other side.

"Your business, *binochiwen?*" a voice inquired.

Penrys scanned the interior of the compound and bespoke the first adult wizard she found. *We'd like to speak with the wizards of this family, please. It's a friendly call. May we come in?*

She tried to hide her amused expression at the startled mental reaction of the recipient.

In moments, the face at the panel was replaced by a young man. "Zannib? Oh. You." He shook himself. "Please wait a moment, *binochiwen*."

The little viewing panel was closed again.

Najud glanced over at Penrys and winked at her.

They waited patiently for several minutes. Penrys shielded them both from any other wizards in the area, but she found none on the streets immediately around them. Other than the six in this compound, of course—the reason they'd chosen it from among other nearby options.

There was a clatter as the inner bar was lifted from the gate and then both doors swung open. An older man bowed to them, his long gray braid attesting to his years. Beside him stood four others, including the young man who'd peered out at them through the gate panel. Each of them bowed as well, and Penrys and Najud returned the courtesy.

A gray-haired woman hastened out of one of the inner buildings, but the old man raised his hand to stop her. "These are foreign initiates of our temple, my wife. We'll be taking them there. No need to stir up the household."

He turned to Najud. "Please, *binochi*, we can talk in private if you'll follow me."

"As you wish," Najud said.

The young man took a torch from the door guard and followed with the others. Penrys kept her attention on the wizards gathered behind the old man, but it was clear they'd been taken by surprise, and there was no immediate threat intended.

A girl of perhaps ten years hastened up to join the party as they made their way to a building in the corner of the compound. When the old man turned to admonish her, Penrys said, "She's welcome to come along. There's no danger."

He stared at her uncertainly, then looked down at the child. "Mouth shut, ears open."

"Yes, grandfather." She bestowed a shy but grateful smile on Penrys.

They paused before the small building with the curled eaves that Penrys associated with temples in Kigali architecture. The old man opened the door, and the young man went inside with a torch and lit two lanterns before ducking back outside to return the torch to the servant who'd followed behind, before closing the temple door to shut him out. In the dim light, Penrys watched the old man open an interior door that led down a few steps into an inner chamber. Without warning, an even light spilled up the stairs into the main room.

Devices, like the Rasesni use. Najud nodded at Penrys's silent comment.

Everyone walked down the steps, and the last one, the same young man, paused to bar the door at the top.

The air was fresh. Built-in stone benches ran down two sides of the room, and above them four more lights gleamed brightly. Shelves covered with books and papyrus scrolls filled the other two walls. Penrys spotted the round opening with a grate on the floor in one corner, and a similar one high on one of the bench walls. Ventilation or escape routes, she suspected, or maybe both.

Najud bowed low to the old man. "Thank you for seeing two foreign wizards, *binochi*. We would have sent you notice to request this visit, but we did not know how to address it, or how it might disturb your… arrangements."

He bowed again. "My name is Najud, son of Ilsahr of clan Zamjilah, of the Shubzah tribe. This is my wife, Penrys, lately of Ellech."

Penrys executed her own bow and said, "We're here in Yenit Ping, along with other foreign wizards, at the request of Tun Jeju, a *notju* of Imperial Security, to speak with the wizards and the chained ones, here in Kigali."

The old man drew himself up in full dignity. "I am Char Nojuk. This is my second daughter, Char Dami, and my nephew, Char Dazu, my youngest sister's third son. These two are my adopted daughters, Char Dachi and Char Danau, and that," he waved his hand at the little girl, "is my first son's second daughter, Char Pangfa. We are rich in women, in my family."

Penrys smiled. "I can see that, *samkatju-chi*. Can you tell me, how long there have been wizards in your family?"

"Granddaughter, fetch the *sumkui*. You know where it is."

He sat down on one of the benches and invited his guests to do the same.

The girl ran to a shelf just within her reach when she stretched up and carefully pulled out a wooden box. She carried it to her grandfather and put it on the bench next to him, and then stayed to watch while he opened it and reverently pulled out a fragile scroll, bound with a red ribbon, and mounted to a rod at each end.

He held it for a moment and looked at Penrys. "This is not the original, but a copy made a lifetime ago. Soon it will be time for a fresh copy. The original is in our room of treasures here in the *samke*, the compound, but only our version in this sanctum records the wizards."

After untying the ribbon, he unrolled the scroll from one rod while his granddaughter carefully took up the slack with the other rod.

"Not many families have been in Yenit Ping as long as we have," he confided, "but then we have been dealers in medicines and similar items for several dynasties. I cannot say for certain who was the first wizard in the family, but we do know when this private sanctuary was built."

He stabbed with his finger at a line on the *sumkui*. "See, just at the start of the Chaik dynasty."

He gave the ignorant foreigners a pitying look, and amplified his comment. "About seventeen hundred years ago."

Penrys could feel her scalp creep back. "That's a long time to keep a secret."

"Not a secret anymore, is it?" Char Nojuk said, suddenly truculent. "This is a disaster, and no mistake. What does Imperial Security intend to do, now that they know we exist, eh?"

"That largely depends on you and the people like you, *samkatju-chi*. Imperial Security is surprised by the discovery of both the chained and unchained wizards, as you might imagine. If they'd known what to expect, they wouldn't have bungled the request for information that was so disastrous for the chained ones, but once that happened, the time for hiding in the old way was finished."

Char Nojuk was silent.

"Or don't you think so?" Penrys asked.

"If you foreign wizards weren't here, they still wouldn't know," he muttered belligerently.

"Perhaps," Najud said. "Or perhaps the disaster for the chained ones would have precipitated a hidden war that brought you all into the light."

Penrys slashed her hand horizontally through the air at chest level. "*Sennevi.* It is done. It doesn't matter what might have been, *samkatju-chi*—we have to deal with what *is*."

There was no response. Penrys could feel the fear in the air, different for each of them, though strongest in the eldest. No one would contradict the patriarch.

Penrys tried again, more gently. "We came calling tonight partly because your family was close to where we're staying, and partly because there were so many wizards watching us everywhere we went that it was just… silly pretending we didn't notice. Tomorrow morning we're going to visit the compound in Chankau Tep where the chained wizards seem to be based, and return the ones held by Imperial Security. I know there are wizards watching them, too."

"What do you want of us?" Char Nojuk said.

"We want to talk with your own leaders. Tun Jeju has the emperor's mandate to resolve this situation, and he wants to do it peacefully if he can. He hopes to bring all the wizards out into the open, the way they are in Zannib or Ndant."

"We're under sentence of death, by order of the emperor," Char Nojuk said. "We put all our families at risk, just by existing. Just by talking to you. Even if we believed you, who would go first?"

Char Dazu suddenly spoke up. "What one emperor decrees, another can put aside, uncle."

Najud said, "I see from these books that you have studied in the traditions of your own nation. I see from the devices on the wall that you have knowledge in the areas of physical magic, like the Rasesni and the Ellech. My wife spent three years in the Collegium of Wizards in Ellech and we understand the lure of libraries."

He leaned forward. "Don't you want to broaden your knowledge?" He cocked his head at Char Pangfa. "Don't you want your granddaughter to live her life without fear of exposure?"

Char Nojuk's gaze drifted to his granddaughter's eager face and then to the floor. "There will be blood at this."

Penrys nodded. "Yes, those that lose power will fight to keep it, and those that fear change will panic. But you have a chance to help steer it."

"No one speaks for all wizards," Char Nojuk said, after a moment, and hope rose in Penrys that they may have turned the corner with him, persuading him to talk.

"There's a council in Yenit Ping, but it's weak. The oldest families speak there, and the rest support them and are represented by them. Consensus on security matters is strong, but in other areas…" He swallowed. "Our family sits on the council, but we have never been numerous or powerful compared to some. Advisors, not rulers. Medicines are sold everywhere, of course, and we have branches throughout the towns, but here in Yenit Ping we are, perhaps…"

"Insignificant." Char Dazu finished his sentence for him impatiently. "We don't count for much, but we have friends, allies. We sometimes swing policy. It was *our* family that pushed through the adoption process centuries ago—to rescue the wizards born into unaffiliated families and bring them into the wizard families. That was an important achievement."

"We've been trying to do something similar with the chained ones that started popping up," Char Nojuk said, after an admonishing look at his nephew stopped his outburst. "The problem was that so many of them were foreigners—hard to adopt those without very awkward questions. We've been debating it for three years, and now it's too late."

"Maybe not, if all of this comes out into the open," Penrys said. "They need support and help."

"What are they? Where did they come from?" Char Pangfa clapped her hand over her mouth after the questions escaped.

"We don't know, young Char," Penrys said. "All of us, and me, too—we just appeared three years ago, often in countries where we look like foreigners, without any memories. Until this morning, I'd only met two others, so I don't know very much yet, myself."

She looked up at Char Nojuk. "All the ones I've seen are indeed wizards, not just chained, and it seems to be random whether any of the ones here are Kigaliwen or something else. We seem to be tossed around the world like carelessly scattered grain, near as I can judge. That's why Tun Jeju summoned the foreign wizards—to hear about chained wizards in their own countries."

She pointed at the lights on the walls. "The chains seem to be devices, like those lamps are. We can't take them off. Some of us seem to have other devices that let us change part of our physical form. Some of us, at least, are stronger than ordinary wizards, once we're trained—don't know if that's intrinsic to us or because of the chain, or both."

She looked at the rapt faces standing before here. "And lots of us are already dead, some from the disaster that followed the

Imperial Security search decree, but many for other reasons. There's a level in the prisons there, where I've spent the last two days, filled with empty chains and dead chained wizards, laid out on tables like so many broken devices."

Char Dami, Char Nojuk's daughter spoke for the first time. "That's why you're here, isn't it."

"I'm here because I was summoned, *we* were summoned… But yes, I want to know who made us and threw us unprepared into chaos. And some of us have already gone bad and killed hundreds and had to be stopped. Those deaths are on the head of our maker, too. I want to know *why*. Yes, I do."

She stopped when Najud put a hand on her arm. "Sorry, I have a serious desire to meet my maker and have a few words with him." A half-smile flickered across her face. "But that may never happen, and in the meantime I am also a wizard, like my husband, and we want to help fix this situation in Kigali, if we can."

"Will you help us with that, *samkatju-chi?*" Najud asked.

Char Nojuk said, "I'll need to consult with others. Don't expect anything to happen right away."

Penrys laughed. "Whoever's watching us is welcome to come out into the open to talk, or just to keep watching. If you can, you might warn the ones watching the chained wizard compound tomorrow morning. Things might get lively there."

CHAPTER 12

"Well, no one's killed us yet. That must be progress."

Najud's sarcastic comment as they walked made it hard for Penrys to keep her countenance. Munraz failed altogether, and Najud frowned at his grin. They'd yielded to their apprentice's pleading to come with them, though Penrys was already having second thoughts about it.

Char Dazu had joined them at the gates of Talqatin's compound when they left. "Someone from our family should be there as a witness." When Najud asked if his uncle had agreed, he just shrugged.

Another person to keep track of, to keep from getting hurt if something goes very wrong. Penrys wished she'd crept out with Najud at dawn and gone to the chained wizards' compound directly without all this fuss.

Zep Pangwit had looked sourly at Char Dazu, clearly suspecting what he was, but for a wonder he'd kept his mouth shut as he escorted them back to Tun Jeju. *Maybe he's feeling out of his depth, too.*

At the steps to the Imperial Security building, Penrys glanced down the street and spotted the same two watchers that she'd spoken to the day before. She lifted a finger to them to tell them to wait briefly, then followed Zep Pangwit inside—some sort of briefing from Tun Jeju before they continued, he'd told them. Najud and Munraz stayed outside with Char Dazu who very clearly had no intent of entering the building.

The *notju* was waiting in an anteroom off the main entrance, a sparsely furnished room with a few chairs and a table near the entrance. Gen Jongto and the eight wizards from Rasesni, Ndant, and Ellech were there with him, to Penrys's surprise—all of them standing as if they'd been waiting for the Zannib delegation. *This can't be good. Only Gen Jongto should be here.*

Tun Jeju greeted her, then walked over to the table and opened a wooden box there. He lifted out an artificial wood and silk imitation of a leafy branch, like the one he had himself carried in Neshilik when negotiating with the Rasesni.

"If you're going to represent us as a neutral party, you'll need a *leipum* for parley. Everyone should recognize what it signifies."

He bowed slightly and handed it to her. She took it from him distractedly, her eye traveling to the others in the room.

"Um, yes…" He coughed politely. "There was some discussion yesterday evening about the wisdom of sending just the Zannib wizards into a possibly unfriendly situation. In fact, there was some insistence on… spreading the risk. From the entire group of our foreign guests."

He looked at them all blandly, and Penrys blinked at the picture she conjured up of this meeting they'd missed while visiting the Char family compound.

"I see. Am I to understand that *everyone* is planning to come along today?" Penrys tried to keep the dismay out of her voice. Aside from Munraz, Najud and she were the youngest wizards there. Would they follow her orders?

Tun Jeju fixed his eye on each of the wizards in the room as he answered. "I have made it very clear that I have designated you as my representative in these initial contacts. Only you. That is the condition to which they have agreed in order to participate."

Penrys said, "Those wizards out there are pretty shy, *notju-chi*, both groups—and with reason. If I saw all of us coming, I might go hide, too."

There were smiles from Chosmod and Mrigasba at her attempt to give in gracefully. She knew she had little choice in the matter. No smiles from the Ndant woman, though, or her two attendants.

Tun Jeju spoke without raising his voice, but his authority held the attention of everyone in the room. "Gen Jongto is my witness, as all of you are witnesses for your countries. We value your advice, but Kigali policy is ours to set, and Penrys here is our initial representative for this."

She cleared her throat. "Um, now would probably be a good time to mention that we've brought along a witness for the Kigali wizard community, too. It would be nice if he weren't frightened away, either."

Gen Jongto raised an eyebrow, but Tun Jeju had no visible reaction at all. "All the better. I will speak with you when you return."

He nodded his head and walked out, leaving Penrys staring at her augmented party, each of them in characteristic national clothing. No chance of something inconspicuous now.

"The five prisoners have been released, Penrys-chi," Gen Jongto said, "and will be coming with us. They'll bring them to us outside."

He waved her forward and she preceded him through the door in Tun Jeju's wake. She forged a light link to the wizards behind her to keep track of them, but refused to look backward to see if they were following.

Carrying the *leipum* in one hand, she opened the outer door of building with the other and pushed her way back out into the early morning sunlight. She was relieved to find the prisoners from yesterday waiting for them there, in the custody of half a dozen guards and held apart from Najud, Munraz, and Char Dazu. They were clean and dressed, but their chains were visible and hands raised to throats made it clear how uncomfortable that was to them. They stood in a widely spaced group, their chains preventing them from bunching up.

Penrys pivoted on her heel and spoke to Gen Jongto. "It's one thing for me to expose my chain, but not them—they've been hiding theirs for years. Haven't you got something we can use to cover them before we march them through the city?"

He ducked back into the building, and then the rest of the wizards came down the steps to join her.

Najud raised both eyebrows, and she shrugged helplessly at him. A quick glance down the street confirmed that their two guides were still waiting.

Gen Jongto came back out with a small pile of brown fabric which he handed to Penrys.

She unfolded the top piece—a square of plain material, large enough to fold diagonally like a scarf. "These will do fine, thanks."

She walked through the screen of guards and presented each of yesterday's students with a cloth, at arm's length. "Wrap it around your chain, if you want to," she told them.

Gen Jongto had followed her and she took a breath—she knew the next request would meet resistance. "We can let the guards go, Gen-chi."

"And if they run?"

"If they run, they run. But we're taking them to the one place that's trying to take care of them, so I expect they'll stay at least long enough to look that over." She spoke loudly enough that all of the erstwhile prisoners could hear her. "Besides, there's no shortage of other chained wizards in the area—can't lock them all up."

Gen Jongto hesitated.

"We don't need the guards. They're not prisoners." Penrys waved her *leipum* lightly and the silk flowers rustled. "Isn't this within my authority?"

He agreed, reluctantly, and spoke to the commander of the guard party. He had to do it twice before he was believed, and the guards withdrew into the building.

"All right, everyone," Penrys called. "Let me just confer with our guide, and we'll get started."

She walked away, expanding her link to keep tabs on all of them. *What a mess.*

Approaching the older woman, she stopped when she felt the beginning of the pressure from the chain that would become pain if she got closer. The *leipum* which she'd forgotten she was carrying attracted their attention. It was clear that they recognized its significance.

"I thought we could do this more discretely and with fewer people, but apparently I was naive in my hope. Those are the foreign wizards—come as witnesses—as well as the prisoners, my husband and our apprentice, and a local wizard, also a witness. Oh, and a witness for Imperial Security."

The woman swallowed. "He told me to bring you, but he didn't expect..." She turned to the young man. "Better warn him, Am Limzu. About twenty folk, all kinds. Under the *leipum*, tell him."

He looked at her reluctantly. "Go along, run off now," she confirmed. "I'll be fine."

"How about some names?" Penrys prodded.

"I'm Kit Hachi, and our leader is Rin Tsugo." She eyed the motley crowd up the street. "We're going to walk all the way with that... flock of exotics?"

Penrys commented, "All we need is a dancing bear and a couple of jugglers, don't you think? A drummer or two?"

A snort from Kit Hachi confirmed her observation.

"Come with me," Penrys said. "Hope you can remember all the names. And find us a route that's a little less public."

They avoided the largest avenues but there were still busy crowds along the streets Kit Hachi selected. The chained ones couldn't walk close to each other, so they were spread out among the others, and the foreign wizards stuck together by country.

They almost lost Najud in a book district, until Penrys sent Munraz back with a message that they wouldn't wait for him. She didn't want to just bespeak him—ever since they left the government district of Mentsek Tep she'd felt an ill-defined pressure building up around them.

At first she'd thought it was the tail they were collecting, the odds and ends of people that trailed behind them, wondering what to make of all these foreigners and the woman with a *leipum* in front headed east to the industrial district. They were polite—Penrys suspected the presence of Gen Jongto in his brown robe had something to do with that.

Then she realized what it reminded her of—the temple school of mages that the Rasesni had set up in Neshilik, when she was teaching the wizards there how to attack a more powerful wizard, like herself. Cautiously she lifted her shield and extended her reach out a few blocks to see what was there.

Ah. That was the problem. Several dozen wizards, and three chained ones, all keeping pace on the streets to either side. As she watched, a few more joined them. Each mind was busy trying to look at her party and make sense of them.

It was like the roaring of a disturbed ocean against a rocky shore, and just as irritating. Finally she raised her hand and halted them all, right in the middle of the street.

She dropped her shield altogether and bespoke every wizard in several blocks. *Back off, please. You're welcome to follow, if you wish. We're headed to Chankau Tep and, after we conclude our business there, perhaps there would be someplace we could speak to each other nearby?* She included a mental image of the *leipum* in her hand and the brown-robed Gen Jongto.

There was a sense of a shocked silence, and she resumed her shield. She nodded in satisfaction. "There, that ought to hold them for a while."

Behind her she could hear Najud explaining to Gen Jongto in an undertone. Everyone else with her had heard the mind-speech directly.

After that, the remainder of the walk passed uneventfully except for the stares of the ordinary citizens of the city.

That Tun Jeju is a sly one—he could have arranged something discrete, but he set this theatrical display up deliberately. Pushing the local wizards before they can plan something, rubbing their noses in the reality that they can't hide any more. Dangerous, and we're bait.

What happens if his foreign guests are attacked? So sorry, we lost your emissary, send another? On the other hand, if not us, then who? Someone's got to winkle out the locals so he can talk to them, get him a foothold in that community. He can't afford to lose the dignity of his office fumbling with that. I guess I can.

The buildings changed character gradually until manufacturing and wholesale merchants outnumbered the remaining retail businesses. The residential compounds that she could see on the cross streets looked dingy, and many were not in good repair. Strange stenches began to appear—scorched iron, nose-wrinkling sulfurous stinks, and something that dried the mouth when you tried to avoid breathing through your nose.

The crowds of following wizards, which included a few chained ones, numbered more than a hundred by the time Kit Hachi paused on one corner and held up her hand.

"That's our *gewengep*," she said, looking diagonally across both streets, "the whole block. It was empty before Rin Tsugo took it over for the brotherhood."

It looked like any compound to Penrys, its gate shut and anonymous—no symbol engraved on the wall by the gate. When she scanned inside, however, it blazed. There must be thirty or more powerful wizards there. And several outside the perimeter, she was amused to see, just in case something happened.

"How do you want this to work?" Penrys asked.

"Maybe I better go find out," Kit Hachi said. "Will you wait here a few minutes, *likatchok-chi*?"

The ambassadorial title was given half-jokingly, but half in earnest, too, and the woman made a little bow before crossing the street kitty-corner to the compound and its gate.

"We're here" Penrys announced. "They'll let us know how they want to handle it. They weren't expecting so many."

Chosmod tilted his head to the unseen wizards in the next streets. "What do they want?"

"I'm sure they're going to tell us," Penrys said, "but one problem at a time."

Char Dazu walked up to her. "Will they let all of us in?"

"Don't know, but I think they'd be fools not to. If they look, they can see that mob of wizards out there. By comparison, we're not nearly as threatening."

He hesitated, then said. "Could you send them another message, Penrys-chi? Tell them I'm here for the Char family as a witness. Rightly it should be my uncle, but it should still help."

She glanced at him. "And don't you wish you'd told him what you were going to do this morning, eh?" She grinned at his expression.

We look forward to speaking with you after we're done here. We have Char Dazu serving as a witness for the Char family, and he will share his observations with you, too. Once again, she included the image of the *leipum* and Gen Jongto in his official brown robes. *We're eager to meet some of the wizards of Kigali. Thank you for your patience.*

Movement at the gate of the compound caught her eye. Kit Hachi stood in the gap of the open gateway and beckoned her in.

CHAPTER 13

Rin Tsugo stood at the back of the inner courtyard of the compound, on the steps of the central building where most of the group activities took place. The compound had once housed a clothing manufactory, and its large workrooms were well-suited to gatherings of people who needed a certain amount of space between them.

His vision of the street beyond the open gateway was restricted, but Am Limzu and then Kit Hachi had told him what to expect. Behind him, through the open doorway to the hall, he could hear the hasty preparations for receiving so many guests. He wished they had better clothing, but that hadn't been high on the list for survival, and it was too late now.

Dar Datsu was with the visitors, and Goi Ofa, which relieved some of his concerns, but there were three others to be taken in, new ones, and he'd summoned his *chirmurno* to join him to look after them.

Sek Seto left his guard post at the gate to stand with Kit Hachi, and their bow, directed to someone on the street outside, alerted him. A quick scan around the walls confirmed that the *gewengep* was surrounded by wizards, but they'd stopped moving in—only the official visitors entered his gates.

He'd noted the chained wizards in the waiting crowd, too—everyone trying to hide from everyone else, like his first weeks hiding in Yenit Ping while he'd tried to come to terms with *what* he was, if not the *who*. The *who* was gone entirely, from the day he'd stolen a name to use in place of his lost one. Maybe now there'd be some answers for him and those in his charge. If they survived this visit.

The first one in was the chained woman with the *leipum*. She was in Zannib clothing, right enough, but no Zan. She looked a bit like Dar Datsu—not very tall, brown-haired, somewhat round of face. Friendly and confidant—well, she must be, walking all over Yenit Ping with that chain exposed. Confidant, or foolhardy.

The Zannib man beside her must be this husband he'd heard about. *I bet there's a story there.* A younger Zan trailed them. She paused to let a *shaibo* join her so that they entered the courtyard together.

A show of power, or a gesture of neutrality? What can Imperial Security want from us that's anything but a threat?

They continued forward into the middle of the courtyard to let the rest of them in. The woman caught his eye and smiled at him. He nodded to her cautiously.

Behind them came the five captives, now apparently released, interspersed with several foreigners and one prosperous Kigali man, quite young, who placed himself with the woman's husband, as if for reassurance.

Dar Datsu and Goi Ofa smiled as they spotted their friends, but the other three captives looked about warily. Rin Tsugo suppressed a sigh—hard enough to bring in any new member, but three at once, in the midst of this disruption… Well, there was no point worrying about it, the *chirmurno* would just have to handle it while he concentrated on the real threat.

He waited until the gates were closed again and all the guests were quiet and attentive, then he bowed deeply to them. "I am Rin Tsugo, and this is my… household. We're grateful for the return of our lost ones and welcome their companions in… duress." *Idiot, there's a shaibo who was probably responsible for that. The less said about it, the better.*

While he paused to recover his composure, hopeful that the lapse hadn't been observed, the woman bowed deeply as well. "M'name's Penrys. You can see what I am, well enough." A smile flickered across her face. "I apologize for this invasion of your… home by so many, unwarned, but we're being pushed by events and it's in everyone's interest to try and control as much as we can for fear of something worse. May I introduce my companions?"

He nodded, and she began with the captives, rather than the most important members of her party. It marked her out clearly as no Kigalino, but he liked her the better for it. When Dar Datsu stepped away to join his friends gathered around the edge of the courtyard, he bowed to her and the wizards with her, first, in a show of gratitude that seemed to surprise her. A couple of the new ones did the same, before Dar Datsu took them in charge and walked them over to the *chirmurno* to take them in and teach them the rules.

Then Penrys named the *shaibo* who nodded neutrally and stepped aside. "He's here to witness for Tun Jeju, a *notju* of Imperial Security," she said. "We'll speak about that in a moment. All of these here are witnesses, in fact—wizards for their countries, like my husband Najud. And Char Dazu, here, witnessing for the local wizards." This was the young Kigalino.

She waved her hand in a circle around her head. "We didn't ask for all that out there to come with us, but there was no easy way to stop it. I told them we'd talk to them next and asked them to wait." She paused and looked at him directly. "Let's hope they do, eh?"

A nervous laugh traveled around the courtyard.

"I'm afraid we don't make very good hostages," she commented "all us foreigners, but maybe that won't be necessary."

It was outrageous, speaking of such a thing so baldly, and he feared the unexpectedness of it had shown on his face. No diplomat, this one. Why was she the one with the *leipum*, instead of the brown-robe? Just because she was chained like they were?

"Oh, I almost forgot," she said, gesturing to the young Zannib man. "This is Munraz, our apprentice. He wanted to come and see what would happen." The young man blushed at the notice. "Me, too. Could we go inside and sit down? I'll tell you all about it."

Rin Tsugo blinked. She was making a claim on his honor, that he would not hold them as hostages, that the young and innocent were not at risk, no matter what the stakes might be. It was masterful, and he could see now why she held the *leipum*.

"Please, Penrys-chi," he said. "We would be honored to hear you, and to introduce you to some of our… community."

He beckoned Sek Seto over while the visitors filed past him. "Call in the outer guard and bar the gate—they should hear this, too."

"But what about our security?"

"Sek-chi, there must be a hundred wizards out there, or more. What exactly do you think we could do, eh?"

At Sek Seto's stubborn expression, he added, "We can't keep them out. Ready all the bolt-holes—if we must, we'll scatter and try to hide. I'll do what I can to keep it from coming to that."

Penrys could see that the cavernous hall with its scarred wooden floor had clearly been some sort of work area once. It stretched to the left and right, and there were small chairs and individual tables stacked the length of the inner wall, no two of them precisely the same. Already some of the people inside had fetched a chair and spaced themselves out along the farther side, well-separated from each other, looking toward the narrow end at the left, where three empty chairs faced into the room.

Kit Hachi, their guide, picked up a chair. "Come sit here," she said, and Penrys followed her toward the left front of the room, near the three empty chairs. Najud, unprompted, picked up a chair and followed, and the rest of her party did the same, though Ijumo carried two chairs, one for himself and the other for Mpeowake.

Penrys made a show of making sure everyone in her party was comfortable while she concentrated on the minds around her, both in the room and outside. The mob of wizards outside was still in place and gradually growing, and this Rin Tsugo seemed to have pulled in his perimeter guards. There were two elsewhere in the compound moving about, and she recognized one of them as the guard at the gate.

Their leader was standing at the end of the hall where everyone could see him, waiting for the noise to die down. When Penrys looked around the hall for herself before sitting down, she marveled at the even spacing between the seated people, all but her own group. *It reminds me of something... what? Of course—honeycomb, like a bee hive. It's as close as they can get to each other, with a little space left for passage.*

She caught Najud's eye and nodded behind them for him to look for himself. "Think we can get any honey out of this hive without getting stung?"

He appreciated the reference and grinned. "*Baijuk* is even better than *khimar.*"

Mead over honey, is it? I don't think it's going to be that easy.

Rin Tsugo moved to the empty chairs and faced the room. He raised his hand, and everyone quieted. "We welcome back our comrades and greet three new ones." He gestured to the front along the inner wall, where all five were seated together, appropriately spaced.

"We also welcome our... unexpected visitors, both foreign and official. I for one would like to hear what they've come to tell us."

He sat down, and Penrys stood up, the *leipum* in her hand. She cocked her head at one of the empty seats near Rin Tsugo with a question on her face, and he gestured an invitation to her. She picked her way carefully between chairs to get there, trying to avoid the contact warnings of her chain, and then faced the audience—almost forty chained wizards.

For a moment she multiplied her memories of the Voice and the young *qahulajti* in *sarq*-Zannib by twenty and shuddered inwardly. *No. These are untrained, and no more hostile than you would expect of any other banned civic group. They're not monsters, any more than you are. Not yet.*

"M'name's Penrys, and I appeared out of nowhere, in Ellech, a bit more than three years ago, like all of you did, I imagine. No clothes, no memory, no name."

Heads were nodding slightly all over the room.

"I was very lucky. I found myself in wizard hands. And then, a few months ago—it's too long a story for right now—I ended up in Neshilik, in the west, and there I met a *notju*, one Tun Jeju. That's another long story, but we ended up defeating, and killing, a chained wizard who had raised an army and killed hundreds in Rasesdad and Kigali."

It was silent in the room.

"After that, Najud and I,"—she gestured at him in the forefront of the audience—"we traveled into the west of central *sarq*-Zannib, and there we encountered another chained wizard, this one a youngster who'd been very unlucky, meeting only animals and not people in her short, new life. She caused the death of more than two hundred people once she came out of hiding. She, too, was caught and killed."

She could feel the dismay in the room.

"I tell you this not to alarm you, but to explain what has happened since. Tun Jeju, on behalf of Imperial Security and the emperor, sought to discover more about these chained wizards. He knew of three—two disasters, and me. Were there others? Were any of them in Kigali?

"In the belief that there were no wizards in Kigali..." She allowed a little time for the nervous chuckles to die away. "He sent for wizards from his neighbors, and for the only other living chained one he knew."

She pointed to the wizards seated in front of her. "To Rasesdad, Ndant, *sarq*-Zannib, and even far Ellech." At each name, the emissaries stood up briefly.

"Meanwhile, he sent a notice to the village headmen, to identify anyone dwelling among them with an unremovable chain. And this was a terrible mistake."

Anger was the emotion uppermost in most of their minds. *And who could blame them?*

"He didn't understand how many of you might be foreign in appearance, as I was in Ellech, and the villagers and townspeople were frightened by Imperial Security interest in strangers with no family ties. He never meant for a wholesale slaughter to be the result. But that's what happened, and it can't be remedied.

"When his invited emissaries arrived, they brought both information and evidence of chained wizards in their own countries. Ask *them* what they've seen—empty loops of chain and preserved bodies, some of them in transition to strange forms." She waved at the five liberated captives.

"Worse," she said, "Only now does Imperial Security realize that wizards have been active in Kigali for a very long time, hiding their abilities, the way you've been doing for this short while. There are hundreds and presumably thousands of them, and they've been watching you wondering where you come from and what you can do. And the official government of Kigali has no knowledge of their leaders, their power, or their interests."

She took a deep breath. "I have an official mission, from Tun Jeju." She brandished the *leipum* until the silk petals rustled. "He wants to bring the Kigali wizards and all of you out into the open and normalize relations. Wizards operate as part of society in the neighboring countries, so why not here? He has the emperor's backing to make this happen. That's why we're here, all of us."

Licking her lips, she said, "And I have another goal, one of my own. I want to find whoever made us and scattered us around the world. I want to have a *talk* with him.

"But that's for later. Right now, there are more than a hundred wizards around your compound, wondering what's going on. I don't know who they are, or what they think about any of this. I'm going to talk to them next, but the whole thing is unstable and dangerous."

Pen-sha! They're at the gates.

Najud's warning brought her head up at the same time as a loud crack sounded from the gates across the courtyard.

She whipped her head around and scanned the situation. Dozens were pouring into the courtyard, well-shielded. Behind her, she heard Rin Tsugo calling to his people over the noise, "Get out, get out. Run!" They scattered to the doors at the back end of the hall and further into the maze of the buildings in the compound.

These untrained people couldn't defend themselves against an attack of armed wizards. She'd have to try and hold the rear for them. Dar Datsu and Lai Tsumai were frozen in place instead of running with the others, but her call broke them out of their trance. "Stand with me," she told them, then she turned to the first wave of attackers coming through the door and took their power, all of it except for the merest remnants.

It staggered them, and they jammed up in the entrance to the hall, after the first few slipped through. The foreign wizards stood indecisively, as if their neutrality would protect them, and she saw Char Dazu place himself in front of them to divert the mob, before they were overrun. Chosmod monitored what she was doing, and escaped to join her, and Mpeowake did the same, but the rest were overwhelmed.

She could feel Najud fighting, feel the slash that he ignored, only thirty feet away, but she couldn't get to him, and there were more wizards coming in from other entries. She caught a glimpse of his turban, and then she couldn't see it any longer. *I'll make them sorry, I swear it.*

Without looking at her four companions, she cried, "Find weapons and defend us. I'll take the wizards."

Penrys stood in place and began disabling every attacking wizard she could find, starting with the ones around the foreign wizards. Draining them of most of their power didn't physically stop them, but it left them so disoriented that most of them dropped out of the fighting. Her chain fairly hummed as it absorbed the energy.

It was an uneven battle on the power front—all it took was time to work through so many of them, as each one's defeat provided power to suck the next one dry. But there were so many, an endless stream, and it took too long.

The ones nearby who could still fight wreaked havoc. A group of them had surrounded the other foreign wizards and started to drag them away, and she targeted them for death by complete power drainage before stopping their hearts, but they blew a path through their own people to get away with their prizes before she could get to them all. All around her she could hear her companions fighting and then a punch of wind sent her violently into the air. In the moment before she fell again, she sent a wave of death as far as she could reach, and then she collided with a wall and it was over.

CHAPTER 14

Penrys woke to a pounding head, a roiling stomach, and panic, opening her eyes at the sound of tense voices that she didn't recognize.

Brown-robes. Everywhere.

I'm alive.

In sudden memory she scanned widely—no Najud, no Munraz. She sat up and groaned at the movement. She was at the base of a wall, so she squirmed until it supported her back.

"Where are they?" she croaked.

A Rasesni face swam into her sight and she flinched for a moment, recalling Neshilik, but then she recognized the man bent over her as Chosmod. "Tell me," she said.

"You kept us alive," he said. "You, me, Mpeowake, and those two ex-prisoners."

"The others?" She was afraid to hear the answer.

"Innurrys and Bildaer fought and died. The Ndanwe woman, Toawe, was killed, unarmed. We think the rest were taken."

"Najud?"

"Him, too. There's no body here. Not sure about your young apprentice, though—no one remembers him fighting."

"How long…"

"It's been maybe three hours since the fight. Imperial Security arrived just a few minutes ago." Chosmod nodded over to a cluster of people working on someone lying on the ground. "Luckily for me, I landed on someone. Not so lucky for Mpeowake however."

Penrys shoved her body up against the wall trying to find the least painful position.

"There are other dead—some of the chained wizards, from wounds, and dozens of the attackers, most of them with no marks on their bodies." He raised an inquisitive eyebrow at her, and she swallowed.

"Nothing else I could do," she muttered.

"I don't doubt it," he replied. "Just wish you'd done it sooner, *brudigna*."

"Done what?" Tun Jeju appeared, and Chosmod straightened up and made room for him.

Penrys ignored the question. "Where are the survivors? The chained wizards?"

"There are eight dead, I'm told. That means how many have escaped?"

She ignored that question, too.

He turned to one of his men. "Get her into a chair, if she's not too damaged, and fetch some water."

The man pulled her up and Chosmod set up a tumbled chair. She stumbled over and collapsed onto it clumsily.

Chosmod looked her over. "Your head is bloody but doesn't seem to be still bleeding."

"I'm well enough," she said. "Just give me a minute." She drained the cup of water that someone handed to her, and it was taken away again. When it returned, she sipped at it and stared out at the room. Her chain was heavy with captured power, but there was no one in her reach to use it on.

Pools of blood were scattered around, trampled by the fighters and now by the dozen or so brown-robes who were going through the place looking at the bodies. A few feet in front of her she spotted the *leipum*—broken and dusty, some of its leaves sticky with blood.

Dar Datsu appeared. His face was battered and dirty, but a very welcome sight nonetheless. He picked up another chair and made to join Penrys, then he followed her gaze to the floor and paused to go fetch her the silk-leafed branch before sitting down heavily.

She opened her hand mechanically to take it, then shuddered and took a deep breath.

"How is Lai Tsumai?" she asked him.

"She's quite a fighter," he said. "Took a slice to her arm, but she brought down at least two of them."

He gestured to the side, where six bodies lay around an open circle. *That must be where we were standing.*

"You killed four of them?" she asked.

"No…" he said, hesitantly. "We killed a couple, but the rest just… died, somehow, at the end."

Penrys closed her eyes. *How many this time? Have I beaten the Voice's record yet?*

"All three of you were out, so we did what we could for Mpeowake and I bound Lai Tsumai's wound. Then I left her in charge and went for help."

"You did what?" she said.

Tun Jeju must have been hovering behind her, out of sight, while she gathered her wits. "He ran to tell us, through the streets. Walked right in and made a fuss."

She turned her head warily to stare at Dar Datsu. "That was… brave of you." *And him only out of the prison a few hours.*

Tun Jeju's patience was clearly at an end, for he took the broken *leipum* out of her hand and said, "I would appreciate hearing just exactly what happened here. Who had the nerve to break a parley under the imperial *leipum* and assault my guests? And where is my representative?"

His fist clenched and the silk-flowered branch broke off and fell to the dusty floor. The ears moved back on Penrys's scalp—she'd never seen Tun Jeju lose his control before.

She straightened in her seat. "And my husband, foster-father, and apprentice, *notju-chi*. Find a clean chair and I'll tell you what I know."

Penrys was in the process of describing her warning to the wizards on the street, where she had showed them images of the *leipum* and Gen Jongto, when they were interrupted.

A querulous old man's voice demanding access brought her head up. *What, out here in the open? It couldn't be… could it?*

Two brown-robes escorted Char Nojuk and his daughter into the hall. They stopped, appalled, at the bloody mess, and then zeroed in on Penrys seated in the corner, ignoring Tun Jeju and the others with her.

"Where is he, *minochi*? Where? I heard he was seen down here, before the riot."

Penrys cleared her throat. "Tun Jeju, this is the *samkatju* Char Nojuk, someone you should meet, and his daughter, Char Dami. *Samkatju-chi*, this is the *notju* I mentioned to you. There's been a …"

"A disaster is what there's been. Where is my nephew?" Every syllable was forcefully stressed, as if clarity could make the answer any more palatable.

She held up her hand. "I believe he's been taken captive, with several of the foreign wizards. Including my husband, whom you met last night."

"I'm so sorry, Penrys-chi," Char Dami said. "Are they hurt?"

"Najud is." Her throat closed up, and she swallowed. "I don't know about Char Dazu. He stepped in front of the foreigners to claim protection for them, I think. It didn't work."

The old man's mouth worked. "You mean they knew there was a Char here and they attacked anyway?"

Penrys nodded. "That's what it looked like to me. I told them he was here to witness before we entered the compound. By name."

She could see this took the wind out of his sails. Tun Jeju gestured to one of his men, and chairs appeared for both of them. Char Nojuk sat down abruptly as if his knees had stopped working, and Char Dami settled herself more gracefully.

Tun Jeju pinned Penrys with an "I'll be coming back to you in a moment" look, and spoke to the *samkatju*. "Do I have the honor of addressing one of our esteemed Kigali *lupjuwen*?"

Char Nojuk blinked at him. "Did she tell you nothing?" He cocked his head scornfully at Penrys. "Yes, of course—the wizards of the Char family have been advisors and councilors for generations. And we'd be hidden still if my nephew hadn't been so imprudent as to join her this morning on a fool's errand."

"I'm sorry, *samkatju-chi*, but that's not quite true," Tun Jeju said in his even tones. "That news cannot be returned to the earth, as if the ore were never mined. Like it or not, we are all now in a new era."

He sent Penrys an unreadable look. "Please, *samkatju-chi*, join us while Penrys continues her story. One of my men will fetch us something to drink." A wave of his hand to his staff started the process of turning that command into reality.

Penrys summarized the story so far and then continued with the details for Tun Jeju.

By the time her hoarse voice had finished the tale, cups had appeared, with both water and a pot of *bunnas*. Tun Jeju assumed the role of host, and offered refreshment to the Char family. Penrys and Chosmod were left to fend for themselves, and they passed cups along to Dar Datsu and Lai Tsumai, who were trying to look inconspicuous—not easy to achieve when they couldn't get very close to Penrys or each other without complaints from their chains. Mpeowake was still being tended to, near the wall where they'd ended up when whatever device had been used had done its damage.

"I don't understand why they didn't just finish us off once we were down," Penrys muttered to Chosmod when she stared at the dead bodies where they'd been standing.

Tun Jeju turned his head in her direction. "You haven't seen the bodies in the courtyard yet. No betting man one who got out would have been tempted to go back in to see if you were actually dead or not. And I doubt there was anyone left alive in here to check."

She swallowed. *And even so, they managed to capture Najud, and Vylkar, and I couldn't stop them. And where is Munraz?*

Two of the brown-robes approached Tun Jeju and waited for his attention.

"Well?" he said.

The senior woman reported first. "We found three different openings into the sewers, with obvious traces of passage. They've had three hours—if they don't return here, we won't be finding them. There may be other exits that weren't used, perhaps blocked by the attackers. I would expect they have plans for how to reassemble somewhere else and maintain contact but unless one of these two here…"

Tun Jeju raised his hand to stop her and turned to the man. "What's the status of the injured?"

The man's robes were bloodstained, and he had an air of weariness. "The Ndanwe woman will recover, but she'll have difficulty moving about until her ribs heal. She's awake and asking questions. We've told her about the death of her young female companion, and she's asked to speak with you."

"Can you bring her here?" Tun Jeju asked.

The doctor shrugged. "We have to get her on a pallet anyway— we can start by moving her over here. We were too late for many of the others."

He spared a casual glance for Penrys and the other survivors. "Nothing needed for these, though I expect they'll be sore for a while. Now, unless there's something else, I'd like to see to the body counts."

Tun Jeju dismissed them both.

"And how do you plan on finding the captives, *notju-chi*?" Char Nojuk was single-minded about what he expected from the apparatus of Imperial Security.

"Who attacked here, *samkatju-chi*?" Tun Jeju shot back. "Who ignores the authority and custom of the Char family, as they ignore the *leipum* and assault my representative and the guests of the emperor?"

An uneasy look crossed Char Nojuk's face. "Now, that I can't say, not for sure. We have disagreements among ourselves, I'll not deny it, but we know better than to start a war we can't win. We just wanted to be left alone."

"That's not what these wizards wanted," Penrys said. "They were told what we planned, they knew we wanted to normalize their position. That's clearly what they *don't* want. There's going to be some kind of demand, based on their hostages—where will they send it? What do they want?"

"How should I know what these motherless scum want?" Char Nojuk responded hotly.

"Don't you think you should find out?" Tun Jeju asked, quietly. Char Dami nodded silently from her seat beside her father.

"Come, *wo-chi*, we should go home and give them the news. There's nothing we can do here. And you need to talk to people."

He jerked his head in reluctant agreement, and glared at Penrys. "I expect to hear from you every day until this is over. This is your fault, you and that feckless Zannib husband of yours."

Penrys held her face expressionless until he'd stalked off with his daughter, and then slumped in her seat. She hoped Tun Jeju would delay his own admonition until the pounding in her head subsided.

Movement caught her eye, and she watched some of the brown-robes carry Mpeowake on a pallet over to their cluster of tables. She was alert but pale, and winced when her bearers jolted to a halt.

"*Notju-chi*," she said, to Tun Jeju, her tone of displeasure unimpaired by addressing him while flat on her back. "Chosmod has told me of the death of Toawe and the capture of Ijumo. This is not the hospitality we expect from great Kigali, and our embassy will be most displeased. We must insist on a prompt pursuit of the captives before greater harm comes to them."

"As you say, Mpeowake-*chi*. Please be assured that we are giving this our fullest attention." Tun Jeju's voice was calm, but Penrys could feel the steel in his mind.

"And you…" Mpeowake turned her head to Penrys. "There is something you should know. One of the missing wizards from Ndant is my sister's son, Kalavo. He vanished almost four years ago, en route to the north. We assumed his ship was lost—it happens—but we never saw his body and so he is on our list of the missing."

She took as deep a breath as her broken ribs permitted. "I saw him here tonight, in the audience, with a chain. And he didn't recognize me."

She lifted her head. "They tell me there's no dead Ndanwo here that could be him, so presumably he got away. I'd like him back, please."

Letting her head fall back to the pallet, she spoke to no one in particular. "And now I'd like to return to my embassy, if you don't mind, and give them the news."

CHAPTER 15

The walk back to the Imperial Security building, under guard from a squad of brown-robes, seemed endless to Penrys, every step matched by the throbbing in her head. She walked with her eyes on the ground, sunk into her own fog. At least she'd stopped throwing up after the first half hour.

Every few blocks she scanned the area, looking for a buildup of wizards again, but found only a few, in ones and twos, and no chained ones at all. And none of the captives. Tun Jeju was with them and the guards were vigilant against physical attack, but she was worried about a second strike.

Tun Jeju had offered to shelter all the wounded, but both Mpeowake, from her litter, and Chosmod declared they would be more comfortable in their own embassies.

Penrys couldn't decide what to do. She was sure the wizards who'd attacked them could identify her as the one who'd killed so many of them. How could she return to the Zannib embassy and make them all a target there? She was uneasy about letting Tun Jeju take charge again of the two recently released prisoners, but she couldn't think of an alternative.

Chosmod had matched steps with Penrys for half a block before she really noticed and looked up at him inquisitively.

"What are you going to do, *brudigna?*" he said, in Rasesni.

Was she still in charge, in Tun Jeju's mind, or had today's fiasco changed that? She remembered her reading in the Collegium in Ellech. *Never show weakness as a leader.*

"We have to find out what they want, and we have to get the captives back."

"Yes, that goes without saying," Chosmod said, impatiently. "What are *you* going to do, right now, to seize the initiative."

She spoke without hesitation. "Search the city for the captives." She tapped her forehead. "If I can find Najud or Munraz, I can find the others."

Chosmod nodded. "Good. I can help with that, and so can Mpeowake, if she will. Maybe even the chained ones, or that Char family."

He searched her face. "And if they've been moved out of range?"

Her stomach clenched again. "Search first, adjust if not found." She took a breath. "You have suggestions?"

The man was fifteen or twenty years older than she was, and remembered more than three years of it, unlike her. She'd take whatever advice she could get.

"I don't think they would go to all that trouble to take captives if they just intended to kill them," he said, judiciously. "But they might move them."

"Can they do that and not have other wizards notice? I'm beginning to think a significant fraction of the city is involved."

"But your Char Nojuk didn't recognize the existence of this group, and I gather he's part of the established underground community."

Penrys paused in mid-step. "You're right. That implies they've come out of hiding today for the first time."

"So we've got allies, I should think, at least potentially, in the wizard community here."

"And enemies. They're not going to talk to me, after today's…" She wanted to say "slaughter" but couldn't bring herself to utter the word.

"Oh, I don't know," Chosmod said reflectively. "How tempted they might be to force you into a vulnerable position in exchange for the captives, don't you think?"

She stared at him.

He shook his head. "You have something of value now, *brudigna*, don't you see? Something they want—*you*. This morning, they only wanted captives. Now they're going to want something else. We can use that."

She stirred herself and started walking again. Chosmod swung along beside her, comfortably silent while she turned the notion over.

"Thank you, Modo—may I call you that?" He nodded.

"It's good to have leverage," she added. She could feel her mind starting to work again. "I've got to keep them from taking what they want before I'm ready to offer it to them, and I've got to keep those other chained ones out of their reach."

"Are you sure they care about them?"

Penrys swept her hand through the air. "Certain. Nothing stopped them from attacking us on the street, once we were gathered as a group. Why invade that compound and make it harder on themselves, unless they wanted to eliminate the chained wizards, too, and decided to strike when both targets were together?"

"Speculation, but reasonable." It was Chosmod's turn for ruminating silently for a while.

"Ask your new allies for protection—that Char family," he suggested. "You have value to them, too— a channel to Tun Jeju, a link to these chained wizards, and a proven fighter against the rogues."

"I've thought about that," Penrys said. "But I don't know that they can stand up to fighting physically this way. What we saw in the compound today, not just weapons but devices—can the established hidden wizards defend against that? And will they?"

She waved her hands to illustrate. "Char Nojuk lives in his family compound. There are wizards in his family, a few, but others, too. I can't go there for shelter any more than I can make the Zannib ambassador and his family into targets. They probably all live like that, hiding within their families."

Her voice rose. "Whoever attacked us today had more than a hundred wizards. It wasn't spontaneous, a 'riot' like Char Notju suggested—I don't believe that for a moment. Who leads them? How many are there? They very nearly overran us all, and we were a lot stronger than the Char family resources. No one family could stand up to that.

"So that'll have to change, too," Chosmod said, with a shrug.

She laughed. "You don't ask much, do you? Is that before or after I cower in the Imperial Security building with my handful of unwilling minions?"

"I can think of worse places to go. At least you'll have disciplined fighters on your side. And wizards will join you, if you work it right."

When they finally reached the Imperial Security building, Tun Jeju paused on the steps to hear their decisions. The guards with

Mpeowake continued in the direction of the Ndant embassy, and Chosmod walked off alone to his own embassy, waving off the guards offered by Tun Jeju.

Penrys turned to the chained wizards. "Dar Datsu, I'll be returning here tonight, after I make a couple of necessary visits while things are in flux and it's relatively safe. I strongly recommend that both of you take advantage of the *notju*'s hospitality this evening, and we can discuss it further in the morning."

The two wizards exchanged weary glances with each other. Lai Tsumai shrugged. They filed up the steps, and several of the guards went with them.

She looked for a moment up the steps at Tun Jeju. "I have an idea," she told him. "Will you still be here in a couple of hours? I'd like to discuss it with you."

He nodded. "Where will you be in the meantime?"

"I want to pick up a few things from the Zannib embassy and explain what's going on to them. And clean up, I suppose." She surveyed the rags of her lovely formal robes. She couldn't imagine what her face looked like, but her hands were bloody and filthy.

"And then…" She took a breath. "What'll be done with the bodies?"

"We'll take those eight bodies into our care and embalm them, pending our reestablishing contact with the leader of the chained wizards, that Rin Tsugo. If he claims them, we'll release them to him.

"The attackers?" she asked.

"Men will be there all night sketching faces and searching them. When we're done, they'll be buried, like any other enemy of Kigali."

Penrys could hear the anger in his voice.

"Our guests… the three of them will be cleaned up decently and presented to their embassies, this evening."

"I'd hoped so," she said. "Mpeowake will explain what's happened to the Ndanum, but what about the Ellech embassy? Two dead and Vylkar missing." She cleared her throat. "I'm as much Ellech as those chained wizards from wherever are Kigaliwen. I should go there myself and talk to them. I'm not sure I'll be welcome, but I have to try."

Tun Jeju nodded. "I'll have an honor guard waiting here for you when they're ready, and you can escort the bodies yourself. We'll talk when you return."

He gestured to four of the remaining guard to go with her. No more nonsense about Zep Pangwit as a guide apparently—seemed she rated more serious protection now.

The guard at the Zannib embassy hesitated when he saw Penrys's bloody face, but he opened the gate to her nonetheless. Mir Tojit was waiting alone in the courtyard. He exchanged an enigmatic look with the guards that had accompanied her, and the squad leader nodded to him and took position outside the gate.

"This may take a little while," Penrys warned him.

"We'll be here, *minochi.*"

The gates were shut behind her and she focused on the *katsom.* "You've heard?" she said.

"A message was sent," he acknowledged, dropping any pretense that he didn't work for Imperial Security. "Will you be staying?"

"No, I can't bring this down on the head of Talqatin and his household. I'm just here to clean up and gather a few things, and then I'll leave."

Talqatin appeared at the top of the steps. He looked her over, and then called to Mir Tojit, "Send someone to her room to help her."

He came partway down the steps and beckoned her in. "It was only yesterday that you mentioned 'a lively week.' I think you underestimated things."

She trudged slowly up to join him, and they climbed the rest of the steps side by side. "Najud and Munraz?" he asked her, quietly.

She shook her head. "Najud is a captive, and injured. Munraz… I just don't know. Not dead, but missing. I haven't found them, yet."

He laid a hand on her shoulder, and the simple human contact almost broke her control.

"Let me make myself presentable," she said, hoarsely, "and then I'll tell you what happened. Then I have to leave."

His head pulled back. "You belong here."

"Not possible. Bad enemies you can't defend against, and I have other options. Ask Mir Tojit—he knows. But… thank you for the offer, *lij.*"

He stopped in the entry hall and let her mount the stairs alone to the room she shared with Najud.

She walked in and sat on the edge of the bed, and waited for the throbbing in her head from the exertion of the climb to beat itself into something less intrusive. Just taking the weight off her feet gave her a light-headed feel.

Once again she did a multi-block scan, and found nothing but the few clusters of wizards she'd seen in the neighborhood before. She pushed it further, seeking Najud or Munraz, but turned up nothing. *Where are you, Naj-sha?*

She snatched up his pillow and clutched it to her chest, inhaling deeply. It smelled of him, and a shudder ran through her body. She rocked with it for a minute or two.

At a polite knock on the open doorframe, she wiped her face and turned away to restore the pillow to its proper place.

One of the maidservants stood there, staring wide-eyed at her ruined clothing and battered face. "I've run a hot bath for you, *minochi*—you'll feel better for it. Come with me."

The guards who escorted Penrys back to the Imperial Security building carried in the few items she'd chosen, and left her with the sixteen members of the honor guard that had been waiting for her. This fancier version of the brown robes uniform was new to her, silken and gleaming.

They left her standing on the steps with four of their number, and the other twelve ducked inside. They returned a few minutes later around the outside of the building carrying two long palanquins, and Penrys caught a glimpse of coffins, before the curtains were drawn to block the sight.

She was tired, but cleaning up had revived her enough to finish this job tonight, at least she hoped so. She was heartsick inside— these men from Ellech had traveled all this long way, partly on her account, and two of them were dead. It was a good death, as the Ellech reckoned such things—they'd died fighting with weapons, back to back—but still, they died and left families behind.

And where was Vylkar, the man who'd searched for her on the mountain and found her, naked in the snow, and then gave her the countenance of his home and served as her *bilappa* at the Collegium? She owed him a great deal and, in his cool way, she knew he was fond of her.

What a wretched reward to be bringing to his country's embassy.

She didn't know the route and let the four who weren't burdened by the palanquins lead the way. The pace was slow and deliberate, and the civilians on the street made generous room for them, though heads turned curiously to watch after they'd passed.

The district was similar to the one where the Zannib embassy stood, and not far distant from it. When they approached the compound's gates, she saw the Kigali sign for a ship etched and colored in the outer wall, and alongside it a snowy mountain peak, an ancient symbol for Ellech and the highest mountains in the world that marked its northern border.

In the central courtyard, all of the embassy staff, both those from Ellech and their local servants, were lined up in two columns, and biers waited side-by-side between them to hold the coffins. Beyond the biers a low fire burned in a pit. While the honor guard transferred the bodies, the ambassador made himself known to Penrys. His hair and tidy beard were completely gray, but still he held himself tall and upright.

"I am Preinnur. Thank you for seeing Bildaer and Innurrys home to us. There is no news of Vylkar yet?"

She swallowed. "No, not yet. He was taken with others, including my husband, and we have only just started to search."

"Can you stay and tell us the story of their deaths, Penrys?"

She steeled herself and nodded—she'd expected this. "I can't stay for the wake itself, ambassador. We have more work to do tonight. I hope you understand."

He spread his hands sympathetically and led her to a platform behind the fire, where everyone could see her, and the light shone on her face as she spoke, to witness the truth of her words.

The quiet conversations ceased, and all that could be heard inside the compound was the crackling of the fire. The Kigali honor guard lined the walls by the gates and all heads turned to her.

"This morning," she said, "Imperial Security sent an embassy to the compound that housed many of the chained wizards of Yenit Ping. All of the foreign wizards invited by Tun Jeju chose to attend under the truce sign of the *leipum* in order to bear witness to this meeting…"

CHAPTER 16

"I need a building," Penrys said. "Maybe two."

She was exhausted but she couldn't go to bed until she'd had this discussion with Tun Jeju. The Imperial Security building itself was almost as alive with activity as in the middle of the day, but the familiar meeting room they shared was empty of all but the two of them.

Tun Jeju looked as if the day's events hadn't touched him, but Penrys knew her own face and posture belied her clean clothing.

Only the *notju's* raised eyebrows betrayed his surprise at her request.

"You see, the wizards like Char Nojuk… they need a base. They can't fight from their compounds—too scattered, they have families with them that aren't wizards, and so forth. You don't expect an army to fight out of its homes, after all.

"In Rasesdad, they have the temples. Temples have leaders, priests, mages, and guards, so the mages are protected, and they also do some of the protecting. The temple schools that are for everyone let mages from different temples mingle, and that provides some stability and cross-fertilization, too."

Tun Jeju's silence unnerved her.

"Temples and temple schools—those are official buildings. Most of the mages are members of temples, and many are priests. Most of them earn a living at least partly from their wizard skills."

She waved her hands in the air.

"Now, what we have here are wizards in families. They earn their living mostly from the family businesses, which they learn at home. What if they had a guild building, just for wizardry? Maybe under the auspices of one of the gods. Then those who want to advance in wizardry can be taught and certified, and those that just want to get on with the family business can go do so."

She cleared her throat. She was on firmer ground here. "In Ellech, they qualify their committed wizards through a series of schools, and then release them to work in the craft or as technologists with some of the commercial ventures. The schools don't have guards, as such, but in a crisis that could change—all the rest of the structure is in place."

"What about *sarq*-Zannib and Ndant?" Tun Jeju said.

"Zannib does schooling one-on-one, through an apprentice system. They've never had a reason to think in terms of mass defense, but there's a functioning tradition of creating ad hoc groups of wizards to contain and eliminate any so-called wizard-tyrants, what they term a *qahulaj*. That seems to work well enough for them, though I don't know if it could grow to accommodate more than one at a time."

Penrys frowned. "I'm not so sure about Ndant, but I think it's not too different from Rasesdad—temple-based qualifications, but maybe no general school."

She yawned and covered her mouth with her hand. "So, what do all of these systems have in common that might work for Kigali?"

Holding out her hand, she began to tick off fingers. "They have public buildings, except for *sarq*-Zannib which doesn't have many permanent buildings like that of any kind. In all of them, wizards are identified and educated, though not all of them choose to live as wizards. They have ways of working together that are compatible with self-defense and separated from their households and families. Again, the Zannib are an exception, being lightly populated and dispersed. And when they work together, they recognize a leadership structure. Even the Zannib."

Tun Jeju finally volunteered a comment. "You're proposing that a single temple take ownership of the wizard… class. Some place that is defensible, that could hold a leadership out in the open, that could identify and qualify the wizards of Kigali."

"And the chained ones, too. Don't forget them," Penrys said. "Don't the main temples of Yenit Ping have branches in the other cities and towns?"

"They do," he said.

"And you could either do education in the same place, or the temple could support a separate building, whichever is more compatible with how guilds are organized outside of the families that work in them."

Tun Jeju mused on the concept for a moment. "The temples are already part of the governing body of the empire. They hold power that is more nominal than real, and this might shift that balance, but there's already a structure in place that could be built upon."

"If you could do this in Kigali," Penrys said, "and if the hidden wizards liked the idea, then there would be a way to actually build a stable addition to your society, out in the open. I haven't proposed anything like this to Char Nojuk, but you could start there and find out."

"This proposal has merit," Tun Jeju said. "We'll speak more about it tomorrow."

He stood, and Penrys followed suit and yawned again.

"Enough for tonight. The guard outside the door will take you to the other two."

He paused for a moment to respond to her unasked question. "And, no, we didn't put them back in the cells.

Her lips twitched. "Just one question—what's happened to Zep Pangwit?"

Tun Jeju spared a brief smile. "Apparently he decided he'd had enough of the excitement in Yenit Ping after he heard about this morning. He requested to be released back to Tengwa Tep."

"Isn't that a shame," Penrys said, with a tired grin.

Munraz stood in the dripping passageway underground and chewed his fingernail in the dark shadows. Kit Hachi beside him carried a torch, and raised it as high as the ceiling would permit while she counted out loud. The man at the end of the line lifted his, too, to help her.

"That's fifteen of us, still," she told Rin Tsugo, quietly.

He swore under his breath. "If I'd made them run the drill more often…"

Munraz watched the shadow of Kit Hachi's head as it shook in disagreement. "We have two more exits at that end of the compound—others will have made it. No one was trying to stop us."

"Too busy making hash out of our visitors," Rin Tsugo said sourly.

Munraz's last glimpse of the hall before Kit Hachi hauled him out the door had been of Najud's turban, visible over the knot of attackers, and Penrys circling at the other end of the room with a look of concentration he remembered and feared.

Did either of them survive?

The trip through the sewers in the raised embankment underneath the buildings of Yenit Ping was neither sweet-smelling nor dry as they passed along the ancient stonework. He was the only one there with no chain, though not the only Zan—one grown woman with her hair in a long braid that could not fully control its untidy waves had curled her lip at the sight of him and ignored him ever since.

He held his mouth shut and hoped they would overlook him. He'd wanted to stay and help his *jarghal*. That guide had no business pulling him away. And now, what would they do with him? *Am I a hostage, myself, to get their own people back?*

Unfortunately Kit Hachi kept a frequent hold on him by his robe, and his attempts to drift backward and let them go on without him didn't work. The last time she'd done it, he lost his self-control and glared at her, but her only response was a no-nonsense lecture. "If you fall behind, youngster, you could wander around down here forever in the cold dark. You stick with us, and we'll sort it out later. Trust me."

He tried to keep his feet and splashed through liquid where he must, trying not to think about it.

Finally, when it seemed as if they'd been walking down there for hours and Munraz's stomach was becoming insistent despite the smell, Rin Tsugo called a halt. He borrowed Kit Hachi's torch and looked at the characters drawn next to a vertical shaft. "This is it," he told her.

"Quiet, everyone," he called back down the line. "I'm going to take a look around."

He climbed carefully, testing each embedded rung, until he reached the platform on top. The doorknob turned in his hand, and he beckoned Kit Hachi up to take the torch away from him, back down into the passage.

When she had retreated far enough to give him darkness, he pushed the door open, and Munraz heard a squeal of hinges that set his pulse racing, followed by soft footsteps that faded away above him. A dim light fell down through the opening. He crept forward to the base of the ladder, and Kit Hachi was powerless to stop him without finding someone else to hold the torch.

"Come back!" she whispered after him.

"I won't go far," he called back softly.

He hauled himself up and waited on the platform, peering through the door. It opened inside a building, but the place must be a ruin, for he could see daylight penetrating from above, through breaks in the roof.

Careful to keep his own shield up, he did a quick mind-scan. He couldn't reach very far—Najud had told him that would improve with practice and age—but he could see all the escapees below, and no one else nearby on his level besides Rin Tsugo.

Munraz tiptoed through the doorway and the movement startled Rin Tsugo who had just turned away from a glassless window.

"What are you doing here?" he hissed.

"Just wanted to help."

"Get back down there. I'm making sure no one else is around."

"They're not. I already checked," Munraz said.

"And do you know how to look for power-stones, for devices that could betray our presence?"

Abashed, Munraz said, "I… I don't know what those are."

"And the Zannib don't do devices, I know." Rin Tsugo sighed. "Go back to the door and wait, youngster. Please."

When Munraz hesitated, Rin Tsugo gave him a good look. "You're not in any danger from us, boy. But you can't go wandering alone on the streets, a Zan in torn clothing, ripe pickings for whoever's after us. We'll get you home, soon as we can. Soon as we meet up with the others."

"Now go," he said, and Munraz obeyed. *Home. Where's that? Still, the Zannib embassy would be a good choice. The ambassador will know what to do, if… No! They're not dead! They're not! I don't believe it.*

But he couldn't shake that vision of dozens of people pouring into the hall, and Penrys and Najud fighting, separately and outnumbered.

Eventually Rin Tsugo returned and called quietly down to Kit Hachi, "Bring them up, and leave the torches below, in case we need to duck in again."

Munraz moved out of their way into the derelict building and walked over to the windows, following them around on three sides. The afternoon was unexpectedly deep in shadows but what light remained showed two other buildings, abandoned and partially collapsed, standing in an overgrown field huddled up against the steep eastern slope of Tegong Him. *We're in the mountain shadow cast by the afternoon sun. No wonder I thought it was almost evening.*

The creak of the noisy hinges drew his attention again, and he saw that the last one up had closed the door again.

Kit Hachi beckoned him over. "Are we staying here?" he asked.

She shook her head. "Our rendezvous is the building closest to the ridge. Gives us the most varied ways of escaping."

"Rendezvous?"

"Everyone who escaped will find a way to meet us there."

"And then what?" he said.

She looked at him, their eyes on a level, since he wasn't done growing. He had a few more inches to add before he stood as tall as his father and uncle, family to him no longer but part of his blood. The only other chained wizard he'd been this close to, besides Penrys, had been the *qahulajti.* Just before he spared her the fate his uncle had planned, by slitting her throat. *In mercy. It was in mercy!*

The muscles of his arms and hands remembered how it felt, holding her chin from behind and slicing the soft skin, how it bled, spurting over his hands, and his eyes dropped involuntarily to Kit Hachi's neck with its gold-colored chain.

"What's wrong, youngster?" she asked, concern in her eyes.

He backpedaled out of reach and turned away. *Always a woman with a chain, one after another. What would she think, any of them think, if they knew?*

"Nothing," he muttered. "Sorry."

"Well, don't worry. You're safe with us, as safe as any of us are. We'll figure it out and get you home."

The floor was hard, and everything hurt. And it smelled bad. The persistent clinking of metal was an irritant, and the side of his head was sore, where the turban hadn't protected it.

Najud finally opened his eyes to figure out what was making the noise. There were other shapes shifting restlessly in the dim space of the stone-walled room. When he moved his leg to shake off a weight, it jingled at him, and he realized he was chained by the ankle to a wall.

The last thing he remembered was the desperate fight. The vivid image of the young Ndanwe Toawe holding her hands out in surrender and being casually slaughtered made him suck in his breath. *Penrys?* Some of the attackers had converged on her and he wasn't sure if there'd been anyone with her.

"Pen-sha?" he called softly.

"Ah, our young Zannib friend awakes."

The quiet voice to his right was Vylkar's, and Najud started to push himself up into a sitting position, then hissed at the unexpected pain that stopped him.

"Careful," Vylkar said. "We had to patch you up as best we could, but some of those cuts were deep."

Najud glanced down at his hands, criss-crossed with torn strips of cloth. The muscle ache reminded him of defending himself against swords with his long knife which was never meant for the task. He checked but the weapons he'd carried under his robes were gone.

A thicker, blood-stained bandage covered his right forearm, but since he could still move his hands, he dismissed it for now. He still wore his robe, but underneath he was bare chested. He felt a tight harness holding a pad against his left side—wet and seeping, his probing fingers told him.

"Had to use your shirt," Vylkar commented.

"Who else is here?" Najud asked.

"Ijumo, Mrigasba, Gen Jongto, and Char Dazu."

"I remember Toawe being struck down."

"Yes, and my colleagues made a glorious death, like warriors of old, fighting back to back with captured swords. Not something a middle-aged scholar can expect in this mundane time. They were smiling, before they died."

His voice trailed off. "I believe I'll set it to verse, as an exercise to pass the time."

There was a pause. Najud worked his way more cautiously up to a sitting position against the wall and wished he could see Vylkar's face.

"Where are the others? Penrys? My apprentice?"

"Chosmod and Mpeowake retreated to join Penrys and, I think, so did a couple of our students from yesterday. Last I saw, they were defending themselves well enough. The chained ones fled— wisest thing for them to do, I think."

"But Penrys and Munraz aren't here."

"Don't know about your apprentice," Vylkar said. "But I don't think you need to be concerned about Penrys. Something was killing our attackers. They were dropping in the hall, and the courtyard was covered in bodies as they dragged us out."

"Penrys," Najud said, decisively.

"Yes, I thought so."

On Najud's left, Char Dazu spoke out of the shadows. "This is a war that's been started. A Char at a meeting of this sort is like the *leipum*—a sign of truce and parley. That's why I came. Everyone will be hunting them."

Gen Jongto's voice chimed in. "The *notju* will be… incensed."

"Glad you made it, Gen Jongto," Najud said. "Where are we? Think he can find us?"

While he spoke he scanned the surroundings but found them well-shielded beyond the room. "That's odd…"

Ijumo's voice came from across the room. "You've noticed the shield, have you? I wonder how they're doing that."

"Any thoughts, Najud?" That was Mrigasba, the white bandage wrapped around his head showing clearly in the dimness. "I seem to remember you having some experience with wizards in groups, in Neshilik."

What did they do, turn that into a training manual in Rasesdad?

"We did some work on it in the Temple Academy, yes. But that was on shielding ourselves, not someone else. This is something else—keeping us in instead of keeping someone out."

He thought about it for a moment. "How many of them are there—anyone know? What do they want, and what are they doing with us?"

"What, indeed," Vylkar murmured. "They've given each of us soup, bread and water—yours is up next to you, by the wall. And a bucket for… other things. The ankle shackle is an unwelcome complication."

Char Dazu said, "They haven't asked us for anything." Najud could hear the affront in his voice.

"So we're just hostages, then," Gen Jongto commented. "That's unfortunate—they seem to have managed to keep one from each embassy for maximum leverage."

"We don't know how, and we don't know why." Vylkar's voice had assumed a pedagogical tone. "Maybe we can find out who."

Najud shook his head. "I'd rather get free first, then worry about it. We are five wizards—I expect we can come up with something."

Mrigasba lifted his leg and rattled the shackle until its chain tinkled merrily. "And what about this?"

Najud smiled in the darkness. "They left me my turban, didn't they? My *anah im-ghabr*? I think I may be able to find a few things to help us out."

CHAPTER 17

"Languages first. It's an essential skill."

Penrys took a deep breath and darted a half-smile at her test subject. "You've just met this man on the road. Who is he? Where is he from? What is he?"

They were one level down below the street in the Imperial Security building, and Penrys was working on basic education for Dar Datsu and Lai Tsumai as quickly as they could absorb it. Chosmod had spent the first part of the morning checking the basics with the two students—mind-speech and shielding—while Penrys sat in a corner of the dusty room and searched fruitlessly for Najud and Munraz, and for any foreign wizards or unusual concentrations of native ones.

When that failed, she offered to take over for the next topic, mind-scanning, and Chosmod volunteered himself as a non-Kigali subject.

She perched on one of the random pieces of furniture in the small room which had been hastily emptied for their use and tried not to sneeze at the dust in the air that had been stirred up. With only one formal Zannib set of clothing remaining, she'd opted for her everyday work clothes, in Zannib style—boots, breeches, a loose vest and a short overrobe. The two ex-prisoners were newly clad in ordinary Kigali garments, with their hair in a single braid, though neither bore a Kigali face. Only Chosmod retained any elegance of dress in his priest's robes.

The biggest difference, however, was the exposed chains of the two students. Neither of them was wearing the high-necked style of tunic that hid the chains, and they'd decided not to cover them with any sort of fabric.

Penrys watched the aborted gestures, the hands partially lifted to check if the chains were exposed, before being dropped. *It's going to take them a while. I wonder if my example is really right for them, anyway.*

"Now watch what I'm doing," she told them.

She opened her mind to both of them and let them watch while she superficially probed the cooperative Chosmod.

First things first. He's clearly male. Even young children usually have a firm sense of identity that includes the basics. It's the mental equivalent of how he holds his body, how he occupies space.

She felt the agreement of her students, and the lingering investigation by Lai Tsumai of what it felt like in a mind of a different gender.

Now, what does his body know? What has been ingrained in the structures of his mind? Feel for the echoes of it in your own body. I feel reaching and pulling in his arms and chest. There are very high mountains in Rasesdad. Is this what it feels like to travel hill terrain as an expert, moving over rock and not just following trails?

Chosmod was listening in to the lesson, and they all felt his amused assent. "We have competitions for climbing difficult cliffs, and I was considered well-skilled, when I was younger, of course."

What else?

Lai Tsumai ventured an opinion. *His hands know subtle, coordinated movement. Rhythmic. A musician?*

Well done. His cheeks and mouth, too. Wind instrument?

That last question was directed to Chosmod. *Several. I'm not very good.*

Doesn't matter. Your mind and body still remember whatever skill you have. It's just as much effort being a bad musician as a good one.

His laugh which turned into a sneeze broke her concentration, and she turned that into some advice for her students. "Next time you have the opportunity, spend some time watching entertainers and craftsmen, to see how it feels from the inside. And then think about what it's like when you yourself become an expert in anything, even if it's only throwing knives or making bread. It'll help you when you meet strangers."

They both nodded.

Let's look at language. How does his mouth form words, his tongue and teeth chew on them? Try it out in your own mouth… what does it feel like? Does it feel like Kigali?

Dar Datsu answered tentatively. *No. More movement in the back of the mouth, almost in the throat.*

Now try and see what sounds go with that—which ones are meaningful, and which are just noise.

Dar Datsu sputtered some random noises out loud, but the guttural feel was clear.

"That's what Rasesni sounds like," Lai Tsumai exclaimed.

"Neither of you know Rasesni," Penrys said. "So watch, from the inside, while he talks. Say something, Modo."

Chosmod obliged with a description of the sun setting behind the Mratsanag Mountains, as viewed from the temple city of Dzongphan.

"Could you follow what he said?"

Dar Datsu nodded slowly. "Yes, I think so."

"Good. If you work on this for a while, you can learn the language this way. Even quickly, once you become expert at it."

"Does that mean I could play his instruments, too?"

Penrys shook her head. "There's no shortcut for your body learning what his body already knows. You can quickly understand the mechanics of how his instruments work, but your fingers and mouth and breathing would all be clumsy until your body learned it the slow way. Same for the language—your accent comes from what your mouth knows about making sounds. You can understand and speak the language you're tapping, but you'll garble it in your mouth until you have enough practice with it."

They spent the next half-hour exploring Penrys's native Ellech and Chosmod's Rasesni and trying to generate sentences of their own in the two languages, until Penrys called a halt with a lift of her hand.

"So," Penrys said. "What's missing from what you know about this man?"

The two students looked at each other, then almost as one they realized. "He's a wizard," Lai Tsumai said. "How do we know that?"

"Chosmod, how do *you* tell if someone is a wizard?" Penrys asked.

"By using some of the techniques you've been teaching, *brudigna*. It's a profession like any other."

Penrys gave him a startled look. "Not directly?"

Chosmod slowly shook his head. "I'm not sure what you mean by that."

"Hmm… Let me find someone nearby."

She scanned the surrounding blocks and located one of the Kigali hidden wizards. *Here, watch, everyone. Do you see that core of* *power, deep inside? If we were using our eyes, we might say it shines.** She showed them what she meant, and they tried looking by themselves.

Dar Datsu naturally tried looking at Chosmod and the rest of them.

"Chosmod-chi shines like the Kigali man. But it's hard to look at you or Lai Tsumai—too bright!"

"You three all look like that to me," Chosmod told him. "I assume it's the effect of the chain?" he asked Penrys.

"I'm not sure what's cause and effect," she said. "All the chained wizards I've met shine brightly, but are there wizards who shine as brightly without the chain? Were we all wizards before we were... taken? Were we bright before and that's why we were taken? Or is the chain responsible?"

She shook her head. "I assume it's the chain, for convenience, but it could be the other option. I'll have to ask Mpeowake about her nephew, what he was like as a wizard before he went missing. He's the only one whose history we know, from before."

Now was not the time to tell them that she could pull the power from those cores into her chain, temporarily or otherwise. *Don't want them experimenting with that.*

"If I shield myself..." She suited action to words.

Lai Tsumai said, "I can barely see your mind at all, even though my eyes tell me you're there."

"And that's what you both need to work on, with each other."

The little digression reminded her of why they were there.

"All right, we need to find the captives, since that way we'll presumably find their captors. That means we need to search for wizards. Problem is, the city's full of them. We're going to have to take it sector by sector."

She linked with all four of them. *Let's start with the immediate surroundings to see what our joint range is, and then we'll refine this down to something systematic.**

Each cluster of a few dozen people included one or more of the Kigali wizards, and every so often a chained wizard shone out as well.

Chosmod dropped out first. "Too many possibilities."

"And that's my problem," Penrys said. "I can go about five miles out, but that's not even a quarter of the city, and there are hundreds of thousands of people here. Perhaps a million or more—it's difficult to judge."

She hunched over and worked her shoulders. "I've tried looking just for Najud, but it's so hard sorting through them. Only the chained ones are easy to find. There aren't very many of them, but they're scattered all over, too."

She caught the eyes of her students. "I've looked in the direction of Rin Tsugo's compound—they're not there any more."

Lai Tsumai said, "I don't understand—it wasn't chained wizards who attacked. Was it?"

"Well, no, I have no reason to think so. There were three of them in the crowd that surrounded us when I told them to back off, if you remember. But there are two or three like that wherever I look, all over the city, and they are just as likely to have been there by accident. Why would they have anything to do with the mob of wizards?"

Chosmod said, "That 'mob' as you call it was well-prepared and must have had leaders. Are you sure those leaders weren't chained wizards? Isn't that how the Voice worked?"

Dar Datsu bristled at the implication, but Penrys only shrugged. "I'm not sure of anything, though I would sooner suspect wizards with generations of knowledge than any number of chained ones, three years old."

Her stomach grumbled audibly, reminding her of how much time had passed. "No, that's not true," she said. "I'm sure of something else… I'm starving."

She could feel the lessening of tension that told her that her change of topic was successful, but Chosmod's query set her thinking. Maybe she should pin down the locations of all the chained wizards as a first step.

Yrmur! Najud, if you've gotten yourself killed, I swear I'll haunt you, rather than the other way around. How bad was that wound? Was he still alive?

She found her appetite had vanished.

Before Penrys resumed classes in the afternoon, Chosmod took an opportunity to join her for a private conversation over the remains of their meal while the other two practiced their silent speech and shields on each other at the other end of the room.

"You said the Char family wizards had devices?" he asked.

"I saw powered lights in their own areas, and there were many books on the shelves in their sanctum. I would expect they can make more than lights, but there hasn't been time to ask yet."

Chosmod nodded. "And that was definitely some sort of device that hurled us off the ground, at the end. You know devices, I think?"

"I was considered something of a specialist in the Collegium, Modo—it's what I experimented in. Haven't done much since I ended up in Kigali, and you know the Zannib don't do physical magic."

The Rasesni man folded his hands on the table before him. "What do the Kigali wizards know that we don't? Where do they get their information?"

"What, not from Rasesdad? I assumed they picked up books and expertise from there, or maybe Ndant. Or even Ellech."

"And no one heard about it? No one talked, for hundreds of years? There's always been some intermarriage on the borders, but still…"

Penrys looked at him. "What are you suggesting, Modo? That they created their own school of physical magic and devices, based on their own discoveries?"

She held up her hand before he could reply. "Wait, maybe you're right… The Ellech don't read Rasesni books on the topic— you don't let those works travel. And there's not much from Ndant in the library at the Collegium, and I would know."

Chosmod smiled in satisfaction at making his point. "So where are they getting power-stones? I assume those devices had them."

"Oh, yes. I could feel them. Wait a minute…"

She cast her mind out to scan the area, this time looking for power-stones instead of people. They glistened like little pinpricks of light, almost all of them in small physical concentrations that she suspected were the sanctums of compounds that held a few wiz- ards. In the first few blocks, she found five such repositories.

Come and see. She invited Chosmod to share her perception of them.

"Well, that might not identify wizards for you," he said, "but you can surely find out where they live."

"That makes sense, doesn't it? But why were you asking about power-stones in the first place?"

"You can't become a senior mage in Dzongphan without some knowledge of politics and leverage." Chosmod was truly doing his best not to seem patronizing to the much younger Penrys, and she gritted her teeth and invoked patience.

"Our *notju*," he said, jocularly, "he's worried about hidden Kigali wizards who might be pulling strings inside the government somewhere. But our bad boys from yesterday… if they're truly not known to the Char family and, by inference, to the other hidden wizards in Yenit Ping, then who's to say who's pulling the strings of those wizards? And them not even necessarily aware of it?"

"Wheels within wheels," Penrys commented. "I can see wizards hiding from the rest of Kigali, given the original imperial ban, but how would the second group hide from the first?"

"Very carefully," Chosmod whispered, theatrically, and Penrys laughed.

"But it's no joke. Look how many there were, and how many died. We killed a lot more of them than they did of us…"

"And that's down to you—both groups met unexpected opposition." Chosmod nodded in approval.

She shrugged, still unhappy at the body count, but becoming resigned to the necessity. "So everyone pauses to go lick their wounds, is that it? While the captives…"

"They have hostages—we need devices. To help us even the odds." He pursed his lips. "Think you can find out where the wizards get their power-stones?"

"I bet they're family heirlooms," Penrys said. "Probably hurts every time they lose one."

She leaned back and looked up at him. "But if that's all you want, I have power-stones. What do you need?"

"You, *brudigna*? Where did you get… Oh."

"I'd rather not say." She remembered the head-sized sack of power-stones gifted to her as illicit reward for her role in putting a stop to the Voice. She wouldn't betray Dzantig, the young mage who'd handed them to her at the end of the fight, in the chaos. They were worth a fortune, anywhere physical magic was used, even if they didn't look like much—small and dull.

It was clear from Chosmod's face that he was reviewing what he knew of that battle, in the official account.

"It's only fair," she added, while he remained silent. "It was a Rasesni spy who first abandoned a stash when we unmasked him,

Najud and I, and then it was the Rasesni Temple Academy that stole those from us when they… betrayed us. Seems only right that we ended up with a few at the end of it all. We did manage to stop the Voice and his army."

"Hmm." A smile flickered on his face. "Then I won't waste my time digging into it. Let me think about something useful we might do with a few of them…"

A noise from the doorway drew their attention. One of the guards preceded Tun Jeju into the room.

"Making progress?" Tun Jeju asked.

The two students stood, and Penrys and Chosmod followed suit. "In some ways," Penrys answered, nodding at the other two chained wizards. "But not at finding the attackers or their captives."

"I have one piece of good news for you, presumably from Munraz." Tun Jeju handed her an unsealed roll of papyrus. "This was sent by a relay of messengers to the Zannib ambassador, and then forwarded here."

By Mir Tojit, Penrys guessed. She opened it and read the Kigali characters. *Not in his own hand, and he can't write Kigali that well yet anyway. If he'd written it in wirqiqa-Zannib, it would have been suspicious to those who couldn't read it, and it was never sealed. So, dictated to some Kigali scribe.*

"I'm with our hosts from yesterday morning, unharmed and free. I know nothing about my two elders. I will contact you again when I have more to tell you."

It was signed with two pictures in a different hand—a set of three mountain peaks, and a spoked wheel.

Tun Jeju commented, "Admirably discreet, but still intelligible to those who know enough. If he weren't disqualified by his honest Zannib face, he might seek a position here."

"You can always send him to *sarq*-Zannib in your employ," Penrys said, absently. "He'd fit in there."

The *notju* let that pass. "What's the significance of the last two signs?"

"His old clan, Rashaban, which translates as 'three hills,' and his new one, Zamjilah, the 'eye of heaven'—named for the wooden frame that holds the *kazr* open at the smoke-hole."

At least Munraz seems to be all right. She could feel her shoulders drop a bit, as if she'd been hunched up under a massive weight. *But Naj-sha…*

"So, as we thought, at least some of the chained wizards escaped altogether, and Munraz is with them, apparently of his own free will."

She glanced over at her two students. She knew Lai Tsumai was new to that group and probably ignorant of their backup plans, but Dar Datsu had been with them for some unknown amount of time.

"I wonder where they are?" she said, watching them openly.

Dar Datsu flushed, then spread his hands. "I'm sorry, Penrys-chi, but I can't…"

"Yes, I know. And for now, I'll honor that. But the time may come when someone will have to make a choice." She fixed him with her gaze and eventually, he nodded.

Tun Jeju watched this byplay expressionlessly. When it was over, he said, "And now I have other news. Please, follow me—all of you. We have a bit of history to make."

CHAPTER 18

Tun Jeju and his staff led the four wizards out of the main entrance of the building and stopped them on top of the public steps. A few others were already gathered there.

At least thirty Kigali in formal dress were gathered on the walkway and spilled out into the street. Penrys spotted four of the Char family, all but the granddaughter, but there were several other clusters as well.

A few bystanders paused to watch, wary of the unprecedented situation.

A quick scan confirmed it—these were all wizards. Out in the open, confronting Imperial Security in public. Peacefully. She blinked. *My, that was fast.*

Char Nojuk walked up the steps to join them. He gave the two chained wizards a jaundiced look, and they backed up nervously, but he otherwise ignored them. He spared a brief nod for Penrys and Chosmod, then he turned and faced Tun Jeju.

The *notju* bowed and presented him with a sealed scroll. Char Nojuk returned the bow and carefully broke the seal on the document and read it aloud in a carrying voice.

> *"Be it known that the King of Earth and Sea today revokes the ban of his Imperial predecessor on the craft of lup and the practitioners thereof. In token of which, the Supreme Deity Lemju has increased the domain of Suimiju, patron of Toilekja Dugom with its Engineers and Pharmacists, and decreed that all the temples of Suimiju throughout the great empire of Kigali provide suitable resources for lupjuwen recognized by their own guild, in the tradition of all craft guilds.*
>
> *"We welcome the support of all the lupjuwen of Kigali in the service of the King of Earth and Sea. Long may they serve."*

The imperial chop in red ink accompanied by the red wax seal with golden ribbons was visible to Penrys as Char Nojuk displayed the document to the crowd, turning from side to side until all had glimpsed it. She could feel the electric excitement running through the wizards, and the surprise of the passersby. She glanced down at her commonplace clothing and grimaced. *Would've been nice to get a warning before being on stage like this, however tangentially.*

Char Nojuk turned back to Tun Jeju and raised the scroll to his forehead. Then he bowed deeply and when he straightened again, he shouted, "Long life to the King of Earth and Sea." The wizards standing a few steps below him repeated the wish three times, louder each time.

Tun Jeju waited for the clamor to die away, and then presented Char Nojuk with another document, this one without the wax seals and ribbons. The *samkatju* read it over quickly, then faced the crowd. "This is the new foundation document for our Guild, which I accept on its behalf."

After letting the crowd react for a few moments, Char Nojuk raised his hand for silence. Tun Jeju summoned forward a man in the crimson robes of a temple priest from the support staff at his side, and presented him to Char Nojuk. The priest nodded to Tun Jeju, and then to Char Nojuk, and presented to the latter a pair of large bronze keys, holding them horizontally in both hands.

"The temple of Suimiju stands ready to receive its new guild."

Char Nojuk took the keys from the priest's hands and raised them to let the crowd see them. Then he bowed to the priest and said, "We thank the temple, and we shall visit it when we're finished here."

Tun Jeju then raised his hand and waited until he could be heard.

"We thank the King of Earth and Sea for this opportunity to fulfill his mandate, as witnessed here by all of you, and by the foreign nations of Rasesdad, *sarq*-Zannib, and Ellech."

Penrys realized she was doing double-duty as a national witness. She followed Chosmod's lead in bowing deeply to Tun Jeju, as all the crowd did. She admonished Dar Datsu and Lai Tsumai. *You, too. You count as wizards by this decree.* Belatedly, the two students joined her bow.

The *notju* held his bow for a count of five, and then straightened up, and everyone followed suit, including Penrys. *What happens if someone doesn't bow deep enough or long enough? Nothing good, I bet.* She almost giggled but managed to hold a straight face.

Char Nojuk turned to her and said in a conversational tone, "Maybe now we can get some action finding my nephew. Come along."

He hobbled down the stairs without bothering to look back, his gait impaired by a stiff knee.

She shrugged and looked at the three wizards. "That means all of us, I imagine. Modo?"

He smiled. "Reminds me of my old teacher, the one I had as a boy. Didn't dare say 'no' to him, either. Let's go see how a guild is born in Kigali, eh?"

Penrys paused and looked back at Dar Datsu. "Rin Tsugo should be here, if he wants the chained wizards to have a proper place here in Kigali. Someone should tell him so, and summon him."

The young man looked at her. "By himself, with all those wizards?"

"Why should he come alone?" she countered. "The imperial mandate made no distinction between types of wizards or any mention of Kigali bloodlines. I may be foreign, but who's to say any of you are? If he wants acceptance, he has to come and fight for a place in the governing structure."

He hesitated, until Penrys pushed at him impatiently. "Go! You know where we're headed." The crowd below them was already moving south to the temple district. "I'll tell them to expect you."

Dar Datsu glanced at Lai Tsumai as if reluctant to leave her alone in this company and the woman make a shooing motion with her hands. "She's right. Go get them."

His shoulder sagged in acquiescence and he trotted down the steps and headed east.

"Think I have time to change?" Penrys muttered to Chosmod, and he shook his head. With a sigh, she beat some of the dust from her breeches, and hiked down the steps to join the back of the exultant crowd of wizards as they marched off.

Penrys's inclination to stay in the rear of the crowd of wizards with Chosmod and Lai Tsumai was overridden by the men and women that poured out of the nearby side streets to join it, constantly pushing then further up in the ranks until they were near the front.

Clearly the word of the events had been broadcast widely by mind-speech.

There was a jubilation in the air, almost a feeling of dance at odds with the advanced age of many of the wizards, as their families came out into the open in Yenit Ping for the first time in many generations. Some had even brought children to witness the spectacle.

The normal traffic on the streets they took to the temple district pulled out of the way, uncertain about what was going on, and clearly puzzled about what linked these particular people together.

Penrys could tell when the news spread among the ordinary people, no doubt from the bystanders who had heard the announcement. Little cries rose up, and Penrys heard words like *"Lupjuwen!* The emperor has recognized a guild of wizards!"

They seemed more astonished than alarmed, and the wizards surged quickly past, almost faster than the news could spread, until they reached the wide avenue parallel to the river and faced the blocks of temples. Char Nojuk led them and maintained a careful hold all the way on the temple priest of Suimiju, bright in his crimson robes.

The priest directed them across the avenue, stopping all traffic, and then past the first block of temples to the second one, nearer the river. The temple of Suimiju was solid and substantial, not as highly decorated as some, but capacious.

Penrys read the characters inscribed over the closed double doors. "The Benevolent Suimiju—Heavenly Department of Industry, Sub-Department of Practical Knowledge." *As Najud would say, the Kigali even have their gods organized.*

Her stomach cramped. *Where are you, Naj-sha? You should see this.*

On either side of the doorway more characters were inscribed. As she started to work her way through them, she realized these must be the guilds assigned here—Engineers, Chemists, Pharmacists, Metallurgists—domains famous for experimentation, research, practicality. *Makes perfect sense. They'll just add "Wizards" to the list.*

Penrys and her companions were carried up the temple steps by the pressure of the crowd behind them. She stumbled and an arm shot out to support her. The elated face of Char Dami appeared. "This is no place to fall," she admonished Penrys, then she turned her attention to her father, poised at the top with the temple priest.

Char Nojuk faced the crowd that stretched across the avenue and held his hand up for silence. When a wave of quiet had swept over them, he held the two bronze keys aloft again so that all could view them, then he inserted one in each door and turned them ceremoniously. The click each one made was clearly audible, and Char Nojuk pushed both the doors wide open, and walked in as if he were coming home. The other Char family wizards followed him, and Penrys was swept in with Chosmod and Lai Tsumai.

Behind them every wizard in the crowd donned a new dignity and, family by family, they ascended the steps and followed Char Nojuk into their new guild home.

Inside, there was a vestibule with wide stairways on either side. Through a further door, Penrys glimpsed an actual temple interior, but the rest of the building was organized for practical matters.

Chosmod muttered in her ear, "I've never tried to enter one of these sub-department temples, as a foreigner, but I've heard how they're laid out. The bottom floor and any sub-levels will be for the temple itself and its operations—the priests, supplies, dormitories, kitchens, and so forth. But all the other floors will be for whatever guilds are supported. Not for their actual craft work, of course, but for their guild functions. Even when the guild memberships are too large for their temple and meet elsewhere, they still conduct the ceremonial parts of their government in the temple buildings."

"It's not a bad arrangement," he mused. "Not very different from our temples in Dzongphan."

The priest led them up the left stairway to the third floor, and then out into the building-wide landing with its matching stairway ascending the other side. Interior corridors penetrated back into the building to left and right, on either side of a large hall in the center whose double doors stood open. He waited at that open doorway with Char Nojuk until as many people as could fit were waiting silently in front of them, and the remainder, on the stairs, had ceased talking.

Once more, he bowed to Char Nojuk. "At the request of Tun Jeju and in recognition that the *lupjuwen* at present have no other arrangements, we have set aside this entire floor for the use of the guild. May prosperity and benefit to the emperor result from all your works, under the benevolence of Suimiju."

Someone in the crowd raised a cheer, and the building rang

with the thrice-repeated sound, echoing in the enclosed space with its hard surfaces.

Even Penrys felt her heart lift. *Don't be ridiculous, this isn't for you.* But she couldn't keep from smiling at the joy and satisfaction in the minds around her. Not that she failed to note the wariness and trepidation that was also present.

Char Nojuk led the way into the large central hall, and Penrys was pushed along with the rest of them. The raised platform at the end was clearly designed for speakers, and he walked up the four steps alongside it and faced the crowd as it filed in. The space could have held twice their number, but Penrys suspected this was only a small portion of the wizards in Yenit Ping, the ones close enough to have joined them at little notice. She positioned herself off to the side at the front, near the steps to the platform. Lai Tsumai was uneasy at being hemmed in by a crowd of wizards like this, and Penrys assured her, "They'll have to go through me first, and Modo and I are foreign witnesses," she told her. *Yeah, and that was true last time, with Rin Tsugo, and look how much good it did. But these are different wizards. I hope.*

One by one, older men and women separated themselves from their companions and walked onto the speakers' platform to join Char Nojuk. By the time the crowd had settled, there must have been a dozen of them. Char Nojuk functioned as the moderator of the meeting, but did not assume the role of guild leader—that clearly belonged to one of the others.

The first hour or so was spent explaining the happenings of the last few days, in particular the invitations to foreign wizards made by Tun Jeju, the disaster with the chained wizards in the villages and cities in response to the query by Imperial Security, and the accumulation of chained wizards happening in Yenit Ping.

Char Nojuk, in telling his part, eventually summoned Penrys and Chosmod up to attest to his words, and Penrys insisted on Lai Tsumai accompanying them. Many had apparently been unaware of the existence of chained wizards and frankly stared at Penrys, as well as Lai Tsumai with her Rasesni features, in the background.

A voice cried out from the center of the hall, "How are the *tekenga lupjuwen* different from the rest of us?"

Now is not the time for complicated explanations. "A bit more than three years ago, wizards with a chain, like this one"—she bared her neck so all could see—"began appearing, in places like Ellech,

Rasesdad, *sarq*-Zannib, Ndant, and Kigali, and maybe elsewhere. They all had a chain like this that can't be cut or removed. They came from a variety of nations and were randomly distributed, and none of us have any memories before that point."

That created a buzz throughout the crowd. Penrys held up her hand to request quiet again. "I'm from no one knows where and appeared in Ellech. Lai Tsumai here, apparently of Rasesni origin, appeared in Kigali—Kigali is all she knows. Many of the chained wizards in Yenit Ping are of Kigali origin, and many are not—they all think of themselves as Kigaliwen."

She took a deep breath. "I've invited the leader of their brotherhood to come here, to this assembly. It may take him a while to get here."

She backed away behind the other speakers while the crowd debated the propriety of letting the chained wizards participate.

Chosmod caught Char Nojuk's eye and gestured that he wished to speak. When he was beckoned forward, he planted himself solidly and said, "I am a mage out of Rasesdad, here at Tun Jeju's request. My colleagues from Ndant, and Ellech, and *sarq*-Zannib— we were requested to advise Imperial Security on ways to normalize the relation between Kigali and its wizards, once it realized that you existed. Of course you existed!"

His broad smile brought some answering chuckles, foreigner though he was. "We all of us went to visit this Rin Tsugo, the *teken* in charge of the chained wizards that gathered as refugees in Yenit Ping. That was… yesterday. We included Char Dazu to witness for his uncle, and Gen Jongto to witness for Imperial Security, and Penrys to extend an invitation for the chained wizards to join the process. We were attacked."

The hall was silent.

"More than a hundred wizards broke the compound doors and invaded. They killed eight of the chained wizards, they killed three of my colleagues—foreign envoys—and they kidnapped several more, including your own Char Dazu. Many of them died, and many of the chained wizards escaped, but that was only the first foray."

He surveyed the hall. "In Rasesni we have an expression—'the enemy of my enemy is my friend.' Do you know who these wizards are? Are they your friends or your enemies? When they come to seek guild endorsement, will you grant it to them?"

He shook his head. "I am only a foreigner, but if the *tekenga lupjuwen* come, and it were me, I would make myself stronger by the alliance."

"What good are they?" Penrys couldn't see the woman who spoke.

Char Nojuk stepped up. "I came afterward and was told that most of them were killed by Penrys here, through the special *lup* of a *teken*. I believe it."

Penrys grimaced.

He overrode the disbelieving noise of his audience. "I saw the dead, but I didn't know them. Kigaliwen, all of them. They're not here among us today, nor do I expect to see them. Who are they, and what do they want? They have taken my nephew, and others."

A disturbance at the entry to the audience hall drew all attention. Rin Tsugo entered, his high-necked tunic unbuttoned to reveal his chain. Behind him came at least a dozen of the chained wizards, in all of their variety of appearance, and Dar Datsu, whose eyes sought out Penrys and Lai Tsumai on the platform. All had let their chains be visible. They walked boldly through the crowd, which parted to let them pass, and Rin Tsugo left them at the base of the steps to join the other leaders on the platform.

Where's Munraz? Wasn't he with them? Penrys couldn't ask at this moment, but it worried her. Maybe there were other groups that had escaped and he was with one of those.

She walked forward to perform the introduction, since Char Nojuk had never met him. "This is Rin Tsugo, the leader of the brotherhood of chained wizards in Yenit Ping."

He was the first chain-bearer the crowd had seen with Kigali features, and it made a difference to them. This was apparently one of their own.

He cleared his throat and addressed them. "We were told of the extraordinary announcement on the steps of the Imperial Security building, of the emperor's establishment of the guild for *lupjuwen*. The *lupjuwen* in our *gewengep* hereby notify you of our intent to join with you, for mutual aid and growth."

And, with that, the room erupted into debate and argument.

CHAPTER 19

Munraz tried not to look down.

He'd waited until Rin Tsugo left in a hurry with a bunch of the others, and then slipped away out of the building in the confusion and hastened toward the edge of Tegong Him, jutting out to its southern point.

Crouching as he burrowed through the brush around the building, he'd tried to keep out of sight until he was far enough away to be truly concealed.

The chained wizards had put no guard around him, though he thought Kit Hachi might have been left behind to keep an eye on him, to judge by the looks she had directed his way when she was talking with Rin Tsugo before he left.

He'd dictated the note to Talqatin at her suggestion, though who could tell if they'd actually sent it? They'd taken his weapons once the other chained wizards had joined them from their escape routes, though they hadn't bound him. He liked Kit Hachi well enough, but he couldn't stay as their almost-prisoner if there was an opportunity to get away, so he'd shaken off the uncomfortable feeling that he was somehow betraying their trust and waited for the right moment.

He looked up now to judge his next footholds, and spared a moment for self-congratulation. They'd searched for him, all right, but no one ever thinks to look up. The side of the tip of Tegong Him was very steep but not quite a cliff, and there was sufficient vegetation to keep him concealed. He'd followed plenty of game up hills like this in *sarq*-Zannib, and his prey hadn't seen him until it was too late, either.

There was no question about where he was in the city—Tegong Him made an unmistakable landmark—but he knew he would be easily marked as a Zan in daylight, and that the search would concentrate on the obvious routes back to the Zannib embassy.

And then he'd thought about the upper city, Juhim Tep. It ought to be possible to go up Tegong here, work his way south to the actual point, and then descend again. By then it would be dark, and he thought he could sneak back to the embassy from there, if he waited long enough. He had a little money in his pockets, but there was no way to conceal his Zannib clothing or appearance.

He'd removed his *anah im-ghabr* before he started his climb and stuck it in his belt—no sense having his silhouette so obviously recognizable if someone glimpsed him. No useful weapons concealed in it, not like Najud's. Next time he'd listen to his *jarghal* when he suggested something like that.

If his *jarghal* was still alive. Or Penrys. He swallowed. *They were still alive and fighting when Kit Hachi dragged me away.*

He shook his head to banish the worry. *One foot after another, and alternate hands. Concentrate on the climb. Even if you're alone in Yenit Ping, Talqatin will help you. You just have to get there.*

Two hours of guild birthing pains were enough for Penrys.

They hadn't shouted Rin Tsugo off the platform and that was sufficient for her. It wasn't her country, it wasn't her problem, they weren't her people. They had to settle all of this for themselves.

She had family to find, and she needed solitude to do it in, or at least less noise than this.

The little group of chained wizards huddled as closely together as they could, off to the side of the platform steps. They held their faces as expressionless as possible, while the Kigali taste for organizational details played out with their future at stake.

She turned to Chosmod, and told him, "I'm leaving. We still have a search to do."

"I'll stay, *brudigna*. They'll be finished with this eventually, and then I can recruit some help. Where will you be?"

She shrugged. "Not a lot of choice. Back to Tun Jeju, I suppose. See if you can find out why he didn't bring Munraz, if he has him." She cocked her head at Rin Tsugo, speaking to the crowd above her head.

"Is it wise to travel alone through the streets?" he asked.

"It's only a few blocks, and with this many wizards here, should be easy to notice any strays where they don't belong."

She worked her way along the edge of audience until she found a door halfway down the hall, and used it to slip out into the corridor. The sound of the meeting with its debates was muffled and the lonely hallway was a relief, though she held her shield in place all the way through the building to distance herself from the unbridled emotions of the wizards.

At the top of the steps outside, she paused and scanned for other wizards in the vicinity. It was emptier than usual except for the temple itself. *No surprise—anyone who heard about this would have come running to participate.*

The walk of a few blocks to Imperial Security was uneventful. Her mind was on the search she needed to make. She couldn't just look through the entire population, the way she'd been doing in her first panicked attempts. *Think about it logically. How would you quarter a city this size to identify a concentration of wizards? There are wizards everywhere, and they live in groups.*

She wasn't paying attention, and almost ran into someone who didn't move out of her way. She stumbled to a halt, and blinked. It was Kit Hachi, with worry all over her face.

"What's wrong?" Penrys blurted out. "You want Rin Tsugo? He's over there with the other wizards, getting the guild going." She waved her arm back the way she'd come, to the south.

"No," the woman said. She took a breath. "I've been looking for you. It's Munraz."

A chill traveled Penrys's spine. "Not... dead?"

"No, it's not that." Kit Hachi plucked at her sleeve, and tugged her close to a building so that they'd be out of the way of traffic.

"I pulled him along with us when we escaped." She glanced apologetically into Penrys's face. "We couldn't fight those wizards—no weapons, no training…"

Penrys sliced her hand through the air in front of her chest. "You did the best thing, all of you, and I'm grateful you took Munraz with you."

"Maybe not, when you hear the rest," Kit Hachi muttered. "We had a rendezvous… We took his weapons away, it was easier to do that than fight about it with some of the others. I tried to explain he wasn't a prisoner, but it wasn't safe for him to walk the streets alone and we couldn't escort him—we'd arrange something."

She glanced down. "It took us all the rest of the day to settle the stragglers down and set up security. Get dinner. You can imagine."

When she looked up again, Penrys nodded.

"Then I helped him with that note this morning—did you get it?" Kit Hachi asked.

"Yes, from the Zannib embassy. Thanks for that."

"Well, I guess Munraz didn't believe we'd bring him back. When Dar Datsu showed up with the news, he snuck away in the excitement. We've lost him. We searched, but…"

"*Yrmur!*" Penrys said, with feeling, then she focused on the problem. "Where, exactly?"

Resignedly, Kit Hachi gave her the details. "See the point of Tegong Him?" She pointed north and both of them looked at the busy face of the steep cliff, with the movement of its traffic hauled up and down barely visible. "Our rendezvous is to the east, well around the tip."

"How can he hide, a Zan in Yenit Ping?"

Kit Hachi spread her hands in reply. "I imagine he's lying low until dark, but it's still a long way."

Penrys shook her head. She could feel the truth in Kit Hachi's account, and it some ways it was just like Munraz—slow to trust, used to relying on himself. *What have you gotten yourself into, nal-jarghal?*

"All right, you've done your duty, *minochi*. I don't know what else you could have done. I'll just… add it to my list."

She looked into Kit Hachi's face, still worried, and told her, "Why don't you go see Rin Tsugo making history?"

Responsibility warred with eagerness in the woman's mind, and Penrys resigned herself. "Come, I'll take you there."

Half an hour later, Penrys was back in the Imperial Security building. The guards passed her through without any fuss and she returned to the empty room that had been cleared for them just this morning.

The thick walls one level underground reinforced the quiet, a welcome relief after a repeat dose of the turmoil in Suimiju's temple. She closed the door and made herself comfortable.

So, Munraz on the loose, hopefully, and all the captives. How do I find them? I can't just clear sectors—people move around.

The area Kit Hachi had described east of the point was within her range, but if there were chained wizards left behind there, she couldn't find them. *Shielded? Maybe. Does the massive rock of Tegong block me? Don't know.*

Certainly she couldn't pick out one stray Zan over there.

She closed her eyes and composed herself to try one more sweep through thousands of people looking for Zannib wizards. She focused on the embassy—no wizards there but could she at least recognize Zannib people in that direction?

Yes, and no. Knowing where to look and what she expected to find, she thought she could detect a Zannib presence, but she could be fooling herself. Wizards, she was sure of—ordinary folk, maybe not. Not in this swarm of Kigaliwen.

And even wizards, if they were shielded, would probably escape her notice. It was hopeless.

A knock on the door broke her concentration, and she got up to open it, and then stepped back to let Tun Jeju in. He closed the door behind him.

"You know," she said, by way of greeting, "I would be glad to go see you, if you summon me. No need for you to make the trip."

A smile flickered over his lips. "Fewer of my people can find me easily this way."

He gestured her toward a chair and chose another one for himself. "I don't imagine the new guild is done talking yet?"

Penrys rolled her eyes. "Maybe this week, sometime. Maybe not, too. The good news is that Rin Tsugo did come, and he was still among the potential leaders on the platform when I left, so it looks like there will be a united guild when they're done, wizards and chained wizards."

"Even though some look like foreigners? That *is* good news."

"That part made them uncomfortable, but I don't think it'll matter in the end. Chosmod and I pointed out that they have actual enemies to focus on instead, and that willing allies should be welcomed, whatever they look like." She reconsidered. "Might matter later, once the euphoria wears off."

She glanced at him. "Chosmod's still there, but there wasn't really anything left for me to do."

He made no reply, so she ventured a question that had been puzzling her all day. "*Notju-chi*, how is it that you were able to get that declaration from the emperor so quickly, and the cooperation of the temple? I can't imagine what it took to do that."

"It helped, though, didn't it?" Tun Jeju replied.

She waited patiently for an actual answer, and he almost obliged her.

"There were reasons, *minochi*. Yes, there was some pre-arrangement, but I can't discuss it with you."

"Hmmph." She'd have to be contented with that.

"And how are you progressing with your search for the captives?" he asked her, in turn.

"Badly. Too many Kigali wizards, as you are discovering for yourself." She allowed herself a brief smile. "Simple brute force is not going to work. I need a way to sort them out categorically…" Her voice trailed off as she thought of something.

"Tell me, *notju-chi*, does this building have a flat roof?"

Tun Jeju raised his eyebrows. "It is peaked in the middle, but a flat walkway extends on all sides."

Penrys smiled broadly. "And I can get onto it, this evening?"

"Does this have anything to do with the wings I heard about?" he asked.

"Well, I can hardly launch from the street, out in the open and all," she said.

The evening meal was the first one Najud was awake for. A well-shielded wizard brought two pitchers of water and a pot of stew with bread on a tray, and unloaded it all onto the floor just inside the doorway. He was careful not to stand within reach of more than one of the tethered captives—Gen Jongto, nearest to the door, who carried one arm in a sling.

He'd placed his lantern outside the door in a corridor, and it was difficult to make out his back-lit features, but Najud thought he was a Kigalino.

"If you lost your spoon or broke your bowl, you're just out of luck."

"How long do you plan to hold us?" Vylkar inquired, politely.

Najud could see the man's toothy grin. "As long as it takes. We ain't in no hurry, us. Better settle in for the long haul. If'n you get sick, that'll just be too bad."

He picked up the tray and the empty pitchers and pot from the night before. "You don't make us no trouble, and we'll keep the food and water coming."

The door clanged shut behind him, and Najud heard the key turn in the lock.

The pottery bowls and cups were passed all the long way around to Gen Jongto, and he carefully filled all the cups with most of the contents of the first pitcher before starting them back the other way via Char Dazu. He emptied the pot of stew entirely, being as scrupulously fair as he could be. The rest of the water would sit there for breakfast and lunch, unless requested. It was up to each of them to decide how much of the stew to eat at once, and how much to save—there had been no more than one meal offered per day, so far. The bread was broken into pieces and handed around with the bowls.

As he passed the cups and bowls back around the circle to his right, Najud reflected on the day's activities.

Ijumo was their clock. He claimed he could tell the rough hour of the day from clues in the air, the smell of the plants. He also said he thought they weren't in the city itself—something about the difference in the plants. Najud had no way to judge his accuracy, and there was no source of natural light to contradict him. Still, he'd predicted the mealtime today, so perhaps he was accurate.

On the other hand, he was also clearly ill. He'd been in a constant sweat, sleeping uneasily for long stretches.

Gen Jongto was patient and reticent. He took his role as the only non-wizard in stride and watched the rest of his cellmates as they grappled with their options.

Char Dazu had stopped blustering about the trouble their captors had called upon their heads and begun to worry. He was the youngest there and clearly out of his depth, but willing to cooperate with any plan the others put forth.

Vylkar remained detached and quiet, muttering verses softly to himself as he worked on the tribute to his fallen colleagues. Najud thought he'd also sustained injuries during the fighting, but he'd been patched up before Najud had woken, and refused to discuss them afterward.

The thick wrapping around Mrigasba's leg attested to his part in the fight, as well as the blow on his head that rose to the surface as a spectacular black eye visible even in the dim light from the outside corridor.

Najud, unconscious, had been the last to join the discussions among the wizards the day before but had made up for the delay by using a pick from his turban to unlock his own shackle and then traveling around the cell to do the same for everyone else. Each man let the shackle lie around his leg in place but unlocked. It wasn't a ruse that would pass inspection, but then no such check had yet been carried out.

In fact, it was difficult to draw any conclusions at all about their captors. The wizards they'd fought at the compound of the chained wizards had seemed… well, the only word that came to mind was criminal. Not to put too fine a point on it, they felt like thugs to Najud, wizards or not.

Certainly their only visible jailer seemed to be cut from the same cloth. Were they the ones that had organized the attack and carried them off?

That question had gone the rounds all day today, and the consensus was that these were hirelings. Which left the issue open—who was in charge? Who had planned all this, and what did they want? Had they made any demands yet?

What Vylkar had said about their wizard attackers falling dead certainly had the ring of Penrys. Why weren't they incensed about losing so many in the attack? He knew he'd done damage, and he was sure his cellmates had, too. Someone was paying a lot to capture and hold them, and they were going to want value for their money.

They could've overpowered the jailer who brought their food and stepped out of the room, but that was premature until they could break the shield itself, or had some plan of physical attack. Whoever was powering the shields around them, they were stronger than the five wizards, even working together the way Najud had started to show them at Mrigasba's urging. *Glad you're not here Pen-sha, but you and your chain would surely be death on this shield.*

There weren't enough weapons to go around. Mrigasba had managed to conceal a dagger, and Najud's turban had yielded two small knives, better than nothing but more for surprise than sustained attack.

It was going to have to be wizardry or nothing. Without discussion, he had assumed the leadership during the day, and no one seemed eager to contest it in an environment where more than wizardry was clearly going to be necessary. Char Dazu was too young and tentative, Vylkar too elderly, and Mrigasba still damaged from his head injury. Ijumo was too ill to attempt it, and Gen Jongto was no wizard.

Najud finished the last of his stew and laid the bowl down. "All right, my friends. Time to report on the state of our health, honestly, starting with Gen Jongto. And after that, back to our shielding exercises. If they drop the outer shield we'll have an inner one to match. And then we can start to look for a weakness in theirs, yes?"

No one demurred, and with a quiet clatter of wooden bowls and cups being laid on the filthy stone floor, they prepared themselves for the evening's lesson.

Munraz had been surprised on his way up the eastern slope of Tegong Him just as the sun finally set. The trail he was following petered out as the surface became more vertical and turned into a real cliff, perhaps two hundred feet from the top. And yet the trail persisted.

Not until he reached the end of it did he find the outlet of a tunnel, not much more than man height and discretely tucked behind a small fold in the cliff. This must be one of the tunnels his *jarghal* had told him about that were rumored to wind through Tegong Him.

He glanced up at the cliff face itself, in the dusk. Not an appetizing choice. Still, the trail did see use, so he needed to expect to encounter people if he entered the tunnel.

He tried scanning his surroundings, the way Penrys had been teaching him. It felt curiously muffled, as though all the rock around him interfered with it somehow. In any case he could detect no one else around, which reassured him.

There was no way for him to make a light, however, not for long. His little fire-starter kit was in his pocket—his uncle had long ago beat it into him that he should never travel without it—but there was nothing to use for fuel except whatever cloth he could spare. The bushes on the slope were green and wet with spring growth, and the prior season's remains of herbage were too small for anything but tinder.

Either I sleep in the entry here and go back down in the morning, or I try to find where it goes. Someone made it for a reason, and they still use it, or the trail would be less obvious.

His stomach growled and his mouth was dry, but he tried not to think about it. *Better inside, I suppose. Can't get any darker than dark. Might as well see what I can find, if I don't go too far from the entrance.*

He stretched out his left hand until he touched the wall, slightly slick. He knew there was an entire small city above his head but for all he could tell he was in a cave near the top of a bare mountain. *How strange to be underground while so high above the ground.* It made him smile.

He took small and careful steps, turning his head every six steps as he counted to make sure he could still see the gray light of the entrance, until a gradual upward curve in the tunnel took it out of his sight.

After a while, a small breath of air touched his face, and there was an indefinable sensation of openness. He'd been careful with his feet as he shuffled along, though he didn't expect a natural opening in a man-made tunnel like this. Now he needed a way to make sense of the new geometry he sensed around him. He stretched his right hand out and encountered nothing but bare space.

A rope would be handy. Who would've thought I'd want a rope for a walk in the city? Or a torch, either.

There was a small square of cloth in his pocket, and now was the time to sacrifice it. Keeping his left foot in contact with the wall, he felt for his striker in the fire kit, and then thought through his actions in advance. Once the fabric caught, he wouldn't be able to hold it. But it wouldn't burn long and he wanted to lift it somehow.

He tugged off his right boot and sat himself down crosslegged, his left knee in contact with the wall. He pinned the boot upside down between his legs, put the bit of cloth on top of the hard sole, and struck sparks over it until it caught.

Then he grabbed the reversed boot with its feebly burning flame by the ankle and stood up carefully, in touch with the wall at all times, and held out the makeshift torch to see as much as he could while the light lasted.

In front of him the tunnel continued into blackness. To his right, a sunken channel pierced the rock, smaller than a man, and headed in the direction of the cliff face, as best he could judge. It was smoothed by the passage of water, and above it, not far from his head and the source of the air movement that bent his dying flame, he saw the metal rungs that ascended the far side of a shaft upward out of sight.

And then the fire died away, leaving behind a smell of scorched leather.

He yanked his boot back on and then stood and stretched out blindly with his arms in the direction of the fixed handholds, counting his steps as he did do, in case he somehow got turned around in the short distance. He took his time, mindful of the water channel on the right and feeling carefully with each foot before committing to the shift of his weight.

It took him twelve anxious shuffling steps to reach the wall of the shaft. He'd missed the metal rungs, but a careful probe with his arms in turn as he hugged the wall turned them up. He looked up, but could see nothing. Either his view was blocked by the structure, or it was open to a night sky.

Up it is, then. The ground is up there, at least the nearest ground. I can't go crawling through these tunnels without light.

He counted the rungs as he climbed. At the twenty-ninth, air movement warned him of an opening, and he clung to the bolted handholds with one hand and both feet while he reached out with his other hand. It took a while to confirm the geometry—there was a cross-tunnel here, its left side higher than the right. It grazed the bore hole and continued downhill. Munraz was no longer sure of his orientation and didn't want to guess which one went further into the mountain, if indeed either of them came out directly.

When he looked up, he thought he saw distant specks of light, not stars exactly, but something. *It smells moist, like soft night air.*

He pulled himself up forty-six more rungs, past one more intersecting tunnel until he felt the soft breathing of the shaft as it inhaled the heavier wet air of evening, through a coarse metal grate, into the unknown tunnel and cave structure below him. At his first attempt to push the grate open, nothing happened.

He stood on the rungs as high as he could and tried to see where he was. No light fell through the grate to illuminate his face, but there was light scattered about, and the sound of people moving nearby, walking steadily and talking.

Would they help him if he called out? He shook his head. *No doubt, but what will they help me into? I need to see what this is, figure out the situation, not just hope for the best.*

His stomach growled and his mouth was dry. *Too bad. I'm just going to have to wait for daylight. I've been worse off than this. I'm not even hurt. Just a little delay, so I know what's what. If I don't like what I see, I can always explore one of the tunnels. In the dark, without a staff or a rope.*

It wasn't an appealing thought. He lowered himself back down to the last intersecting tunnel and prepared himself to wait, choosing the downward side of the tunnel to minimize any chance of rolling the wrong way in the dark.

He was tired, but too wound up to contemplate sleep. He dropped his shield and tentatively reached out to the upper city above him. There were people everywhere, like Mentsek Tep below, and several were wizards.

At his own level and below, he thought he could feel others. *Traveling in the tunnels?* Compact groups of them moved inexplicably up and down. He was puzzled until he remembered the cages he'd seen ascending the southern cliff. *At least I know which way is south.* He strained to reach Penrys at the Zannib embassy, but it was too far away for him.

Is anyone even looking for me?

Cautiously he raised his shield again, and tried to get comfortable enough on the bare rock, with his turban for a pillow, to sleep the night away. His hand reached out to the wall to keep contact with it, and fell upon on a small shard of rock there. He cupped his hand around the stone in the dark, and drifted off.

CHAPTER 20

After her solitary meal, Penrys took advantage of the guide sent by Tun Jeju to show her the way to the roof.

When he opened the door for her, she stepped out onto a slate walkway. The evening was quiet and a breeze blew from the west, fresh and moist. Five stories was enough height to let her sense the darkness to the south that marked the river. No moon was visible, but there was enough ambient light to see Tun Jeju waiting for her.

"I admit to being curious about the wings," he said, and she laughed.

"My pleasure," she said. She pivoted on her heel and told the guard, "I may be out for hours. Can I open that door from the outside to get back in?"

"He'll stand watch on the inside and wait for your knock," Tun Jeju answered on his behalf.

"All right, then." Penrys stepped away and invoked her wings. She stretched them to get the kinks out, and noted Tun Jeju's attention. "You can touch them, if you like. It's just feathers."

"Thank you, *lupju-chi.*"

A chill went down her spine as the Kigali term for wizard was applied to her for the first time.

Tun Jeju walked around her, and briefly ran his hand down a wing tip.

"I don't understand how they are attached," he said, as he moved back to give her room.

"No one does, *notju-chi,*" she called back over shoulder as she took a running jump into the air and launched herself into flight.

She overflew the entire city and its suburbs, from Junlin Tep in the west to Chankau Tep in the east, and from the river to well back on Tegong Him and Juhim Tep. It didn't take as long as she'd feared—the city was broad but not nearly as deep.

Against a dim background of ordinary minds, the wizards and the chained wizards both stood out like stars on a cloudless night.

There weren't many chained wizards—in fact she easily located the rendezvous point of the *gewengep* east of Tegong Him which contained most of them—but the hundreds of conventional wizards were surprising. Most of them seemed to be in small clusters. When she dipped low to test a theory, she found that she was mostly finding wizards in their larger families, within a compound, anywhere from two to twelve, home for the night. There were exceptions—people traveling or stationary in ones and two—but almost all of them at this hour were at home.

The guild meeting at Suimiju's temple was over for the night and set to resume tomorrow. Chosmod had filled her in when he dropped by before returning to his embassy for dinner. "Hard to say how far they've gotten," he'd said, "but I take the absence of bared weapons as a good sign."

Everywhere she flew, there were no concentrations of wizards in larger than family compound quantities, except in three locations. The first was in Chankau Tep, where a cluster of compounds seemed to house three dozen wizards, many of them shielded. She counted buildings from the river and local parks so that she could identify it from a map.

The second was on the edge of Chankau Tep and the central Mentsek Tep. Fifty or more were actively working in a group of four linked compounds, and Penrys could make out sparks and fires as well as other activity.

Finally, when she overflew Juhim Tep, she found wizards scattered about, and one compound occupied almost entirely by wizards, apparently settled for the night. In addition to the unusual quantity, at least forty or so, it was noticeable for how many were shielded. The little drop-outs that were shields to her mental scan were well distributed in that one.

Once again, she counted buildings from apparent landmarks. *The emperor and the rest of the court are up here somewhere, and much of the army. Maybe I'll get to see that in daylight.*

She turned south from there and counted streets until she was sure she'd found the Imperial Security building again. *Wouldn't do to land in the wrong place.* She chuckled at the image of some bureaucrat from some other government department trying to make sense of it.

She landed nimbly, for a change, and tried the door. Locked. A rap on it resulted in a cautious opening, and the guard stepped out of the way to let her in.

After trailing him down to the ground floor, she waved him off and went down one more flight to her cold and solitary bed, underground in the stone-walled room. The story from the Ellech delegation of the chained wizard waking, and dying, inside a stone tomb haunted her, and she left the lantern lit in the corner of the room while she tried to yawn herself into a decent sleep.

"That's part of the Armorers' compounds."

The map expert that Tun Jeju had called in put his finger on the city map spread on the familiar meeting room table.

Penrys couldn't recall his name—she was too focused on remembering her coordinates from the night before. She'd described her evening's activities to Chosmod, and to Mpeowake who had walked in unexpectedly this morning, her torso stiff and bound.

"Active at night? Many wizards?" Penrys asked.

The man glanced at Tun Jeju for confirmation, then explained. "They don't live there, they work there. Some of their work—smelting ore, refining metal—that runs in long batches regardless of the hour, so there's always activity at odd times of day or night."

He blinked at her uncertainly. "I don't know about *lupjuwen*... But other than that, what you saw seems normal to me."

Penrys suppressed a smile. The man was unnerved by the implications of this meeting, that someone had flown over the city and wanted to find parts of it on a map, but he was still doing his best to adjust.

Chosmod cleared his throat. "There were armorers at the temple yesterday, so the craft certainly includes mages. Device-builders, I would imagine."

"So, not an unusual concentration," Tun Jeju supplied, and Penrys agreed.

"Then what about this one?" Penrys moved her finger along a grid of streets until she found the landmarks from last night and singled out a cluster of several compounds.

Tun Jeju leaned forward with interest. "The center of Chalen Tep, the criminal district?"

The map expert nodded. "Yes, *notju*—gambling and debt collection, murder for hire, stolen goods distributors."

"And they are *lupjuwen*?" Tun Jeju riveted Penrys with his eyes.

"Well, lots of them seem to be." The silence that resulted seemed to need filling. "What, you expected all wizards to be upstanding citizens of the empire? Name me one class that doesn't have its criminals."

She checked his emotions. No, that wasn't it—he wasn't surprised.

"But do they have our lost emissaries?" Tun Jeju asked.

"That's a more difficult question. I looked closely but I couldn't find any trace of our people." She held up a hand. "Doesn't mean they aren't there and shielded, and there were shields there. I'd still like to look from the ground."

Chosmod said, "You mentioned murder for hire. Could they have hired out to attack us, even if they don't have the captives?"

Penrys added, "Weren't you going to identify them, the dead ones? What did you find out?"

Tun Jeju gave her a measuring glance before he replied and she held her expression immobile. *Yes, I killed most of them. You don't have to remind me.*

"We knew some of them, and when we brought in the City Guard they placed quite a few more. All known criminals."

At Mpeowake's repressed snort of dissatisfaction, the *notju* expanded on his explanation. "Imperial Security is more focused on external threats and internal treason. Criminals are the proper concern of the City Guard. The problem remains that we have captives we must find, and a motive we must identify."

Penrys thought his mind didn't quite match his words, as though he knew more than he said, then she laughed at herself. *Of course he knows more than he's sharing. What would I expect? The downside of organization, Naj-sha—rigid, inflexible, and secretive.*

Why aren't there any demands from whoever holds the captives? Are they still alive? And Munraz? Talqatin had no news of him. Are they even further away, smuggled out to sea? Carried inland?

"Penrys?" Tun Jeju's voice recalled her attention.

She spoke her thoughts aloud. "Do we know that the captives are still in the area? Not taken away by river or carried into the interior?"

"Every boat at dock and on the river has been inspected, and the ships in the ocean harbors, just in case. That order was given at the first alarm, before we left with Dar Datsu to see what had happened." Tun Jeju almost gave the impression of compassion for

Penrys's anxiety, but she couldn't be bothered to check his mind to see if it was real.

"We also have inspections for all wagons leaving the city." He shrugged. "No city this size can truly seal its edges, but we don't think they've been removed."

So they're still here. Or they're dead.

For a moment, an involuntary wash of black swept over her, and she fought to keep her eyes open and her teeth from clamping together. It wouldn't help, and they all had colleagues in the same situation.

"So," she said with false calm, "what about the third location?" She leaned over the map and hovered uncertainly above the Juhim Tep street grid. "Here, I think."

The map man identified it. "Warehouses and retailers." He looked over at Tun Jeju. "Nothing distinctive about this."

"But there were wizards there last night, lots of them, and many were shielded, not like the simple groups in the family compounds." Penrys straightened up. "Tell me about this part of the upper city."

Tun Jeju paused and then seemed to be choosing his words carefully. "Chosmod-chi, were there courtiers at the guild meetings yesterday, or anyone else from the upper city?"

"No, not that I could tell. But yesterday was just a few families and clans—clearly there are others who hadn't heard the announcement yet. I assume more will join them. They'll all want to be part of the guild, surely."

"Not the criminals," Mpeowake interjected. "A proper guild wouldn't let them participate. In fact, it would actively try to suppress them."

"Better to police your own," Penrys said, in agreement. "Who else can? That's the Zannib policy."

"And the opposition won't join either," Chosmod added, nodding slowly, his eye on Tun Jeju. "So there *is* opposition, *notju-chi*, and it's not a surprise to you?"

Tun Jeju's expression froze into a mask.

Chosmod persisted. "Opposition to you or to the emperor?"

"We are the same," Tun Jeju grated out. "I am the emperor's servant, his *posom*."

"So," Penrys said, "you knew there was a threat and that it involved wizards. And now maybe it has blown up in your face." She could tell from his mind that she'd made a hit.

She closed her eyes for a moment, then rubbed her hand over her face. "What's done is done. We want our people back. Please, tell us what you know. We can still help each other, and we've no reason to wish your emperor harm."

Mpeowake's expression was stony, and Penrys remembered the dead Toawe, but the woman held her tongue.

Wise woman. You have another colleague yet to rescue. We all do, hostages to both Tun Jeju's secrecy and to his enemy, whoever that is.

Tun Jeju gave them little satisfaction other than to say there were internal issues involved about which he couldn't speak. When Penrys persisted, he rose and claimed another appointment, and simply walked out.

The map expert stared after him, then looked at the three unsatisfied wizards, and reached for the map.

"You stay," Penrys told him, and crossed the room to close the door. "What's the best way to get here"—her finger stabbed the gambling district—"without being obvious?"

Chosmod nodded approval, and the man nervously sketched out a route down the larger avenues that would be unremarkable in the middle of the day.

"I would prefer not to walk all that way," Mpeowake said, and Penrys gave her a closer look. Her posture was as upright as before, perhaps more so with the bindings around her torso, but her rib was clearly paining her, and the sweat on her face told of the strain.

"If we're not going to get help from the *notju*, then we'll do without," Penrys said. "I can bring horses from the Zannib embassy, or we can get a palanquin for you, whichever you prefer."

"Or we could escort you back to your embassy to rest, which might be a better idea," Chosmod said, politely.

"No, it's my responsibility to see this through for both the living and the dead." Penrys had always felt a cool restraint from Mpeowake, but for the first time she approved of her, for her dedication to her people.

"A palanquin would be most welcome," Mpeowake said.

Penrys glanced over at the map expert. "Thank you, you can go."

He reached for the maps again, and she stopped him. "We'll keep these, for now." He protested but backed down when all three of them stared at him, pointedly. He bowed hastily and left them in possession of both the room and the maps.

"That clever old man." The voice rang with a mix of disgust and grudging respect.

Tsek Anbu admired Tsek Uchang's calm. The open casements of the room admitted the spring breezes, fresher up here in Juhim Tep than in the lower cities. Scrolls suitable for the season decorated the walls, and the graceful furniture stood in contrast to the waves of anger from the other two people in the courtier's smaller reception hall, the private one for intimate gatherings.

"Your father, the emperor?" Tsek Anbu asked. "I imagine he had help from that *notju* of his."

"Ever since his little triumph in Neshilik, Tun Jeju has been gaining ground at Noi Shibu's expense. My father listens to his old Imperial Security advisor and nods pleasantly, and ignores him."

The sweet musical tones of Tsek Okim overrode her son's sour complaint. She was still an attractive woman, even in her fifth decade. "I warned you, didn't I, that if Noi Shibu was weak enough to welcome our offer, he would be vulnerable to his own ambitious officers, and so it is proving."

"Why not remove Tun Jeju altogether and gain some breathing room?"

Internally Tsek Anbu shook his head. Tsek Uchang was too fond of the simple violent approach, impatient with the subtlety that kept the fabric of society knit together. But he was strong and vigorous, and it's not as though it would be a change in dynasty. Bastards had ruled before, and would again. Under the control of the magnates, of course. As it had always been.

But these things took time. His own father had spotted the potential in his niece and groomed her for the imperial bedchamber. Not only had she born the emperor a bastard son almost as old as the official heir, but she'd managed to pass the *lupchit* along, making her son the first *lupju* who might claim the throne.

At the death of his father, Tsek Anbu had inherited the management of his cousin and her son. He'd trained him in the hidden traditions of his clan, but the man made an indifferent *lupju*. It didn't really matter—they had many better *lupjuwen* in the clan—but it was difficult to keep a rein on him. The family wealth in military supply contracts was more than respectable, and they were powerful among their peers, very powerful, but they weren't courtiers, and too much of Tsek Uchang's time was spent out of his influence, with only his mother to supply a counter-balance to the inflated flattery that surrounded even a bastard of the imperial line.

Time for another lesson in strategy. "The imperial decree that granted the *lupjuwen* a guild was very, very clever. Any *lupju* that doesn't seek to join the guild will be automatically suspect, requiring him to remain hidden, vulnerable to exposure and blackmail. If he does join, he'll be under the scrutiny of others. It cuts the ground out from under our family and our allies, up here."

"I recognize Tun Jeju in the speed with which this happened," Tsek Okim said. "Removing those uncontrolled *tekenga lupjuwen* so that ours would be unchallenged… it was the right thing to do, and I commend you, cousin, on your planning. You achieved the primary goal—embarrassing the *notju* by demonstrating his impotence to protect his own foreign guests. How can the emperor endorse him after that?"

"But we lost so many, cousin," Tsek Anbu objected.

"It matters little. They weren't our family." She smiled coolly. "If nothing else we've aided the civil order in the lower cities by the death of so many criminals. No, it was the escape of the *gewengep*'s leader, that *teken* Rin Tsugo and his people, that was unfortunate. Still I have no doubt we can hunt down the remainder before they become a threat. The last thing we want is for them to establish themselves."

Tsek Anbu shook his head. "Too late, I fear. I hear that Rin Tsugo is helping the guild with its foundation rules. The faster the *tekenwen* join, the sooner they'll be under the protection of the whole."

Tsek Uchang interrupted his mother's cousin. "Unless we can discredit them, make them outcasts that we can pick off at our leisure. That would solve one problem."

He glanced at Tsek Anbu as if to assert that he did, after all, understand what it would take to assume the imperial throne. "And if we can make them responsible for Tun Jeju's failure, then we would have a very tidy solution indeed."

Penrys waited as Chosmod paid the porters and dismissed the palanquin. They stood at the corner of a middling-sized avenue and a well-traveled cross-street. The district was seedy, the compound buildings in need of repair, and the people currently abroad looked as if they had yet to face their first meal of the day in any but liquid form.

"All the action's at night in places like this," Penrys said, and Mpeowake contented herself with meeting the eyes of the passersby with a cold glare.

Chosmod said, "From here I can make out five brothels, several drinking establishments, and at least three spots dedicated to gambling, in addition to whatever else they support."

"So you're familiar with places like this back home, then?" Penrys commented, deadpan.

Mpeowake stared at her, but Chosmod chuckled. "Well enough, *brudigna*. I wasn't always this dignified." He rubbed his hands together. "Let's go find us an alley where no one will bother us. They'll mostly be sleeping at this hour, anyway."

They found a closed place down a mid-block lane whose signs advertised lucky sticks and coins, fortunes to be had, and companions for gentlemen. Two low walls funneled customers toward the main door, and there was room for all three of them to sit on the walls, shadowed and inconspicuous.

"The way I see it," Penrys said, "we can be obvious and fast, or we can be subtle and slow. Either way, I want to be thorough— everything with a shield needs a good look."

"But they're shielded, you said. That means we can't look." Mpeowake glanced at Chosmod to check that he agreed.

Penrys shook her head. "Not from me, not without a good deal more organization than they've got. Want to see? We'll try it quiet for starters."

She linked with both of them and let them watch, then she reached out stealthily for the nearest wizard.

**Kigali-native, this one. He knows knives, see? Not interesting. Let's try this one—she's shielded. Now, see, it's easy to break a shield, but she'd feel it,* *like a slap. So we want to just sort of slip on in like this… Hmm, sex and finance and management. Seem like someone who runs a brothel, Modo?*

A bemused reply returned. *Yes, could be. She'd have reason to be shielded, in the company of other wizards, some of whom are probably stealing from each other.*

Distasteful, these people. Mpeowake's disdain colored her thoughts.

Aloud, Penrys replied, "Yes, it's a dirty job. But our people might be here—it has to be done, yes?"

"Yes," said Chosmod. "We can always wash afterward." He projected an image of a bucket pouring water into his head, and Penrys snorted.

Mpeowake contented herself with saying. "Let's get on with it, then."

Penrys sobered and said, "I'll work systematically west to east, up and down in columns. I'll try to do it quickly, since there are so many of them. You two make special note of anything that seems important."

She closed her eyes to concentrate better. *Here we go.*

<h1 style="text-align:center">CHAPTER 21</h1>

A couple of hours later, Penrys called a halt to their scan through the wizard population of the district.

She closed her eyes and rotated her head until the vertebrae in her neck clicked. When she took a look at Mpeowake, she was alarmed. "You should have stopped me earlier," she said.

The woman was pale and sweaty, but she raised a hand. "Better to finish it before they started moving around more. I'll recover, but I'd like to return to my embassy."

"As soon as we've talked about it for a moment, we'll get you a palanquin," Chosmod promised, and Mpeowake nodded in weary acceptance.

"All right," Penrys said. "Here's what we know. What was your final count, Modo?"

"Not quite two hundred wizards, including five chained ones. No sign of our people."

"Hold on a moment—I need to check something else." Penrys did a quick scan. "I can see hundreds of power-stones, mostly scattered around, and that means lots of devices. I'll bet they have a lot to do with the gambling odds for some of the games of chance."

She took a breath. "I think we have family wizards here, just like the non-criminal ones. They're born into their trade, and those that are wizards get a special education. The difference is, I think they run the craft families, rather than just sharing them."

Chosmod nodded. "So, you're not just born a gambler, but if you show wizard blood and sufficient talent, you may become a leader in your family."

"There are plenty whose primary skill seems to be weapons. The enforcers, I suppose."

Mpeowake made an effort. "I saw nothing incompatible with the attackers at the *gewengep*."

"I agree," Penrys said. *Many of them felt just like the ones she'd stopped… killed. Equally untalented, equally vulnerable.*

"More than one family was included," Chosmod said. "That means they're organized enough to work together. Probably have a history of that for fulfilling the larger contracts."

"Not quite mercenaries," Penrys said, "but fighters after a fashion."

"The brutal scum of the underclasses," Mpeowake summarized.

Chosmod chuckled. "Let's get you into a palanquin and then home. Penrys, you stay here with her while I find one and bring it along."

The two women eyed each other after he trotted off, apparently indifferent to being a Rasesni on his own in a bad part of town.

"Well, it is the middle of the day— I don't imagine he'll be attacked in public and all."

Mpeowake gave her a glance and decided she was joking. In actuality, Penrys kept tabs on him while he was gone the way she did on Najud in a dangerous situation.

Her fist clenched in impatience. "You know what's next, don't you?" she said to Mpeowake.

"Up to Juhim Tep to do the same thing. But you won't be able to sneak up there. All travel is up and down in the cages. They'll know you're coming."

"Well…" Penrys demurred. "There are other choices, other directions."

"Around from the north, through the military encampments, or up from the west with the vegetables?" Mpeowake suggested.

"Or from above." Penrys said.

"Ah, yes. I was forgetting that. But not in daylight, surely."

"Indeed." Penrys bit her lip. "I haven't decided yet—partly depends on what Chosmod wants to do, if he wants to come along."

"I've been to court," Mpeowake said. "They patrol the streets up there, and the security around the emperor is strong and attentive. There won't be anything like this to hide in." She waved her hand around their dirty hidey-hole. "No easy way to be inconspicuous."

"I'm not going to wait for dark," Penrys said. "It may be only a few hours for us but…"

"Yes, a long time, perhaps, for our friends." Mpeowake adjusted her position. "I regret I cannot come with you."

Munraz positioned himself beneath the grate and scanned the street level above him. *Another pair of guards. I should never have slept past dawn, but who could see the sun in here?*

He could finally see the lock that held the grate shut. The keyhole was reached from the inside of the opening. *As though you might be above or below it when working the key.*

He'd long since worked it open. When he'd woken, his hand was still on the small stone from the wall. He'd made to pocket it out of some impulse, but found his pocket overfull of small items, which he emptied on the tunnel floor into the small patch of light that leaked down from the grating.

While he'd absently stuffed the rock into the empty pocket that resulted, he'd rooted through the old contents and found one of the spare picks his *jarghal* had given him, feeling that his own *anah im-ghabr* was already overstuffed with metal. *I'd forgotten that was there. That's a lucky find. If I hadn't wanted to take the rock, I'd never have emptied the pocket.*

The thought made him dig the stone out again and look at it in the light. It seemed ordinary, at first, but there was something about it that made it feel right in his hand. *Can it be a lud? Here, in a Kigali tunnel?*

He shook his head, unable to decide whether or not the little gods that manifested in a found object could travel so far. But he put the rock back in his pocket again and made sure it was secure.

The pick from Najud made short work of the lock, but the same light that made it possible to see what he was doing lit his face for anyone to see who came close enough, so he remained cautious as he spied out his situation and stayed as low as he could.

The bore hole he was in seemed to operate as some sort of storm drain for a public square in the upper city. It was full of activity—a platform was being hammered together and decorated at the far end from where he was, and merchants and food vendors were doing a lively trade along all the sides he could see.

The smell of cooking was maddening, but he could hardly lift the grate and come out in broad daylight, Zan that he was by face and clothing, and not cause an unwelcome stir. It would have to wait until dark, but at least the way was open for him.

He tried to finger-comb his curls into a braid and wrap his robe in a more Kigali fashion, but he knew it would only work in dim light, if it worked at all. He spent most of the day in the tunnel where he'd slept, coming up every now and then to watch the activity in the square as the platform was completed.

There would be some sort of ceremony here tonight, he decided. Good—he could just be part of the crowd as they departed. Better to escape aboveground than try the tunnels, better to go forward than back.

"You can't do the upper city the same way," Chosmod said. "We'll stand out like raisins in a bun."

The two of them had sent Mpeowake on her way, and paused indecisively not far from the Imperial Security building—Penrys was reluctant to enter it.

"No, we can't," she agreed. "I need a Kigalino wizard. A female one."

Chosmod raised an eyebrow. "Should I ask?"

"I think you might be better off not knowing. Perhaps you could distract Tun Jeju instead."

"I don't understand his internal politics," Chosmod said, "but I recognize the smell well enough. He's got problems somewhere."

"Spies?"

"Maybe. Almost certainly—it's an accepted fact in Kigali institutions." Chosmod shrugged. "I'm more interested in something else."

Penrys waited, expectantly.

"Why haven't we met his superiors since your arrival?" he said. "All the wizards he sent for had to wait for the Zannib ones, the last to come. We were shown the sights of the city, entertained in various functions by each others' embassies, the Zannib one included, and welcomed with great ceremony by the head of Imperial Security, Noi Shibu."

Penrys was mystified. "So? We haven't been here long, after all."

"My sources tell me that the emperor and Noi Shibu meet frequently. Tun Jeju used to attend these meetings, ever since his work in Neshilik. But not recently."

"So you think, what—Tun Jeju is no longer in favor, that there are spies reporting what we're doing?"

"The second, certainly. The first, I'm not so sure. The *notju* is no amateur at professional survival. It's not an accident that he left us on our own to check your findings this morning."

"Which he can't be seen to endorse." Penrys nodded slowly. "Don't know if you're right, Modo, but it makes sense." She looked up at him. "All the more reason for me to do this next bit on my own."

"You find out what you can about what's going on from Tun Jeju, if he'll tell you. I'm going up there, somehow." She gestured at the cliff face of Tegong Him many blocks to their north. "If I'm not back by tomorrow, well, at least you'll know where to start looking."

"Shouldn't try this by yourself," he said.

"I have a plan, and there's no way to include you." Penrys smiled as she thought about what she intended.

Penrys watched Char Dami's face and lightly touched her mind to see her reaction.

"You want what, *teken-chi*?" Her polite bearing registered surprise.

They sat together in a small public room in the Char compound. Penrys had counted on Char Dami leaving the more detailed aspects of the continuing guild meetings to the *samkatju*, her father. The other wizards were all still attending. *More stamina than I have. I don't see how they can stand each other after all that public speaking. Glad it's not my problem.*

"I need to explore the upper city this evening, Char-chi, and I don't want to do it as an obvious foreigner. There are wizards there, many of them, and I'm looking for Char Dazu and my husband, and all the other captives, if they're there."

"Does Imperial Security know about this?"

Penrys laughed. "Well, that's not entirely clear. If they don't, they will. Let's just say that I think I have permission. And if I'm wrong, I don't much care."

At Char Dami's dubious look, she added, "I saw wizards there last night, and more of them in Chalen Tep, the criminal district. We investigated that group this morning, Chosmod, Mpeowake, and I. Not model citizens, those. Might have been the ones hired to attack us, but the captives aren't there."

Char Dami pursed her lips in thought for a moment. "There's a festival tonight, did you know? The *Lenju ka Yukmat*, the Festival of Lights—a celebration of the season. There'll be fireworks and feasting all over Yenit Ping, but the emperor himself will host the event in Juhim Tep. People will be ascending Tegong Him all evening to join him, and coming back late."

"But that's perfect. Big crowds, what's another short Kigalino with an odd face?" Penrys looked Char Dami directly in the face. "Can you help me prepare, Char-chi?"

The older woman rose abruptly and clapped her hands. When a maid servant slid the door of the room open, she told her, "Ask Char Pangfa to meet me in my chambers, right away."

After the servant vanished, Char Dami turned to Penrys and smiled. "I've invited my young niece to help us. She would never forgive me if she'd been left out of the adventure."

She led the way to her room and the next hour passed in a whirlwind of activity.

It had been quickly decided that Penrys would be more plausible as a servant than as a more notable citizen. "Some come from ancestry that is better unexamined," Char Dami had commented, tartly.

The result was a raid on the housekeeper's clothing, a woman similar in height and general shape to Penrys. The housekeeper was well-compensated for the privilege, and soon Char Pangfa was demonstrating the right way to walk, with the modest demeanor suitable for a respectable servant. "Keep your head down when you approach anyone in colorful silks or any sort of headgear," the child said. "That's always safest, my grandfather says."

The hair was a different problem. Penrys was forced to demonstrate why her ears needed to stay covered, even with a braid, and the Char Pangfa was fascinated with her furry fox-like ears, the same color as her hair.

Char Dami asked, "Do all the *tekenwen* have such ears?"

"I haven't asked them all, but every one I've looked at does. It seems to be universal, like the chain."

"We'll just have to braid over them, then. It's odd, but not as strange as the rest of your face. Some of the hair oils are tinted, to conceal gray, you understand—that should help darken your hair."

Penrys had the brown hair, round face and pale coloring of her unknown ancestry.

"Find me your water paints, niece." The request sent Char Pangfa scurrying off.

"We have to change the color of your skin," Char Dami told Penrys. "Too light, and the wrong tone."

When Char Pangfa returned, her aunt showed her how to add pigment to a clear cream. After some tests on Penrys's hands, they coated her hands, face, and neck with the result, and then drew lines to tilt the impression of her eyes and add some shading to hollow her cheeks a bit. The last touch was to darken her eyebrows from brown to Kigali black.

When they finally let her see a mirror, Penrys blinked in surprise. She didn't make a very attractive Kigalino, but she no longer looked like a foreigner.

She raised her hand to her throat with the prominent chain. "What about this? It's got to be hidden."

Char Dami looked at her niece. "What do you think?"

The child cocked her head on one side. "A woman like that wouldn't wear silk. A cotton scarf would be best."

The older woman nodded. "A colorful one would suit the occasion, too. Go choose one."

Char Pangfa rummaged through the indicated chest and returned with something vibrant in reds and yellows, and Char Dami arranged it carefully and securely so that no trace of the chain was visible.

When Penrys raised an eyebrow at the loud colors, Char Dami cleared her throat apologetically. "They'll be so busy looking at the scarf in astonishment, they won't notice your face."

"Thank you, *minochiwen*," Penrys said. She smiled and bowed to each of them in turn. "I am deeply appreciative of your help."

Char Pangfa wrapped Penrys's old clothing into a tidy packet and presented it to her with a grin. "Will you come back and tell us what happened?"

"Child!" Char Dami chided. "That is not the *teken*'s concern."

Penrys bowed deeply to Char Pangfa and promised her. "I'll return when it's over, and tell you all about it."

Outside the Zannib embassy, Penrys contemplated her options.

There was something important she needed from her packs, but she didn't want Mir Tojit to know she was there. He certainly reported to Imperial Security, but she had no way to know if he was loyal to Tun Jeju or part of whatever else might be going on there, if Chosmod was right.

A quick local mind-scan placed Talqatin alone in his *kazr*, in the little garden alongside the southern wall of the compound, and she turned the corner and walked casually to the other side of that wall.

No one had given her a second look as she proceeded through the streets from the Char compound, and she didn't want them to notice her now. She stooped for a few small rocks from the edge of the gutter and waited for the few people in the street to pass, and then she popped one stone blindly over the wall the direction of the *kazr*.

She was in luck—she heard the thump as it hit the canvas-covered felts and felt Talqatin's startlement. Unfortunately he settled back down to his work, and she cursed under her breath.

Another rock flew over the wall, and missed, and she followed it with a third that was successful. This time he rose and stood in the doorway.

"Baijukti, is that you? How old *are* you?" The tone of affectionate rebuke painted a vivid picture for Penrys of a mischievous young girl dropping rocks down on her father's *kazr* while he tried to get his work done.

"Sorry, it's one of your guests, *tawirqaj*," she called softly over the wall. "Can you come and speak to me at the gates, and not let anyone know, especially your majordomo?"

There was silence for a moment, then he said, "Stand near the gates but out of sight. I'll find an errand to send him away."

She watched from across the street as the main gates were opened. Mir Tojit strode out with a young servant to carry things for him, and the gates were shut behind them. The two of them walked south toward the town, and then one of the gates gaped open and Talqatin appeared there and searched the street, up and down.

Even as Penrys walked directly toward him, with her head down and her demeanor modest, he ignored her until she was just a few yards away, and then an expression of surprise crossed his face that gratified her immensely. *I'll have to tell Char Dami how well it worked.*

She bowed to him in character and held out her hand as if supplicating him for something.

"Sorry for the roundabout communication. It's a long story, and I don't know enough about whatever factions there are in Imperial Security to trust any of their men assigned to you."

His lips quirked. "You do make a somewhat unlikely Kigalino, and yet I didn't know you for a foreigner. Any news about Najud or Munraz?"

"You know what Munraz wrote, but I've heard since that he slipped away a day ago from his well-meaning rescuers. I would have expected him back already, so it's puzzling what might have delayed him." She drew a breath. "About Najud and the others, nothing. You?"

He shook his head. "What are you up to?"

"I'm headed up there." She hooked her thumb toward the distant cages ascending the cliff face of Tegong Him. "I looked at it last night, in the dark, and now I need to see it up close. There's a nest of shielded wizards up there."

She cleared her throat. "I don't dare go in, don't know who all you've got in there and who they report to. Sorry to ask it of you, but could you take this package of my old clothes and perhaps fetch me something from my packs?"

He suppressed what Penrys thought might have been an eye-roll in other circumstances. "What do you need?"

"Thank you, *tawirqaj*. Trust me, it's diplomacy by other means." She quickly sketched out for him which pack she meant in their work room, and where the pouch of power-stones could be found. "It's too large for me to carry the whole thing around. What I need is a small pouch that would fit in a pocket—just scoop up a handful and pour them in."

"Wouldn't some weapons be more useful?" he said with some exasperation.

"Oh, I have those, too. These are just a different kind. Mind you bury the big sack carefully in the pack afterward, please. In the wrong hands…" *You have no idea what they could do. Or what they're worth.*

CHAPTER 22

"Why is it taking so long?"

Najud's complaint was for Vylkar's ear alone. Most of the day had been consumed in quiet conversations among the prisoners in twos and threes, interspersed with some of the exercises Najud had initiated to polish their group shield work. Considering that they were all senior in their professions, there was little to hold them in that.

Vylkar glanced over at Najud. "Patience, my young friend. Politicians move slowly."

"But not Penrys," Najud muttered, and Vylkar's solemn face broke into a smile.

"Nothing has changed, I see. She was always impatient of restrictions and the slow pace of others."

"What was it like when you found her?" Najud asked. "I've heard her version of the story."

Vylkar shifted his position and the ankle chain chinked. The shackles were no longer latched shut, but they kept up the pretense for now.

"It was like watching a star blaze up and then be muffled of most of its light. It roused both my mother and me, and I took my men from the country estate to go looking for it. When we found her, she had no expression at all, and wouldn't talk. She didn't even shiver in the snow."

He pursed his lips. "I'd never heard of anything like it before, nor did I find much later, when I looked. It never occurred to me she would be a wizard until I went to probe her mind, and she snapped her shield in place."

He looked around their cell. "An impenetrable shield much like this one."

"You remember what I told you about the *qahulajti* we found, in the west of *sarq*-Zannib? Did you know that Penrys gave her a name, just before the end? She called her Vylkerri, after you."

"I didn't know that." Vylkar said, somewhat taken aback.

Najud glanced at his face. He could understand why Penrys was grateful for his mentorship, but not unduly concerned with his feelings. It was clear she was more a puzzle for him than a member of his family.

"Why is it she chose the library and research over teaching? Was she not welcome at the Collegium?"

Vylkar permitted himself a small smile. "There was some debate about it. Her shield was stronger than anyone's, her reach longer, and so forth. You can imagine this disturbed my colleagues. They were at a loss for how to… place her.

"There was much she didn't know of a mundane nature, of course, but that was a need that could be filled by books. There was little they could show her regarding basic wizardry skills—once seen, easily mastered. So, on the one hand she was beyond the students in the classes, and on the other, the least little thing might be a surprise to her.

"They didn't dare put students in her charge, for not knowing what she might do. But she didn't belong in their classes either. The best thing for her seemed to be the library. When they decided to classify her as a *hakkengenni*, an adept in the old tongue, that satisfied them. Foolishly, I thought—to name something is not necessarily to understand it."

Vylkar glanced at Najud to make sure he took his point. Najud nodded, to encourage him to continue.

"When I heard she was forming professional relationships with the older researchers, I was pleased. They told me she brought new, and sometimes shocking, interpretations to bear on what they were doing from what she was reading, but that's a common perception of rival scholars."

He pursed his lips with a look of discomfort. "I didn't quite realize just how deeply she was experimenting with devices, nor did I know anything about the wings. I'm afraid I just thought of her as unique, as a…"

As a specimen, not a person in your care, or a contributor to the Collegium's knowledge. Najud didn't want to be rude enough to say it out loud.

"So it was a surprise when she vanished," he suggested.

Vylkar nodded. "The device she was building was undisturbed, but there was a fresh layer of dust, as though a wind had blown through the room, and there were no footprints. One researcher in a nearby rooms had heard a dull sort of pop but couldn't place it. It was a complete mystery to us until her letter arrived, a few months ago."

A cold place, this Ellech, and a cold welcome. But Pen-sha was right—it could have been so much worse. All he had to do was think of the *qahulajti*, lacking human contact at all until it was too late, to agree with her.

To his left, Gen Jongto spoke over the napping Char Dazu. "I don't believe the *notju* meant for any of you to be put into danger by his invitation. He has the emperor's mandate, but this is a very large potential change in the political balance in Kigali. There will always be entrenched players who want no change, and hidden players with their own agendas. Our captors could be any of a number of groups I can think of, and there are probably others I don't know."

He leaned forward to speak over the recumbent Char Dazu. "We need to know who's holding us, and why."

"Not just for the politics," Najud said. He waved a hand at Mrigasba and Ijumo, across from them. "That fever isn't getting any better, and all the wounds need tending."

Mrigasba shrugged. "I'm well enough, if I don't have to move too much, but I'm worried about Ijumo." He said it quietly enough that the Ndano didn't wake from his restless doze.

Najud tested the cuts on his arm and in his side with the pressure of his hand. Sore, they were, and they might break open still, but other than the stale smell of blood on the unchanged improvised shirt bandage, he thought they were healing, slowly.

"The longer we stay here, the weaker we will be," he said. "We should ambush our jailer on his next visit."

He'd suggested it before, with little success, but this time more heads nodded—everyone's but the sleeping Char Dazu and the oblivious Ijumo.

Accordingly, they all casually drew themselves up to attention at the noise outside the door well in advance of their evening meal. Even Ijumo roused himself blearily.

The jailer was not alone this time. A chained wizard of Kigali appearance accompanied him.

He gloated in the open doorway, his feet spread confidently. Najud could feel the man's personal shield inside the group one, and knew there was little they could do, even united, to break through that.

"I need a volunteer," the chained wizard said. When he met with silence, he chuckled. "Actually, I don't. Let's see who would be least missed."

Najud felt his probe as it went by, and could follow it by the flickers of discomfort on the faces of his fellow-captives.

The man's focus fell on Ijumo. "Not doing too well, are you? So should it be you, from a sometime-ally, or you," he swung his head to stare at Mrigasba, "from a sometime-enemy?"

He spat and turned back to Ijumo. "Easy enough decision. If I don't spend you now, you might lose all your value. So, Ndano, it's your turn to do something useful for Kigali."

Mrigasba leaned over his neighbor as if to prepare him and Najud saw the slight movement of his hand, concealed by his body from the two at the doorway, that shoved Ijumo's shackle all the way shut to preserve their secret.

The jailer kicked Mrigasba out of the way and unlocked Ijumo's shackle, then hauled him up to his unsteady feet.

Even in a fever, with an expectation of disaster, Ijumo took his time to brush off the dust and resettle his disordered clothing and smooth his hair. He bowed tremulously to his companions and straightened up as best he could, then followed the jailer and the chained wizard out on his own two feet. The door clanged behind him.

Char Dazu burst out, "We should have done something."

"Like what?" Mrigasba muttered.

Najud said quietly. "He went like a warrior," and Gen Jongto nodded his head.

"A good man," Vylkar said, judiciously.

"Are they going to kill him?" Char Dazu asked.

Vylkar replied, "Always best to assume the worst and be prepared," and Char Dazu turned away from the cool voice.

Uncomfortable truths. Vylkar may not be a warm man, but he sees clearly enough.

Najud swallowed and set himself to wait for the arrival of the dinner jailer, and another chance.

The preparations were going well, Tsek Anbu thought.

His biggest concern was the whereabouts of that *teken* from Zannib, whatever she was. His last certain information was from the morning, when she'd reported to Tun Jeju and then vanished with the maps.

It was distressing that she had found… something in her overflights, but his own *tekenwen* assured him she hadn't returned overhead all day—probably waiting to do it again in the darkness, and they'd be ready for her this time. The reports from Chalen Tep made it clear how she spent her morning. At least, they knew the Rasesni and Ndane *lupjuwen* had been there, looking over the joints, and he assumed the foreign *teken* had been with them.

He smiled to himself, alone for the moment in his reception room at the Tsek family compound. The foreign *lupjuwen* were no match for his three *tekenwen*, nor were the rest of them, wasting their time in that irritating guild. Only the other *tekenwen* concerned him, the ones that had wandered into that *gewengep* from the countryside and the city slums..

He slapped his knee, no one present to watch him give vent to his feelings about the failure to exterminate them while they were weak and unwarned. He'd made his displeasure abundantly well known to his allies. *Serves them right that they lost so many. Too bad it didn't get me what I wanted.*

Not all of it, anyway. The captives were useful, and he'd start demonstrating that tonight.

If he could only keep Tsek Uchang and his mother under control. His father's plan had worked to set the foundation, but he hadn't lived long enough to try and manage the spoiled, touchy, grandiose creature his young relative was becoming. His cousin had enough sense to restrain her son, when she could, but that was proving more difficult by the day.

He just couldn't see beyond his immediate interest. The impatience of youth—it might still derail his plans. The young fool thought Tun Jeju dead was better than Tun Jeju discredited. He *liked* the opportunity to reduce his obstacles to bloody wrecks rather than to make them work, willingly or not, for his own benefit.

Well, tonight should satisfy him, then—keep his mind off immediate succession. There were a lot of other heirs to eliminate first, and it was safer to do it bloodlessly if he could. The emperor's favor could do what an army could not, if the bastard would only cultivate it.

What an ingenious arrangement.

Penrys stood with the hundreds of other people from the lower towns in the long and orderly lines that waited for the hoists to bring up the next load of passengers for the festival in Juhim Tep.

Three cables of rope and wire passed over a triad of pulleys deployed from sturdy arms that reached out from the towers that stood near the edge, each cable reportedly capable of bearing the entire weight of a fully-loaded double cage system, according to the conversations around her, as the experienced elders informed their juniors.

What sparked her admiration wasn't just the scale of the system, one of three on the southern point of Tegong Him, with two others on both the west and east faces, but the way each was joined to a second cage as a partial counterbalance. A bullock-driven screw system applied force to either the descending cage, if it was lighter than the ascending one, or to the rising one if it needed a brake to keep from being overpowered by a heavy descender.

The principles were clear to Penrys, but she marveled at the ability to build on this scale. *One of the strengths of empires, thinking for the long term with public works. Were the builders well-paid, and disappointed when the job ended? How long did it take?*

She wondered if any of the hoists had ever broken its cables, but she didn't want to speak unnecessarily and possibly attract attention to herself with an accent.

When it was finally her turn, she filed into place and listened to the cries of mingled amazement and terror from her thirty or so fellow passengers, many of whom were visiting the upper city for the first time. It was a much more perilous feeling to be held in a reinforced wooden cage suspended hundreds of feet from the ground than to be freely flying over it. If the cage fell, her wings would be of no use to her, trapped inside with everyone else.

She swallowed and concentrated on what she knew about the layout of the streets in the upper city.

By the time she found the square where the Festival of Lights ceremony would be held, darkness had descended upon the city, and the braziers at street corners and the torches carried by officials provided what light there was.

The shops surrounding the square itself mounted torches from their balconies that blazed in sufficient quantity that the crowd packing the public space could see well enough. People jostled each other to get as close as possible to the two platforms erected along two adjacent sides—the stage for the festival performances, which occupied most of one of the narrow ends, and the viewing platform for the emperor and his family and guards which almost abutted the corner with the stage, at one end of the long side of square. Unlit torches with shields at their back lined the ground in front of the performers' stage, to provide directed illumination once they were needed.

From where Penrys stood, almost at the edge of the stage, the emperor's platform was directly across the narrow end of the square from her. Canvas on frames extended behind the stage platform on her left to hide the preparations from the audience.

The square itself was a milling mass of people in holiday dress. All classes seemed to be there, both well-dressed families clustered together as well as poorer folk trying to get as close to either platform as they could. Around any part of the edges unoccupied by the two platforms, vendors sold food and drink to the eager crowds.

Penrys backed away into the darkness as best she could while still keeping an eye on both platforms. She planned to leave the ceremony while everyone was distracted so that she could quarter the streets on her own looking for the wizards. But she'd never attended a Kigali event like this, or seen the emperor, and she couldn't resist just being a spectator, for once.

Horns in the distance announced the arrival of the emperor's party, and a respectful silence fell upon the crowd. Penrys turned to watch, with everyone else, as a procession of palanquins in yellow or amber silk, tassels dangling from each upcurved corner of their roofs, halted at the steps to the viewing platform and guards surrounded the passengers as they were handed out. The palanquins themselves, with their bearers, were collected on either side of the emperor's platform, as an extension of his presence.

Even with everyone bowing deeply, Penrys was frustrated at being too short to see the emperor and his court well, and she stepped up on a curbstone, before belatedly bowing like everyone else to keep from standing out. As a thin, elderly man in yellow robes ascended the steps, surrounded by taller and brawnier guards, she stepped down again without looking away, and stumbled over a storm drain grate that brought her to her knees.

"*Yrmur!*" she cursed, and placed her hands on the grate to push herself up, but fingers rose out of the darkness below to touch hers and startle her into rigidity.

"*Jarghalti?*" Even as a whisper she recognized it.

"Munraz! What…?"

I'll tell you afterward. It's unlocked, but I can't open it while people are watching.

She stood up cautiously, and faced the platforms like the other people, keeping one foot in contact with the grate. Invisible fingers clutched it.

What happened? She narrowed her reach as much as possible to keep their conversation shielded and private.

Munraz told her of his escape from Kit Hachi and explained his delay.

Penrys listened to the story and the destruction of her plans that went with it. She'd heard the rumor of the existence of a tunnel network but she didn't trust that she could join Munraz and use that as a way off Tegong Him. *Who knows how many there are, or where they go, or if we can get out when we want to, even if her student could pick the lock here? We could starve down there or, more likely, run into other trouble it they guard parts of it, as they surely must.*

She said none of this to Munraz, though, wanting to encourage him for his initiative even if it was imprudent. *It was wise of you to stop when you did, and wait to see what the situation was. You must be hungry, though.*

And thirsty. She could hear the real need behind the reply.

Wait—I'll be right back.

She stepped outside the square for a moment to buy two skins of ale and a net bag holding eight meat pasties, "for the family," as she told the sellers.

Striding casually back to the grate, she positioned herself so that her feet stood just beyond the grate's hinge and the back of her robes reached the curb and masked the latched side as much as possible.

Open it up just a little and use my robe to conceal it. I've got something for you.

I can smell it!

His eagerness brought a smile to her face. *Growing young men. I bet he's ravenous.*

Her position on the edge of the stage platform was unpopular—too small for the larger groups, and too poor a view of the performance that was to come. In the near perfect darkness, it wasn't too hard for a stealthy hand to emerge and take her purchases, one by one, and lower the grate back down, unobserved.

Don't eat it all at once, your stomach may need time to adjust.

There was no reply. Too busy eating, Penrys thought, and she rolled her eyes.

Now that that crisis was resolved, she mulled over her larger plans. She'd intended to slip away while the focus of so many was drawn to the ceremony, so that it might be easier to walk the streets to scan more closely all those interesting collections of wizards and shields she'd seen last night. But if she took Munraz with her, an obvious Zan, it made her precautions to pass for a Kigalino pointless, and she didn't see any easy way to hide him.

Equally she didn't see how she could leave him behind to wait for her. What if something happened to delay her return? Or worse...

She sighed. She'd have to linger after the crowds left and then help him, maybe support him as though drunk, with her sleeve for partial concealment. But would that work on the cages, when everyone stood at close quarters?

Well, it couldn't be helped. Maybe they'd just have to brazen it out. He could be a Zannib visitor, come to see the sights and headed back for the embassy, and she the servant paid to guide him. That was worth trying.

Nothing could be done until they could lift the grate and get him out of the tunnels without anyone noticing, so they were going to be stuck here for a while. *Sorry, Naj-sha. I've got to deal with the responsibility at hand first.*

If Munraz had stayed with Kit Hachi, he'd have been back at the embassy by now, and me free to see if the captives are here. He meant well, but... Two full days now—anything could have happened to them.

And if Naj-sha isn't coming back from this?

Her fists clenched and she berated herself for indulging in pessimism, but her rational thoughts couldn't fully rule her emotions.

The crowd, which had resumed its loud buzz of excitement, hushed, and Penrys stepped up onto the curb again to look at the emperor's platform. The men and women in yellow silk were clearly members of the family. Some of them wore a darker color of yellow, almost an amber, but Penrys didn't know what the distinction indicated, except that the yellow-robes sat to the front, surrounding the emperor on his elevated chair, and the rest were placed further back.

The platform was surrounded on the back and sides by a solid rank of guards, and on the ground in front, where they wouldn't block the view, a double rank of guards maintained a distance between the platform and the spectators. The guards looked like wasps to her, in their black robes with yellow slashes and insignia. Courtiers and officials of some sort sat on either side of the imperial family, wearing elaborate robes of all colors, barring only solid yellow—that seemed to be reserved to the dynasty itself.

The emperor stood. He was slender and elderly to Penrys's eye, but not frail. He spoke firmly—something about the victories of the light against the darkness and the blessing that resulted for all of Kigali, bringing strength to the empire and comfort to all Kigaliwen.

His voice didn't carry well to Penrys over the noises closer at hand—the final preparations of the stage troupe hidden by the canvas-covered extension behind the platform. A few props were already positioned on the visible stage—a painted wooden tree, nearest to Penrys, an ornate bench, and a table on the far side with objects under it, hidden from the audience by a cloth around three sides.

The performance was a series of brief tableaux, narrated by an announcer in a loud singsong voice, to the accompaniment of raucous instruments concealed behind the stage. Penrys was surprised by the style of the thing—she had expected something more refined for the emperor's pleasure—but then it struck her that this was probably a rural style, something traditional for the common folk whose holiday this must be.

With that conclusion, she listened more carefully to the story being told. The master of light was a thin fellow in a bright silver mask, dressed in robes of orange, yellow, and white. He was kind to the poor, firm with the misguided, and eager to contend with the mistress of darkness. This latter was a woman, dressed in black and red. Her mask was black, its features outlined in gold in a ferocious scowl.

In the various scenes, sometimes the Light was ahead, and sometimes the Dark, and the audience cheered the one and booed the other. In what seemed to be the final crisis, Penrys watched, quite as absorbed as the spectators, while the master of light was tied to the prop tree, a captive of his enemy.

Something seemed not quite right—she thought the knots almost seemed real rather than a stage illusion—but she was distracted by the actions of the mistress of darkness who reached under the table from behind and pulled out a sword. That, too, seemed more solid and weighty than she expected, but before she could quite formulate her thoughts, the woman in black flourished her sword in the air and tore off her outer robe. She was dressed in bright red, in Zannib style, and when she reached for her throat and tore off the last bit of black, Penrys was shocked to see a familiar chain.

Dimly she heard the confused murmurs of the audience behind her.

She froze as the woman approached the captive master of light from the side and wielded her sword with delicacy, slicing cleanly through his throat. Screams erupted from the crowd as those closest to the stage confirmed it was real blood that pumped out of the sagging body.

When the woman yanked the mask off her victim, Penrys recognized in horror the Ndant features of Ijumo.

The announcer flung something down to the center of the stage which burst loudly and raised a cloud of smoke, behind which he and the mistress of darkness ducked while the crowd erupted in chaos.

The explosion seemed to have been the prearranged signal for the fireworks that capped the event, for behind her Penrys could hear the whistles and explosions that launched over the southern cliff face of Tegong Him, and see the colored reflections at the far end of the square, where the guards were tightly clustered around the emperor's party while people fled in all directions.

She couldn't move. She was mesmerized by the stream of blood that had flowed down the sagging body and the rivulet that moved along the surface of the platform in her direction, seeking an exit. It seemed to her that it was headed directly her way, as if to accuse her of delay and uselessness, as if there would be enough blood that it would flow down the platform past her and down the storm drain, past Munraz, and then through the tunnels and on down the side of Tegong Him, a red flow that could never be stopped. Red flowing down and down.

A hand grabbed her ankle. "Get in here, *jarghalti*."

When she didn't react, Munraz said, "That was supposed to be you!"

She should pursue the woman who had impersonated her. She should track her. *Was she really a chained wizard, or was that part of a costume? She must know where the captives are. If any are still alive.*

Her skin was cold and she couldn't make herself take a step. *How much time has passed?*

The square was half-empty now, and some of the imperial guards were beginning to turn from their duties as protectors to come and see exactly what had happened. All this while, the cheerful fireworks behind her banged and exploded, and their reflected colors decorated the stonework of the buildings around the square.

A pinch on her calf made her look down into Munraz's scared face, peering up from the storm drain. "*Jarghalti*... Penrys, get in here. Hurry!"

I've just become the most hunted woman in Kigali. It seemed as if she had all the time in the world to make up her mind, and she shook her head to clear it. The approaching guards would have a view of this spot in just a few moments.

She swerved a couple of steps to an abandoned vendor's booth and tore off a piece of its flimsy wooden canopy support before returning and lifting the grate far enough to slip inside.

"Out of the way," she spat, and set her foot on the first rung without checking to see if he'd complied.

CHAPTER 23

Everything was ready. They'd finalized all the plans and settled or shelved all objections, and all Najud was waiting for was the entrance of their jailer with the evening meal.

They still didn't know where they were, but Gen Jongto was firm in his assertion that he could find shelter anywhere in Yenit Ping, and they had little choice but to trust him, and hope that they hadn't been carried somewhere else. The fact that three of them were obvious foreigners was a problem, but one they could do nothing about.

Najud had his own difficulties. He believed that the shield around them was tied to the place rather than to them as individuals, and if they just moved beyond its range they would have a lead before the captors could react. But he couldn't prove his assumption right, not even to himself, and it was not the sort of weakness a leader could admit to.

They're careless. They've got at least one chained wizard with them, and they've gotten used to relying on that strength. He recognized the temptation from working with Penrys.

Mrigasba had shut down all speculation about what might be happening to Ijumo. "Put it out of your minds," he'd said. "It can only weaken you."

He'd caught Najud's eye when he said it, and Najud had returned a tiny nod. Char Dazu to his left was inexperienced and young, but willing to try. They didn't want to unnerve him with dire thoughts. Vylkar and Gen Jongto were as calm as ever. The ankle shackles had been removed but left in place by the legs they were supposed to restrain to keep the illusion as long as possible.

Najud held one of the small knives from his turban—he'd given the other blade to Gen Jongto.

What's keeping our jailer?

The sound of footsteps coming toward the door raised all their heads, and Najud had to hiss and gesture to make Char Dazu lie back and feign sleep, stretched out with his feet toward the wall. Two men entered, their usual keeper and an armed guard.

Gen Jongto moved aside slowly, as if weary and beaten down, and the wizard stepped toward him to hasten the process. The guard followed him in past the doorway, and Gen Jongto watched for the signal from Najud that there was no one else lingering outside.

At his nod, Char Dazu reached out along the floor and tripped the jailer, and Gen Jongto pounced upon the guard, with Mrigasba to back him up. Najud, Vylkar, and Char Dazu flung themselves on the wizard and imposed a shield around him so he couldn't summon help. He fought and squirmed, trying to raise a cry if not a mind-shout, and Najud worried he might shake them off yet, if he could reach a knife, so he picked his moment and stabbed his short blade through the man's eye and tried not to think about it.

As soon as the blow was struck, Vylkar and Char Dazu abandoned the dying man to help the others, and Najud smothered the man with his body until the throes were over and pulled the knife from the socket.

When he finally stood up to look, he found Gen Jongto casually going through the guard's equipment and distributing everything useful. He eyed Char Dazu, and told him, "You'll fit these clothes—I won't."

The young man swallowed. "What do you want me to do?"

Gen Jongto told him, "You'll be the guard leading the prisoners somewhere, if anyone sees us. It's not much by way of misdirection, but it'll buy us a few seconds, maybe, if we need them."

Char Dazu nodded unsteadily, and began stripping the body of its outer clothing. He used his own discarded clothes to wipe the blood off, and Najud recognized the effort he was making to maintain his calm in the violent circumstances. He gripped his shoulder as he walked past him, in silent approval.

"Ready to travel?" he asked Mrigasba.

"As well as you are," the Rasesni shrugged.

A noise penetrated the building that held them, muffled by the stone walls—bangs and whistles, firm, then fading away, and repeated.

Gen Jongto lifted his head and grinned broadly at them all, a shock after his usual sober demeanor. "I know where we are—this is Juhim Tep, and the *Lenju ka Yukmat*, the Festival of Lights. Get me out to the streets and I can hide you."

Vylkar looked surprisingly natural, despite his gray hair, with the guard's longsword on its belt wrapped around his waist. He turned to Najud. "Shields up. You hold them, and we'll do the fighting."

As a group, under their shield, they stepped out of the cell into the corridor. Char Dazu was in the lead in his persona as guard, but Gen Jongto had a hand under his elbow, guiding him without words. No one was out there, and they turned left, the way the jailer had come, until they reached an outer door.

Gen Jongto tried the handle—it was unlatched, and Najud could tell his opinion of that level of security by his expressively raised eyebrow. He couldn't spare too much attention to the details, since the surrounding shield that had silenced them for two days was starting to attenuate. If they came to the notice of the chained wizard who had taken Ijumo away, it would all be for naught.

They pushed through the doorway and into the back of a compound that seemed largely deserted. Gen Jongto held his hand up to stop them, and then peered cautiously around the corner of the building before returning.

"There's an outer door. We were in some kind of storehouse. The door may be guarded…"

Najud muttered, "Please look, Char-chi." He didn't dare take his attention from their group shield. The noise of the fireworks was louder outside, and distracting. It almost seemed as if he heard shouting some distance away.

Char Dazu's presence pulled away and then rejoined him. "One man nearby," he announced.

"Then you will walk up to it in your official capacity and summon him out." Gen Jongto's voice left no room for disagreement. "I'll be behind you, humble and beaten, with my hands crossed behind me as if bound."

He left Char Dazu no time to reconsider, almost pushing him forward, until they reached the smallest booth of a guard post inside this back gate.

"Yeah? What do you want?" The belligerent guard was still chewing a mouthful of his dinner as he walked outside.

"Will you make me yell at you across the yard?" Char Dazu did his best impression of an arrogant superior, and the gatekeeper straightened up and approached. Gen Jongto waited until he came within unsuspecting reach and made short work of him with the knife in his unbound hands. The two Kigaliwen carried the body back inside to evade detection, and then joined the other three at the gate.

Gen Jongto looked at them and smiled wolfishly. "Shall we leave, *binochiwen*?" He unbolted the gate and opened it, and they all slipped out into the dark streets, and pushed the gate shut behind them.

Char Dazu dropped back to Najud while Gen Jongto led them through the back streets, searching for some landmark he knew. "Do we still need the shield?" he asked Najud.

"If I drop it in order to look around, and attract the wrong notice, well… Better to keep it up and look around later." Najud glanced back at Mrigasba who was moving a bit unsteadily. Vylkar had an arm around his waist, and when he looked at Najud, he cocked his head forward, as if to say, "keep going." Najud nodded back and did his best to keep up with Gen Jongto, casting about up ahead like a questing wolf.

The fireworks were winding down, but he still thought he heard the sound of an angry crowd. Gen Jongto had come to a halt up ahead, just short of a larger road, and when he caught up, he asked him, "Do you hear that, too?"

"Yes, and I overheard people talking in the street. Something happened at the festival, something serious. I should find out what."

Najud reared his head back. "And leave us all dangling out here?"

Gen Jongto kicked the storm drain at his feet. "Still have your little pick, in that treasure house you call a turban? They took my key."

Najud, slow to follow, looked down into the column of blackness. "The tunnels are real?"

"That's where we're going. You *lupjuwen* will go down and wait for me—don't leave the bottom of the ladder and watch your footing! I'll come back as quickly as I can."

He pointed out the lock, and Najud bent down and got to work with his clumsy bandaged hands while Gen Jongto walked briskly back toward the disturbance. Vylkar and Mrigasba joined them, and

Najud continued to work on the recalcitrant lock while Char Dazu relayed the conversation.

With a muffled click, the lock yielded, and Najud let Char Dazu lift the grate despite the resistance of its rusty hinge. His arm and side were feeling the work he'd put them through since the killing of their keeper, and he thought the wounds might both be bleeding again. "You first, Vylkar. Stop when you reach the bottom. Mrigasba will follow you."

Vylkar made no objection and backed down the shaft he found, feeling carefully for each rung. At a depth of perhaps three stories, he called up softly, "Send him down."

Najud braced Mrigasba's shoulders. "Not much further."

The Rasesni gritted his teeth. "And I was always so fond of heights."

"Good thing these are depths instead, then." Najud grinned at him and sent him on his way, listening for any sounds of pursuit. He could still hear the noise of a disturbance at a distance, and the occasional loud conversation of people passing on the cross street.

Eventually Vylkar called up again. "Follow me down," Najud told Char Dazu, "and as soon as I get a few steps below you, lower the grate as you come. Gen Jongto can lift it for himself when he returns." *If he returns. If not, then what? Wander through the dark tunnels till our beards grow white? Pop up in daylight into the arms of our captors again?*

Some version of this litany occupied him all the way down, until he set his foot on the solid tunnel floor, only to trip over Mrigasba seated there. "Sorry," the man muttered, and Najud helped him clear a space for Char Dazu. They all collapsed in a heap and set themselves to wait.

A good hour passed, just long enough to stiffen up nicely, before a voice called softly down. "Still there?"

"We're here," Najud called back, just as quietly.

The grate above opened to let in one person, and then closed again. In a few moments, Gen Jongto was with them. Najud was still concentrating on holding the shield, and it was too dark to see Gen's face, but he could feel the strain in the air.

"What did you find out?" he asked.

Gen Jongto paused before speaking. "Ijumo is dead. I'm sorry, Najud, but the witnesses think Penrys killed him."

Najud's muscles clenched in rage at such an accusation, but before he could act, Vylkar laid a hand on his shoulder. "Wait. Can't you hear in his voice that he doesn't believe it himself?"

It was true, and Najud subsided again, still twitching. He clung tiredly to the shield he was maintaining with the other wizards and tried to regain some equilibrium.

"Tell us the full story," he said hoarsely.

"I spoke to two of the imperial guards. The performance before the emperor was the usual broad rural presentation, with the masked masters of light and darkness. In this case, it was a mistress of darkness, but that's not completely unheard of.

"At the end, when the dark is supposed to attack the light and then suffer defeat, the woman used a real sword to cut the throat of the man in the mask of the light, tied with real ropes to a stage tree. Under the mask, it was Ijumo, and the woman wore a chain like your wife. The body was still there—I saw it."

"And the woman was Penrys?" Najud was finding it difficult to speak.

"Oh, I doubt it," Gen Jongto said, and there were intakes of breath all around. "The witnesses say she never took her mask off, and the chain could be a fake. Everyone was too shocked to look behind the stage in time to catch the actors. The musicians played from the rear and couldn't see what was happening, and everyone else fled—the announcer, the woman, the man who played the master of light until the end, and whoever helped them prepare."

He shrugged. "The guards said they expect to find a troupe of dead players around somewhere. But meanwhile there are rumors flying around and no one knows what the truth is."

"If they see her on the street..." Najud couldn't finish the sentence.

"Yes, that would be a problem. But the news will travel fast and she'll probably hear it." Gen Jongto seemed to be treating this all rather casually, Najud thought.

"Meanwhile, we have to give some thought to next steps. I know these tunnels, but we need light to navigate them."

"Which we haven't got," Vylkar said, wearily. "We may have to break up our group shield soon—it takes a great deal of effort— and revert to individual ones. We're too close to the compound where we were held, for my taste, but at least we're hidden in an unlikely location. It's always been my experience that people forget to look up or down when seeking someone, and we're well 'down' now.

Mrigasba chose that moment to close his eyes and pull out of the group shield. Najud monitored him to make sure he raised one for himself before he sank into sleep. "Can you keep watch for a while, Char-chi?" he asked. "You're the most wide-awake of the four of us."

He could feel himself fading, so he dropped the group shield altogether and curled up on the hard stone floor.

"I could've done it tonight. I was right there!"

Tsek Uchang in his amber robes thankfully no longer paced the floor when he was agitated, but he hadn't grown out of his impatience in any other way Tsek Anbu could detect.

The atmosphere in his reception room was tense, reflecting the mixed results of the evening's events. *How can I get him to focus on the small steps that will take him where we want to go? Shortcuts lead to disaster—he should know that by now. What has my cousin been teaching him?*

"The two guards which are mine were there. We could have removed the emperor while everyone was distracted."

"Yes, and then what?" Tsek Anbu replied, goaded into a testy reply. "Did you plan to go through all the heirs up on the platform? Who would finish the young ones still at home? You haven't even been legitimized yet—until you assume the yellow, no one will take you seriously as the successor."

He took a breath and added soothing tones to his voice. "We can get all of this done, but not if you try to shorten the process. Look what we've accomplished tonight—another foreign wizard ripped from the shelter of the emperor and killed, and their biggest weapon, that *teken*, neutralized. No one will trust her now."

"But you've lost the rest of the foreign *lupjuwen*." Tsek Uchang sneered and it was all Tsek Anbu could do to hold his temper. That news had stung, but he concealed the smart.

"It doesn't matter. We've proven we can seize the emperor's guests and abuse them, and no one can prevent us. We've seized them once, and we can do it again. They don't know who we are, but we can find them whenever we want to."

He was waiting for his *tekenwen* to report the overflight of that Penrys tonight, and her capture or death. That's why his coverage of the captives had weakened—one *teken* for the mistress of the dark, and two to search for the foreigner. Even if she escaped, her influence was gone. He smiled at the thought. Should he add his third *teken* to the other two, or send her to search for the escapees? No, better to strengthen his guard tonight—he meant what he'd said, that he could capture the foreign *lupjuwen* again later. Where could they go, after all?

"I don't understand why you care so much about one Zannib woman," Tsek Uchang complained.

"Indeed you don't understand. I'll be sure to demonstrate for you, as soon as we get her."

Tsek Uchang on the throne, and a separate *lupju* guild in the upper city, and his family in charge of both. Those were the stakes he was playing for.

He sighed and turned himself to applying some unctuous flattery to his imperial fool. *Can't afford to lose any prestige with him now. I'm going to need him firmly in hand to make this happen.*

Penrys went to work just around a tunnel bend from the the intersection with the grate, feeling her way carefully behind Munraz. "I'm going to be making light," she'd told him, and I don't want it to leak upward."

She thought about next steps—she was going to need light to make a *bendu*, a device that would shed light. How to start the process?

"D'ya have anything that'll burn?" she asked Munraz. He'd said little since she'd swarmed awkwardly down the shaft with her armful of sticks pulled from the wreckage of the vendor booth.

She dropped the wood bits at her feet now and lowered herself to the floor. Munraz was probably waiting for her to talk about the murder, but she had more urgent things on her mind. Later, maybe. She could feel both his shock and his wariness of her, but she pushed it aside and made sure the shield around the two of them was tight and impervious.

"I've already burned the loose material I had with me," he said. "I could start on my shirt…"

"No, wait. Let me think." She had plenty of power-stones—what could she do without an actual device? She should've made a lighting device framework before she came, a *rysefeol*, but there was no help for that now.

What was a device but a way of holding power-stones in tension at set distances to provide efficient control? A stone by itself… she could make it glow for a while, if she didn't mind spending the power, and there was plenty of that in her chain. It would get warm, or course. Better if she could stick it to a wall so that it shone above her work, but the walls felt smooth.

"How did you hold the lights you made?" she asked Munraz.

Instead of an answer, she heard Munraz sit down. There was was a rustle of clothing, and then a boot was shoved in her direction, upside down. She grabbed it, startled, then followed her nose to the smell of charred leather.

"Perfect," she said. She carefully loosened the thongs that tied the small pouch of power-stones she'd had Talqatin get her, and she fingered out a single stone before carefully tying it shut again against an accidental spill.

She pushed the stone down into the surface of the burnt sole, and then handed the boot back to Munraz. Instead of releasing it, she kept her hold and guided his hand with her free one so that he could feel the power-stone lying there, precariously attached. Then she let him take the boot away.

"I'm going to load that stone until it shines, and we can treat it like a torch while I make some real devices for light. I'm not sure it'll stick, so try to keep that sole level. Don't get your hand too close, now."

"I'm ready," he said.

Penrys smiled grimly to herself—he sounded anything but ready. She drained power from her chain into the stone until it began to glow. There was no way to tune it, without the structure of a device, so it produced heat and light indiscriminately.

She cast a superficial glance around the tunnel, fading into gloom in either direction, and then pulled out the smallest of her knives and went to work on the broken sticks.

By the time the smell of burning leather could no longer be ignored, she had two power-stones secured in the slots of an ad hoc device. With a little fiddling, she managed to adjust it so that it produced a cold light that was in no danger of consuming the wooden *rysefeol* framework that held it. She left the rest of the stick fairly long, rather like a short torch, to make it easier to carry for a long hike.

"I'm going to kill the one you're holding now," she told Munraz. He'd maintained a tense silence the whole time, and she imagined his conflicting motives—not wanting to distract her, not wanting to talk about what had happened but needing to, not sure how she might react—but she had no patience right now to indulge him.

Anger burned in her like the torch she'd made of his boot, and she couldn't afford to let it out quite yet, or even think about it. She stamped it down and focused on the task at hand. There would be time to dwell on it.

"Don't know if there will be anything left to wear, but we can let it cool down for a while and see." She stopped feeding the power-stone and sucked any energy it still held back into her chain. When she took the boot from Munraz's hand and examined the sole by the light of the new device, she was pleased to see the power-stone hadn't quite charred its way through the full sole.

"I'll take the stone back once it can be handled, but you're in luck. Might not keep out water anymore, but I think you'll still find it useful. Now take this."

She gave him the device to hold overhead by its long handle and busied herself making two more—another one with a long handle, and a small one that could be held with the palm of a hand. She slipped that one unpowered into a pocket, in case they ran out of boots to use for emergency torches.

There was no way to tell how long the devices would continue working on a single charge from her chain, but she suspected it would be an hour or two, and that was nothing to her.

"If we run into trouble, I'll try to turn them off by draining them, but if you cover the shining stone with your hand, that'll be surer and probably faster. Shouldn't be hot to the touch."

Now she felt equipped to travel, but where to? In what direction? "Have you got a bit of cord to tie these sticks into a bundle?" she asked Munraz. "I'm not leaving them behind—might come in handy."

He shook his head. "Burned it all."

Oh, well. Penrys unraveled the colorful scarf given her by Char Pangfa, the one that was hiding her chain, and twirled it diagonally into a strap to fasten the sticks together.

She looked over Munraz. He still had both skins of ale, one somewhat deflated, and there were still six pasties in the net bag. He followed her glance and said, diffidently, "Never know where the next meal might come from."

"Very wise."

"What are you going to do?" he ventured.

He wasn't specific and she dodged the deeper part of the question. "First we find out what else is down here. Then we decide where to go."

She scooted up against one of the tunnel walls and made herself relatively comfortable. "Come watch," she said, and felt his attention over her mental shoulder. She walled away her personal feelings and started at the bottom of the mountain.

For searching, direction is easy, but estimating distance is hard. There's nothing below us but rock and whatever it contains.

She showed him the little rodents that were scattered around the perimeter. *What does that tell us? Means there's nothing to eat on the inside and there are openings to the outside. We can't tell if there are tunnels this way—we can only tell if there are minds.*

As she drew their attention closer to their own level but still below them, she found three scattered people, moving slowly—none of them wizards.

They're not as high as we are, but it's hard to say by how much. Probably they're nothing to do with us. Now let's look at the cages on the hoists.

She moved their view to the edge of the mountain point, and the clusters of minds moving up and down—very disconcerting to see.

No surprises so far. What's on our own level, more or less? That's where I expect problems, not to mention the ground above. We'll catch the top levels of tunnels, and the lower levels of basements.

She tightened her shield around them. It limited her reach but reduced her visibility to other wizards, and the knowledge that there were chained wizards up here was a powerful caution.

From where they were, outward to the cliff face, there were only a few blocks of buildings, apparently unoccupied below ground.

To the north and northeast, however, it was a different story. She felt the tingle that warned of wizards very near the surface as she swept north from the west, and she found more above ground on the same bearing and apparent distance, as if they occupied different levels of the same space. Three of them, she thought, were chained wizards, but she made only the most cursory examination of them lest she draw their attention.

When she swung further east, she found another cluster, below ground, and these she recognized. *Najud!* Munraz's excited thought was echoed by her own.

Yes. Now quiet, please.

She focused on them—four wizards and one other. She knew Najud and Vylkar immediately, and it took but a moment to establish the others as Char Dazu and Mrigasba. The other man must be Gen Jongto, otherwise unaccounted for. They were tired, hurt, and hungry, and several were sleeping.

They had no shield, and that struck her as very foolish. Her own couldn't extend that far, but if they were closer together…

Well, sleeping or not, she had little choice.

Naj-sha… Wake up, Naj-sha. What kind of trouble have you gotten yourself into now?

She listened for him as he slowly shook himself awake.

He projected cautiously. *Pen-sha?*

He felt less than healthy, but her heart sang, the part of it that wasn't wrapped up tightly with anger. *I've been looking for you.*

She felt his hesitation, before he added, *Have you heard about Ijumo?*

Her rage flared up before she could rein it in again. *I was there. I saw it happen. I'm still there, in the tunnels, with Munraz.*

We escaped. Haven't gotten very far. Gen Jongto knows the tunnels, apparently.

Penrys had a vision of Imperial Security trainees memorizing maps. Well, why not? It might be literally true.

How can we get together without leaving the tunnels?

Her question hung unanswered and she tried to wait patiently for a reply.

Gen Jongto wants to know where you are, exactly.

Beneath the storm drain at the far edge of the stage at the Festival of Lights. That good enough?

More silence.

Gen Jongto knows where that is. He says your tunnels and ours connect. Do you have lights?

She smiled humorlessly and projected an image of Munraz holding a device torch.

Good. We don't. He says he can guide you, turn by turn. Me, I think that's too risky.

Penrys considered. With a light, they could mark the tunnel intersections and make their way back to their starting point. Theoretically.

Let's do it. She lifted her own *bendu* torch and the bundle of sticks, and waited for the first instructions. It would give her something to think about, other than bloody death and bloodier revenge.

<h1 style="text-align:center">CHAPTER 24</h1>

"Two hundred twelve, two hundred thirteen, …" Penrys counted her steps under her breath. It was apparent that three of Gen Jongto's memorized steps made four of her own, so she had to convert his measurements before counting.

So far, each intersection in the tunnels had been just about where he said it was, adjusting for step-length. The void of minds south of the cliff at this level made overall orientation simple, and she was able to confirm checkpoints with the relayed instructions from Gen Jongto, who was clearly relying on a map of some sort he'd seen.

Najud must have felt something of her reined-in turmoil, but she turned away his questions for now. She caught him up with the fate of the others as she went along, and she imagined him reporting the news to the rest of them. It would've been better to tell them directly, but she was unnerved by the closeness of the wizards she'd sensed not far from their location—must've been where they were held—and relied on a tight link with Najud alone. They already knew about the deaths in that part of the attack that had resulted in their capture, but the survival of Chosmod and Mpeowake was welcome information.

She left it at that—wizard guild news and all the rest could wait until she wasn't concentrating on counting steps.

Her route had taken her up and down vertical passages, not all of which seemed to be part of a drainage system, and through one locked barrier which Munraz was able to pick open. At one point, Gen Jongto's instructions took her some distance in the opposite direction, with the repeated assurance that it really was the best way.

When she tried extending her shield to Najud one more time, she was close enough that it worked. She stopped on the spot and swayed, chanting "three hundred thirty, three hundred thirty, three hundred thirty…" so as not to lose count. All she wanted to do was lie down somewhere and sleep. She felt like she'd been wandering through tunnels forever.

"What's wrong?" Munraz whispered.

"Nothing. Just give me a moment," she replied. She pushed the shield out to cover them all, then started walking again.

Turn left and you're on the last leg, Gen Jongto says.

Najud's tired but calm mental voice was like a beacon guiding her into harbor. It had taken maybe two hours to cover a distance of less than a mile on the surface, and she begrudged the moment it took to scrape one more blaze on the wall of the intersection to mark their back route. Each pause like that was fueled by a stubborn determination that seemed to be reaching its limit, but she'd done it, the whole long way, and she wasn't going to stop now. Who knows—maybe Munraz's entrance would prove to be the closest exit, after all.

How far to the last bend in your section? You all should come to me there, so the light won't leak upward and give us away.

She felt the non-verbal agreement, and waited. Via Najud, Gen Jongto sent her one hundred and sixty-eight more steps to a curve, and she stopped there. From where she stood, with her device torch held beyond the bend, she knew her light would be visible to the others.

Under her shield, she felt them slowly make their way to her, and she retracted the area covered by the shield as they shortened the distance. Her light would only give them a target, not illumination, so they had to move carefully.

Munraz grunted an incoherent apology and trotted out to meet them and guide them with his own torch. He used his hand to shield it from shining upward, but it was still a rash risk to take. She couldn't summon the energy to rebuke him, and just hoped for the best, and waited for them to arrive.

The surprise on Najud's face when he halted at the sight of a unexpected Kigalino brought a tired smile to her face. "Sorry, forgot to warn you."

She burrowed into his arms, cautious of the obvious bandages, and inhaled his scent—stale, rank, but still her husband, with a scratchy beard. Someone's hand pried the device torch from her fingers and she let it go and just lost herself mindlessly for a time.

The growling of Najud's stomach brought her out of it. She blinked, and realized that everyone was eating one of Munraz's pasties, and now he was offering the last two to them.

She released Najud, and he made short work of his, but when Munraz offered her the last one, she shook her head. "I can't eat." She knew she should, but her body shut down at the thought. The skins of ale made the rounds, too, and she made herself drink some.

After that, she pulled out the small light device from her pocket and powered it. She took a quick look at everyone. Mrigasba was the worst—there must have been serious concussion under those bandages. He assured her he was improving, but she was dubious. The others looked like they could travel well enough, though not for a while.

"We need sleep, all of us. We'll collapse where we stand, else," she said.

Najud and Gen Jongto exchanged looks. "Better to get further away," Gen Jongto said.

"No point. They've got three chained wizards up there." She waved to indicate the direction. "My range is about five miles. What's theirs?"

She shrugged. "I've got you all shielded now, and I can hold that even asleep. One can only spot a shield as an unexpected void, and who expects people underground? But if they look hard enough, they'll find us."

Her voice was fading into hoarseness, but she cleared it and went on. "Your grate's still unlocked, right? If they spot that, they'll see your marks in the dust below it. We can't get far enough away to make a difference, not the way we are right now."

Gen Jongto nodded. "She's right. Sleep as best you can, for as long as you can. We'll talk and make plans in the morning…" He paused, as if realizing there was no sunlight here. "When we wake up."

"Do you need to charge the power-stones?" Najud asked Penrys.

Of course. She did it, then said, "Don't know long the charge will last, but if you wake up to darkness, don't worry—I can power them again, soon as I wake up."

Nothing could make the gritty stone floor comfortable, but she picked out a spot along a tunnel wall and lowered herself cautiously. Najud joined her, and at least a part of each of them was cushioned by the other as they put the long day behind them.

The stiffness of cramped muscles eventually penetrated Penrys's sleep, and she blinked in the dim glow of the torch devices that were starting to lose their latest charge.

With a light touch of her mind, she confirmed she was the only one awake at the moment. All was quiet, apart from the comforting buzz and rasp of assorted sleeping men.

The satisfaction of finding them alive was more than counterbalanced by the wretched death of Ijumo. Every time she thought of the escaped captives, the image was overlaid with the sheet of blood, consolidated into one stream and slowly flowing across the stage from the slumped body.

Maybe Najud and the others could tell her more about their captors. What did they mean to accomplish by that murder—other than blackening her name?

Her gorge rose again in anger and she stamped it back down. *I doubt it's personal for them. They just wanted me out of the way, disarmed, for whatever reason. Did a pretty good job of it, too. But it's as personal to me as a heartbeat. I won't let them dishonor me that way.*

It took a few deep breaths to calm herself. *I may have come to Kigali as a favor to Najud and to repay Tun Jeju for the caravan licenses, but it's serious now. They've earned my complete attention, poking me with a stick like a bear in a den. No going back until this is settled, in their blood.*

She sensed a change and looked up to see Gen Jongto watching her. "Why are you dressed as a Kigalino?" He spoke quietly, so as not to waken the others.

With a soft snort, she said, "I overflew Juhim Tep the night before and identified a nest of wizards. Thought all of you might be there, so I wanted to come back and check it out on foot up close and anonymously. That's why I was here. I stopped to watch the show and literally stumbled over Munraz."

Her momentary grin was erased by the memory of what followed. "Must look a nightmare by now—some of this paint's probably wearing off. No scarf anymore either." She gestured at her bundle of sticks with its colorful binding. "Not that it matters—can't go out in public now, anyway. Not after that performance."

A thought struck her. "But you can, or Char Dazu."

"No money," Char Dazu murmured, sitting up and trying not to disturb anyone else. "They emptied our pockets when they took our weapons."

"Everything but your husband's turban." Gen Jongto's eyes crinkled in amusement. "Do all Zannib travel like that?"

"I will next time," came Munraz's voice out of a shadowed area. "I was wrong to turn down my *jarghal*'s suggestion."

"I hear you, *nal-jarghal*, and I'll hold you to it." Najud sat up and leaned against the tunnel wall, placing a hand on Penrys's knee.

"I have money," Penrys said. "A reasonable amount. Certainly enough for someone to get us food and water, maybe some clothes or bandages. Don't know what's going to be needed to get out of here, though."

"And you have power-stones, I see." She heard a tone of approval in Vylkar's voice and saw him stir in the dim light. "How many?"

"Wasn't sure I'd need them but I made a special stop once I had my… illusion painted on. Sent Talqatin off to pour a handful into a pouch for me."

"You had the Zannib ambassador run an errand for you?" Vylkar asked, dryly. "And why would he have power-stones, considering the Zannib attitude toward *raunarys*, the physical magic?"

"They were *my* stones, from my packs," she said, defensively.

Mrigasba cleared his throat. "Over in Rasesdad, there's some debate about that point. But certainly they're going to be useful now, I don't deny."

"That's what the wood is for, that you brought." Vylkar stated a conclusion, not a question. "What did you have in mind?"

"Wait, we're getting ahead of ourselves." Penrys yawned. "Since we're all up, let's take the time to pool our information and decide what to do. We need a plan."

Najud squeezed her knee. "You first, *bikrajti*. We've been… out of touch." The Zannib word reminded her of the days of tracking the rogue chained wizard through the snow with him and the others just a few months ago.

"*Bikraj*," she said. "It's a good word, with a fine taste in the mouth."

"Do you know," she told the others, "what the Zannib wizards do when a wizard goes bad and people start dying? They band together to stop him, because if they don't, who can? It's done out of duty, part of their responsibility as wizards."

Her audience was silent. "I'm *angry* now. My honor and name have been abused. My family has suffered. Both my adopted countries have been insulted, and people have died. More than that… whatever's going on, it's clear that wizards are at the heart of it, both the chained and the others. I need to understand what's going on, and why—we all do.

"Up until the attack a couple of days ago, I was content to help Tun Jeju ease the transition of the Kigali wizards and the chained ones out into the open. His country, not mine. His wizards, not mine."

She slashed her hand through the air across her chest. "*Sennevi.* It is done. This is my fight now, not Tun Jeju's. If the Kigaliwen can't settle the problem, then I have to. *We* have to."

Vylkar replied calmly. "I don't see any other way."

When she looked at Najud, he nodded in agreement.

"Mrigasba?" she asked.

"Chosmod would approve," he replied.

Char Dazu hesitated. "What about the *lupjuwen*, the wizards of the country? I know they would want to help."

"That's right, I forgot," Penrys said. "None of you know what's been happening. There's a new guild for the wizards, with the emperor's endorsement. They've been getting organized, after the Kigali fashion ever since the attack. The chained wizards, too—Rin Tsugo is there. And your uncle, Char Nojuk, is moderating the whole affair."

She filled them in on the founding of the guild, her discovery of the wizard concentrations in Yenit Ping, and what she discovered when she visited the criminal Chalen Tep district with Chosmod and Mpeowake.

"We've been busy," she concluded. "Not like the lot of you, lying about in comfort up there." She hooked her thumb upwards with a smile.

Gen Jongto pursed his lips. "There are things I should tell you all, even without the proper authority. It would be a mistake to take any steps without understanding the politics, and I don't believe the *notju* has been very open with you about that. Too much is at stake."

He paused, and Penrys filled the void. "Let me shed some light on the problem." She charged the power-stones from her chain, and regarded the tired, bearded faces that swam out of the gloom.

"What time it it anyway? Is it still night?" She dug out her small light device and charged it, too, then gave it to Munraz. "Go to the grate—quietly!—and see if it's daylight yet. Don't let the light be seen!"

Munraz stood up stiffly and stretched before he took the device from her and walked around the bend of the tunnel. While he was gone, the last skin of ale was passed around and drained, and everyone shifted position to relieve their aching muscles, trying to find a spot of least discomfort supported by the tunnel wall on one side or the other.

Quiet footsteps approached. "It's still dark, but it smells like dawn," Munraz said, and he handed the device back to Penrys who laid it to shine upwards from the tunnel floor beyond them, in the direction they'd been traveling.

Gen Jongto cleared his throat and began speaking in a low voice. "The emperor has his guards, of course, and so does each city, but Imperial Security—we're the guards of the nation, the protector of internal order. Naturally we're aligned with the emperor, at least when the emperor is clearly doing the will of the gods, as a father rules his house.

"It's a delicate balancing act. With the great magnates and the military leaders, we are the tripod that the peace of the empire rests upon. The emperor expresses his will, but it is the rest of the great powers that cooperate to make it happen.

"And we are, all of us, only human. However we strive to do the right thing, ambition and corruption dominate human affairs. A magnate may rise with the emperor's favor, so it is in his interest to cooperate with the emperor's will, but if he thinks he can only rise under a new emperor, well… The military may benefit from an external campaign, but if the emperor wishes peace with his neighbors, then… And even Imperial Security is not immune.

"We're approaching a transition. The emperor, long life to him, will not live forever, and the usual factions are beginning to appear."

Penrys asked, "How does the succession work?"

"The emperor makes his will known and a new member of his family succeeds him."

"Sometimes." Vylkar's skepticism was such a familiar part of him that Penrys's mouth quirked at it.

Gen Jongto acknowledged the sardonic comment with a nod. "If the chosen one is the eldest son, or one who has been recognized as the heir for many years, then the transition tends to go smoothly. As long as his views are well understood and all the other powers have come to an accommodation with them.

"But if his views would upset the balance, in the judgment of the powers, or if his views are unknown, or if there is a dispute among the successors backed by different factions, then bloody chaos results. It's happened before, and it may be happening again.

"In this case, the designated heir is unobjectionable to the current powers—that's not the problem. But there are always new powers who would like to break into the top ranks. And *that's* what we're facing, Tun Jeju believes."

Najud muttered for Penrys's ear alone, "Like starting a new caravan and upsetting things."

"One of the emperor's recognized bastards, Tsek Uchang, is making a push to be legitimized. He's about the age of the heir, and his mother is part of the Tsek family of military suppliers. Their compound is up here in Juhim Tep, near the army headquarters. We're sure the clan is planning a push with Tsek Uchang as their excuse to pull themselves into the top ranks. If they can seat the next emperor, the thing is done."

"Is that necessarily a problem?" Penrys said. "New blood, and all that?"

Mrigasba muttered, "Disruption, factions, chaos. A coup is always bloody."

"Surely the emperor knows all this," Char Dazu said.

Gun Jongto nodded. "Tun Jeju took advantage of his presentation to the emperor after the victory at Neshilik to seek a private audience and lay out his concerns, and the emperor shared his own observations of the situation."

He hesitated as if reevaluating his decision to share information, then he forged ahead. "The emperor expressed his surprise, since Noi Shibu had been telling him something entirely different, dismissive of this threat. Noi Shibu, you understand, is two levels above Tun Jeju."

Mrigasba nodded sagely. "He's been bought, by the Tsek family."

"How do you bring an accusation about corruption here? How do you fix it?" Penrys asked.

"You don't," Vylkar said. "Power and money must be brought to bear against power and money. And blood usually results. The lessons of history."

Gen Jongto nodded. "And that's what we want to avoid. Tun Jeju has been in communication with the emperor ever since, while the emperor pretends to believe the reports of Noi Shibu. This is not without cost—suspicion is growing about Tun Jeju from some of his superiors, and that's the last thing we want. Factions within Imperial Security are a fearsome thing—they know all the secrets."

"Why now? Why foreign wizards now?" Najud asked.

"Because we've disbelieved for a long time, in Imperial Security, that there could be no *lupjuwen* in Kigali. We left the the situation undisturbed as long as things were stable. But now's the time, because our spies tell us odd things about some of the clans in Juhim Tep, that the leaders within the families have secret meetings to which only some of the family are ever invited."

"*Lupjuwen*," Char Dazu said. "There are *lupjuwen* up here. Why not? Many of the old families have them, so why not here?"

Penrys stood up to stretch her muscles. "So the combination of an ambitious family with an heir of its own for the empire, and the fear that wizards might be involved—that's what precipitated it. Right?"

Gen Jongto nodded. "We didn't know much about the *tekenwen* obviously—you're the only chained *lupju* Tun Jeju had ever met. He thought if he could let the *lupjuwen* come forward on their own and claim a place, it would either force any of them up here to do the same for their own advantage, or require them to hide and thus tie their hands. We bungled the recruiting call for the *tekenwen*, but the emperor agreed with Tun Jeju's reasoning and backed it with the guild license."

"No wonder that was so prompt," Penrys said. "If the Tsek clan has wizards, what about the bastard? Is he one?"

Gen Jongto shrugged. "No way to know. All I can say is that I recognized the family symbols on the compound we escaped—the Tsek clan. And all of you tell me they have *lupjuwen*."

"Wizards and chained wizards," Najud said.

"Three chained ones," Penrys added. "And I don't think they're self-taught amateurs like the ones Rin Tsugo's picked up. I think they've had three years of a wizard's education, just like I did."

She glanced at Vylkar who said, dismissively, "Native texts instead of the well-established education in the Collegium."

Char Dazu replied with some heat, national pride besting deference to an elder. "Our texts go back almost two thousand years, in the private collections. Do yours? We spend much of our youth and adult years studying underground in the compounds." He cast a rueful look at their surroundings. "Not quite as underground as this, I grant you."

There was silence for a moment while bodies shifted, seeking in vain for softer surfaces.

Najud ventured a question for Gen Jongto. "I assume we can't just gather the wizards from the guild and mount an assault. Wouldn't that be the proper responsibility of the guild when faced with criminals or renegades?"

Penrys shook her head. "You couldn't bring a bunch of untrained chained wizards in to attack well-prepared ones, and I can't easily picture people like Char Nojuk launching into some sort of disciplinary war."

She turned to Char Dazu. "What about the Armorers' Guild? Wizards and weapons both—they must understand violence, surely."

"Not this kind," he said. "That's not the answer."

"There've been wizards at war in the past, yes?" She looked at Mrigasba, but it was Vylkar who answered.

"You've seen the heaths where nothing grows, *hakkengenni*, even if you haven't read every book in the Collegium. Wizard wars have a distressing tendency to continue until few wizards remain, and the prosperity of the whole nation suffers for generations. You should read more history."

Mrigasba endorsed this depressing view. "Our mages are aligned with different gods, so we enjoy the additional element of religion added to our mage wars. A serious mage war is nothing the world wants to see, ever again. The devices alone, and the damage they do…"

He glanced at Vylkar and the two of them shared a look of understanding.

"How much power does the emperor really have?" Najud asked Gen Jongto.

The man replied, slowly, "It's a mistake to think of the emperor as a figurehead, a purely ceremonial position. A subtle man can find many ways to shape events, indirectly. Look at the grant for a guild—how that change will spill out across the nation and, incidentally, hobble the actions of the wizards of the Tsek family, if they let it.

"He won't issue a command that is at any risk of being disregarded, but he can bring the will of heaven into his pronouncements, if he feels it right, and the people will listen."

"I *will* have justice," Penrys said, "and all of you want peace and order. Can an appeal be made to the emperor? Seeking redress for, I don't know, the violation of guest rights for invited foreigners? Something like that?"

Gen Jongto pursed his lips. "Make it a matter of judgment for him, righting a balance that has been disturbed, angering the gods... That might work, give him an excuse to launch some sort of action."

He looked around at them. "All of you should participate, to make it more solid."

Char Dazu added, "And the guild wizards, too. This is part of their duties, to ensure balance and righteous actions. Will the *tekenwen* join in?"

"Last time I saw Chosmod, he said Rin Tsugo was on the platform with all the other leaders, hammering out the rules," Penrys said.

Vylkar told Gen Jongto, "Penrys is the best positioned to present the petition—a foreigner, a chained wizard, a guest whose rights have been violated, and the subject of a dishonorable libel which caused the death of another foreign guest. Plus she represents Zannib, Kigali's oldest ally. And Ellech."

That last surprised Penrys, and she stared at his imperturbable face.

"So we bring a petition, then what happens?" she said. "He can't enforce anything, can he?"

"No, but you can ask for a *lirshik*, to give the heavens a chance to make their will known. That's a trial by sword or other weapon." Gen Jongto turned the idea over in his mind. "You couldn't challenge Tsek Uchang—he would be off limits by blood. But the

Tsek clan is another matter. You would represent yourself and all the foreign wizards. Your challenge would naturally go to the patriarch of the clan, Tsek Anbu, but he would need to choose a champion to oppose you. And so would you, for a physical fight. Unless, I suppose, this would be a fight between wizards… I don't know what the precedent would be."

Penrys shook her head. "I'm likely to be stronger than the wizards in the clan, but it's their chained wizards I'm wary of. Can a champion be a hireling? Or are they maybe married into the family?"

Najud said, "And there are three of them. Are we to believe they will fight fairly?"

Mrigasba shook his head. "Unlikely. Accounts of mage wars are full of the most outrageous stories about cheating."

Vylkar said briskly, "Therefore this needs to be settled as a public affair of honor and justice, with as much precaution as possible. And it will take place in front of an imperial audience which, guarded though it may be, will be vulnerable to attacks from the contesting wizards, and any other wizard who chooses to interfere."

Char Dazu nodded as Vylkar spoke. "So the guild wizards must serve as guards for the court and the rest of the audience."

"If the imperial succession is part of the problem," Mrigasba said, "then I can all too easily see an attempt being made on the emperor at the same time. And that makes the designated heir an ally, if we can find some way to speak with him."

Gen Jongto stood up. "I think this is as far as we can take it for now. It's a decent skeleton of a plan, but our next steps have got to be getting out of reach of our recent captors and communicating with Tun Jeju and everyone else."

Penrys laughed as an idea came to her. "Where better to conceal a few extra wizards than with a bunch of others? Think the Armorers' Guild would hide a few more, Char Dazu? It'll make it harder for any other wizard to find us—too many blades of grass in the glade."

"I would want to check with my uncle," Char Dazu said, "but I think that's workable."

"Then all that's left is getting out of here," Gen Jongto said. "Tun Jeju's going to need time to set things up. You should all disappear while he starts the process."

Penrys caught Munraz's eye and rolled her eyes at the lack of specifics. "So, just how *are* we going to get from here to there?"

CHAPTER 25

Penrys recharged the light devices again while Gen Jongto sketched out his plan for getting out of Juhim Tep.

"These storm drain tunnels we're in were created when the city above us was built. Only a handful of grates can be opened, and those are locked, so people think of them as water drainage and nothing else. They don't connect to the buildings, as far as most people know. It's the other tunnels that have most of the rumors."

"Smugglers, spies, secret assignations, assassination plots." Char Dazu ticked off a list. Penrys smiled at the relish in his voice. *Sounds like there are popular stories on the topic.*

"There's some truth to all that," Gen Jongto admitted. "The other tunnels are independent of the ones we're in. Each is its own system, with its own exits, made for its own reasons. But they do intersect, mostly by accident. To qualify as one of the *notju*'s section leaders, I had to travel the whole warren of them, so that the maps can be updated."

"Where will we come out?" Najud asked.

"I have in mind an exit on the south wall, near the eastern edge. Into the Armorers' cluster of compounds."

He raised a hand in caution. "That's if no new obstacles have been erected since the last time I was in the tunnels. It's going to take many hours, and we're going to need supplies. I'll do the shopping—I doubt they'll notice me if I change my appearance."

Munraz used his fire kit to burn a rag torn from the bottom of Mrigasba's under-robe. Gen Jongto unbraided his hair and spread the gray ash liberally throughout it before rebraiding it. He followed this by turning his brown outer robe inside out to expose a clean, tan lining.

When he stood up and walked with the stiffness appropriate to an older man, Penrys agreed with him that he was unlikely to be recognized by anyone he encountered in the streets. The tricky part would be to avoid detection exiting or re-entering the grate.

She went with him as far as the grate to scan the area for people, and especially wizards. It was early in the morning, the dawn light just starting to show. She found nothing nearby, so he climbed the metal rungs attached to the side of the shaft, lifted the grate, and slipped out, lowering it silently back to its place.

She thought he was unlikely to return before mid-morning. *If he doesn't make it back, we'll just have to retrace our steps to where I met Munraz, and then follow his route out to the eastern cliff.*

Char Dazu had offered himself, if Gen Jongto didn't return and they needed to try again. "I've been passing as a someone who is not a *lupju* all my life."

She'd told him that Gen Jongto had all her money, and there would be no second ventures. It wasn't strictly true—she'd held a little back for emergencies. She hadn't forgotten that she had the remains of a Kigalino face painted on her, and the right clothing, but she doubted she could pass in daylight. She'd need her scarf back, too—the one wrapped around the bundle of sticks.

A trek of hours without water was not appealing, but she wasn't going to send a young and hunted wizard up to meet his captors. Better the long way than to lose another one.

Four hours later, Penrys was heartily tired of narrow passages.

Gen Jongto had easily managed food but he could only carry so much water without attracting attention. He'd had to buy ale-skins and replace their contents from the fountains provided for the public. He had the most difficulty locating a seller of clothing without spending too much time. In the end, he'd settled for clean rags, thinking of bandages, and a couple of sturdy bags.

They'd attended to the various injuries and replaced the bandages. A little bit of the water had been spared for rags to wipe off faces and hands, before they set off.

Now they were as begrimed and filthy as if they hadn't seen a bath for weeks.

Some of the tunnels along the route Gen Jongto followed were no larger than they needed to be. "Good thing smugglers made these," Najud said to Penrys. "Had to make them big enough for men carrying things."

"Small men," Vylkar commented sourly, his forehead in constant peril from the ceiling.

Everyone in the party had his own device torch by now, and Penrys's small belt-pouch of power-stones was half empty. So far there'd been only one roof collapse of unknown extent that had required a detour, but that had cost at least an hour all by itself.

The connections between the tunnel systems were varied. In one case, the intersection was through a hole in the floor. In another, there was a locked framework with bars. Penrys used a power-stone to enhance her skill at moving the internal components of the lock around.

Najud and Munraz kept up a running commentary while she worked, offering to take over with actual lock picks. She ignored them while she concentrated on the delicate work, but was distantly aware of Vylkar taking her own side, describing what she was doing. When it finally turned over, reluctantly, she smiled in satisfaction. "The workings were easy—it's the rust that was hard. Thought I might need another power-stone to force it."

"That's not quite how we would do it," Mrigasba offered. Char Dazu had his own opinions to volunteer, as well, and it took Gen Jongto's sober and worn voice to recall them all to the task at hand.

"You can compare technical notes later," he said. "This takes us into the next to last of the tunnels we want. I'd like to come out in daylight, *lupjuwen*, if you please."

This particular tunnel was unappealing—low-ceilinged and dank. It smelled stale, as if no one had been in it for years.

"Can we trust the air?" Penrys asked.

"We may need to sacrifice a stick and light a real torch," Najud said. "If fire can breathe, so can we."

Reluctantly, she pulled the longest of the remaining sticks from her bundle, now reduced to just a few small pieces of wood. Instead of tying her abused scarf around them, she spread it out and piled the bits that were left onto it, then tied the corners of the cloth into a parcel.

Munraz cut some strips off a cloth rag and used them to bind the rag around the end of the stick. He reserved some fragments for tinder and used his fire kit to ignite them, and then the torch itself. Moving up behind Gen Jongto, he held the open flame carefully and watched it as it guttered.

"Don't like the looks of that," Gen Jongto muttered. "This air should be fresher—the next tunnel beyond connects to the outside. This one didn't use to be this bad."

"Should we retreat to a different route?" Char Dazu asked.

"It would cost us at least a couple of hours, and it would come out somewhere not nearly so convenient." Gen Jongto stroked his face and considered.

Penrys pushed. "If the distance is short, I say we give it a try. Let's see what it looks like at the other end."

Munraz kept his grip on the makeshift torch, and held his device torch in the other. "Only one of us should go, so the others can pull him out if they have to. It can't be you, Gen-chi—you're the only that knows the tunnels. I'm the youngest and least useful. This is my task."

Penrys lifted her hand to stop him and then aborted the gesture. He wasn't a child. Before she could think of what to say, Najud spoke. "Take care, *nal-jarghal.*"

Munraz gave a jerky nod, and pushed politely past Gen Jongto, into the new tunnel. Penrys monitored him as he went. He stopped after no great distance, but she felt no alarm in him, and he began to move back towards them.

When he reappeared, the torch was still alive and glowing, just bare wood now with the rag burned away. He rejoined them in the adjoining tunnel and wiped his face with his sleeve.

After a few deep breaths, he told them what he'd found. "Someone's built a wall, right across."

Gen Jongto scowled. "That's it, then. We'll have to go around."

Penrys ignored him and shared a glance with Vylkar. "What do you think, *bilappa*? We've got plenty of power-stones."

Before he could reply, Mrigasba asked, "What did you have in mind?"

Soon the three of them, with Char Dazu, were deep in the technical details of just what sort of device would be best.

They had Munraz repeat his description of the wall in as much detail as he could. "It's not joined to the tunnel at the top or sides," Mrigasba summarized. "Sounds like drywall construction. Might be pretty easy to bring down."

"Unless it's thicker than you think," Vylkar pointed out.

Penrys shrugged. "Even if it is, the first device may demolish enough to open up the airway, and then we can deal with what's left more easily." She began sorting through the wood fragments she had left and shook her head, then she chose a device torch to sacrifice instead and went to work, sitting on the floor of the tunnel. The others leaned over her holding their device torches and suggested improvements or offered warnings freely, all of which she ignored.

Gen Jongto joined Najud and Munraz who were taking no part in the discussion. "Can they really bring down a stone wall with a bit of wood and a few pebbles?"

Najud half-smiled. "We don't do this sort of work in *sarq-Zannib*, but I wouldn't be surprised."

Penrys heard them and looked up. "It's actually not too difficult, if you're willing to sacrifice the power-stones. That's what makes it expensive. An arc of stones in the right shape can focus the force of another stone that's pushed to destruction. If you can confine it inside a crack, you can get a nice explosion."

"My wife," Najud said, "The bringer of lightning."

She laughed. "Better thank the Rasesni—without a handful of their power-stones, it would be a lot harder." Behind her, Mrigasba cleared his throat.

More soberly, she told them. "I can't use them all, either—we might have to try more than once."

When she was done, she held in her hands a stick that had been originally set up as a device torch. Most of the long handle had been cut off and shoved into her sash for re-use. The far end held an arc of seven stones. The wood inside the arc had been shaved down to make a depression, in the middle of which a larger power-stone was embedded so that the outer arc was focused both across and downward into the singleton.

"It's tricky," she said. "You have to get the right geometry for the stones, and then the facets have to be well-cut. This is the best I can do with what I have on me."

She glanced at Najud. "I've never done this before, only read about it. Couldn't spare the power-stones to give it a try."

Char Dazu shook his head. "I still don't see how you're going to trigger it."

"That part's easy," she told him. "The wall's not far. I'm going to set it in place, then I'll power the stones from here." She tapped her chain.

A thought occurred to her. "Now listen, all of you. The books are full of warnings about what happens. When it attacks the wall, it will displace the air, just the way that a large rock displaces water when it falls into a lake. When the air changes like that, it can hurt you."

"Knock you down?" Munraz said.

"Not just that. You have air inside your body, too. What the books say is, you have to cover your ears to protect them, and open your mouth to let the air inside match the change in the air outside. And that's what I want all of us to do."

She held their eyes long enough to get gestures of consent from all of them.

"All right, then," she said. "Let's see what happens."

As she walked alone down the oppressively dank tunnel, her device torch in one hand and the new device in the other, Penrys chewed on the thoughts she hadn't shared with the others. This was her best set of power-stones for the purpose, from the ones she had on her. Any second or third attempt would be weaker, or might fail altogether, and she didn't know if she could face another couple of hours wandering around these tunnels.

She wasn't really hungry or thirsty yet, just tired and filthy. It was her mental control that bothered her, the fraying at the edges. It was harder and harder to banish the sight of Ijumo's murder and the roiling anger that was making her muscles twitch. Making the device had required fine movements, and for a while she hadn't been sure she could do it.

Najud had his own injuries dragging him down, but he knew there was something seriously wrong—his little pats of comfort in passing had been unexpected but welcome. She couldn't talk about it with him yet, not while they were all trapped here. It wasn't fair to put another burden on him like that.

She shook her head impatiently. *I'll think about it all later.*

There it was, looming out of the dark into the light of her device torch—a rough drywall. *You could attack it with a pick. If we had a pick.*

Well, this will be a very expensive pick, then, won't it?

Her mouth quirked for a moment, and she sought a piece of chinking along the lowest part that she could remove. She found one thicker than her hand and wiggled it out. When she stuck her hand in the resulting gap, it seemed deeper than the flat stone she'd pulled out. *Perfect.*

Carefully, she pushed the device inside, and then replaced the chink as deeply as she could without displacing the device.

It was hard to breathe, she discovered—she'd stayed too long. She turned and pushed her way through the inert air toward the distant light of the device torches, not sure if she was going to make it, gasping.

One step, and another. You can do this. One more step.

Suddenly she felt support on one side, hastening her along. Najud's grip. When she got to the metal frame, hands reached down and pulled her out.

"Breathe!" Najud's face loomed over her. "Big breaths."

She obeyed, and gradually she felt more alert and noticed the worried expressions. "Sorry. Nasty down there."

With Najud's help, she stood up and leaned on him. "It's in place. We need to move away before I trigger it."

When they settled down again, several yards further down the upper tunnel, she looked at them all in the light of the device torches. "Remember, cover your ears and open your mouths. And watch your heads—it might bring down loose rock elsewhere, too. Hard to say how powerful it will be."

She hung her head and concentrated on the distant power-stones. The power she poured from her chain into the focal stone pushed out to the arc of stones surrounding it and was reflected back, and she kept pumping power into the loop, reinforcing it until…

With a low thud she could feel in her bones, the air became solid for a moment and knocked her sideways. An impenetrable haze of dust surrounded the device torches, and then it was cleared away in a draft of freshening air.

"You did it!" Munraz cried, and Vylkar murmured, "Well done."

Gen Jongto just shook his head, then he picked up his device torch and headed back to the intersection. They all followed him into the lower tunnel, the draft of air in their faces. When they got to the wall, they found most of the central section in rubble, the rocks spilled out all over the floor.

Munraz scrambled up the slope of loose rock and stuck his head and torch out the other side. "We made it all the way through," he said, when he tumbled back. "We'll still have to clear some of these rocks out of the way to get by."

He suited action to words by thrusting his device torch at Najud and lifting a rock to heave it to one side. A work party quickly developed for the able-bodied. Najud protested being assigned to torch duty like Mrigasba, but was overruled by the others. "Bad enough you probably opened those wounds again pulling me out of the tunnel," Penrys told him. "We need light on both sides, so make yourself useful."

She kissed his cheek surreptitiously when he glowered at her, and went back to hauling rocks aside.

It was tedious, dirty work, and even with rags wrapped around their hands no one escaped scratches and abrasions.

Char Dazu asked Gen Jongto, "Who would have built this wall, and why?"

"No way to know. It's recent, no more than eight years old—that much I'm sure of from my own experience. When I get back and look at the updated maps, I may be able to pin that down more exactly if anyone's gone this way more recently."

Mrigasba held the torches up on his side and said, "This is prepared stone, from outside, not rubble from the tunnel walls somewhere. Quarried stone. Some of it's even shaped and cut."

Gen Jongto paused a moment to wipe his face. "Leftover building material, most likely. That'd be the easiest thing to lay your hands on. Doesn't take much to build a wall."

Then he looked down at his rag-wrapped hands and the rocks remaining to be shifted. "Well, I suppose that's easier said when you're planning the project than when you're actually moving the material."

Penrys said, "The wall looked finished from this side. The gaps were chinked. Built from this side?"

Mrigasba asked, "All the way up?"

"Well, I was looking at the lower courses."

"Look at the edges," he said, directing her attention to the still intact portion alongside the tunnel walls.

She finally saw what he meant—the chinking stopped about halfway up. "You think they finished the lower part completely, then pulled themselves out and closed it behind them?"

"We'll know when we see the other side. If the chinking goes all the way to the top, then that's how it was made."

She nodded, and bent over another stone.

They managed to carve a passage out by disassembly without creating more than one additional partial collapse, and two of the power-stones were recovered from the rubble—one intact, and the other shattered. Penrys pocketed them both, surprised that any had been found at all.

Gen Jongto scrambled through first, with his device torch, and called softly for the others to join them. Penrys noticed Munraz hanging back conscientiously to take the rear guard position and refrained from smiling. *Who's going to sneak up on us from behind?* Still, it was good to know that Najud or Mrigasba couldn't fall behind with Munraz on watch.

When she reached the other side, she lifted her torch to inspect what was left of the wall and found Gen Jongto doing the same. "Mrigasba was right," he told her. "Built from this side, in the narrowest part of the tunnel. I wonder why?"

He shook his head. "Doesn't matter right now, I suppose." He glanced at the five foreigners and laughed. "If your embassies could see you now."

Penrys surveyed the dusty faces, torn rags, and sagging postures all around her. "Don't think we look too impressive, do you? Let's go change that, Gen-chi. How much further?"

"Not far at all," he said. "The last intersection should be about a hundred yards."

After they trudged behind him a little while, he was proved correct. The small tunnel continued on its way, but there was a fork to the right that connected to a larger, well-worn ancient tunnel that ran both ways—southeast toward the cliff, and north, deeper into Tegong Him. It sloped down gradually to the southeast, and that's the direction they took.

Penrys could tell from the minds beyond the cliff within reach of her scan that they were approaching ground level for the lower town. Fifteen minutes later, the tunnel widened into a broad excavated hall, with actual tables and chairs. Several floor-standing candle holders with dead stubs and old dripped piles of wax beneath them attested to the lighting arrangements. She ran a finger across one of the tables and it came back only slightly dusty.

The tunnel exited this hall with a sharp bend to the left and came to an end, at a wide wooden door, hinged on the other side. The door was oddly constructed, to Penrys's eye—almost as if the wood were woven instead of solid, with gaps nearly the size of her hand wherever the pieces crossed.

"Ventilation?" she asked Gen Jongto.

He shrugged. "Probably. Let's find out if it's locked."

Vylkar held up his hand. "What's on the other side?"

"A warehouse, *lupju*, and I hope Char Dazu can come up with the name of a few friends in the Armorers' Guild, because they're not going to be happy to see strangers arriving out of this door."

CHAPTER 26

In the end, Penrys and Char Dazu working together did the equivalent of knocking on the door. Penrys reached out to shield all the wizards in the immediate vicinity, and Char Dazu announced himself under the shield to the nearest ones.

Char Dazu of the lupjuwen of the Pharmacists' Guild presents himself and companions at your back door on urgent business and seeks audience of the samkatju of the Armorers' Guild.

Penrys chuckled as she felt the wave of astonishment flow through the wizards who were targeted. "Well, that got their attention," she said. The disturbance reached most of the wizards under the shield that hadn't been targeted just a few moments later as the word spread, like the ripples from a rock thrown into a pond.

It took a little time for the surprise to be digested. And then a cautious mind-voice replied. *We are honored by your visit, Char-chi. Please allow us a moment to prepare to properly receive you. May we know the identity of those with you? And were you, perhaps, responsible for the strange noise a couple of hours ago?*

Char Dazu looked at Penrys with a question in his eye, and she shrugged. "Might as well tell him."

Yes, that was us. I'm traveling with Gen Jongto of Imperial Security and several foreign lupjuwen. It is, I fear, a lengthy tale.

So we would imagine. We look forward to hearing it.

Penrys felt twenty or more people converging on the other side of the door, and a growing illumination became visible through the air gaps of the door. "Here they come. Let's try for a little diplomatic dignity, now." She glanced around at the ragged vagabonds and snorted.

With a snap of bolts pulled open, the door creaked back and the light of their device torches merged with that of the sconces along the walls of what seemed to be a warehouse with fully loaded shelves and a wide passageway down the center, aligned with the door.

The sconces were still coming alive as the escapees walked into the building from the tunnel, Penrys noticed. No doubt the wizard powering them was doing it as quickly as he could. She pulled the power back from the power-stones in the device torches and they went dark. *Munraz, please gather them. I'll need to salvage their power-stones later.*

While that was happening, she joined Gen Jongto and stood behind Char Dazu in support. An older woman and two men in a similar configuration waited partway down the corridor while two impromptu columns of guards lined up on either side.

The reception trio wore ordinary Kigali dress, but the guards seem to have been assembled on the fly from people working in all sorts of capacities within the compounds of the Armorers' Guild. Some were in uniform clothing, as if they really were guards, but many were in working clothing, some still in stiff leather aprons, the sort used by blacksmiths. A few looked as if their evening convivial activities had been interrupted.

All of them, Penrys was interested to see, were wizards.

Without apparently watching the guards directly, the woman leading them waited until all of her escort had arrived, and Char Dazu and his party waited equally patiently as if nothing were more normal than to emerge from the clandestine tunnels of Tegong Him in rags and dust and demand an audience.

In her own good time, the woman bowed to Char Dazu. "I am Wok Tomai, the sister of our *samkatju*. With me are Wok Panwit and Wok Sojit."

Char Dazu bowed in return. "It's an honor to meet you, Wok-chi. Let me present Gen Jongto of Imperial Security, and some of our visiting foreign *lupjuwen*—Penrys, her husband Najud, and their apprentice Munraz from *sarq*-Zannib, Vylkar of Ellech, and Mrigasba of Rasesdad."

Penrys waited for her cue from Gen Jongto, and then joined all the others in bowing to Wok Tomai.

"The *lupju* Ijumo is not with you, Char-chi?" The woman knew more than Penrys had expected.

"Ijumo was publicly murdered last night, *lupju*." Gen Jongto spoke without softening the news. "By an impostor pretending to be Penrys."

"I see." The woman's carefully neutral response made Penrys's jaw tighten, but she said nothing.

Wok Tomai looked them over again and came to a decision. "I will convey your wish to speak with my brother to him. Meanwhile, I see that some of you are injured and perhaps you would care to bathe? We'll do our best to provide you with adequate clothing until yours can be… repaired."

Burned, more likely. Penrys was all too conscious of the appearance they presented.

Char Dazu bowed to her again and belatedly Penrys joined in when Gen Jongto did. "We are obliged to the hospitality of the Armorers' Guild," he said. "It would indeed be very welcome to… wash the dust of our journey away before disturbing the *samkatju* with our presence. Our urgency can wait that long."

Penrys felt a flash of humor from Wok Tomai. The woman called over her shoulder, without looking, "Wok Limdo, please fetch the physicians on duty to the night-shift barracks and clear out anyone who might be inside, with my apologies. And send Wok Lorchit to me there."

A guard in workman's clothing near the front of the left-hand column bowed silently and trotted off.

Wok Tomai bowed again to her unexpected guests. "Well. Please follow me, *binochiwen*, and excuse our lack of ceremony. We are a practical guild, as I'm sure you will have heard. Better to make sure our visitors don't collapse on our doorstep before they can speak."

Penrys felt almost human again.

Apparently the craft workers of the Armorers' Guild were provided with a place to sleep and bathe, if they chose not to return to their own dwellings. The requirements of the industrial processes they executed overrode the social schedules of work hours, and it was normal for the barracks, assigned by work-shift, to support several people off-shift. There was even a common eating area for all three shifts together, where simple food was available at any hour.

Men and women bathed separately, and Penrys had been alone but for an uncomfortable-looking male guard at the door and a female servant within to help her. It was an indescribable pleasure to sluice off the remains of the Kigali disguise and all the filth of the journey through the tunnels—a return to civilization.

She'd tried not to think of the rivulet of Ijumo's blood whenever she looked at the streams of water pouring over her.

The garments that had been hurriedly provided were ordinary drab working clothing for the female workers. She retained her weaponry and belt with its pouches, and the scarf wrapped around the remaining fragments of wood. "Would it be possible," she asked the servant, "to get any sort of rough bag? My companion Munraz is carrying around some sticks for me, and I need to keep the ends of them—he can show you. But it's too much for pockets. My companions had something…"

"I'll see to that for you, *minochi*." The servant bowed before returning Penrys to the care of her guard.

The guard conveyed her to the common eating area where a corner had been cleared off just for their party, to keep their conversation from the ears of anyone else. The room as a whole was well-occupied, not just with the off-shift workers who would naturally be there, but also with the curious, Penrys suspected.

Vylkar and Gen Jongto had arrived before her, each with his own armed escort. She smiled to herself to see that Vylkar lost none of his dignity even with wet hair and clad in impromptu Kigali clothing, rather too short for him. Gen Jongto was at home in the clothes, of course, his damp braid tidy and restored to its natural color.

Pitchers of *bunnas* and water on the table and small platters of tidbits made her mouth water. "This is just to tide us over," Gen Jongto warned her. "I expect something more serious is being prepared, and you will want to be properly appreciative, so…"

"I'll try to not to overdo it," she reassured him. "Where are the others?"

"Mrigasba and your husband are with the physicians," Vylkar said, "and Char Dazu is supervising. When I last saw your apprentice, he was watching a man carve off the working ends of those torches— something about carrying them for you."

He looked at her. "Why not just dig out the power-stones? Less for you to carry."

"I noticed some of the device torches behaved a little differently from the others. I wanted to inspect my setup in detail and do some comparisons, see if I can figure out why. Maybe it's something useful to know."

Vylkar was silent for a moment. "Sometimes I believe your adventures have changed you out of all recognition. And then there are moments like this, where I believe you haven't altered at all. Give you a place to work and the right books, and who knows what you might come up with. Don't you miss all that? The advancement of knowledge?"

She half-smiled at him. "I will always feel the curiosity and thrill of discovery—you're right. But if I'd stayed in the Collegium, I would have missed my husband. I can't go back to that life, *bilappa*, and wouldn't want to."

"But the nomadic life of the traditional Zannib? I can't picture it." Vylkar shook his head.

"I'll admit, it was an adjustment, life in a *kazr*. You should come by the Zannib embassy and see the one Talqatin keeps in his garden, as an office. Can't carry many books that way, but it's not a bad life, and you don't travel in the winter. Some Zannib don't travel at all."

"Besides," she said, "did you know that Najud has ambitions to found a school at the base of his new caravan route, in the west of *sarq*-Zannib? He's always wanted to see the Collegium. I'll never lose my desire to tinker with the limits of what wizardry can do, or the design of devices, and if we can build another research institution, in a city that might someday rival Qawrash im-Dhal as a center of trade, I can think of worse legacies."

She leaned forward. "Vylkar, the most important research I will ever do will be the answer to the question of the chained wizards— where we come from and who made us, and why. When I think of those chains, heaped up on a table in the cells below Imperial Security, and all the dead wizards that wore them... Those people are nothing more now than broken devices, like the torches Munraz is breaking up for my convenience—turned out without regard to the consequence, and discarded without thought, like a burnt-out power-stone."

Her throat closed up with unexpected emotion. *I need sleep. I need to distance myself from the events of the last couple of days. And here's Gen Jongto, listening to every word.*

She slashed her hand through the air at chest level. "Enough. *Sennevi.* I can't solve that puzzle today. We have enough problems to deal with for now."

Turning her shoulder to Vylkar to break off the topic, Penrys caught sight of Munraz coming their way, with his escort. His eyes were wide, taking in every detail, and she was happy to see that he carried a plain canvas bag in his hand. His wet curls looked strange with his Kigali clothing, but he seemed none the worse for wear.

He was followed at no great distance by Char Dazu, accompanying Najud and Mrigasba. All three looked much better. Char Dazu had acquired dignity and stature over the last few days, despite his youth, and the two injured men looked weary, still, but livelier. All the men except the bearded Vylkar were clean-shaven again.

Penrys wouldn't embarrass Najud in a room full of strangers, but her questions must have been apparent on her face, for the first thing he told her was, "We're fine, both of us—much improved."

She glanced down at his hands, freshly wrapped, with salve visible in odd spots.

"I didn't say I was healed yet, Pen-sha, just much better."

It was oddly intimate to see him in public without his turban, his shoulder-length curls damp and coiling. She didn't trust herself to speak, and contented herself with pushing the chair beside her out from the table with her foot and inviting him to join her there.

They refreshed themselves with bits of food for a quarter of an hour while the rest of the people in the room cast surreptitious glances their way. The lines on all their faces told their own tale of lack of sleep and stressful captivity, but the brief interlude revived their spirits, and Penrys thought they were ready when Wok Tomai rejoined them, and everyone rose respectfully.

"Have you received everything you need?" she asked.

Char Dazu said, "We are most grateful for this opportunity to prepare for our audience with your brother."

"I am to conduct you, when it is time, to the *samkatju*. We took the liberty, in the interval, to summon a few others to hear your story, under the safety of our roof."

At Char Dazu's raised eyebrows, she continued. "Perhaps you have not heard, in your… absence, of the new Guild?"

"Penrys told us," he said.

"With all respect to the *teken*, I think she may not know the most recent news. We have settled the initial matters of governance for the guild. Your uncle, Char Notju, is advisor—I think that will not surprise you—and my brother, Wok Tori, is now *samkatju* of the whole guild, not just of our house."

Char Dazu inclined his head. "I did not know, Wok-chi. That may simplify matters."

"Indeed. In that capacity he has summoned both your uncle and Rin Tsugo, the *samkatju* of the chained ones. The *tekenwen* have decided to form their own sub-guild within the larger *lupjuwen* one, counting themselves a specialized group, a *gewengep*, a brotherhood instead of a family clan."

She glanced at Mrigasba. "Our messenger encountered Chosmod in Char Notju's company, and he was insistent upon coming. He has just arrived and is currently making a case for Mpeowake and Tun Jeju to be invited as well."

Gen Jongto bowed and said, "This is exactly as we would have wished. I hope care is being taken to avoid spies? We have reason to think all of our movements are being watched, including possible spies within the embassies and other *lupjuwen*."

Wok Tomai waved a hand in the air. "We weren't born yesterday, *shaibo*. The brown-robes didn't invent security, whatever their pretensions and title."

Penrys watched Gen Jongto's face freeze in courteous impenetrability and choked down a laugh. She wondered how Tun Jeju would get along with her.

Char Dazu bowed to her, dignified even in his rough borrowed clothing. "We're ready, Wok Tomai."

Penrys plucked the canvas bag out of Munraz's hand and took charge of it, after adding the poor abused scarf with its scraps of wood. They filed out, and she heard the silence of the witnesses in the room break into excited conversation before the door could shut behind them.

CHAPTER 27

Wok Tomai, accompanied by their escort of guards, led her unexpected visitors through more than one linked compound without ever setting foot out of doors.

Penrys formed the impression of buildings dedicated to smelting and refining, full of heat and metallic stinks. There was a clamor of hammers striking in uncoordinated individual rhythms.

While they were in the area of the raw ore working, a constant traffic accompanied them, making room for Wok Tomai's party to slip through as if they were insulated from all friction. Men, and some women, with smuts on their faces and scars on their protective leather aprons looked up in surprise when they saw them, but hurried along to wherever they were going without stopping.

The further they got from the heat, the more the workshops were dark, their fires not needing to be maintained all day and all night for efficiency. The workers vanished along with the fires, until only a light evening foot traffic crossed their paths. Eventually they crossed over from the working buildings to the offices and reception rooms of the guild.

The sconces on the walls of the corridors here were dimmed to a quiet nighttime glow. Char Dazu looked startled to see them, and then Penrys remembered that in his compound the visible devices like lights were only used in areas that expected no one but wizards. In this compound, such things were common and out in the open, even in a warehouse, like the one they arrived in.

She wondered about the candles in the hall in the tunnel, just the other side of that warehouse door. Perhaps not everyone who used the tunnels, whatever their purpose was, happened to be a wizard, and alternate lighting was needed.

No wonder this place had blazed with wizard activity when she overflew it two night ago. *Was it only two nights ago? How is that possible?*

Her whole body cried out for sleep, but this meeting couldn't be delayed. She eyed the doorway up ahead, its two doors spread wide in welcome.

She followed the others into an elegant room of some size, its walls hung with subdued fabrics with highlights of gold and silver over red. Soft rugs in reds and blues were scattered so thickly that the gleaming hardwood was barely visible. Sconces with power-stones provided an even light, and in the center of the room were groupings of wide, low wooden chairs with small tables, arranged to face each other in informal arrangements.

Penrys was struck by the similarity of this room to one she'd seen before, in provincial Neshilik. She'd met a Rasesni named Menchos there, some sort of intelligence officer, and she remembered the archers hidden behind the walls who had stayed their hands when she'd provided the right answers to his questions.

A quick scan showed no such trap here, but the spike of alarm served to concentrate her attention on the rest of the people.

A man of roughly Wok Tomai's age must be the *samkatju*, she thought. He was speaking with his sister. Chosmod grinned at her as he walked by on his way to greet Mrigasba, and then the two of put their heads together to confer.

She turned her head at a bustle of noise at the doorway, and watched Tun Jeju and Mpeowake as they were escorted in. Mpeowake stopped dead at the sight of her, and Penrys could feel the blood drain from her face. She bowed to the woman, and said, "I was there, hidden, when the impostor killed Ijumo. There was no way to stop it."

Tun Jeju broke step while she spoke, as if to prevent any trouble, but Mpeowake froze for a moment, and then nodded coldly and walked stiffly by. Her face was drawn, and Penrys couldn't tell if it was the pain from her ribs, or the reminder of her colleague's death, or both.

Next to her, Penrys could hear Najud exhale. "Well, that was fun," she muttered for his ear alone.

Kit Hachi approached Munraz with a smile. "I was responsible for you, young man, and you vanished on me. I'm relieved you seem to have come to no harm, but it was a poor trick you played. We were about to send you to Penrys, until you made that impossible."

Munraz blushed. "I'm sorry, Kit-chi, but I didn't…"

"Didn't know if you could trust me, eh?" She laughed. "Well, no damage done, and I hear you've had some sort of adventure as a result."

One by one, Gen Jongto and the wizards were presented to Wok Tori, and invited to find a seat. They sorted themselves into groups, first Wok Tori and his sister, with Char Notju and Char Dazu to one side, and Rin Tsugo and Kit Hachi on the other.

All the foreign wizards clustered together after Char Dazu, with Najud and Munraz at the far end, and Penrys. In the gap between Penrys and the other chained wizards, Tun Jeju and Gen Jongto took their chairs, with Chosmod and Mpeowake.

Once everyone was seated, servants positioned along the walls conveyed dishes of spicy food and both hot *bunnas* and cool fruit drinks to the individual tables beside or in front of each seat. At the completion of the task, they walked out through service doors at the end of the room, and closed the doors behind them.

For several minutes the murmur of polite conversation filled the room while everyone did justice to the food. Penrys was grateful she'd been able to sate some of her hunger so that she could match her manners to her surroundings and not be overwhelmed by her appetite.

Wok Tori raised his head and looked at Rin Tsugo, who said, "Penrys, would you raise a shield over us, in this room? Kit Hachi will keep it up, so that you don't need to be distracted, but you are better at this than we are—better for you to set it."

Somewhat startled, Penrys complied. *Here, like this.* She showed Kit Hachi how to maintain it, and monitored it for a few moments to make sure it would hold.

Rin Tsugo watched, and reported to Wok Tori, "It's done."

"Doesn't mean those chained wizards up in Juhim Tep can't break it," Penrys said, "but you'll know if they do it."

Wok Tori said, "Now, how shall we hear this tale, hmm?"

Tun Jeju stood. "I have not yet received my report from Gen Jongto. Perhaps we could begin there?"

At the *samkatju*'s nod, he turned to Gen Jongto. "Your full report, please. We have no secrets from anyone here on this matter." He addressed everyone in the room. "I remind you all of the emperor's expressed support for all the *lupjuwen*, as demonstrated by the guild license."

He sat down and waited for Gen Jongto to begin.

With apparent reluctance to leave his dinner, Gen Jongto stood and began the story of how Penrys had convinced everyone to dispatch the foreign witnesses to the *gewengep* compound of the chained wizards, and how he and the wizards were captured in an attack.

Penrys listened. She'd already told Vylkar of the eulogy at the Ellech embassy for his companions, but this was the first time Mpeowake had to hear from witnesses about the slaughter of Toawe, her hands raised in surrender as she was cut down. The planes of her face shifted as her teeth clenched, and underneath the general shield, Penrys could sense her raising her personal shield for privacy.

Their audience listened to the description of the captivity and their jailer in silence, until Gen Jongto told of the chained wizard choosing casually between Ijumo and Mrigasba. Now, of course, they knew what the choice was for, and Mpeowake took it as another private blow.

I didn't realize how much she would care about them. I thought she was too… cold for that.

Penrys castigated herself for her easy dismissal of the woman.

Gen Jongto took the tale as far as the escape into the tunnels and stopped. "We should hear from Munraz and Penrys, before I continue."

Wok Tori waved his hand in assent, and Penrys kicked Munraz's ankle. He looked to Kit Hachi in mute appeal, and she stood up with him.

"I'll start this," she said, and she told of the escape from the compound, dragging Munraz along for his own safety, and how they had planned to return him to Penrys, before he escaped on his own.

When she sat down and left Munraz standing alone, he swallowed and in a reserved voice he went quickly through the scrambling climb of the east side of Tegong Him and the tunnel opening that he followed, until he met up with Penrys. When no one asked him any questions, he sat down quickly, in relief.

Now it was Penrys's turn, and she talked first about the overflight that identified the three centers of more-than-family wizardly presence. "This was one of them, *samkatju*," she said, "but I was assured there was nothing unusual about that, so I began the detailed search in Chalen Tep with Chosmod and Mpeowake, where we suspected the actual attackers came from."

After describing that part of the investigation, she half-smiled for a moment, remembering the visit to Char Dami and Char Pangfa. "I reasoned that I couldn't check the third group of wizards up on Juhim Tep without attracting unwanted attention, so I went looking for a little help to masquerade as a Kigalino."

She watched Char Notju's face as she told of the help she got from his daughter. He'd clearly already heard the story from her side, but no one else had. "So I was able to ride the cages up to the top without exciting any suspicion, and I started toward the place I'd found the night before. But I passed the plaza where the Festival of Lights was to be celebrated, and I was distracted by the show."

Trying with only partial success to keep her voice from thickening, she described the stage performance, and then the murder, and her encounter with Munraz.

After a pause, she continued. "I made some device torches in the tunnel, and then I looked for them directly." She cocked her head at the foreign wizards. "When I found them, Najud relayed Gen Jongto's instructions for how to get to them through the tunnels, and Munraz and I did that."

She sat down abruptly, worn out from reliving the murder, and waved a hand at Gen Jongto to go on from there.

He took the rest of the story, up to the explosion that took down the wall. He paused, as if to give Wok Tori an opportunity to explain why there was a wall there, and if the Armorers' Guild had built it, but the man volunteered nothing on the topic. Gen Jongto finished his part of the story and sat down.

Tun Jeju stood up, then, and looked around the room. "Would you like to know what's been happening, up on Juhim Tep, since the Festival of Lights?"

The rhetorical question caught everyone's attention, and he continued without pause.

"The emperor was shocked, of course, but as soon as it was seen that he was not the subject of the attack, he turned the investigation over to Noi Shibu, the head of Imperial Security."

Suddenly it occurred to Penrys that all the talk from Gen Jongto about the *notju*'s awkward position relative to Imperial Security's internal politics had been private. And here Tun Jeju was spilling it out into the open. If he didn't succeed in this, there was little chance of him surviving, personally.

"My superior commandeered the emperor's guards who made the first reports of what they found, and this he delivered to the emperor—that the foreign *tekenga lupju*, Penrys of *sarq*-Zannib, had somehow infiltrated the performance, aided by accomplices, and killed the foreign *lupju* Ijumo of Ndant as a clear threat to the safety of the emperor, a warning of what the *lupjuwen* and *tekenwen* planned."

Gen Jongto said, "But the guards I spoke to didn't say that. They were much more skeptical of who the killer was—they noticed the mask never came off."

Tun Jeju patted the air to silence him, and he subsided.

"Noi Shibu offered to set up an Imperial Security guard inside the palace, to supplement the emperor's own guards. And the emperor accepted. Over a hundred of our men are there now, almost as many as the guards who sport the yellow." He paused. "They do not report to me, but to certain others in our organization.

"I am also told that Tsek Uchang has prostrated himself before his father and expressed a wish to defend him from a position of legitimacy, where he can be more useful." Tun Jeju's voice was colorless.

"The emperor responded that any who wished to support the throne would be welcome. The *gap kwosum*, the ceremony for legitimization, is scheduled for tomorrow afternoon. It will be a small affair, due to the urgency of the moment, at the expressed wish of the honoree."

All over the room, people shifted uneasily in their seats.

"To be followed shortly by the emperor's death, no doubt. And then, maybe, civil war." This came from Wok Tori, and there were murmurs of agreement elsewhere.

"How do you know all this, *notju*?" Char Nojuk asked.

Tun Jeju shook his head slightly with a small smile, and sat down.

"Why does the emperor cooperate in his own death?" Char Dazu asked his uncle, bewilderment in his voice.

"He has little choice, and some of his allies have clearly betrayed him. He's looking for support wherever he can get it." Char Nojuk cocked his head at Tun Jeju.

Penrys thought about these events, precipitated by the trigger of Ijumo's murder, and her blood boiled. She stood abruptly.

"Well, and what do all of *us* want?" she said. "I'm just a foreigner, but I think I can summarize it well enough. Wok Tori, you want the success of the new guild, yes? And, of course, of the Armorers' Guild as well. Rin Tsugo hopes for the same thing, for the *tekenwen*. Our *notju* here wants to root out corruption, if he can, for his own organization.

"All of you want stability in the empire, peace under the emperor, and an orderly transition when the time comes." She waved a hand to include the foreign wizards. "And we want that, too—a peaceful Kigali—and I'm sure we all wish the wizards of Kigali well."

She took a deep breath. "These are policy matters we can all agree with. But me, I'm not a diplomat, I don't have a guild to lead—I'm not even a citizen. It's not enough for me!"

She glared at them all. "We've been attacked, out of someone else's policy, and innocents were killed. My family was attacked, and my name was dishonored. A foreign wizard was coldbloodedly murdered, all out of that same policy, to force events that aim at your emperor's death and the setting up of a new emperor, to allow one family to rise to power over another, regardless of the cost to everyone else.

"I don't care about the politics in here." She thumped her chest. "I want justice! Futile as that is, unlikely as that is—that's what I want. What is your emperor but the will of heaven? And what does heaven want of mortals? I bet your heaven wants justice more than it wants politics. From the point of view of heaven, politics are simply what it takes to create a world of justice, a place where men live morally and provide, however imperfectly, the sort of justice that would meet the approval of heaven."

"Or am I wrong?" She glanced at their faces and nodded at what she saw there. "The people want to see justice done. That's who the emperor *is*, at the most basic—the ensurer of justice, under heaven. All the rest is a necessary evil, the *means* by which it happens. Justice is the *goal*."

She ran out of impetus and sat down. Vylkar stood unexpectedly. "Well-reasoned, and I agree. Ellech and I require a judgment for the deaths of my colleagues."

"And Ndant and I for mine." Mpeowake rose stiffly to make her statement formally, and sat again.

Chosmod rose with Mrigasba. "Unlawful attack, says Rasesdad."

"And imprisonment, says *sarq*-Zannib." This from Najud.

Rin Tsugo took up the call. "Many of my *gewengep* were slaughtered for no reason other than that baseless attack. I join the cry for justice on behalf of Kigaliwen everywhere, and the *tekenwen* in particular."

Tun Jeju rose slowly, and bowed to Penrys. "Then if Kigali is to reply, let's discuss the practical methods, the political methods, of bringing these matters to justice, shall we?"

Once Penrys's outraged cry had precipitated a unified goal, the discussion returned to ways and means briefly, until Wok Tori put a stop to it. "It's late, and many of our guests require sleep. I propose we reconvene early tomorrow morning with initial plans. Our time is limited if we hope to do something before Tsek Uchang consolidates his position tomorrow afternoon."

Tun Jeju took Gen Jongto away with him, claiming a need for access to the tools and records of his headquarters. Penrys didn't envy him the job of engineering some sort of takeover of his own superior officers. Could it even be done?

Rin Tsugo and Kit Hachi approached Penrys. "You should come back with us, to the gewengep, where it will be harder to find you. If tekenwen from Juhim Tep look for you here, you'll stand out as the only teken among the lupjuwen."

Penrys yawned. "I have a better idea. Why don't the two of you stay here? That way there'll be three of us to confuse anyone who's searching."

She added, while the two tekenwen looked at each other. "I just got Najud back. I'm not leaving, and I'm not separating him from the men who shared his ordeal, either, in case you were about to suggest it."

In the end, they agreed to stay. All the foreign wizards elected to avoid their embassies for fear of spies among the Kigali staff, and guides showed them to a suite of rooms normally reserved for shift managers, as a way of surrounding them most closely with a cloak of Armorer wizards.

Eventually Penrys found privacy with Najud in their own room. "Off with your robe," she told him. "Don't get any ideas, I just want to see those wounds."

Silently he removed the Kigali work clothing and she laid her palm flat on his side around the wrappings to feel for heat. There was no trace of fever, and the arm wound seemed to be healing, too. "Truly, you feel well, considering?" she asked.

"I've bathed, the injuries are fading, I've had plenty to eat, and…"—he swooped down on her suddenly—"my wife is in my arms. I have nothing to complain of."

The warmth of his bare flesh and the clean scent of him loosed so many of the tense constraints that had been holding her up all this time that her knees sagged. To her own surprise, tears of relief started to trickle down her face, and Najud, when he felt the moisture on his chest, murmured reassuring noises in her ear until she had recovered herself.

"Sorry," she muttered, as she swiped at her face. "I was worried, and we've been so busy since then…"

"It's flattered I am that I can reduce my wife to tears by my absence." He helped her off with her own clothing, and the two of them slipped into the narrow bed nestled together. Najud wrapped his bandaged arm around her, and the unaccustomed tickle of the dressing was unable to keep her from falling instantly asleep in the longed for comfort of his body alongside hers.

CHAPTER 28

By early morning, Penrys was feeling considerably livelier. She made her way with Najud to the common meals area that served all the work shifts, and found most of the foreign wizards there ahead of her.

Kit Hachi was chatting with Munraz, and Chosmod and Mrigasba had Rin Tsugo pinned down in a discussion of the capabilities of the *tekenwen*. With relief, Rin Tsugo hailed Penrys as she claimed two chairs. "At last—you can settle these issues for them. I don't know the answers."

"Hmm?" Penrys said, absently, her nose already busy with the savory smells of Kigali cooking. "Like what?"

"Like how to combine the strengths of more than one wizard," Chosmod said.

"Oh, for that you want Najud. That's his specialty. He likes to talk about it." She gave her husband a poke and abandoned him to the conversation while she walked across the hall to a series of tables with platters and plates.

Many of the dishes available didn't suit her notion for eating this early in the day, but selections from one simple fried pork platter and another of egg and grains cooked together took her fancy, and she filled two thin flattened circles of steamed dough with her choices, and rolled them up onto her plate.

When she turned back, it took her a moment to locate the table of her colleagues, all the way across the hall. The room was perhaps a quarter full, several dozen people, and she sensed their curiosity, mostly hidden under their courteous manners. *What do they know about me? Ally of their samkatju, or despicable murderer? Do they know they're also providing cover for me, for all of us?*

With a subdued snort she began picking her way between them with her plate in one hand and a mug of juice in the other.

Got you!

The mind-speech heralded a blow that pierced her personal shield and dropped her to her knees. Her eyes darkened and the noise of the diners and her broken crockery faded from her awareness, until all she was left with was a perception of three other minds attacking from all sides against her own crumbling defenses.

She reached out for more power, pulling in all the wizards in her path as she searched for Rin Tsugo and Kit Hachi. She was careful not to drain them completely—they weren't her enemies—but it wasn't enough. If she could integrate the other two chained wizards, though, maybe…

The attack was far from subtle, a matter of overpowering her until they could reach inside and stop her heart. She needed to make that impossible and then to counter-attack.

If she could.

Where were they? Ah! That was Kit Hachi. She felt the woman's alarm as she barreled in and pulled at her chain's power, and then she turned her mind to Rin Tsugo and did the same to him. With that, she began to reconstruct her own shield and push the attackers out, but it was rough work.

She noticed when Najud joined in voluntarily and bespoke the other wizards she'd seized to tell them what was happening, and how they could help. Things smoothed out on her side after that, and she began to gain ground against the uncoordinated attack of the three chained wizards up in Juhim Tep.

What are your names? Penrys smiled grimly at the surprise she encountered. No doubt they weren't used to having their enemies talk back to them while they were trying to kill them.

The attack was renewed, but now Penrys was past the tipping point of building her defenses and it was just a matter of time before they were repulsed. *No, I don't think so. No win for you this morning. Might want to reconsider what you're doing. Come join the new guild instead—better for your health in the long run, whatever your employers may have told you.*

Just before they broke off, she felt bewilderment, dismay, and fury on their end.

Good. Let them do the worrying for a change.

Meticulously she sought out each wizard she'd tapped and restored the balance of his power from her chain before releasing him, taking care not to overfill anyone. She worked her way through them all, a couple of dozen or so, until she reached Rin Tsugo and Kit Hachi. *Here's what left.*

Penrys had never tapped a chained wizard before, but the procedure seemed to be the same. Most of what she'd borrowed she returned to them.

Finally, she opened her eyes. The first thing she saw was the remains of her breakfast, scattered on the floor with the broken plates and never tasted. Then the noise of the room assaulted her ears as everyone tried to speak at once.

She was sitting on her heels, having collapsed from her knees, and she pushed herself clumsily to her feet and leaned on the nearest chair once she was upright. When she spied Najud making his way to her, she waved him off, and pulled the chair around so she could sit in it.

It struck her as humorous how she could see so clearly the line of wizards she'd tapped, leading in a straight line to the table of her colleagues, and she started to laugh, until she saw the uneasy glances sent her way and choked it off.

Najud had ignored her signal, and walked up to her in the chaos. "Well," she greeted him, a smile still on her face, "I've learned something."

"Yes?" he prompted.

"They've never met someone like you. They're not organized." She sobered then. "It was all three of the chained wizards, two women and a man. I asked them their names—they were so surprised a victim would talk to them while being attacked that they had nothing to say."

"Organized?"

"They came at me at the same time, but separately. And it was just brute strength, no finesse. If they'd been operating as a single unit, or if they'd pulled power from the wizards they're working with, it might have been a very different story."

"They'll learn." The certainty in Najud's voice brought Penrys down from the euphoria of having survived. "And then what?"

"They know we're here now. We can't stay."

Penrys had just finished filling in everyone who had missed the excitement at breakfast. They were gathered again, as planned, in the same hall as the night before. The consensus of the previous evening had partially evaporated—the goal was the same, but the means were in dispute, and the attack changed the timetable.

Wok Tori had questioned her closely about her ability to borrow power from other wizards and was chewing on the ramifications.

"You fought them off successfully," he said.

"Yes, *samkatju*, but they'll know better next time. If they learn how to work together and steal power the same way—and they saw me do it—then I won't be able to stop them."

"We have more *lupjuwen* here than most of the other families combined," Wok Tori said, indignantly.

She sighed. "You have no way to combine their strengths and, without that, they have no defense from chained wizards. And if they learn to drain your wizards, they can kill them. I could hold your wizards in a shield together, as long as the attackers don't gang up, but I'll be needed elsewhere."

Tun Jeju looked at her speculatively. "But if you're here, you can't be up on Juhim Tep, causing trouble."

"That's what I just said," she snapped.

"You're not looking at it right. It's an opportunity." He pursed his lips. "Bait. One thing that's been worrying me is how to keep them from being prepared for our resistance. If you're here, then you are obviously not planning to be there, so they might relax their guard."

Penrys rolled her eyes. "Oh. Of course. I can always arrive at the last minute, can't I?" It would only take her a few minutes to fly to a rendezvous point. "This would still be in broad daylight, you know. No way to hide it."

Tun Jeju shrugged. "That's the least of our problems. Remember, you're still being sought in all quarters for your heinous crimes. I don't see how this makes it any worse."

She snorted. "I suppose not."

They worked together on the necessary details. The foreigners were given materials for notes to their embassies, requesting formal clothing for the messenger to deliver, and insisting upon secrecy from the embassy servants. The wizards, except for Penrys, would meanwhile evacuate to the *gewengep* compound to prepare and wait, until Tun Jeju himself would return to convey them up to Juhim Tep with an escort from Imperial Security and from the Armorers' Guild.

The emperor would hold the ceremony in the Court of the Flowering Trees, an external courtyard on the edge of the palace, one wall of which was pierced with narrow columns that left the interior visible to anyone standing on the other side. For public occasions, a large and decorous crowd would gather outside the wall to view the imperial ceremony.

Tun Jeju had an access point in mind where he would be permitted to enter the imperial palace. He didn't say, but Penrys envisioned palace guards with mixed loyalties. A rendezvous point was set in a warehouse a few blocks away, where Penrys would join them at a set time beforehand.

"I'll send you maps," he said, "so you can see exactly what you'll be looking for, from the air. And the words you must use in issuing the protest and the challenge."

Penrys nodded absently, her mind on waiting here alone for the next few hours. To her surprise, Rin Tsugo raised an objection. "The two of us should stay with Penrys," he said, gesturing at Kit Hachi. "If they attack, all three, before the ceremony, it would be best for three *tekenwen* to meet it. And up in the palace, we can be a sort of honor guard."

"But you can't stay with me until the last minute," Penrys said.

"Well, no, but most of the day, anyway. We can join Tun Jeju and the rest as they leave the *gewengep* compound. That should distract them just as well without leaving this defense weak."

He turned to Wok Tori. "In fact, *samkatju*, I have been considering some of the services the *tekenwen* in the guild could be offering. Guarding against hostile *tekenwen* seems one obvious choice. We would be pleased to do this for the Armorers' Guild today, if you wish."

"And we accept," Wok Tori said. "Perhaps Penrys could spend some of your time together helping you practice your skills so that the next attack will be easier to handle."

Rin Tsugo let the pointed suggestion slide off him as he bowed politely to acknowledge the informal contract.

The balance of the morning passed quickly. Penrys worked with Rin Tsugo and Kit Hachi after the foreign wizards left for the *gewengep* compound. Najud had been unwilling to go, until Penrys suggested he use the time to teach them all more about working together as a unit—that won his reluctant agreement.

By mid-day, a messenger from Imperial Security brought both her second best clothing from the embassy—all that had survived—and several documents describing the ceremony they planned to disrupt and the challenge she would have to make.

The two *tekenwen* were taken elsewhere in the compound to be fitted for formal attire of their own by tailors provided by the Armorers' Guild, and Penrys was left alone for a while in the empty reception room, buried in her reading.

All this time she had kept a shield up over this part of the compound, and now she felt a quiet probe, a subtle "still there?" touch.

Where else would I be? Ready to tell me your names, introduce yourselves? You already know mine. She could feel the echo of all three of them, though only one took the lead.

Did you enjoy the death of that decent man, the one you murdered on the stage? Did you know I was there, and watched?

Consternation came back over the connection, and she pushed harder. *You, the woman who is too cowardly to name herself—you know it's too late for you? When we meet, I will erase the dishonor of my name in your blood.*

The reply that came was tinged with a man's flavor. *Against the three of us? We are well-learned, well-practiced. As good as you.*

Penrys felt her temper rise. *You're not 'good' at all. And I've killed stronger chained wizards than you. Death comes to all.*

Deliberately, she severed the contact and tapped her chain to increase the strength and reach of the shield.

Kit Hachi apparently felt the change. *What's happened?*

Penrys received a brief image of fabrics and mirrors. *Our friends from above, all three of them. Wanted to see if the bait was still in place. Hopefully they're so busy staring at me they'll forget to look everywhere else.*

She returned to the legal documents, trying to memorize the correct form for the challenge. Tun Jeju could help her get it right when she needed it, she hoped. The street map showing the rendezvous and the outdoor courtyard with its viewing area for the public was critical—she'd be flying in daylight. The less time she was visible in the air, the less time there would be for setting off some sort of riot.

CHAPTER 29

It was nerve-wracking waiting around, all dressed up.

Penrys had dismissed Rin Tsugo and Kit Hachi to join Tun Jeju's party as they passed the Armorers' Guild after picking up the other wizards at the *gewengep* compound. She had to allow them almost an hour to reach the base of Tegong Him, ascend via the hoisted cages and get to the warehouse where she would meet them.

She monitored Najud as they went, but she was leery of initiating any mind-speech—she wasn't sure what could be overheard by their enemies up in Juhim Tep, and she didn't want them wondering where everyone else was.

Wok Tori had joined Tun Jeju's group, so it was Wok Tomai who accompanied her out to the nearest courtyard in this compound when it was time for her to leave. No one else was visible, but a cursory mind-glance revealed an audience at every window, trying not to obtrude. *Oh, well. Let 'em look.* She pulled her shield tightly around her mind.

"Thank you again for your hospitality, *minochi*," she said, and she bowed to Wok Tomai.

"Come back safely, with your task accomplished." Wok Tomai bowed in return and stepped back.

Penrys invoked her wings and pushed the spectators out of her thoughts. She took several running steps and pulled herself into the air.

As soon as she cleared the compound's walls, she aimed for the eastern side of Tegong Him, skimming it as closely as she dared and keeping below the level of the upper city on its top. Nothing but industrial areas passed beneath her.

When she judged she'd come far enough she flared up and over the top of the steep slope. As she'd hoped, she was north of the city walls, over the military barracks and training grounds. Most of the army was headquartered here, serving the additional duty of guarding Juhim Tep and the emperor from any land approach on the north.

She'd calculated a route, based on Tun Jeju's street map, that took her low over broad buildings, designed to mask her from people at street level. That was the path she followed now, until she found the compound with the warehouse that was to serve as the rendezvous point. No one was visible, and she landed in the courtyard, stumbling a bit as her formal clothing hampered her usual movements.

The warehouse—indeed, the whole compound—was empty, as she verified with a mind-scan. *I must be early. It was a tradeoff between alerting our enemies with Tun Jeju's large group or my flight. Let's hope the alarm isn't spreading from my part of it.*

She dusted off a spot on the steps of the courtyard at the warehouse entrance, and settled in to wait.

After a quarter of an hour had passed, she was unable to suppress her nerves. *Where are they? What's taking them so long?*

They weren't going to risk any direct mind-speech, but she did a simple monitor in that direction and couldn't locate them. Too many people, too far away. *If there were a problem, wouldn't they have tried to tell me anyway?*

And then a horrifying thought struck her. *How far can they reach? What if they're more than a mile away?* That was Najud's range. She didn't know Rin Tsugo's limits.

After half an hour, she knew she was on her own. Maybe they'd been ambushed somehow, below. Meanwhile their opportunity was vanishing. Once Tsek Uchang was legitimized, the emperor's days were surely numbered.

She didn't know how Tun Jeju had planned to enter the palace—she couldn't use his methods. Without him, there was no one to oppose the emperor's guards, no one to deflect the Imperial Security guards that had been added under his corrupt master. And the challenge… that wouldn't work without backup to ensure no interference from the Tsek wizards—it was hopeless.

And if she didn't try, she might as well kill the emperor herself.

She didn't know the man—he meant little to her as a person, no matter how well Tun Jeju and others spoke of him. But she cared about the wizards she'd met, both the Kigaliwen and the foreigners. She wanted the chained wizards to find a place for themselves. All that would be derailed by the faction up here if it succeeded in putting an emperor of its own in place.

These were all good reasons, but she paced restlessly in the open compound, unable to make herself act alone. Not her country, not her wizards.

And then the rivulet of blood from the slaughtered Ijumo flowed across her inner sight and accused her. *Yrmur! They* are *my wizards. That was* my *name that was filthied. They can't just take my name from me, make me complicit. I* am *complicit if I don't seek justice.*

Her blood boiled freshly, as if the murder had just been done again.

Even if I fail, I will go down fighting. Before her better judgment could kick in, she ran a few steps and launched herself into the air again.

This time she made no attempt this time to hide herself. She swooped low over several of the markets on the east side of the palace, her ultimate destination. People pointed up at her and cried out. She flared up directly above the outer courtyard, so that her target would be obvious to the people watching.

In the moment before she landed there, she had time enough to see the crowd gathered outside the viewing wall, and the calm arrangement of people within, their faces just lifting in surprise. She marked the emperor's seat on its raised platform and aimed for precision in her landing on the clipped grass, and achieved it, not six feet from the foot of his throne. She deliberately left her wings exposed for effect, poised partially closed over her back.

Ignoring the noise behind her, the sound of the panicked guards drawing weapons, she fell to both knees and bowed low enough that her forehead touched the ground before raising it so that her voice would carry. "Justice!" she cried, loudly enough for the disturbed public crowd, watching from the other side of the pierced wall, to hear. "I accuse the Tsek family of crimes against the emperor's peace. I beseech the emperor to hear my claim."

She held her bent pose unmoving while the hairs on the back of her neck prickled in alarm. Out of the corner of her eye, she saw the spearpoint that touched her side, just short of driving through her ribs.

The noise stopped suddenly, and the spear withdrew. She lifted her head just enough to see that the emperor had raised his hand and motioned the guards back. He waited until order in the courtyard had been restored, and the silence there radiated out through the viewing wall into the watching audience.

When he was satisfied, he said, "Rise, *tekenga lupju*. I will hear your claim."

"I am Penrys of *sarq*-Zannib, and of Ellech, summoned by Imperial Security as one of several foreign *lupjuwen* to advise in the new guild of all the *lupjuwen* in Kigali."

"I did not summon her." The man who denied her wore the brown robes of Imperial Security.

"Peace, my friend," the emperor murmured. His face was impassive under the gray hair and the complex raised head covering, all stiffened flaps and ritual form.

Penrys knew the other man had to be Noi Shibu. Other courtiers sat in his area of the viewing platform, but her eye was drawn to several men and women, even children, in yellow robes— the heirs. She spared a glance for the one man on the platform in the darker amber robes of a recognized bastard. At all costs, she must keep him from concluding this ceremony. A much older woman in amber sat behind him—his mother?

"Four days ago," she said, "a delegation of all the invited foreign wizards, from Kigali's allies of *sarq*-Zannib and Ndant, and from Ellech and Rasesdad, attended an assembly of *tekenga lupjuwen* to encourage them to join with the other Kigali *lupjuwen*. We were attacked by a rabble of *lupjuwen*, hired by the Tsek clan out of Chalen Tep."

"That is a lie," the amber-robed woman hissed.

The emperor raised his hand again, and she subsided.

If they're going to dispute my every sentence, this could take a while. She clamped her teeth on the black humor that threatened to show on her face.

"Many were killed, including three of my colleagues, and several were captured. They were held captive for two days, their wounds untended, in one of the Tsek buildings here, in Juhim Tep, where they were shackled to the wall and supervised by a *lupju* jailer, shielded from searches by a group of *tekenwen*."

She'd been pitching her voice to carry, and she could hear a sort of echo in the distance, her own words being relayed to those too far back in the crowd to hear her directly.

"Two days ago, the captives were visited by a *tekenga lupju* who chose one of their number, Ijumo of Ndant, and led him away.

That evening, the captives managed to escape."

She took a breath to steady herself. "I also had come in search of them, having discovered the concentration of *lupjuwen* and *tekenwen* in the Tsek compound. As it happens, I was in the crowd during the Festival of Lights, and I witnessed the foul murder of the bound Ijumo by a *teken* working for Tsek Anbu, wearing clothing meant to suggest me.

"I claim justice for my colleagues, Kigali's foreign allies. I claim it for the Kigaliwen who were wantonly slain in these attacks. I claim it for my own name and honor. Most of all, I claim the right to make the emperor acquainted with the mischief and treason plotted by one of his subject clans that wishes to divide *lupjuwen* from the righteous control of their guild and encourage them in criminal activities."

She waited for the relay echo to finish.

"This I swear to be true!" She bowed again and remained kneeling, until the emperor gestured with his hand for her to rise. His expression was impossible to read.

From behind Penrys, an urbane voice spoke. "My clan is accused, and I claim the right to respond."

She turned around and confronted a plump and prosperous Kigalino, middle-aged and confident. This would be Tsek Anbu, the *samkatju* of his clan, she thought. That woman in amber robes on the platform was, what, his cousin?

He walked up to her as if he had no fear of her whatever, as if she were unimportant. "Where are the proofs?" he asked, reasonably. "Are we to take the word of an uninvited and unsupported foreigner, one who is sought for treasonous murder? What are the oaths of foreigners, or their notions of honor?"

Penrys, under her shield, took a moment to verify that this man was indeed a wizard, as were the two in amber robes behind the emperor. She didn't dare distract herself looking for the three chained ones that had to be nearby, perhaps in the public audience outside the wall.

The emperor asked her, "And where are the other *lupjuwen* you say were captive? Would they not come with you?"

Straight to the weakness of my claim. Now what?

"They were to have joined me here and have been prevented. I am sure that this man could tell you more about that." She gestured at Tsek Anbu.

"You see how it is," Tsek Anbu said. "These good allies of ours didn't wish to support this nonsense and are probably unaware of her actions."

Penrys remembered the documents she'd been studying all day, and Tun Jeju's insistence on a public solution. "Challenge!" she cried. "I call challenge upon him, for impugning the truth of my statements."

That gave him pause. Then he bowed to the emperor again. "Gladly will I accept challenge, but this is a *tekenga lupju*, as all can see. I will need a champion."

He approached the viewing wall and raised his voice. "Is there, by chance, anyone who will champion the Tsek clan to refute these falsehoods?"

By chance! A well-prepared backup, more like it. She watched a soberly dressed Kigaliwen couple standing an unnatural distance apart from each other approach the walls. The man unfastened the top of his tunic to reveal a chain. "We are here to witness this joyous occasion that adds another heir to support our emperor. I would be honored to do my best to support you and the emperor."

Tsek Uchang spoke to his father. "In a sword challenge, all may judge of the actions of the contenders, whether they are honorable or not. In a challenge like this, how will we be able to tell that there has been no impropriety, no… falseness?"

The emperor inclined his head to listen. "And what do you suggest, my son?"

The young man called out to the crowd. "Is there one who can serve as overseer of this challenge?"

Without surprise, Penrys watched another woman make herself known in the audience. "I am so qualified," she said, never taking her eyes from Penrys while she bared her neck to reveal the chain. A tight, satisfied smile played on her lips.

Penrys declared, "These are the three *tekenga lupjuwen* employed by the Tsek clan. This last woman is the one who impersonated me on the stage at the Festival of Lights."

"So you say, foreigner," said Tsek Uchang. "I think this is just a way of trying to evade the charges of murder against you. If you survive the challenge, you will find justice, indeed, of a rather different kind."

He assumed a bored expression. "Let's get this over with and return to the ceremony."

Two guardsmen were dispatched to an outer gate to bring the three chained wizards in. The instant they had revealed themselves as *tekenwen*, open space had opened around them, but they feigned not to notice and let themselves be led around into the courtyard where they all three spaced themselves apart by a few feet and bowed to the emperor.

He looked each of them over closely and asked their names. They disclaimed any connection with the Tsek clan while Penrys watched resentfully. He paid most attention to the woman who had nominated herself as overseer of the challenge, and then caused a seat to be brought for her, on the platform next to him, and another to the right of the space before him for the wife of Jut Sejo, the man who'd accepted the champion's role.

When everyone had been seated, and only Penrys and Jut Sejo remained standing before the emperor's platform, the emperor dropped his civil mask and assumed a sterner aspect. At a nod to one of his ministers, two resonant sticks were clacked together, three times.

Into the resulting silence, he spoke so that all could hear him, with all the majesty of his role. "Heaven has heard a call for justice, and insists that we respond. If there is treason in the land of Kigali, we will find it out."

His glance went to the public audience. "This challenge will be to submission or death. There will be no interference from anyone, and most especially from any *lupjuwen*. Our overseer will hold herself bound to prevent that."

"Anyone who interferes will be subject to severe penalty, not excluding death."

Penrys muttered, bitterly, "Heaven puts its thumb on the scales, like everyone else."

The emperor turned his head to her, but she did not apologize. She let her wings vanish—they would be a useless distraction—and faced Jut Sejo.

Her raised shield was proof against his first probe, and she pushed back immediately. There was nothing for the spectators to see, but her own attack induced him to step backward in response.

She moved forward to match him, and searched for ways to penetrate his shield—draining his own power would be the only way to truly stop him, like any wizard. It was a good, strong shield he had, not something she could just overwhelm, and she concentrated on finding a weakness in it somewhere to break the stalemate.

If I just pick at it here, I bet I can crack it. Wait, what's that? The so-called wife? Two against one, is it? Not so easy to break my shield, eh? Yrmur! Where did that knife come from?

She dodged the blade that Jut Sejo pulled once, but the pressure from the second chained wizard blinded her long enough that he managed a slash on her arm. It flashed cold, and then began to burn.

Scrambling back to create a little space, she drew the knife at her back and prepared to meet him, blade to blade. The emperor's guards shifted to provide a shield in front of him, but otherwise did not interfere.

That's why it was the man who was the chosen champion, not the women, who were stronger wizards. Now his height matters, and his reach.

The insight was too late and useless.

I've got to neutralize the second one.

She couldn't draw on the shielded *tekenwen*, but there were other wizards. She reached for the ones in the crowd first, a dozen or so, leaving them enough to stay alive, and used that to blindside the seated woman. She sprawled in her seat and then rose and dropped all pretense of non-interference.

Penrys needed more wizards. Tsek Anbu's clan—that was close enough. Their group shield wasn't strong enough to withstand her, not without the help of the chained wizards here, and she tore it away and drained them all, trying not to kill them, but there wasn't enough time to be delicate about it.

With that surge of power, she swatted down the second woman and broke her shield. Once inside, she drained what she could, but her own chain could only hold so much, and too much was left for safety—the woman would recover too quickly.

A cold shock radiated from her right arm. Too much focus on the woman, and he'd slashed her there a second time. Her hand couldn't hold the knife, and it dropped before she could bring her left hand to grab it. There was no noise at all, except the sound of the knife hitting the ground, and she seemed to be moving slowly, as if the very air were thick.

Before the pain could hit, she formed all the power she now had into a bludgeon that smashed through his shield. There was no way to drain him, nowhere for it to go, and so she stopped his heart. He managed one more step toward her before he collapsed.

Penrys clamped the double wound on her forearm with her left hand to try and stop the bleeding. Her eye fell randomly on a guardsman along the wall and she puzzled over his face. His expression was shocked, but he wasn't looking at her, at the fight. He was looking past her.

She turned to follow his gaze, and there was the emperor, still seated with dignity. The third chained wizard, the one who had murdered Ijumo, rested a knife against his throat. She was silent until she saw that she'd gotten Penrys's attention, and then she spoke, and all the noise that had been at bay rushed in along with her words.

"You know I will do it," she said. "You of all people."

No one else on the platform dared to move.

It's a device. The chain is a device. Move, bind, destroy—that's what devices do.

That was one thought. And then… *If she twitches, he dies. It'll take too long to break her shield.*

Penrys pulled power from the dead man's chain and poured it into the woman's body, a simple *push* like the sort used to propel blades on a ceiling fan, but much more powerful.

Faster than a gust of wind, she was hurtled upwards over her seated neighbors and backward off the platform into the stone wall behind it. She hit with an audible crack and slid downward, leaving blood smeared on the stone where her head had impacted.

That was… interesting.

There are other enemies still on the platform, within reach of the emperor.

She turned her attention to Tsek Uchang and his mother, and the emperor lifted his hand. "Their lives are mine."

"They're too dangerous," she replied, "Let me defang them for you, for now."

She was twitching with power, and could hold no more. By restoring the power for the wizards in the crowd that she'd started with, she made enough room that she was able to drain the two wizards. It left them impotent under the eyes of the emperor's guard, now freed to move again with the threat of his immediate death removed.

The surviving chained wizard, half-drained, sat unmoving and unshielded, also under guard. A look of shock was still on her face.

"I summon Tsek Anbu." The emperor was unruffled, as if nothing had happened.

Penrys watched the *samkatju* approach. *Give him his due, he's man enough to face his ruin.*

She looked a question at the emperor, and he nodded. Again she drained another wizard. Tsek Anbu seemed to barely notice.

He has other things to worry about. Penrys smiled to herself.

"Heaven has demanded justice, and justice has been served. The murderer of our Ndant guest has been found guilty, and treason has indeed been revealed."

A wave of his hand sent more guards to surround Noi Shibu, whose reaction was one of stoic resignation. A fresh column of guardsmen filed in and placed themselves in front of the borrowed Imperial Security guards that lined the solid stone extending to either side of the viewing wall with its rapt crowd standing beyond.

One of the newly-entered guards approached the emperor and whispered something in his ear. He raised his hand for silence again.

"Some of our invited guests for this ceremony were detained and have only just arrived."

Penrys turned to face the bustle of activity that was sorted out by the guard captain at the entry.

Tun Jeju trod in with Gen Jongto in his train. Behind him came another file of Imperial Security guards that joined the emperor's, along the walls, burying the suspect contingent two-deep. He reserved a group of four that accompanied him to the emperor's platform, where he bowed deeply, and then took Noi Shibu into his own custody and removed him from the platform.

The foreign wizards entered next in formal attire and walked in silence, to stop short at the trampled space where Penrys stood. They bowed to the emperor as a body, and withdrew to one side, behind Penrys, all except Najud. He busied himself with picking her knife off the ground and using it to cut off the remains of her sleeve which he wrapped tightly around her bleeding arm before taking a position behind her.

The last group in was comprised of wizards. There were some, like Wok Tori, who were properly dressed for the ceremony, and several who were in their ordinary clothing, as if they'd been swept impromptu into this confrontation. Wok Tori with Char Nojuk and Char Dazu in support, and Rin Tsugo with Kit Hachi joined

Tun Jeju across from Penrys, surrounding the chair where the surviving chained wizard sat, joining the guard there.

With relief, Penrys felt Rin Tsugo taking charge of the woman who, despite her apparently submissive demeanor, still held more power than she was comfortable seeing so close to the emperor. She wasn't sure Rin Tsugo could control her, but Kit Hachi was there and she'd noticed other chained wizards in the party. It was probably safe enough.

All this time Tsek Anbu had been standing at attention before the emperor, with his dead champion to his left, and Penrys and the other foreign wizards to his right.

The emperor waited until all the commotion had ceased.

He singled out the obvious Ndant delegate and spoke to her. "This man," he said, indicating Tsek Anbu, "set in motion a plot, one consequence of which was the death of your colleague, by that woman's hand, and the attacks that were made on you and your companions." His hand indicated the barely visible crumpled remains of the chained wizard on the ground beyond the platform.

"We will speak with you later, all of you, to provide you with the details. We of Kigali are shamed that our invited guests should meet with harm and we offer our deepest apologies."

He waved Tsek Anbu into the custody of his guards who drew him to the side where Rin Tsugo and Wok Tori stood. Tsek Uchang and his mother were escorted there as well.

"Tun Jeju," the emperor said, "my guests are usually more prompt in their attendance. Could you explain?"

Tun Jeju presented himself again and bowed. "This *posum* proffers our collective apologies, *liju*. I see that Penrys-chi must have made her own entrance, but we were compelled to use the *nanglik chok* at the cliff of Tegong Him and discovered that we were anticipated. It took some little time, and assistance, before we were able to… proceed."

"I look forward to hearing the story in more detail later. Meanwhile, we have prisoners to detain, and I do not believe we are competent to do so."

Wok Tori bowed from his position on the side. He walked out to join Tun Jeju and bowed deeply again. "The guild is eager to take up its responsibilities in suppressing criminal activities. We have brought many with us, enough to control these prisoners of yours."

Penrys cleared her throat, and the emperor turned his eyes to her. "You have something to say, *tekenga lupju?*"

She bowed. "I just wanted to mention that there are a few dozen wizards in the Tsek clan buildings that need looking at. I, um, stripped them of power to defend myself. Might not all be alive." She waved her left hand over her shoulder. "In that direction, over there."

Wok Tori buried a smile. "We will take them in, as well."

"You may house those as you see fit, Wok-chi—we will expect reports. For these my one-time relations, however, we expect your representatives to attend us here, to assist with the interrogations and imprisonment."

Wok Tori bowed once again and returned to his place.

Penrys was still standing, as she had been since the challenge, and longing for this audience to be over, but the emperor turned his attention to her again.

"If heaven's thumb was on the scales, *teken-chi*, it was necessary. They needed to be exposed, publicly. It was not intended that you assume the risk alone, but that was not my doing. The more honor to you."

She bowed deeply to him. "I apologize for my presumption. I was just not…"

"Overeager to die?" he suggested.

She smiled wanly and staggered a bit. Najud stepped forward to give her an arm.

"Your husband, I presume."

Without waiting for a response, the emperor waved over his guard captain. "Please escort our *lupjuwen* guests to rooms where they may be refreshed, and where my… champion may have her injuries seen to."

"Tun-chi," he called. "I have immediate duties to see to, but in two hours time I will expect you to attend me to perform a proper introduction to these allies of yours. Meanwhile… sort this out for me." He gestured expansively at all the people, and bodies, in his courtyard.

He rose from his low seat and walked serenely to his personal archway. Those on the platform bowed as he departed, and everyone else bowed as he approached, and held the posture until he had passed. As a turn in his path took him briefly in the direction the viewing wall, the public audience also bowed in respect until he turned away again and vanished into the interior, trailed by his guard.

CHAPTER 30

Too little and too late to be of any use.

Najud nursed uncomfortable thoughts as he waited for Penrys to return from the emperor's healers. *She had it well in hand without us.*

He was glad for the outcome, of course—Penrys alive, the emperor preserved, the Kigali *bikrajab* in charge of their own, even the chained ones, with a place in the society, if they can keep it. But he couldn't help feeling it would've come out much the same way if he'd accompanied his sister Rubti and the others on the *Biziz Rahr*, the Grand Caravan, and left her here on her own.

Whenever he'd seen her deep in some technical discussion with Vylkar, he'd felt like an ill-educated country boy on his first visit to a great city. Did she miss the resources of Ellech and the Collegium? Was he wrong to tie her to this notion of a new caravan and its base in the west?

This is pointless. It's not her I doubt, it's me. Men have married powerful women before and remained men. And they manage it by the work they do, not by envying their wives.

Movement at the doorway to the elegant room with its several low tables caught his eye. Penrys walked in alone and paused there, searching the room with a furrowed brow until she spotted him, and a broad smile broke out on her weary face.

It lifted his own spirits. *I have to believe she's made her choice, and she's happy with it. I've seen it in her—I know it's true.*

Her torn outer robe, in the Zannib style, had been replaced with a wide-sleeved floral Kigali robe that placed no constraint on her bandaged arm. The hair around her face was damp from a quick washing.

He made a place for her at the table he shared with Munraz. Servants had provided small platters of food for each of the seating areas, and the rest of the foreign wizards were gathered in two groups—Vylkar with Mpeowake, and Chosmod with his countryman Mrigasba.

Penrys sat down heavily and looked at the samplings of fried bits and sauces as if it were too much effort to reach for anything. She was white with reaction after a hard struggle—he recognized that pinched look around the eyes.

"You should eat something, it'll make you feel better," he advised.

She visibly pulled herself together. "Do you suppose this is left over from the celebration for the ceremony that never happened?" The thought made her chuckle.

Munraz said, "I'll put some samples for you on a plate, *jarghalti*. It's… tasty, most of it."

"How's the arm?" Najud asked.

"Not so bad. The slashes were impeded by my sleeve, and they're not very deep. Not saying it doesn't hurt, but it won't take that long to heal—you know how I am."

He knew. In a couple of weeks, you wouldn't be able to find the scars.

"Reckless, is how you are. You can bleed to death as well as anyone. What possessed you to try that without backup?"

She sent him an apologetic glance. "What choice did I have? And what happened to all of you, anyway?" Taking the plate that Munraz handed her, she popped a morsel in her mouth as if to evade any further justification of her own actions.

Najud skewered her with his eye to tell her he wasn't deceived, but proceeded to tell her the tale.

"So, picture us all, in our best clothes—the foreign *bikrajab*, Tun Jeju with Gen Jongto and, oh, at least thirty brown-robes, and Wok Tori and Rin Tsugo with Kit Hachi. That's a full load for one of the cages."

He heard the other conversations in the room subside as they listened. "There we were, at the base of the southwest hoist, the one you can see from our embassy, waiting for the empty cage to come down. And then our bright *nal-jarghal* Munraz here observed that it wasn't moving. The cages were stopped, suspended between top and bottom."

"I don't understand," Penrys said.

Chosmod spoke from his table, "The Tsek clan had broken into the building housing the crane and taken it over from the workers. They kicked them out and mounted a guard."

Najud watched her sort through the ramifications. "And you had no way to reach them. What about the other hoists?"

He shrugged. "The nearest one was a mile away, and you could see well enough from where we were that its cages weren't moving either. I think Tun Jeju was almost pleased to have his belief that the ambush would be today confirmed, but for once I thought he was at a loss."

Chosmod laughed. "Until Vylkar stared at him as if he were dense and said, 'surely we have plenty of wizards around to deal with this.' That didn't help the *notju*'s understanding any, but Kit Hachi understood what he meant. She bound all of us together, and we could see the minds of the men who were keeping the cages from moving, wizards all."

Vylkar smiled tightly. "That was all very well, but seeing wasn't acting. We weren't strong enough. Wok Tori sent out a call for any wizard in the area, and Rin Tsugo did the same for the chained ones. Najud helped pull them into the bond, and I guided the winnowing."

In response to Penrys's puzzled expression, Mrigasba said, "We killed the members of the Tsek clan we found there, guards and all. The workers broke back in and restored the hoists."

Najud finished the story. "So many of the volunteers wanted to come along, it took us two trips. That's why we were late."

He cleared his throat. "And we come in to find two dead chained wizards and another subdued. Time for us to hear your story."

Penrys described what happened once she decided to leave the rendezvous, and everything that followed her cry for justice.

Najud was horrified at the risks she'd taken, considering the completely predictable treachery. Characteristically, Vylkar was more inquisitive about the technical means she employed.

"You seem to have learned more about the chains, then. You always thought they were devices."

"Now I'm sure of it," she said.

"But they're not related to power-stones."

"Who says power-stones are the only way to make devices?" she countered.

Najud interrupted. "You two can debate this later. Do we ever get to go home, do you suppose?"

"To *sarq*-Zannib?" Penrys asked him.

"'I'd settle for the embassy for now."

Vylkar shook his head. "We'll have to wait for the emperor to dismiss us, and that won't happen until Tun Jeju has things under control out there."

Despite the pleasure of being clean, tended, and fed, Penrys was ready for this day to be over, and the whole week, too.

Instead she stood as respectfully as she could manage with the rest of the foreign wizards in a row before the emperor who was seated in fresh yellow robes on yet another raised platform in yet another elegant room.

Does he ever conduct an audience from ground level?

Tun Jeju was there, too, with Gen Jongto behind him, standing to their left but closer to the emperor than the foreign wizards. On their right, similarly placed, was a little group of wizards—Wok Tori for one, with his advisor Char Nojuk, Char Dazu at his uncle's shoulder, and Rin Tsugo with his second, Kit Hachi.

No other members of the emperor's family were present. The emperor occupied his dais alone, surrounded by flat cushions— seats for the missing.

For a moment, Penrys entertained a vision of the emperor having wiped the slate clean of everyone who had been on the afternoon platform, family and all.

Most of them would have been innocent. He can't have.
Can he?

At a nod from the emperor, Tun Jeju stepped forward and bowed. "Allow me to present our guests to you, *liju.*"

As he named each of the foreigners, the wizard bowed and said nothing. Mpeowake's bow was abbreviated in deference to her healing ribs.

Penrys and her companions were last. The emperor commented, "'Penrys'—not a very suitable name for a friend to Kigali. It will present difficulties for the scribes."

Tun Jeju coughed deferentially. "May I suggest a more civilized name? 'Sar Luplen' has a more comfortable feel in the mouth. And 'Sar Tobek' for her husband."

Penrys managed a straight face with difficulty. The personal name rendered as "shining magic" for her, and "lucky" for Najud, a literal translation of his Zannib name. Someone on the *notju*'s staff had given some thought to this.

The emperor appeared to consider these names for a moment, and then nodded. "Yes, that's better. If there are no objections…"

She glanced at Najud and they bowed together. In this room full of wizards they didn't dare share their private thoughts, but she had no difficulty reading his insufficiently suppressed amusement.

"My foreign minister and Tun Jeju will be visiting each of your embassies to discuss reparations and to assist in any way we can with your return home. We are shamed to have been the unwitting cause of injury to the representatives of your nations and are in the process of ensuring that the people responsible are… held accountable for their actions."

Penrys tried not to picture dungeons and chopping blocks.

"And you, Tun-chi, what is the state of affairs within Imperial Security?"

A small, satisfied smile flickered on the *notju*'s lips. "As you commanded, we have left Noi Shibu to your care, though I have men with him even now, asking him questions—politely—and taking notes. It may be that we will need to ask those questions more than once. And perhaps less politely.

"Many of my superiors and peers are undergoing questioning in our own hands, backed by your authority. I should have a preliminary report on the extent of the conspiracy for you by morning."

The emperor nodded acceptance. "And the Tsek clan and its wizards?"

"The clan buildings and compounds are thoroughly occupied by my people and by wizards appointed by the guild." He cocked his head at the guild representatives across from him. "We have found no other *tekenwen*, but there are many *lupjuwen*, besides the five we found dead when we arrived."

Penrys shrugged internally. They weren't innocent. She hadn't intended their deaths deliberately, but she wasn't going to mourn them.

"It may be," Tun Jeju continued, "that we haven't found all of them, if any were away from the compound, though we accounted for the ones that rigged the hoists. We have searches underway throughout the city, upper and lower.

"Meanwhile we're just starting to go through their commercial records and their correspondence. And, of course, the questioning. You will receive a preliminary report on what we find tomorrow."

"That is satisfactory." The emperor raised his hand and addressed them all. "We are well-pleased with this afternoon's work."

Fine. So can we go now? The excitement of seeing the exotic emperor of fabled Kigali up close had worn off about two hours ago. *More freedom to get out of here, less ceremony. Though the guild members do look pleased with the results.*

She glanced sideways at Najud and took in the gratified look on his face. *Ah, well, I can stand it a few more minutes for his sake. And Munraz's. If his eyes were any rounder, they'd roll out of his face.*

"I'm sorry to have taken so much time," Penrys told Najud, in the privacy of their rooms at the Zannib embassy.

Their reception by Talqatin and his family had been warm. And relieved. Penrys had been startled to find a new Kigalino *katsom* directing all the staff—Mir Tojit was unaccountably absent. *Part of Tun Jeju's cleanup?*

"Time from what?" Najud asked. He sat crosslegged at the low table in their work room transferring notes from wax tablets to a more permanent form in ink on papyrus sheets.

"You wanted to find merchants and goods for the caravan next year, set up some working partnerships. And look what I got you into." She squirmed, looking for a more comfortable position in the padded chair, trying to keep her throbbing arm from distracting her.

He raised his head and looked across at her. "We weren't summoned to make my caravan easier. Now I can really start that work."

He laid down his quill, and a smile flickered around the edges of his mouth. "How long do you think we've been here?"

"I don't know, I've lost track." She tried to count but so much had happened it was hard to separate the events.

Deadpan, Najud looked at her. "We crossed the river seven days ago."

Impossible. "That can't be right." *Can it?*

He took her through it, and she was convinced. While she was still shaking her head, he added, "And our position is much improved as a result." He started to tick off his fingers. "We have names—that's more important than anything else. It's the rare foreigner who is granted a Kigali name. Merchants will be willing to work with us and take a chance on a new caravan route. And there will be tangible rewards in a day or two, you'll see."

"The names matter that much?"

He shook his head at her unsophisticated understanding. "They mean we've been recognized by someone important, and there is no one more important than the emperor. The story of how we earned them will also become known. They give us standing, status. Merchants will be *eager* to partner in the hopes that the caravan will be successful because of our own good fortune. That's how they'll look at it."

He leaned toward her over the low table. "We're *bikrajab*—foreign wizards who've been granted Kigali names. I'm sure that's never happened before. That's an elevation of the status of all wizards in Kigali. And the story itself… the story will spread, of how the first thing the wizards did once the guild was licensed was to defend the emperor from his enemies, and defense of the emperor is defense of the nation.

"Oh, no, those names aren't just for us—they're for the benefit of the whole wizard community. The emperor and Tun Jeju are very subtle. No one is offended, because no one has lost anything, but their own goals are furthered. We foreigners didn't clean up the mess—their own guild did. We just… helped. That's how the tale will be told."

"But all those chained wizards, all those bodies… and the tables covered in chains." She couldn't get the images out of her mind.

Najud shrugged. "I believe Tun Jeju's account, that they made a bad mistake in how they tried to identify them. But it's Rin Tsugo who has to live with it, and if his *gewengep* can put it behind them, then… The work he's doing to help the guild will save the rest of them."

He stared at her as if she were dense. "They're going to have an established, working community of chained wizards, in a Kigali suddenly conscious of what wizards can do. A professional group, as you like to say. Would you have thought that possible, a week ago?"

Slowly, she shook her head. "Never. I can't get my head wrapped around it, now. What will Chosmod tell his superiors back in Rasesdad, after their experience with the Voice?"

"If he has any brains, and I think he does, then he'll do what I'm doing—spread the Kigali news as broadly as he can. If there's a home for chained wizards in Kigali, of all places, then why not in Rasesdad? Or *sarq*-Zannib? They don't have to become monsters, a threat to everyone else, like that poor *qahulajti* Munraz had to kill."

"I wonder if Mpeowake will see it the same way," Penrys said.

"Who can speak for Ndant? But we can only do what we can do. Speaking for myself, I'm pleased with the outcome. Now if I can only convince the *Ghuzl mar-Tawirqaj*, the assembly in *sarq*-Zannib. I don't know most of them, but Talqatin does. We'll have to work together on his official reports."

He stood up then. "That's for another day. We have our own healing to do before we can get too busy with other affairs. I don't plan on leaving the embassy until you look less... worn, and I can bow without wincing—sends the wrong message to a merchant you're trying to impress."

His grin provoked an answering one from Penrys. She pushed herself clumsily to her feet. "Sounds good to me. Maybe Munraz can make progress with Baijukti, if he's stuck in the embassy with her for a couple of days."

"Be careful what you wish for, Pen-sha," Najud said as he slid his uninjured arm around her waist and guided her into the other room, where a welcoming bed awaited.

CHAPTER 31

Penrys waited for Vylkar on the raised steps of the Imperial Security building the following afternoon. She was back in her accustomed Zannib work clothing, all of her more formal attire having been destroyed, and the small bag clutched in her fist weighed more heavily to her than the three neck chains Gen Jongto had allotted to her from the heap of the dead in the underground level could account for.

She fingered her own chain nervously, exposed to public view again. *Where is he?*

Najud was off speaking with merchants, and he'd taken Munraz with him. She'd told him she had something to discuss with her old mentor, but hadn't given him the details. He'd simply nodded and wished her a profitable afternoon, and a certain amount of guilt weighed upon her for not filling him in. *Time enough afterward once we find out a little more. If we do.*

Eventually her eye was caught by the tall, thin form coming from the direction of the Ellech embassy. She trotted down the steps to meet him, and to turn him to the northeast, to the location she had in mind.

"Did you have any difficulty getting what you needed?" he asked her as they walked through the traffic toward the Armorers' Guild.

"Chains from Gen Jongto, my own power-stones, and a few tools. Plus something to take notes with," she said. *The Zannib wax tablets have their uses.*

"Where are you taking us?" he asked.

"Remember the deserted buildings the *gewengep* escaped to, the ones Munraz described? Just around the corner of Tegong Him, on the east side, past the Armorers' compounds. I wanted privacy."

She cleared her throat. "What else can you tell me about that book's author?"

Vylkar had sent a note to the Zannib embassy that morning the contents of which had sat uneasily with her ever since.

"I'd puzzled over where you got the notion that power-stones weren't the only way to feed a device, and then I remembered Gialfinnur's book was once in the Collegium library, and wondered if you'd read it."

He eyed her as they walked, and she nodded. "I read everything I could find about devices. That one, too."

"So I expected. He's a crank, you know—no one followed up on his assertions. Part of the *yrmkenrolek* school, the crooked learning."

"Yes… He had no evidence, but the theories were interesting. They stuck in my head. All this was before I ever tried seriously experimenting with my chain, you understand. No one really wanted to work with me on that." *Easier to just ignore my inconvenient uniqueness, not a fit for the standard categories. They had more important work to spend time on. That's how the redenrolek school works, the orthodox learning—it's a wonder they ever discover something new.*

"So I took my experiments in other directions," she said.

They walked a moment in silence, the Armorers' Guild off to their left as they passed the first of its compounds.

"I was surprised to hear you knew the man," Penrys said. "And that you knew the book, to be honest."

Vylkar hesitated. "I never met him—he was gone before I got there. His older daughter Elkif shared some of my classes at the Collegium."

"Really?" Penrys smiled.

Vylkar lowered his eyebrows. "Nothing like that. She kept to herself."

He glanced at his feet as he walked. "There were three of them—the two daughters and a son. I only studied with the oldest one."

"Perhaps you don't know…" he said. "They followed in their father's footsteps after he was barred as a *raegar*, a master, and tried to develop his theories. Eventually they, too, were expelled for *yrmkenrolek*, before they finished their studies. Frankly I'm surprised you found the book—it shouldn't have been there. I saw it before it was banned."

"It wasn't in the catalogue," she said. "Someone had shoved it back behind the books on the shelves. I only saw it because I wanted to see what else was there that I might have missed, and pulled all the books out, one by one."

"You think it was hidden deliberately?" She monitored Vylkar lightly and was surprised by a brief whiff of fear.

He didn't answer directly. "Do you remember the details of what he suggested as alternatives to power-stones?"

Penrys dodged to avoid an overburdened man carrying something heavy on one shoulder and took her time about answering. "He'd looked at a lot of broken power-stones with magnifying devices and strong lights. His sketches showed complex crystal structures, more elaborate than the ones of other common materials, like salt and some of the gemstones. His theory was that power-stone internal structures were what made them work, and that a good one had more regular structures than a poor one."

She glanced briefly at Vylkar. He was walking with his head down, indifferent to the noise of the busy streets around them.

"It began with him proposing better ways of judging intact power-stones, and the best ways to cut them, and how to use them uncut, if necessary. Then he started to experiment with how crystals are formed, with various solution mixtures, as I recall. I skipped over that part—it didn't really go anywhere. I mean, the techniques were useful to know, but they all seemed to be dead ends."

Ahead of them the traffic was thinning out and, to their left, the looming Tegong Him withdrew to the north. She veered left looking for the best surface roads to approach the eastern side of it—Munraz had gotten there underground and hadn't been able to help with that when she'd asked him this morning.

"What I remember, other than his basic argument, was what he said about crystalline structures in some metals. It was entirely descriptive, rather than experimental. I hadn't realized before that metal had such structures, that they were a part of how edge sharpness was created in weapons. That's why I remembered it so well—it was my first exposure to the notion. He wrote at some length about the processes that smiths used to control their work.

"Then he stopped—it was frustrating. I slammed the book closed hard enough to raise dust, as I recall. He would have done experiments, I thought—why didn't he write about them? I didn't have access to the resources he did. I couldn't do them myself. I looked for other books by him and didn't find them."

Vylkar's face took on an uncomfortable expression. "That's because he did do the experiments. They were before my time, but

I heard about them from my teachers. He claimed successes, and wanted to show them off. Probably write another book. There was some sort of presentation for the *raegrar*, the senior teachers, and they threw him out. No one would speak of the details, and when I worked up my nerve to ask Elkif—this was years later, he was long gone—she refused to discuss it."

Around them the streets were almost deserted. "I'd been surprised that his children were allowed to study at the Collegium," he said. "It was explained to me that there'd been an argument behind closed doors about it, whether the children should be punished for the *yrmkenrolek* of their father."

"But I don't understand," Penrys said, her focus divided between finding the spot she was looking for and this glimpse into Collegium history. "Why suppress new knowledge like that? If he succeeded, if he was right, then that would open an entirely new avenue of investigation. Surely useful discoveries would come from it?"

"Such as exactly how to store power in metal, under the same sort of fine control as a power-stone?" Vylkar inquired, dryly.

Once his words penetrated, Penrys stopped in her tracks. Her fingers crept up of their own accord to her chain. "You think…" She swallowed and tried again. "You think he went on to create something like this?"

"He had followers. When he left, some of them did, too. I never heard much about them as a student, but then when I thought to ask, Elkif was gone, too."

He took a deep breath. "Some of those who govern the Collegium think that by denying someone the library and the workshops, they can prevent them from traveling unsanctioned paths. I don't agree. It's not that hard to get information—why you can even send your children looking for it if you're willing to wait."

A shiver passed down her spine at the tone of his voice.

"And it's not hard to set up your own workshops," he said. "Ellech is a big place. No, what I disagree with is banning certain avenues of study—better to learn them, too. The knowledge isn't good or bad of itself, though its uses might be. Better we build more ethical students than worry about what they're studying."

He eyed her. "Didn't you ever wonder why no one stopped you from your research and your experiments? Not everyone has that experience at the Collegium."

"I thought it was just that not everyone's interested." She could hear the chagrin in her voice at her own obliviousness. She'd gotten used to working alone, those three years, and stopped wondering at it.

"There'd been second thoughts about the case of Gialfinnur. I wasn't the only one who wondered about your chain and put the two notions together in unsubstantiated speculation. We didn't know what the chain could do—neither did you, after all—so we weren't sure it was a device. But if it was, then what connection might you have to Gialfinnur? Did he send his children in the previous generation, and now you?"

They stood unmoving in the street, and the rare passer-by gave them scarcely a glance.

"And then I disappeared," she said, slowly.

"Yes. And didn't that create a stir. I heard all the theories—you were a spy who staged a mysterious exit, you were a victim, you'd been dissolved into your constituent parts in a failed experiment, and good riddance to a thorny problem."

Penrys snorted at that last one.

Vylkar let a smile flicker on his face in response. "But we just didn't know. And then your letter came, and that was in some ways worse. Unknown wizardry, another chained wizard who was a threat. More late night arguments in the Collegium's governing council. When the invitation came from Tun Jeju, I was eager to find out more. And now it's raised more questions than it's answered."

"I feel like a sheltered child," Penrys muttered. "I wasn't aware of any of this, back in the Collegium. It's an accident that I've even heard of Gialfinnur, via that book."

She rounded on him, in the public street. "You all would be better off dropping all the pointless secrecy and just asking. Maybe we could have found out more that way, working together."

Vylkar spread his hands. "We still can."

She reared back her head. "What, in Ellech?"

"That's where Gialfinnur is still rumored to be, if he's alive, with whatever resources he gathered around him."

"But I can't just leave… it's thousands of miles." *And Naj-sha's caravan has to get launched.*

"Let's just do today's experiments and worry about that after." He gestured down the street, in an invitation for her to continue her guidance to the private spot she had in mind.

"Is this far enough away?"

Vylkar's voice betrayed his uneasiness as he watched with Penrys, almost fifty feet distant from the small patch of weed-covered ground where one of the chains had been laid. Penrys had shoved a stick in the ground through the middle, so she could mark the spot from a distance.

They stood on each side of the glassless window opening of one of the decrepit buildings that she thought was probably one of the ones Munraz had described. Only their heads were exposed.

"When Veneshjug did this, with the chain from the body of the Voice, it exploded on him."

Vylkar glanced at her across the gap of the windows. "And yet, you tell me these chains don't trigger the proximity alert that the chains on a living wizards do. What about the Voice's, after you killed him?"

"I'm afraid I was distracted by my injuries. Don't know when it stopped hurting, exactly."

She swallowed and put that behind her. "Can you feel the chain?" She waved her hand out the window gap.

"Not that one, not the ones in your bag, and not your own," he told her.

"Want to see what it looks like to me?"

He nodded, expressionlessly, and she let him in through her shield. Her own chain felt as much a part of her as her heart or liver, and like an organ she could feel how full it was.

The external masterless chains were different. Each had a… flavor. Not exactly a personality—she wasn't sure if she could have recognized their original wearers if she'd met them while they lived—but they were easy to tell apart. The chains had no intelligence, but she almost felt like apologizing to the one she might end up destroying.

You know how it feels when someone else manipulates a power-stone.
She felt his assent.
This is similar. I'll try to move the stick with it.

Her first attempt did nothing, and then it occurred to her that perhaps it had no power left—drained by its wearer's struggles?

She poured some power into it from her own chain while Vylkar watched, and tried again. The stick moved.

"So, a chain in isolation can hold power, and can *move* an object as a raw power-stone might," Vylkar said.

"We already knew this—I used Jut Sejo's chain after he was dead to *move* the so-called judge away from the emperor."

"Then how did that Rasesni mage manage to destroy the chain and himself, the way you described it?"

Penrys said, tentatively, "Think you could try to do what I just did?"

He blinked, then looked toward the distant stick. He made no offer to share his mind with Penrys while he worked.

They saw the light before they heard the crack, and ducked behind the wooden walls, just before a few thuds announced the arrival of fragments.

"Yes, it was a lot like that," Penrys said, dryly. "So, I don't think unchained wizards should try this."

"Better warn Tun Jeju," Vylkar said.

Penrys had a vivid image of the entire Imperial Security building collapsing lopsidedly into a pit after that collection of chains in its lower level was set off. "Um, yes. Good advice."

She opened one of Najud's wax tablets and used the stylus to make a couple of notes before closing it again.

"That was the first experiment," she said. "The next one will be expensive."

She ushered her mentor out of the ruin of a building and spent a few minutes examining the wall. With her knife, she pried several single links out and gave two of them to Vylkar. "Something to remember me by, *bilappa*."

"Are they equally explosive?" he asked.

"Now that's a good question. Let's find out."

She carried a single link to the area where the first chain had been placed and hunted up another stick. Then she rejoined Vylkar at the window gap inside the building.

Still can't feel it?

Vylkar shook his head.

Neither can I. She tried to invoke it like a power-stone, but there was nothing to grasp with her mind.

"Looks like destroying the chain breaks some key part of its functional integrity. I guess the single links are safe enough."

She trotted back to the spot with her carry bag. She picked up the link and placed another intact chain on the ground. This time she took a small handful of power-stones and covered the long sides of a single link with them. Then she picked everything else up and took it with her, stooping to scoop up another single link and one double that caught her eye from the ground on her way back.

"I know that you can use loose power-stones to melt metal," she told Vylkar. "I used that to cut through shackles in Neshilik."

"That destroys the power-stones," Vylkar said, disapprovingly.

"Yes, yes, I know. But I want to find out what happens." She grinned. "I already know I can't cut the metal with a chisel, or even make a mark, so something unusual is holding them together. These chains were forged somehow, though, so heat must have been used to shape them. Mundane heat? Couldn't test my own neck that way, and haven't had time to do the experiment with the fragment I had."

"You're just going to use the power-stones, not the chain itself?"

Penrys nodded. "Here goes."

She invoked the power-stones, and felt it the moment they broke the integrity of the chain. This time, instead of an explosion, there was a flare of white-hot light, and they felt the heat even at the distance as if a torch were inches from their faces.

Do I smell smoke? She dashed outside as it subsided and examined the building. There were scorch marks, but nothing seemed to have caught. The grass surrounding the fire burned, but between them they were able to stamp it out.

When they approached, they found the power-stones destroyed, but not the chain. The one link was melted into two half-links, and the chain itself exhibited no blackening, shining up from the charred ground.

When Penrys checked, the chain was no longer active, in her mind.

"We killed this one," she told Vylkar. "But I don't think I'll be using this method to remove my own. It wasn't this hot when I melted conventional chains—the chain must have fed its own power into it."

"And would you want to rid yourself of the chain, now, given what you've learned?" he asked her.

I don't know anymore. She left the question unanswered.

CHAPTER 32

"Good news," Najud told Penrys as he sauntered into their quarters at the embassy just in time to clean up for dinner with Talqatin and his family. His arms were filled with bundles.

"Hmm?" Penrys was sitting crosslegged on their bed, playing with what was left of the chains from her afternoon's experiment.

"Yes. Most of the merchants I talked to have heard of *kassa*, but few have tasted it. I brewed samples at seven businesses—may I never see it again. Well, at least for several hours. They want it, more to the point."

"But your caravan won't be trading with them," she said.

"Not directly, but we can supply the *Biziz Rahr* which does. That's a good thing. And if they like it, here in Yenit Ping, they'll like it all the more in Neshilik."

She laid the intact chain out on the bed clothes, and the long length of the one that she'd managed to cut apart, and then the little heap of single and double links, and the two halves of the melted link. She ran the chains and fragments through her hands, absently, and then looked up when she noticed he'd stopped talking.

"What've you got there?" he asked.

After a deep breath, she told him about her afternoon with Vylkar, about Gialfinnur and his book, and about the experiments they'd performed.

He dropped his parcels on the floor near the chair and sat down. "What're you thinking?"

Penrys bestirred herself to concentrate on him. "I'm thinking it's good news that your planned caravan goods look like they'll be successful."

He waved his hand in the air dismissively. "No, what are you *really* thinking?"

She held her tongue. She couldn't ask it of him.

With a snort under his breath, he leaned back. "You want to go to Ellech, don't you? See if there's any truth to Vylkar's suggestion."

"It can wait," she whispered.

"Why should it?" He shook his head at her. "Listen to me, Pensha. We have a full year before the first caravan can start from the west of *sarq*-Zannib. Most of what needs to happen can be done by my agents ahead of time."

"It's much too far away," she said.

He freed up both his hands to gesture. "Let me explain the distances to you. From here to the harbor at Kwattu on the northeast coast is about fifty-sixty days, via the Kwatka Kote lowlands. I've always wanted to see that. Then six to eight weeks by ship to Stokemmi in Ellech. Say you spend a month or two there. That's six months, now. Then coming back all the way to the caravan base in the west, that's another five months, at worst."

He grinned at her. "See? Plenty of time. Besides, if we're delayed returning and late getting the caravan started, it's not like we have any precedent we need to follow. Or competition, yet. We're only planning a single caravan per year. For now, anyway."

She stared at him.

"Seriously, once the caravan gets going, it will be hard to spend many months away. This may be our only chance for who knows how long to take a long trip like this." He lowered his voice confidingly. "And, besides, I've always wanted to see the Collegium. If we're going to supply our caravan base with a school—found a real city—we'll need books and contacts. Maybe even visiting teachers."

"What about Munraz?" she asked.

"If we can pry him away from Baijukti long enough, we'll ask him. I think he'll want to come, but it'll be a long time of travel for such a young man."

Penrys reflected to herself that Najud was only eight years older than his apprentice and rolled her eyes.

"If he doesn't, we'll send him up the route of the Biziz Rahr with fast horses to rejoin Rubti, Ilzay, and Haraq. It's been well under two weeks—shouldn't be hard to catch them, the rate they travel and the stops they have to make. But it would mean an interruption to his apprenticeship. His choice, but he should come along, don't you think?"

"Travel broadens the mind," Penrys commented dryly.

"When was Vylkar planning to leave?"

"He thought to travel as far as Kwattu with Mpeowake, before she takes a different ship back to Ndant. Maybe a week from now, or a little longer?"

Najud rubbed his face. "That should work, but we'll be busy. Clothing, trade goods for Ellech, supplies, more horses… and lots and lots of letters, many duplicates to different places to make sure that at least one reaches the intended target. I wonder if Talqatin has a scribe I could borrow for some of that?"

"How can we afford this?" she asked.

He gaped at her. "Pen-sha, for the masters of a caravan that doesn't yet exist, we're quite prosperous. We still have almost all the gold from Neshilik, herds in quantity waiting for us, and rather large tokens of gratitude from the emperor. More importantly, we're getting invaluable connections to the merchants in Yenit Ping, with the emperor's blessing, friends in Rasesdad—strange as it still sounds to say that—by way of Chosmod and Mrigasba, and soon a useful acquaintanceship in Ellech."

"And I still have a substantial weight of power-stones," Penrys said, getting into the spirit of the thing. "And those are highly valued in Ellech."

"There, you see?"

"You sure you want to do this?" she said.

"What, travel around a quarter of the world to places I've never been but always wanted to see?" Najud laughed at her. "I think I'll manage to enjoy it."

A slow smile spread on Penrys's face.

"I wonder how many chains I can get out of Tun Jeju, before we leave?"

GUIDE TO NAMES & PRONUNCIATIONS

PRINCIPAL CHARACTERS & PLACE NAMES & TERMS

PEOPLE - ELLECH

Bildaer (BILL-dair)
One of the companion wizards who accompanies Vylkar to Yenit Ping.
Elkif (EHL-kiff)
The daughter of Gialfinnur, who carries on her father's studies.
Gialfinnur (GYAHL-fin-noor)
An old scholar who wrote a book on devices and was banned for yrmkenrolek, crooked learning.
Innurrys (IN-noor-rewss)
One of the companion wizards who accompanies Vylkar to Yenit Ping.
Penrys (Ryssi) (PEHN-rewss)
The chained adept. Wizard trained at the Collegium of Wizards.
Preinnur (PRAYN-noor)
The Ellech ambassador to Yenit Ping.
Vylkar (VIEWL-kar)
Senior wizard at the Collegium of Wizards. Patron of Penrys.

PEOPLE - KIGALI

Am Limzu (AHM LIHM-zoo)
A chained wizard hiding in Yenit Ping.
Chaik (CHYKE)
An ancient imperial dynasty, ruling circa seventeen hundred years ago.
Char Dachi (CHAR DAH-chee)
Adopted daughter of Char Nojuk. A hidden wizard.

Char Dami (CHAR DAH-mee)
Daughter of Char Nojuk. A hidden wizard.
Char Danau (CHAR DAH-now)
Adopted daughter of Char Nojuk. A hidden wizard.
Char Dazu (CHAR DAH-zoo)
Nephew of Char Nojuk. A hidden wizard.
Char Nojuk (CHAR NOH-juk)
Patriarch of the Char family, which specializes in medicines. A hidden wizard.
Char Pangfa (CHAR PAHNG-fah)
Granddaughter of Char Nojuk. A hidden wizard.
Dar Datsu (DAR DAH-tsoo)
A chained wizard hiding in Yenit Ping. He seems to be ethnically related to Penrys.
Gen Jongto (GHEN JONG-toh)
A man on Tun Jeju's staff.
Goi Ofa (GOY OH-fah)
A chained wizard held prisoner in Yenit Ping.
Jing Tajip (JING TA-jip)
A chained wizard hiding in Yenit Ping, working as a groom.
Jut Sejo (JOOT SEH-joh)
A chained wizard working for the Tsek clan.
Ki Sechat (KIH SHE-chaht)
The personal name of the Emperor of Kigali.
Kit Hachi (KIT HAH-chee)
A chained wizard hiding in Yenit Ping.
Lai Tsumai (LIE TSOO-mye)
A chained wizard held prisoner in Yenit Ping. She seems to be of Rasesni origin.
Lir Pako (LEER PAHK-oh)
A chained wizard held prisoner in Yenit Ping. He seems to be of Ndant origin.
Lembonka Tenstsu Gom (LEM-bon-kah TOON-tso GOM) - Department of Industry
The heavenly department of Lembonka Tentsu Gom. One of its sub-departments is Toilekja Dugom, to which wizards are assigned.
Lemju (LEHM-joo) - Heaven's Lord
The supreme deity of Kigali.

Mir Tojit (MIR TOH-jit)
The majordomo for the Zannib ambassador, in charge of his Kigali staff. Also a member of Imperial Security.

Nip Jochat (NIP JOH-chaht)
An officer of Imperial Security in Tengwa Tep.

Noi Shibu (NOY SHEE-boo)
The head of Imperial Security for Yenit Ping.

Paik Kanau (PIKE KAH-now)
A chained wizard hiding in Yenit Ping.

Rin Tsugo (RIN TSOO-goh)
The leader of the hidden brotherhood of chained wizards in Yenit Ping.

Sar Luplen (SAR LOOP-len) – Shining Magic
The Kigali name given to Penrys.

Sar Tobek (SAR TOH-bek) – Fortunate, Lucky
The Kigali name given to Najud.

Shwa Uchi (SHWAH OO-chee)
A hidden wizard.

Sek Seto (SEHK SEH-toh)
A chained wizard hiding in Yenit Ping.

Suimiju (SOOEY-mee-joo) - Lord of the Mind's Eye
The deity responsible for the heavenly sub-department Toilekja Dugom, the patron of craftsmen with a high degree of expertise, such as pharmacists, chemists, engineers, and wizards.

Toilekja Dugom (toy-LEK-jah DOO-gom) - Subdepartment of Useful Knowledge
The heavenly sub-department of Lembonka Tentsu Gom. Its patron deity is Suimiju.

Tse Lorping (TSEH LOR-ping)
A chained wizard held prisoner in Yenit Ping.

Tsek Anbu (TSEK AHN-boo)
A wizard, the patriarch of the Tsek family, specialists in military supplies.

Tsek Okim (TSEK OH-kim)
A wizard, the cousin of Tsek Anbu, and mother of the imperial bastard Tsek Uchang.

Tsek Uchang (TSEK OO-chahng)
A wizard, the son of Tsek Okim and the emperor. A recognized imperial bastard.

Tun Jeju (TOON JEH-joo)
The *notju*, intelligence master, and imperial representative for Chang Zenju's expedition.
Wok Limdo (WOK LIM-doh)
A servant in the Armorers' Guild.
Wok Lorchit (WOK LOR-chit)
A servant in the Armorers' Guild.
Wok Panwit (WOK PAHN-wit)
An officer in the Armorers' Guild.
Wok Sojit (WOK SOH-jit)
An officer in the Armorers' Guild.
Wok Tomai (WOK TOH-mye)
The sister of Wok Tori, second in command of the Armorers' Guild.
Wok Tori (WOK TOH-ree)
The head of the Armorers' Guild, brother of Wok Tori.
Zep Pangwit (ZEP PAHNG-wit)
A guide detached from the office of Imperial Security.

PEOPLE - NDANT

Ijumo (ee-JOO-moh) - Shark Tooth
The *munduo*, or West Wind, of the Ndant wizard delegation.
Kalavo (kah-LAH-voh)
The nephew of Mpeowake, missing and apparently converted into a chained wizard.
Mpeowake (m-peh-oh-WAH-keh) - Sparkling Foam
The leader of a group of wizards, very senior in her temple.
Pume Chowe (POO-meh CHOH-weh) - Black Cloud
The storm goddess who is the patroness of all wizards.
Toawe (toh-AH-weh) - Coral
The *shimawe*, or East Wind, of the Ndant wizard delegation.

PEOPLE - RASESNI

Chosmod (Modo) (CHOHS-mode)
A senior mage in the intelligence services of Rasesdad.
Mrigasba (Mrigi) (m-RIG-as-bah)
A senior mage in the intelligence services of Rasesdad.

Surdo (SOOR-doh) - The Voice

 The chained wizard-tyrant who wreaked havoc in Rasesdad. The name was given by the Rasesni — his actual name was unknown.

The Voice

 See "Surdo."

Veneshjug (Vejug) (VEH-nesh-joog, VEH-joog)

 Priest and senior member of the Mage Council exiled from Dzongphan. His god is Venesh.

Vladzan (Vlada) (VLAHD-zahn)

 Device Master (*Grakkedo*) at the Temple School in Kunchik and member of the Mage Council exiled from Dzongphan.

PEOPLE - ZANNIB

Baijukti (bye-JOOK-tee)

 The daughter of the ambassador of *sarq*-Zannib in Yenit Ping.

Haraq (hah-RAHK)

 A survivor of the Kurighdunaq disaster, brother of Luram.

Ilzay (eel-ZYE)

 A friend of Jirkat.

Kurighdunaq (koo-REEG-doo-NAHK) - World-bow (Rainbow)

 A clan in northwestern central *sarq*-Zannib, part of the Undullah tribe.

Munraz (moon-RAHZ)

 An apprentice wizard, nephew of Jiqlaraz, from clan Rashaban, tribe Dhajtawhaz.

Najud (nah-JOOD) - Lucky, Fortunate

 A master wizard of the Zamjilah clan, in the Shubzah tribe.

Nazghib (nahz-GEEB)

 A tribe in eastern *sarq*-Zannib. One of its clans is Umaqlud.

Qulsharma (kool-SHAR-mah)

 The wife of the ambassador of *sarq*-Zannib in Yenit Ping.

Rashaban (rah-shah-BAHN). Three Hills

 A clan in northwestern central *sarq*-Zannib, part of the Dhajtawhaz tribe.

Rima (REE-mah)

 A merchant's widow, from the Umzabul clan.

Rubti (ROOB-tee)

 Najud's second sister.

Shaldaj (shall-DAHJ)
The father of Talqatin, ambassador of *sarq*-Zannib in Yenit Ping.
Talqatin (tahl-kah-TEEN)
The ambassador of *sarq*-Zannib in Yenit Ping, of clan Umaqlud, tribe Nazghib.
Umaqlud (oo-mahk-LOOD)
A clan in eastern *sarq*-Zannib, part of tribe Nazghib.
Umzakhilin (oom-zah-khee-LEEN)
The *zarawinnaj*, migration leader, of the Kurighdunaq clan.
Zamjilah (zahm-jee-LAH) - Eye of Heaven
Najud's clan, part of the Shubzah tribe.

PLACES - ELLECH

Asuthgrata (AH-sooth-grah-tah) - High Region
Upland district of mixed grazing and woodlands, famed for its hunting.
Drosenrolkentham (DROH-sen-rohl-ken-thahm) - Wizard-learning-place
The Collegium of Wizards in Tavnastok.
Dunnarfeol (DOON-nar-fayol) - Winter's House
The highest mountains in the world, forming the north border of Ellech.
Ellech (ELL-ekh)
A northern nation tucked along the southern margin of the Dunnarfeol mountains, with precipitous timber- and grass-covered slopes running down to a deep-water port. Famed for industry and research, with a well-armed merchant navy to seek out new markets.
Lodentaf Gaer (LOH-den-tahf (Gair)) - Ice-Wealth River
The river which runs from the Dunnarfeol Mountains past Tavnastok to the capitol harbor city Stokemmi.
Nachompolek (Lappyri) (NAH-khom-poh-lek LAHP-pew-ree)
The harbor, where the Lodentaf and Baegyl rivers meet the sea.
Stokemmi (STOH-kem-mee) - Mother of Cities
The capitol city, on the east bank of the Lodentaf Gaer where it meets the Nachompolek harbor.

Tavnastok (TAV-nah-stok) - City of Wealth
Inland city based on river commerce and industry, in the Asuthgrata region.

PLACES - KIGALI

Chalen Tep (CHAH-len TEHP) - Red Light Town
One of the criminal districts in Yenit Ping, known mostly for gambling and prostitution.

Chankau Tep (CHAHN-cow TEP) - Thousand Smokes Town
The "industrial" district of Yenit Ping, east of Mentsek Tep, along the Junkawa. Foundries and manufacturing are the primary industries. It has its own harbor.

Dimtok Himbun (TEH-gohng HIM) - Ironstone Range
A range of hills, easy of access except for their southern extent which ends in Tegong Him, the cliffs of which dominate Yenit Ping and support the Imperial district of Juhim Tep. An important local source of iron and other minerals for Kigali, exceeded in quality only by the disputed Galat region.

Gonglik (GOHNG-lick) - The Steps
The largest city in the Neshilik region, named for the extensive stretch of rapids and waterfalls on the upper reach of the Seguchi River which inhibit navigation. It lies south of the river and extends to the north at Kunchik, with the first permanent bridge over the Seguchi River, 1800 miles from its mouth.

Jonggep (JONG-ghep) - The Meeting of Waters
The largest inland city, at the junction of the two main branches of the Junkawa River: The Seguchi and the Neshikame.

Juhim Tep (JOO-him TEP)
The "upper town" district of Yenit Ping on the front tip of Tegong Him. The Imperial Palace and elite temples, associated bureaucratic offices, and the supporting servant and trade districts. Some of the military barracks are inside the northern defensive walls that stretch from the western edge of Tegong Him to the eastern edge, but there larger military encampments to the north of the walls, as well as extensive suburbs and a branching network of lesser settlements that reach all the way out to the first of the mines.

Junkawa (joon-KAH-wah) - The Mother of Rivers
The longest river in the world, with two main branches: The Seguchi and the Neshikame. It finds its outlet at Pingmen below the walls of Penit Ying.

Junlin Tep (JOON-lin TEP)
The "garden" district of Yenit Ping, west of Mentsek Tep, along the Junkawa. Local agriculture for the city and livestock breeding, especially for the military, is the primary activity. It has its own harbor.

Jusham Jan (JOO-shahm jahn) - The Low Pass
Caravan route between *sarq*-Zannib and central Kigali, west of Jonggep, the Meeting of Waters.

Kigali (kih-GAH-lee) - Land of the Ki Dynasty
Set in the mid-latitudes of the southern continent, Kigali is a wealthy and hard-working nation with a history of political stability and expansion. The Junkawa River and its hundreds of tributaries provide internal communications, and well-placed ports support its strong mercantile interests.

Kwatka Kote (KWAHT-kah KOH-teh)
The eastern rift valley running from northeast Gentu Bay to southeast Pingmen harbor.

Kwattu (KWAHT-too)
The busiest port city, in the northeast on Gentu Bay at the mouth of the Kwatna River in the eastern Kwatka Kote lowlands.

Mentsek Tep (MEN-tsek TEP)
The "lower town" district of Yenit Ping that includes the primary harbor on the Junkawa, the civic buildings and temples, and the trading and residential districts between the harbor and Tegong Point.

Neshilik (neh-SHEE-lik)
The western district of Kigali, surrounded by mountains and traversed by the Seguchi River. Often disputed with Rasesdad.

Nitsep Tep (NIT-sep TEP)
A border and market town between Kigali and *sarq*-Zannib.

Pingmen Hanjong (PING-men HAHN-jong) - City View
The bay or series of harbors carved out by the Junkawa River.

Tegong Him (TEH-gohng HIM)
The final prominence of the low Dimtok Himbun range, whose terminating cliffs rise hundreds of feet above Nitsep Tep, the

"lower town" of Yenit Ping. Juhim Tep, the "upper town" of Yenit Ping occupies the top front of the point where the cliffs are steep.

Tengwa Tep (TEN-gwa TEP)
The small city across the Junkawa from Yenit Ping. It is the most important trading town for the Grand Caravan of the *sarq*-Zannib.

Yenit Ping (YEH-nit ping) - Endless City
Capital city, on both sides of the Junkawa River, overlooking Pingmen harbor.

PLACES - NDANT

Shokona Hanjong (SHOH-koh-nah]
The main bay in eastern Ndant.

PLACES - RASESNI

Dzongphan (DZONG-fan) - Temple Quarter
The capital city, which includes the mother temples of all the gods, in Nagthari.

Mratsanag (m-RAHT-suh-nahg) - The Wild Ram's Horns
The second tallest mountain range in the world.

PLACES - ZANNIB

Qawrash im-Dhal (cow-RAHSH eem-THAHL) - Well in the Steppe
The city in the eastern region from which the largest caravan to eastern Kigali originates.

(Mard) Ussha (mahrd OOSH-shah)
Capital city, founded by Kigali, on Pago Bay on the east coast near the Kigali border, at the mouth of the Harin River. Also known as Zudiqazd mar-Sarq, the Winter Camp of the Nation.

(Hilj) Wandat (heelj wahn-DAHT) - Enclosed Sea
Very large almost landlocked sea in the far west, bordered also by Rasesdad.

Sarq-Zannib (SAHRK-zahn-NEEB)
The Zannib nation. It occupies the bottom of the southern hemisphere and is neighbored on the north by both Rasesdad

and Kigali. The western third concentrates on fishing and small farm agriculture, while the remainder is steppe and grasslands.
Zudiqazd mar-Sarq (zoo-dee-KAHZD mar-SAHRK) - Winter Camp of the nation
See Mard Ussha.

WORDS & PHRASES - ELLECH

Bendu (BEN-doo) - Device
A device for performing *raunarys*, usually made of wood.
Beolrys (BAYOL-rewss) - Mind-skill
The wizardly skill of mental-magic, things of the mind such as mind-speech.
Bilappa (BILL-ap-pa) - Father of learning
Mentor, patron.
Drepfarar (DREP-fahr-ar) - Lost souls
Spirits, haunts, ghosts.
Ellechen guma (ELL-ekh-en GOO-mah) - Ellechen language
The language of Ellech.
Emkenrys (EHM-ken-rewss) - Moving
One of the aspects of *Raunarys*.
Felkenrys (FEHL-ken-rewss) - Binding
One of the aspects of *Raunarys*.
Hakkengenni (HAHK-kehn-gen-nee) - One who knows
An archaic term for a wizard with unusual strength in mind-skill and thing-skill both. Usually translated as "Adept."
Raegar, Raegrar (RA-gar, -grar) - Master, Masters
A senior scholar in the teaching/research system, often a teacher of others.
Raunarys (ROW-na-rewss) - Thing-skill
The wizardly skill of physical-magic, things of the real world, such as moving, binding, and destroying.
Redenrolek (REH-den-roh-lek) - Straight learning
Teachings that are considered orthodox or correct.
Rysefeol (REW-seh-fayol) - Device framework
A composite framework, usually made of wood, a level of complexity greater than a *bendu*.
Sennevi (SEHN-neh-vee)
"It is done." The customary final phrase that marks the end of a traditional tale, often accompanied by the slash of a hand.

Strekenrys (STRECK-en-rewss) - Destroying
One of the aspects of *Raunarys*.
Thennur holi! (THEH-noor HOH-lee) - Wasted sweat!
An exasperated curse.
Yrmkenrolek (EWERM-ken-roh-lek) - Crooked learning
Teachings that are considered corrupt or immoral, sometimes
on insufficient grounds.
Yrmur! (EWER-moor) - Broken, Wrong!
A curse.

WORDS & PHRASES - KIGALI

Binochi(-wen) (bee-NOH-chee) - Sir, Sirs
An honorific.
Chirmurno (cheer-MOOR-noh) - Fish catcher
The nickname for the person in charge of new members of an
organization or family, a recruit master.
Duimur(-wen) (DOOY-moor(-wen)) - Fish in a school (singular,
plural)
A nickname for ordinary civilians.
Gap kwosum (GAHP KWOH-soom) - Taking the yellow thread
The legitimization of imperial bastards, giving the same
standing as a true heir. It joins them to the imperial genealogy,
the *sumkui*, the thread book. Clothing all in yellow is the
prerogative of the emperor and his legitimate family.
Recognized bastards dress in amber.
Gepten (GHEP-tehn) - Market Fair
A seasonal market place serviced by traveling traders.
Gewengep (Hoikensuika Gewengep) (hoy-ken-SOOEY-kah
geh-WEN-ghep) - Brotherhood of the Harmonious Mind
Any voluntary association of people united by a common cause,
often sharing a meeting or dwelling place.
Gwatenno (gwah-TEN-noh) - Traveling traders
Merchants who make their living on the *gepten* circuit.
Katsom (KAHT-som) - Head servant
The majordomo or other top servant in a household.
Kigalino (kih-GAH-lee-noh) - A Kigali person
An individual citizen of Kigali.
Kigaliwen (kih-GAH-lee-wehn) - Kigali people
A group of Kigali people, or the collective citizens of Kigali.

Kigali yat (kih-GAH-lee-yaht) - Kigali speech
  The language spoken in Kigali.
Lenju ka Yukmat (LEN-joo kah YOOK-mat) - Festival of Lights
  A seasonal celebration which includes a play about the victory
  of good over evil and a fireworks display.
Leipum (LAY-poom) - Silk petal (branch)
  An artificial version of the branch-in-leaf that is used to
  symbolize a truce.
Liju (LEE-joo) - Country Master, Emperor
  The title of the Emperor of Kigali.
Likatchok (lee-KAHT-chok) - Face of the nation (to others)
  Ambassador.
Lirshik (LEER-shik) - The sword decides
  A formal trial by combat.
Lup (LOOP) - Magic
  Magic, the art of wizards..
Lupchit (LOOP-chit) - Magic blood
  A reference to the bloodline that produces wizards.
Lupju(-wen) (LOOP-joo(-wen)) - Magic master(s)
  The term for wizards.
Minochi(-wen) (mee-NOH-chee(-wen)) - Madam, Ladies
  An honorific.
Nanglik chok, nangchok (NAHNG-leek CHOHK) - Going-up wagon
  The term for the cages that are hoisted up and down the cliff of
  Tegong Him. There are two on each connected loop, for weight
  balance.
Notju (NOTE-joo) - Master of secrets
  A military title roughly equivalent to Intelligence Master.
  Usually this is an imperial representative.
Posom (POH-som)
  A deprecatory reference to self when addressing someone of
  higher status — "your servant", "your slave."
Samkatju (sahm-KAHT-joo) - Family master
  The patriarch of a family, its leader.
Samke (SAHM-keh) - Kin home
  A multi-generation compound for a large family. In some
  regions, it is combined with buildings that are part of the family
  business.

Shaibo(-wen) (SHY-boh(-wen)) - Brown clothing (singular, plural)
Brown-robe, a nickname for the members of Imperial Security.

Sumkui (SOOM-kooey) - Thread book
A document, typically in scroll form, that records the genealogy for a family over many generations.

Tekenga Lupju(-wen) (LOOP-joo(-wen)) - Chained Magic master(s)
The term for chained wizards. Nickname *Teken*.

Togebi (toh-GEH-bee) - Big brother
Also used as a nickname for a captain within an organization, as in togebi-chi.

Wanbum (WAHN-boom)
The small gong that hangs on the wall next to a door, intended to be struck with a knuckle.

Wo (WOH) - Father
Also used as a nickname for the leader of an organization, as in wo-chi.

Yankat, Yankatmi (YAHN-kaht, yahn-KAHT-mee) - Headman, -woman
The person who leads a village.

WORDS & PHRASES - NDANT

Mbaewe (m-ba-EH-weh)
The leader of a group of wizards.

Munduo (mun-DOO-oh) - West Wind
The god of the indigenous people of Ndant, used metaphorically as the title of a second-in-command, typically paired with a *shimawe*.

Ndano (n-DAH-noh)
A Ndant man.

Ndanum (n-DAH-noom)
The Ndant people.

Shimawe (shih-MAH-weh) - East Wind
The goddess of the invaders who came from the eastern sea and settled Ndant, used metaphorically as the title of a second-in-command, typically paired with a *munduo*.

WORDS & PHRASES - RASESNI

Brudigdo (BROO-dig-doh) - Mage
  The standard title for a male wizard (mage).
Brudigna (BROO-dig-nah) - Mage
  The standard title for a female wizard (mage).
Sedchabke (SEHD-chahb-keh) - Mind stop
  A drug that both paralyzes the body and inhibits all use of
  magic. A tool of discipline for errant mages.

WORDS & PHRASES - ZANNIB

Anah im-ghabr (ah-NAH im-GAHB-er) - Flower of the head
  The turban, common but not universal headgear among the
  Zannib.
Baijuk (bye-JOOK)
  Mead, a drink fermented from honey.
Bikraj, Bikrajti (beek-RAHJ(-tee)) - Wizard, wizardress
  The common title for a wizard.
Biziz (bee-ZEEZ)
  A merchant caravan.
Biziz Rahr (bee-ZEEZ RAH-er) - Big caravan
  The Grand Caravan that runs three seasons of the year from
  Qawrash im-Dhal through eastern Kigali and *sarq*-Zannib.
Bunnas (boon-NAHSS)
  A low wild shrub native to *sarq*-Zannib whose berries are
  collected and dried as part of the *taridiqa*, the annual migration.
  The infusion of ground, dried, berries in hot water is high in
  caffeine. Popular throughout the southern countries and a
  significant trade item for *sarq*-Zannib.
Dirum (dee-ROOM) - Herd-mistress
  The senior woman responsible for all the clan's herds while on
  taridiqa.
Dirum-malb (dee-ROOM-mahlb) - Apprentice to the Herd-
mistress
  A younger woman learning the position of *dirum*.
Ghuzl mar-Tawirqaj (GOOZ-el mar tah-weer-KAHJ) - Circle of
Speakers
  The national tribal assembly in Ussha.

Jarghal, Jarghalti (jar-GAHL(-tee))
The title for a master wizard (wizardress).
Kassa (KAHS-sah)
A bushy plant grown on mountain slopes, the leaves of which are used, dried, for a stimulating infusion.
Kazr, Kazrab (KAH-zer, kahz-RAHB) - Yurt, Yurts
A structure similar to a yurt, made of a wooden framework encased in felt.
Khash, Kashab (KHASH, khash-AHB) - Sword, Swords
The curved sword that is the typical weapon of the nomadic Zannib.
Khijr-Zannib (KHEE-jer zahn-NEEB) - The grasslands of *sarq*-Zannib
The steppe terrain that dominates the northern territories of *sarq*-Zannib.
Khimar (khee-MAR) - Honey
Honey is a special substance, favored by the *lud* for its unusual locations and properties, and for its use in fermenting mead.
Lij, Lijti (LEEJ, LEEJ-tee) - Sir, Lady
A term of respect. *Lij-mar-lij* — Master of masters. Derived from Kigali *li* and *ju* — Country-king.
Lud (LOOD)
Numinous objects or locations, often referred to as "little gods."
Nal-Jarghal (nahl-jar-GHAHL)
The title for an apprentice wizard.
Nurti, Nurtin (NOOR-tee, noor-TEEN)
Younger sister, youngest sister.
Qahulaj (kah-hoo-LAHJ) - Taboo
Wizard-tyrant, one who does taboo things.
Sarq-Zannib (SAHRK-zahn-NEEB)
The Zannib nation.
Tawirqaj (tah-weer-KAHJ) - One who speaks for others
Representative, ambassador.
Tigha (TEE-gah)
Older brother.
Wirqiqa-Zannib (weer-KEE-kah-zahn-NEEB)
The Zannib language.

Zamjilah (zahm-jee-LAH) - Eye of heaven
The central crown at the top of the *kazr* that holds the rafters together and lets the smoke escape.
Zan (ZAHN)
An individual member of the Zannib nation.
Zannib-hubr (zahn-NEEB HOOB-er) - Free or Swift Zannib
The Zannib who continue a nomadic tradition of annual migration.
Zannib-taghr (zahn-NEEB TAHG-er) - Slow Zannib
The Zannib who live a settled life.
Zarawinnaj (zah-rah-wee-NAHJ) - One who rides in front
The leader of the *taridiqa*.
Zudiqazd (zoo-dee-KAHZD)
The winter camp, from which the *taridiqa* begins and ends. It houses those who do not go on the migration.

IF YOU LIKE THIS BOOK…

MORE GOODIES

You can find **more information** and **maps** at:
KarenMyersAuthor.com/link-broken-devices/.

Continue reading for an **excerpt** of the first chapter of **On a Crooked Track**, the next book in **The Chained Adept** series, and find out more about it here:
KarenMyersAuthor.com/link-on-a-crooked-track/.

Sign up for the **newsletter** to stay informed of new and upcoming releases and to get occasional bonuses, like free short stories:
KarenMyersAuthor.com/signup.

Let other readers know what you think by leaving them a review where you bought the book.

CONTACTING THE AUTHOR

You can contact Karen Myers at KarenMyersAuthor.com or by email at KarenMyers@KarenMyersAuthor.com. You can also follow her on Facebook: Facebook.com/KarenMyersAuthor.

ALSO BY KAREN MYERS

The Hounds of Annwn

To Carry the Horn
The Ways of Winter
King of the May
Bound into the Blood

Story Collections
Tales of Annwn

Short Stories
The Call
Under the Bough
Night Hunt
Cariad
The Empty Hills

The Chained Adept

The Chained Adept
Mistress of Animals
Broken Devices
On a Crooked Track

Science Fiction Short Stories

Second Sight
Monsters, And More
The Visitor, And More

See KarenMyersAuthor.com for the latest information.

EXCERPT FROM ON A CROOKED TRACK

The Chained Adept: 4

Available from Karen Myers and Perkunas Press

Wood everywhere—the solid pier on which Penrys was trying to find her land legs, the ship moving gently beside it in the harbor at Ellech after almost two months at sea, and the entire forest of a city spread out before her, topped by the clusters of signal towers like groves of mountain spruce trees.

It smelled like home, all that wood—weathering away in the buildings, or freshly cut in the long arm of the hoist that was even now swinging cargo off the ship, or burning as firewood and flavoring the crisp spring breeze.

Home was in the woolens everyone wore, retentive of the odor of hard work and dinners long past. It was in the hair and beard dressings of the dock workers, leavened by the exotic aromas of some of the southern cargo, destined for the perfume manufactories.

Penrys inhaled deeply, feeling the rightness of the environment deep inside her. She hoped they'd have a day or two to spend in the harbor cities at the base of the two rivers before moving upriver to Tavnastok, but that would depend on her mentor, Vylkar, visible on the wharf at the end of the pier making arrangements for their cargo.

Najud and Munraz were having troubles of their own adjusting to an unmoving surface. "Come on," she said, picking up her pack. "The sooner you start walking, the easier it will get."

"Does it work that way for you?" Munraz asked, gamely picking up his own gear.

"Don't know—I've only read about it." She chuckled at his outraged expression. "I've never been on a ship before, not at sea. Never been in Stokemmi, either."

Striding off down the pier, she called over her shoulder, "Let's go explore."

She made a game of anticipating exactly where her feet would meet the planks until her body adjusted to the change of terrain and she stopped stumbling. Her footing wasn't improved by her hard-soled boots, donned for the first time in a while after the bare feet or soft shoes of shipboard life.

The three of them clattered to a stop behind Vylkar. Two piles were accumulating before him as they came off of the hoists. The larger one, goods destined for trade here in the city, were to be stored in the warehouse used by the Collegium for its own supplies. Cargo handlers were stowing the horse packs onto two wagons to move them there, and the draft horses waited patiently, their breath visible in the chilled air.

The laborers joked with each other as they worked, swapping insults that would bring a blush to a hardened campaigner. Many ships were in harbor, and this wharf, one of several, was busy, filled with people earning a living and working up a sweat doing it.

It was noisier, smellier, and far more vivid than the river harbor at Yenit Ping, and Penrys wondered what Najud and Munraz made of it. Except for the sea at their back and the size of the city, it could almost be Tavnastok, two hundred and fifty miles upstream from the mouth of the Lodentaf, just visible as a gap in the wharves far to the west along the shoreline. She'd seen sights like these there, running errands for the Collegium.

Their personal bags went into a hired two-wheeled pony cart. They would walk alongside it toward the center of Stokemmi to wherever they took rooms.

"We've fallen into the hands of talking bears," Najud muttered. "Loud, smelly bears. Great big tall ones."

"I warned you about the beards." Penrys surveyed the wharves with a stranger's eye and noted how many people were clearly natives (most of them), male (most of those), and bearded (all but the children). The few men of other nations, mostly officers from some of the ships in harbor, looked astonishingly youthful with their shaven faces.

"You'll find plenty of foreigners here, and they shave," she said. "I was never sure if that was out of fastidiousness, or because they couldn't raise a competitive beard and were afraid to try."

Some wore their beards in braids, or loose down their chest. Others had neatly trimmed, no-nonsense specimens. And here and there, especially for the citizens who'd come down from the city on business, elaborate grooming and stiffening fashions were on display.

"Do they breed for it?" Munraz asked, in a hushed tone that said he wouldn't be surprised by an affirmative answer.

"Hard to say. The boys compete with pride to see who can sprout first, and survey their fathers and older brothers with envy. Maybe the less hairy ones have had a harder time finding a bride, and so they're all bearded now."

She smiled at the open alarm on his face. "Don't worry, you can keep a beardless face and foreign clothing—no one will think it strange. Foreigners mean money, here—trade and business and interesting foods."

Najud looked unconvinced. She wondered if he thought he had to cultivate a beard to measure up, and then she wondered if he could. She'd seen him in stubble, but she'd never seen a bearded Zan, just the somewhat patchy results of a couple of months of neglect. That would never work here, in Ellech, and they didn't expect to be here any longer than that. Better to choose a different display of manhood.

Ah, but how do you tell a man that? She suppressed a smile.

"What will you wear?" Najud asked her. "Ellech or Zannib clothes?"

And then it hit her. When Najud met her, she wore Ellech clothing, the same sort of work clothes she'd worn for the three years since Vylkar found her. The only years she had memory of— all her life, as it were. She'd adopted local clothing in *sarq*-Zannib, and her life was with Najud now. She'd never expected to return to Ellech, so the matter had never come up.

"Zannib," she said, firmly.

Najud eyed her skeptically. "You should use Ellech styles if you like, might be a nice change for you. Might make it easier to work with the Collegium."

She wavered. "Well, maybe—I'll find something I can wear at need. But with my foreign face, I'll never pass for Ellech anyway." Unlike the tall, fair Ellech, Penrys was brown of hair and eyes, round of face, and below middle height. The two men with her had the olive skin and loose curly black hair of a typical Zan.

Only Vylkar, just concluding the cargo assignments, looked at home with his tidy graying scholar's beard. He turned now to survey his companions.

"Ready?" he asked.

They added their packs to the cart so they could walk unencumbered beside it. The small piebald cob leaned his shoulders into the load, and the carter clucked encouragingly from his well worn perch behind him.

"Is it far?" Munraz asked. He was tall, for a Zan, and not quite at his full growth yet, but Vylkar topped him by almost a head.

"We'll stop at the trade hall in the central square, up near the bridge, and take rooms nearby for the night. You'll want to see the trade goods properly stowed, too, before looking at what's left of the day's markets."

Vylkar glanced over at Penrys, and added, "You'll find it not too different from Tavnastok, I think."

She shook her head. "In Stokemmi, with no deadline, no errands for others, and my own money in my pocket—I think I'll find it very different indeed." She could feel Najud's amusement through the light link she held with him.

The cartwheels rumbled up the wooden road, adding their bit to the resonant din of all the traffic to and from the wharves. Their own footsteps were drowned out.

The harborside warehouses and trade offices along their route gave way to a sort of seamen's district of rooming houses, taverns, and shops, with open street markets visible down some of the cross streets. The faces on the streets there were of many nations, including the bearded Ellech, but she looked in vain for anyone resembling herself or the Zannib beside her. The smells of the food were of as many nations as the men, and her own stomach made its presence known as she inhaled sharply.

They saved their breath as the street continued to climb, not very steeply, away from the harbor, and gradually the main core of the city began to grow around them like a maturing forest—first the many craft shops, many of them integrated into the first floor of the dwellings they passed, and then some of the craft halls and larger markets. Up ahead, the street opened up even as the buildings gained in height, rising to three and four stories, or even higher. The decorative flourishes carved into the doors were matched by touches of wooden inlay for variety, or even painted color and gilt.

Traffic in both directions was brisk, but no one gave their party much of a look, even with the exotic Zannib robes three of them wore.

Penrys wore her chain openly. When she'd left Ellech a year and a half ago, she was the only chained wizard anyone knew of—a seemingly unique and local specimen.

That had all changed, drastically. Her chain meant nothing to this crowd, but it was the reason she was here—to chase down a possible lead on who might have been involved in the creation of dozens of wizards like her, chained wizards, from all nations, scattered where they didn't belong about four years ago, with no knowledge of who they'd been before.

Two months of shipboard speculation were past, and now it was time to get to work.

Find out more about this book here:

KarenMyersAuthor.com/link-on-a-crooked-track/

ABOUT THE AUTHOR

Karen Myers is a fantasy and science fiction author, best known for her heroic fantasy novels.

After a degree in Comparative Mythology from Yale University and a career as an industry pioneer building software companies, she has devoted herself to writing speculative fiction. Her stories feature heroes in real and imagined worlds filled with magic, space travel, and adventure.

When she's not writing, she enjoys hunting, fishing, photography, and playing her fiddle.

Karen lives with her husband, dogs and cats in an old log cabin in the mountains of central Pennsylvania, surrounded by wildlife. Bears, coyotes, deer, and possums visit often, and when she fiddles on her porch, the wild turkeys talk back.

She can be reached at KarenMyers@KarenMyersAuthor.com.

www.ingramcontent.com/pod-product-compliance
Lightning Source LLC
Chambersburg PA
CBHW061012120726

47910CB00006B/1897